# Novus Arcanum

**By: Michael Maxwell**

**Editor: Erin Dotson-Kelly**

## Prologue

Magic is real and has always existed. There have been periods throughout history where the use of magic was widely known and accepted. There have also been times where the use of magic has been twisted into something demonic or devilish. By the early 20th century, however, any notion of magic use, whether good or bad, had been dismissed, by the public, as myth and folklore.

Magic was thrust back into the spotlight at the start of the 1960s when the United States was well into the Civil Rights Movement. Fear and prejudice ruled the nation, and on Sunday, September 15th 1963, four members of the Ku Klux Klan decided to take matters into their own hands by planting dynamite at the 16th Street Baptist Church in Birmingham, Alabama. The bomb was outfitted with a timer, but before the Klansmen could flee the scene, two individuals with the ability to use magic intervened. One of the men removed the dynamite from the church using apportation, an arcane method allowing instantaneous travel from one location to another. The jarring nature of magical travel caused the bomb to detonate. The other man of magic used ward magic and created a spherical, invisible barrier around the area, preventing the explosion from passing beyond it. Unfortunately for the Klan members, their route of escape put them within the sphere of magic, and they were killed by their own device.

A great number of people witnessed the event, and overnight, the press had all of America talking about sorcerers. In a very short time, the entire world knew that magic was real, and it was met with same kind of ignorance and intolerance that led to the Civil Rights Movement. Known sorcerers were often denied services, persecuted, assaulted, and even driven into hiding.

A government study in the late 60s found that not everyone had the ability to wield magic. Sorcerers were either born with the ability or not. This fact only added fuel to the fires of discrimination against sorcerers. Even as race relations improved over the years, the interactions between sorcerers and humans did not improve.

By the 1990s, the divide between people with magical ability and those without it had improved, though not greatly. It was during this time that many innovative corporations started bringing sorcerers on board to improve their products with magic. This greatly improved the public opinion of magic-users; however, it was still not without protests and boycotts of products created by them.

Today, many sorcerers live openly; however, anyone with known magical aptitude is closely monitored by the government. Recent polls indicate magic is still not trusted by most Americans, and a string of terror attacks across the world by a radical sorcerer sect has not helped matters. This is where our story begins…

## Chapter 1: Scorched Earth

A few hundred spectators and news reporters are gathered on the south White House lawn in anticipation of the President's press conference regarding the recent terrorist attacks around the world. Over the past six months, a radical group calling itself the Eye of Ruin has launched three major magical attacks on two continents. The first attack in Paris claimed the lives of 86 people. A second attack on the Kremlin in Russia three months later killed over 200 people and injured dozens more. The most recent act of genocide, just two days ago, took 439 lives in Nigeria.

The White House has been uncharacteristically quiet about all three events, offering little more than condolences for the lives lost. Many believe that President Thompson's pro-magic ideals have prevented her from speaking out against the sorcerer-run terrorist group, so when it was announced that she would be making a statement, everyone came out in droves.

It's quite the perfect day for an outdoor press conference. The cool breezes of an early October day in D.C. keep everyone comfortable as they await the President. The changing leaves of fall occasionally flutter down onto the White House lawn from the trees that were full and green only a month before. Some photographers and camera crews are seizing the opportunity of the picturesque moment until things get underway.

The Secret Service is on high alert for this event with not one, but two sorcerers on staff to help ensure safety. In the early 2000s the military started recruiting certain types of sorcerers to use in military operations. Sentinels, who specialize in ward magic and Evos, who wield evocation magic. The Secret Service prefers to hire Sentinels who are fresh out of the military for guard duty. It's always recommended to have more than one Sentinel on staff for the President, as having multiple layers of ward magic up is best when preventing security breaches by other forms of magic.

Ward magic is rarely used for offense, but is very effective resisting other forms of magic. Barriers mostly come in two types: stationary and active. Stationary barriers are set on a fixed location and will remain there until they are destroyed or removed. Active barriers are stronger and mobile, but they require a spellcaster to concentrate on them in order to maintain the protective ward. A powerful Sentinel can use their wards and barriers to repel attack spells from Evos and block the teleporting abilities of Transporters, who wield apportation magic. Ward magic is also typically undetectable except by other Sentinels who possess the same spells. It can also be used to remove wards and barriers cast by less skillful sorcerers.

The agent charged with securing the south lawn on this day is thirty-two year old Sentinel, Eric Davis. His dark hair is cut short just as it was during his time in the Army. He looks a bit uncomfortable in the suit and tie uniform of the Secret Service, but he's grown accustomed to wearing it. He scans the crowds from the stage area with intensity, concealing his blue eyes behind black sunglasses to avoid any glare that would hinder his sight line.

Before radioing the Sentinel guarding the President inside the White House, Eric decides to do one more sweep of the exterior defensive barriers. Eric slightly raises his right hand which begins to glow with a bluish hue. More powerful spells will often require an incantation to produce the desired result; however, more simple effects, such as detecting magic you already have in place, can be accomplished with a bit of focus. Eric senses the invisible, nearly indestructible magic wall he placed around and over the stage where the President will be giving her address.

Satisfied with the defenses, Eric signals the other Sentinel. "Jones, we're set here," he says into a hidden microphone attached to an earpiece. "How's it looking on your end?"

"Everything is five by five." The voice of Jones is heard over the communication device.

"Alright," Eric says. "Merlin is on approach."

Eric gives a hand sign to the Secret Service agents at the doors to the interior of the White House. The agents acknowledge the sign and open the doors. Within a few moments, President Janet Thompson emerges from within the White House wearing a gray skirt suit. She has shoulder length brown hair that is neatly tied back. The weight of her command can be seen in her hazel eyes. When she ran for office, she avoided the topic of magic use when at all possible. In fact, she learned to be quite adept at dodging the issue. It wasn't until she was sworn into office that she revealed her pro-magic stance. Since that time, she's faced false claims that she herself is a sorcerer, political opposition from all parties including her own, and even threats on her life. Despite it all, she continues fighting for the rights of all people, whether magically inclined or not.

The President approaches the microphone adorned podium with determination. She takes a long, solemn look out over the crowd before speaking. "My fellow Americans. In recent months, the nations of the world have been plagued by attacks from a terrorist organization. We will not let these attacks go unanswered. Right now, the Departments of Defense and Sorcery are hard at work to shed light on those that would hide in darkness. We are cooperating with other defense forces from around the world including the British, French, and Russian Ministries of…"

Her speech continues on, but as it does Eric begins to sense a magical force. Before he can even react, a section of air on the inside of his magical barrier begins to waver and distort as though reality is bending around it. "Transporter!" Eric cries out to alert nearby agents.

A circular, shimmering rift opens up a few feet off the ground with what appears to be a shadowy warehouse on the other side of its water-like surface. Three figures clad in black tactical gear and facemasks emerge from the portal. Another silhouette can be seen in the warehouse before the gate closes. It's most likely the Transporter who created the portal. The three terrorists are greeted by a team of Secret Service agents standing between them and the President. The agents draw firearms. "Incaendo rivus!" The masked men speak a quick incantation in unison without breaking stride as they rush the President.

Streams of flame propel forth from the palms of the three terrorists, and, before any member of the Secret Service team can get a shot off, they are engulfed in fire. These masked men are all Evos, sorcerers commanding evocation magic. Also known as *attack magic* or *battle magic*, evocation is the most common form of magic and uses things like fire, ice, and lightning to deadly effect. It is thought that many stories of the Greek pantheon of gods, including Zeus and his lightning, were just powerful Evos using their abilities to rule over normal men and women through fear.

Eric draws his service pistol while putting himself between the attackers and the President. The terrorists turn their attention to him, still spewing fire from their hands. Eric aims and takes a quick breath before shooting at one of the masked men. The bullet flies true, striking the assailant in the head, ending his fiery onslaught.

A second team of Secret Service agents move out from within the White House, opening fire on the two remaining terrorists.  One of the men uses the other as a shield while simultaneously directing his flame stream towards Eric and the President.  Eric wraps himself around the President.  "Praesidium," Eric speaks quickly, forming an energy shield around him and the President.

The terrorist's jet of fire appears to have no effect on Eric's shield upon striking it.  The terrorist has no chance to try again as a bullet rips into his leg, breaking his focus.  He looks to see his former shield and compatriot on the ground bleeding out.  "Letum displodo!" the terrorist exclaims as he drops to his knees.

The terrorist slumps over, but before anyone can breathe easily, a massive explosion emanates from within his body.  The force of the fiery detonation demolishes the southern face of the White House, shatters through the nearby magical protection barriers, and engulfs a large portion of the panicking crowd.  When the dust and debris start to settle, Eric's energy shield can be seen in the massive crater where the stage once stood.

Once certain there is no more danger, Eric dismisses the shield around him and the President.  He helps her stand.  "Madam President, we have to move," Eric says still scanning the area.

He receives no answer.  "Madam President," he repeats while turning to look at her.

The President's face is frozen in horror as she looks out over the devastation that was once a mass of reporters on the White House lawn.  Ash fills the air.  Countless scorched bodies litter the ground as far as the eye can see.  In the distance, screams and cries for help overwhelm even the approaching sirens of first responders. She barely manages to get out the words: "My God…"

## Chapter 2: Aftermath

The Department of Sorcery is located near the Pentagon in Arlington County, Virginia. It's a new department of the government, having only been open for the past 5 months. It is designed to keep tabs on people with magical abilities and to improve public relations with the magical-wielding community.

Edward Chamberlain, a silver-haired man with an air of authority, is the Secretary of Sorcery. He's uptight with no magical ability and was chosen specifically for the position due to his neutrality on the issue of magic use. He's a life-long politician who has always had his sights set on a Presidential Cabinet position. He was less than pleased with his appointment as Secretary of Sorcery. While he bears no ill will towards magic-capable individuals, he also knows that being anywhere near their issues in the current political climate can be a career ender. He hasn't let this fact interfere with his effectiveness in running the DoS, but it certainly hasn't improved his already gruff demeanor.

Edward barrels through the double-doors of the Department of Sorcery command room. He wears a rather expensive navy blue suit and moves with an urgency that is surprising for a man of his age. Whether through flash or intensity, Edward likes to make his presence known in any room he enters. Hot on Edward's heels is Celeste Winters, a female staff aide in her early twenties, carrying a stack of file folders with an open notepad on top of them.

The command room is a torrent of activity. Two walls of the enormous room are covered with large screens streaming various media feeds covering the attack on the White House. Rows of workstations bustle with staff members gathering intelligence on the situation. A conference room walled-in by glass sits opposite the monitors. Inside, analysts pour over files, intelligence reports, and maps of D.C. that litter a long black table.

"Initial reports show 150 dead and 64 injured," Celeste says frantically as she follows Edward through the command room.

"The President?" Edward questions without looking back.

"She's okay," she replies. "There was a Sentinel on her detail who shielded her from the explosion."

"Thank God for that," he says with relief.

Edward makes his way into the conference room, straight for a woman sitting at the head of the table. Andrea Oliveros, a young Hispanic woman, is a Prophet, a sorcerer that wields divination magic. Prophets have abilities that allow them to see through the eyes of others, see into the past, and, occasionally, see into the future. Andrea, eyes closed, has both hands on the table touching various photographs of the White House attack. In a leather jacket, jeans, and low-top sneakers, she sticks out amongst the staff that is mostly dressed professionally. "Tell me you have something," Edward says to Andrea as he approaches her.

"Focusing at the moment," Andrea replies curtly.

Unlike everyone else in the room, Andrea has reason to be a bit hostile. In her late teens, she committed a series of felonies using her abilities. She'd spent the last four years behind bars until Edward had her pulled out to work for the DoS shortly after its creation. She doesn't get paid for her services, but it does keep her out of prison.

"Let me rephrase that," Edward states in a stern tone. "I need you to tell me something."

Andrea starts to have a vision, seeing through the eyes of one of the terrorists in the photographs. She is in a poorly lit warehouse, standing next to two other masked men. In front of her stands a figure in a sleeveless, hooded sweatshirt. The details of this person's face are concealed in the darkness, but it's apparent they have a wiry frame. Lean arms go through a series of arcane motions as an incantation is spoken from beneath the hood.

"I see a warehouse," Andrea reports to Edward as she continues to see the vision.

"Magna rapidus ostium," a youthful, male voice whispers arcane words from within the shadowy hood.

As the spell is recited, light pours into the room from a portal being opened, revealing the White House on the other side. "There's a Transporter opening a gate to the White House," Andrea says.

No sooner does the gate appear than the three masked terrorists rush through it, ending the vision. Andrea looks up at Edward who is lording over her, waiting for more information. "That's it," she says matter-of-factly.

"A warehouse and a Transporter?" Edward asks incredulously. "That's it?"

"Yeah, that's it." Andrea stands as she responds. "You wanna give it a shot?"

"What is the point of having a Prophet on staff if you can't see things we can use?" Edward questions in a raised tone.

"I'm not a miracle worker!" Andrea fires back. "I can't just see anything I want. You have me working off blurry photos for Christ's sake!"

Andrea swipes at the photos on the table, flinging them towards Edward. "You know this works better if I focus on something the host has touched." Andrea sighs. "And I'm pretty sure whoever's behind this has wards in place to block people like me. You're lucky I can see anything at all."

"I don't need excuses." Edward puts his finger in Andrea's face as he speaks. "I need answers."

"Then get me something from one of these guys, and we might get lucky," Andrea says, pushing Edward's hand away from her.

"They blew up," Celeste says timidly. "I don't think there's anything left."

One of the nearby analysts hangs up a phone before interjecting, "Actually, we just got a report they found a partial corpse that they believe to be one of the terrorists."

"Get me that body," Edward responds.

The analyst picks up the phone again. Edward turns towards Andrea. "Can you work with that?" he questions.

"Maybe, but wouldn't a Reaper be a better option?" she responds.

"It would be if I had one."

"Your big government organization doesn't have a Reaper squirreled away in the darkest corner of Carcer?"

"Why don't I stuff you back in one of those dark corners, and you can tell me!"

Reapers are the rarest type of sorcerer. They use a magic called necromancy, known as *death magic* to the few who believe in its existence. Not much is known about what Reapers really do, but it's thought they can communicate with, and animate, the dead. This kind of power is constantly sought by just about every government in the world, though no one has yet been able to find someone who can wield it. As it stands, both the FBI and Homeland Security have been tasked with bringing any potential Reapers to the Department of Sorcery for immediate processing. Most leads turn out to be false. Just people seeking attention; however, after the events at the White House earlier in the day, all information is being diligently followed up on.

"Now, unless a miracle happens, you are what we have," Edward dictates to Andrea. "So when that corpse arrives you will get all touchy-feely with it to do your thing, or you go back in the box. Your choice."

***

Meanwhile, inside an underground facility back at the White House, doctors look over the President for any injuries. The miniature hospital wing is intended to be able to treat the President, First Family, and White House staff in the event of an emergency. It's not a large space, having only a few rooms, but it is outfitted with the latest medical technology and a 24-hour staff. Janet sits on a hospital bed while being examined by two members of the medical team. A handful of Secret Service agents and military personnel stand guard in the room and near the door.

Eric enters the room, stopping at the Secret Service agents covering the door. "How is she?" he asks.

Janet stands up and waves the medical staff away from her. "I'm fine," she says, mildly irritated. "Frankly, everyone needs to stop treating me like I'm going to break."

"We can't do that Madam President," Eric replies. "It's our job to keep you safe."

"And today, you did that. Thank you."

Unfortunately, her words don't offer Eric much encouragement and only succeed in making him feel worse than he already did. He may have saved her life, but he feels responsible for every other life that was taken today. He manages a small smile and a nod to hide how he really feels about his failure.

In a huff, Secretary of Defense, Allen Barber enters the room. He's a middle-aged, anti-magic Democrat appointed to his position solely to take some of the heat off of President Thompson's pro-magic stance. The Secretary of Defense doesn't hide his disdain for the magic community, and he's routinely at odds with his Commander-in-Chief. "Janet, I'm relieved you're okay, but I warned you about this." Allen steps between Eric and the President. "The more we embrace this sorcery crap, the more we open ourselves up to these kinds of attacks."

Eric steps back as the rest of the Secret Service and military look around the room in anticipation of the President's response. "And if we didn't embrace it, I wouldn't be standing here right now," she retorts. "Ignoring something doesn't make it go away; it just makes you more vulnerable to it."

"I'm not talking about ignoring the problem." Allen doesn't back down. "I'm talking about removing it altogether. You've seen my proposed Project Revelation-"

"I've seen it, and I rejected it," she interrupts. "Now is not the time to discuss this, Allen."

One of the first items to cross the desk in the Oval Office after Allen's appointment was his proposal for a secret military project intended to study people with magical abilities in an effort to infuse their magic with weaponry for combat. Not only was the project budget astronomical, but the methods outlined for magic extraction were bordering unethical. Ever since the President passed on it, Allen has been vaguely pushing it in other forums, trying to gain support.

"I think, after the events of today, it's the perfect time to discuss it!" Allen raises his voice.

"No!" The President's volume makes everyone else in the room feel small. "After the events of today, we need to find these terrorists and stop them! The DoS is already investigating, as well as the FBI and Homeland Security. I suggest you get on board as well."

"The DoS?" Allen almost laughs as he says it. "Come on, Janet. Your little pet project has been around for almost half a year, and I think we can both agree it hasn't produced the results you were hoping for."

"We are done here," the President responds dismissively.

Allen looks around the room as though he's expecting everyone else to rally to his cause. No such support comes, and the Secretary throws his hands up to signal he is backing down. He turns to leave, but stops in front of Eric, glaring at him. After a moment, he simply shakes his head and walks out of the room.

"Sorry you all had to see that," the President addresses everyone in the room.

She wears a brave face to keep up morale, but these constant battles with members of her own Cabinet wear her down. After moments like these, she starts to second guess herself. Not only does she have the weight of being the first female President of the

United States on her shoulders, but going to bat for sorcerers' rights just makes her day to day that much more trying. Can she actually change the world for the better? Does she have the right to try?

"No need to apologize, Madam President," Eric replies.

"The press is going to want a statement," she says moving towards the door.

"The press secretary's topside," Eric says as he escorts her out of the room.

***

That night, after being hounded by countless investigators and members of the press, Eric finds himself at the Public Bar less than a mile away from the White House. It's a popular destination in D.C. because of its three floors, each offering different nightlife options. The bar is usually quite busy with lines out the door, but, on this night, it's eerily quiet. A handful of patrons sit at the bar of the main floor looking up at the three flatscreens on the wall behind the bar. Every screen is covering the tragedy at the White House. A somber news anchor in his early 40s reports while footage of the destruction play on a loop next to him: "No one has yet claimed responsibility for the attack that left 174 dead and 83 injured; however, authorities believe it's the work of the group calling themselves the Eye of Ruin, also behind the attacks in Paris, Moscow, and Nigeria. We go now to a statement given by the White House press secretary earlier this afternoon…" the report continues, but Eric is no longer hearing it.

All sound from the room is being drowned out by screams in his head. Screams of all the innocents immolated right in front of him while he remained safe and sound within his protective barrier. Sure he'd saved the President, that was his job after all, but he should've been strong enough to save everyone. At least that's the thought that continuously repeats in his head as he replays the scene of destruction over and over until…

A loud crack, followed by the sound of shattering glass, fills the bar, drawing everyone's attention to Eric who looks down to discover the bottle of beer he was nursing has been broken in his hand. Cheap beer and broken glass now litter the bar top in front of him. The bartender rushes over with a rag. "Easy buddy!" he chastises. "I think you're cut off for the night."

"I'm…sorry," Eric's voice trails off as he stares up at the news report and his mind starts to go back to that dark place. "Can we turn this shit off please? Or change it. I don't care to what, just anything but this."

"First, you make a mess of my bar and now you're making demands," the bartender responds aggressively. "Who the hell died and made you king of the bar?"

It's very easy to replace a feeling of sadness or regret with anger under the proper circumstances. The bartender's words just happen to be the perfect trigger. It takes everything Eric has to restrain himself from pulling this guy across the bar and knocking his teeth down his throat. "It's not the bartender's fault," Eric thinks to himself. "He's just doing his job. Let it go."

Eric takes a deep breath to calm himself. "Never mind," he replies.

Pulling a twenty out of his wallet, he tosses it down on the bar. "Sorry for the trouble," he says before walking out.

## Chapter 3: Don't Fear the Reaper

The FBI received an anonymous tip that a Reaper might be living in the bayous of Louisiana. Since there has never been an actual reported sighting of a Reaper anywhere in the world, no one in the FBI knows how the situation should be handled. It is thought that they are very dangerous and should be apprehended with extreme caution.

A convoy of four black SUVs makes its way along a dirt road in the swamps of Southern Louisiana. The government vehicles come to an abrupt stop in front of a dilapidated shack near the shore of the area's murky waters. The exterior of the rickety structure is adorned with Vodou symbols and animal bones. The stretched skin of an alligator is strung up on wooden poles carved from tree branches and placed in front of a window-sized opening on the side of the shack. There is a single open doorway facing the road covered with a dingy brown cloth.

Nearly a dozen FBI agents in gray and black suits emerge from the SUVs with an assortment of firearms drawn. The agent in charge shields himself behind the front vehicle's door while holding up a megaphone. "Emmanuel Henri," The agent says in an authoritative tone. "This is the FBI! Come out with your hands in the air!"

The next few moments seem to last an eternity. None of these agents can use magic, nor have they ever dealt with a sorcerer before. They're expecting the devil himself to walk out and turn everyone to dust.

The tension is finally broken when someone slowly steps out from inside the shack. He's not a monster. He's a man. In fact, he's an older man of a swarthy complexion with long, graying hair. He is dressed plainly in some wrinkled brown slacks. His long sleeve shirt has a banded-collar that was once white, but hasn't seen bleach in quite some time. Emmanuel walks out slowly with his hands up. His eyebrows are raised in a quizzical fashion as he looks around for some kind of an explanation. "If dis is about da alligator," Emmanuel speaks with a mild Haitian accent. "Eet was self-defense. He attacked me first."

As unassuming as Emmanuel actually looks, all the agents see is the stereotype of every witch doctor they have ever seen in the movies and on television. "Mr. Henri, you are to come with us right now," the lead agent says with a waver in his voice. "If you attempt to use any of your…uh…voodoo, we are authorized to use force!"

Emmanuel is no stranger to racial prejudices and profiling being a black immigrant from Haiti; however, this is the first time he's been at gun point by the law as a result of it. He'd find the whole situation laughable if he wasn't so insulted. Insulted or not, he knows it's best to just cooperate. "Lead da way," Emmanuel says with a shrug.

The agents are not relieved by his compliance. They keep their guard up as he approaches the SUV where the lead agent still hides behind the driver side door. With his hands still in the air, Emmanuel looks around at all the nearby agents and, with a small chuckle, says "Voodoo? You watch too many movies."

Emmanuel is escorted by the FBI to a private airfield where he is then put on a private plane bound for Arlington, Virginia. Within a couple hours, Emmanuel is back on the ground and being driven to the Department of Sorcery. While he hasn't been treated as a prisoner, no one has been particularly friendly or forthcoming to him about his destination.

***

A short time later, in an autopsy room at the DoS, Andrea stands in front of a metal table where some partial charred remains sit. There are two other empty, metal exam tables in the room. While it's bright in here with lighting focused above the tables, it still manages to feel gloomy. Most of the surfaces are metal, making the room feel cold. Edward stands just inside the room, near a set of double-doors, watching Andrea very intently. Her right hand rests atop the blackened torso of the dead terrorist. Her eyes are closed with her brow furrowed as she concentrates. "I'm getting the exact same vision as before," she says, opening her eyes. "Just from a different point of view."

Edward is on the verge of showing his disappointment and frustration when there's a knock on the door behind him. He immediately perks up. "Help is here," he says turning to towards the swinging steel doors.

Before Edward came down to hover around Andrea while she works, he received a phone call. It was from the FBI informing him of their apprehension of Emmanuel. Needless to say this put a spring in his stride as he made his way down to the sub-level of the DoS to micromanage.

Two FBI agents escort Emmanuel into the room, and despite the hours they've spent in his presence, they still look extremely uneasy. Emmanuel looks around the room, still baffled as to where he is or why he's here. He catches a glimpse of Andrea and the scorched cadaver behind the smirking, slick-suited man before him. Edward takes a step towards Emmanuel. "Mr. Henri, thank you for coming in on such short notice," Edward says in an overly considerate tone.

"I was not given a choice," Emmanuel responds.

At Emmanuel's words, Andrea lets out a slight laugh, which is met by a sharp glare from her boss. Edward's pleasant façade returns as he slowly turns to face Emmanuel again. "I do apologize for that," Edward says as he ushers Emmanuel towards the exam table. "But this is a matter of national security, and your abilities are needed right now."

Edward motions to the limbless blackened torso atop the metal dissecting board. Emmanuel steps up to the table, opposite

Andrea. He briefly looks down at the corpse before looking back up at Andrea then to Edward. He realizes the incorrect assumption that's been made, but since he's come all this way he might as well have a little fun. "Dis one ees dead," Emmanuel says with a shrug.

"Exactly," Edward replies slightly irritated. "That's why you're here."

"What are you wanting me to do exactly?" Emmanuel feigns confusion.

"Talk to it." Edward is in no mood for games and struggles to keep his composure.

Emmanuel looks around the room as though he is expecting someone to chime in with some sense of reason, but no one does. He shrugs again and leans down towards the table. "Ello? Is anyone dere? No?" Emmanuel straightens and looks to Edward. "It ees still dead."

"Don't toy with me!" Edward gets in Emmanuel's face. "I know that you Reapers can speak with the dead!"

"I do not know where you are gettin' your information," Emmanuel replies calmly. "But I am not a Reaper."

"What do you mean?" Edward asks suspiciously.

"Did you people just assume dat because my religion is Vodou, dat my magic must represent death?" Emmanuel raises his voice slightly. "I am a healer. A Mender."

Upon hearing it, Edward knows the truth of Emmanuel's words though he ignores it. Menders use healing magic to bind wounds, enhance the body's regenerative properties, and even modify the human body on a cellular level if used by a powerful enough sorcerer. It's true that the healing magic of a Mender is often confused with that of a Reaper, but Edward refuses to believe that the FBI would make such a major mistake. "Impossible," Edward says dismissively.

"I will prove eet," Emmanuel says. "I can heal dat cut on your 'and."

"What cut?" Edward asks as he displays his hands to show the lack of any injury.

Emmanuel quickly grabs a scalpel off the table's instrument tray and slashes Edward across the top of his right hand. The Secretary growls from the pain, and the FBI agents have found the reason they've been looking for to draw weapons on this magic-user. Emmanuel wastes no time grabbing Edward by the arm. He begins speaking the arcane words, "Celeri instaurabo."

Edward winces, feeling the sliced skin and veins in his hand begin to stitch themselves back together. It isn't exactly painful, but the accelerated rate of healing causes some discomfort. The FBI agents are ready to fire, but Edward waves them off with his left hand. Within a few moments, Emmanuel releases him and takes a step back. Edward looks over his hand as though he's never seen it before. There is no cut. No scar. It's as though it never happened. He'd admire the sorcerer's power if he weren't so pissed off. "See," Emmanuel says motioning to Edward's hand. "All better."

"So it would seem," Edward replies with restrained rage. "Get him out of here!"

The FBI agents quickly grab Emmanuel and aggressively lead him through the double doors. "And the next time the Bureau wants to help," Edwards shouts off after them. "Don't!"

Andrea lets out another laugh. Edward spins around to face her. "And just why didn't you see that coming?"

"Oh I did," she replies with a grin. "I just wanted to see it actually happen."

If anyone else spoke to him in such a manner, they would be fired or soon wish they had been. While he doesn't take it lying down, his reliance on Andrea's unique abilities, does afford her more leniency than most. "Just for that, you can stay down here for a few more hours until you see something useful!" Edward says as he storms out of the room.

"That's real mature!" Andrea calls out after him.

Edward makes his way topside, heading up to the 5th floor of the building. He knows the President will be expecting answers that he doesn't have. On one hand, he has no leads for the terrorist attack; on the other hand, he might be able to use the tragedy to get approval for his sorcerer taskforce. Though if he judges her mood incorrectly, presenting the idea could be career suicide. His nerves get the better of him, and he lets out a long tirade of expletives during his elevator ride.

Edward's office is a sizable, lavishly decorated room. A large mahogany desk sits in front of a window wall looking out over the Potomac River, the Washington Memorial in the distance. The other walls in the room are lined with dark wood bookcases each filled with various volumes on political law and history. While much of the décor in the room appears overly expensive, the items atop the desk seem simple in comparison. A name placard, a telephone, a keyboard and mouse, and a flat-screen computer monitor take up very little of the desk space.

Edward falls into his plush leather office chair, swiveling around to look out the window. It's dusk, and the night lights of D.C. are beginning to come alive. Edward runs a hand through his hair before grabbing a hold of it as though he's going to tear it out. He lets out a long sigh. "I need a goddamn miracle," he says under his breath.

*** 

The following morning, on the other side of the country at Westview High School in Portland, Oregon, fifteen year-old Catherine Moore sits in science class, doodling strange symbols in her notebook. She wears an oversized black sweater with tattered blue jeans and combat boots. Her shoulder length hair is dyed black and hangs in her face as she scribbles. Occasionally, she looks out the classroom windows at the dark clouds in the sky and the rain falling on the glass. Her thoughts are elsewhere. She doesn't even seem to be focusing on the runes she's sketching; her hand moves as though it is being guided by some invisible force.

It is frog dissection day so the rest of the room is bristling with activity. Each of the ten workspaces has two preserved frogs laid out on metal trays, waiting to be sliced open. Teenagers, both eager and repulsed, are teamed up three to four students per table. The pungent smell of formaldehyde permeates the closed classroom. At the front of the room stands a lanky, disheveled man in his forties who is supposed to be teaching the class. He pays little attention to the children as he's too busy nursing a mild hangover and pondering how his life ended up here.

Catherine is partnered up with two girls who could not be more different than her; a prissy blonde and brunette in colorful designer outfits that are irritated by Catherine's very presence. Their feelings towards her aren't malicious, just the average disdain for teens outside of their social circles. At this particular moment, the girls are upset because they want no part of cutting into a dead frog, but their lab partner isn't pulling her weight either. "Hey, weirdo," the blonde says to Catherine. "Are you going to come help us or what?"

"I don't think the frog would appreciate us cutting into him," Catherine replies without looking away from the windows.

"Um, it's dead," the brunette says with condescension.

Catherine turns to face the girls. "So the dead don't feel?" Catherine asks rhetorically.

"No. They're dead." The blonde says shaking her head. "God, you're such a freak."

A strapping teenage jock from the table behind sneaks up behind Catherine with a frog in his hand. She's once again focused on her notebook and doesn't notice him. Her lab partners see him, however, and fight to keep from laughing before the gag has been sprung. "She just likes frogs." The brunette nudges the blonde as she speaks. "She hopes she can kiss one and it'll turn into a prince."

"Let's find out!" The blonde shouts to commence the operation.

The jock pounces on Catherine from behind, shoving the preserved amphibian into her face. She springs up from her stool, pushing him back, but not before the damage is already done. The entire class erupts in laughter, finally grabbing the teacher's attention. "I guess that one's not a prince!" The blonde howls through her laughter.

Catherine collects her notebook, stuffing it hastily into her backpack before making a beeline for the door. The science teacher halts her just shy of her exit. "Where do you think you're going?" He tries to sound as authoritative as possible.

"The office," she answers.

"Why?" he asks, oblivious to preceding events.

Catherine doesn't answer. She can't. Her face is flush; her skin hot to the touch. She's been teased and called names on occasion, but never embarrassed on this scale. She looks back at her classmates who are all still hysterical. The jock is reenacting the whole scene while the girls at her table are practically falling off their stools. In a moment of sheer rage, Catherine snaps, storming out of the room. Her head is full of vengeful thoughts.

The jock holds a frog near his face, pretending to be Catherine about to kiss it. Suddenly, the milky eyes of the dead amphibian shoot open. The jock's bravado melts as he locks eyes with it. In a flash, the frog opens its mouth and its tongue shoots out slapping the teen in the face. The jock lets out a shriek and drops it to the floor. The waning laughter in the room explodes once more, though it is short-lived. The students' merriment turns to horror as every frog in the class comes to life, and almost in unison, begins to leap at the blonde and brunette.

Catherine stands in the locker-lined hallway just outside the closed door of the science room. The gleeful mockery from within has morphed into panic-stricken screams. Catherine laughs to herself as she begins making her way to the front office of the school. She did it again. She's not sure how. It just happens sometimes. And while what she did to those frogs may seem miraculous, she didn't actually restore life; she simply animated them for a short time. She's never seen the effect last more than a few minutes. She normally hates when it happens, but today it was well worth it.

***

Later that day, back at the Department of Sorcery, a team of technicians pour through security footage, news streams, social media sites, and various other sources in order to locate potential sorcerers for monitoring. The tracking room is made up of six workstations, each with a number of screens displaying different information. One to two technicians work each station, using certain keywords to search through audio files, video files, and photographs for possible hits. A supervising technician patrols the room, following up on any significant intelligence brought to his attention.

While reviewing an NSA audio file, a technician excitedly calls to the supervisor, "I think I've got something here!"

The lead technician makes his way over to the workstation, grabbing a headset as he gets there. "Play it," he says in a low tone.

The young technician starts the audio file from the beginning. It's a one-sided recording of a phone call. A mature female voice says: "Mrs. Moore, this is Principal Wright from Westview High. I'm calling about your daughter, Catherine. There was an incident today in her science class. I have multiple reports from her classmates and Mr. Richardson that she, and I'm quoting here, 'brought a number of dead frogs back to life and attacked some students with them.'"

There is a short pause as though the person that was talking is now listening. "Yes," Principal Wright starts up again. "Well no, no one actually saw her do it, but the police have been called to investigate. After all, we can't have students attacking other students with zombie frogs."

The senior technician pulls the headphones off. "Send that file to me right now," he orders with urgency.

He rushes over to his desk behind a partition at the back of the room. He picks up the phone and dials Secretary Chamberlain's office.

After a few rings Edward answers. "This is Chamberlain," Edwards says.

"Sir, you said to let you know if we found anything," the tech responds as he locates the audio file on his computer. "And I think we finally have confirmation of a Reaper sighting."

"Are you sure?!" Edward questions with enthusiasm.

"As certain as we can be without physical confirmation." The tech forwards the audio file to the Secretary. "There was a report of frogs being brought back to life by a fifteen year old girl in Portland, Oregon. I'm sending you the file now."

"I'll review it, but don't wait for me," Edward responds. "Have a local team pick her up. I want to talk to her right away."

## Chapter 4: The Dragon King

Catherine sits in a barren interrogation room, at a metal table bolted to the floor. There is an empty chair opposite where she sits and a mirror along one wall that Catherine glances at from time to time. She's seen enough cop shows to guess that it's probably a two-way mirror and people are watching her from the other side. What she doesn't know is why she's here at all. Sure, she skipped school after the incident in science class, but how did that merit getting swept up by men in black suits and sunglasses, flown to some undisclosed location, and locked in a room for hours? She is bored, hungry, and the hard edges of the chair are starting to dig into her legs.

Both relief and fear wash over her as the door finally opens. Edward enters the room, and, as he is wont to do, makes an impression in his flashy blue pinstripe suit. He quickly closes the door behind him, and Catherine wastes no time in expressing her displeasure. She jumps up out of her chair. "What the hell's going on here?! Where am I? You can't keep me here! I didn't do anything!"

Edward slowly turns towards her and steps up to the table. "Now that's not entirely true is it, Catherine?" he asks calmly.

"I ditched class," she answers. "So what?!"

"I'm not interested in any of that." Edward motions for her to sit back down. "I want to discuss what happened during class…with the frogs. I understand you brought some back to life."

"I didn't bring them back to life," she says as she drops back into her chair with frustration.

"Oh?" Edward replies quizzically. "Witnesses reported otherwise."

"They weren't alive…I just made them move…and jump at some bitches that deserved it," she says. "I'm not even sure how I did it. Is that a crime?"

"Well, it breaks some laws of nature," Edward jokes. "But I think the world has been long past that for a while now."

Catherine is not amused. "What am I doing here?" she questions, crossing her arms.

Edward takes a seat across from her. "I need your help," he says in a gentle tone. "You are a sorcerer, and it just so happens the type of magic you wield is very rare. People with your arcane abilities are called Reapers, and you are the first the modern world has ever seen. That makes you very special."

The more he speaks, the more uncomfortable Catherine becomes. She has known about her abilities for a few years ever since her grandmother started speaking to her from inside the coffin at her own funeral. A short time later, she accidentally brought the long deceased family dog back from the dead. Though it wasn't really alive; just like the frogs, it was a walking corpse. These events are often preceded by strange words in her head, in a language she doesn't understand. She feels compelled to speak these incantations, after which they vanish from her mind's eye, leaving her unable to repeat them. Not that she would want to. It would be a lot for any young person to handle. She acts tough on the surface though inside she is anything but. "Catherine, I need you to speak to someone who has recently passed away." Edward continues.

"I…" She hesitates. "I don't want to."

"Why not?" Edward pushes.

Her façade crumbles as tears well up in her eyes. "Because it scares me!" She jumps again this time knocking her chair back. "I didn't ask for these abilities! I can't control these abilities! I don't want to talk to your dead body! I just want to go home!"

Edward slowly stands up while retrieving the white handkerchief out of his suit pocket. He moves around the table, offering it to Catherine. "Look, I can't begin to understand what you've gone through, but right now I'm asking you to be brave." Edward tries to comfort her. "What I need you to do would save many lives. You would like to save lives wouldn't you?"

"Yes…" Catherine calms a bit.

"Then help me just this once, and I promise you'll never have to do it again." He lies rather convincingly. "We'll get you some help to learn control, so you won't have to experience anymore of these waking nightmares."

Catherine takes a long moment before responding. She definitely doesn't want to talk to another dead person, but if this imposing figure can actually help, then it might be worth a single conversation. "Okay, I'll try," she says with a slight hesitation. "Just as long as you can make this stop."

Edward doesn't have the ability to help her, nor does he know anyone who could. In fact, even if he had the means, he certainly doesn't have the desire. If she is what he thinks she is, then she is far too valuable. He knows that honesty will not work in this situation, so he does as any good politician would: he continues lying. "I promise."

***

Within the hour, Edward takes Catherine down to the sub-level where the body is now in the morgue, a few doors down from the autopsy room. He has taken the liberty of having Andrea called down there as well. One entire wall of the room is lined with square metal doors, each leading to the cold chamber where corpses are kept preserved before and after examinations. A slight chill emanates from a single door that is currently open. The extended body tray reveals the frozen partial remains of the terrorist from the White House attack. A young morgue attendant in a white lab coat sits at a desk on the opposite side of the room, filling out some paperwork on a clipboard. Andrea and Catherine stand on either side of the tray while Edward is positioned at the head of it. He looks to Catherine who still seems hesitant about the whole situation. "Don't worry," Edward offers comfortingly. "I'll be here the whole time, and my friend Andrea here is a sorcerer. She'll help make sure you're safe."

Andrea shoots an irritated glance at Edward. She doesn't appreciate the lies he's throwing at this young girl. If, for some reason, the use of death magic were to go awry, there is nothing she could do to help, and he knows that. Catherine is too focused on the horrific sight before her to notice Edward shrugging at Andrea in response. "Go ahead," Edward gently pushes.

Catherine slowly holds a trembling hand out over the body and closes her eyes. She envisions what Edward is asking her to do, and words appear in her head. Even after knowing the spell, she hesitates casting it, as seeing the spirit rise out of a corpse is the most jarring part for her. "Nex narro," she finally says, the incantation almost catching in her throat.

As her words finish, a soft red glow surrounds the charred remains. The terrorist begins to manifest as a red spectral form lying in line with his body. His partially translucent phantom limbs and head seem to merge with his burnt torso. His ghostly visage is no longer hidden behind the mask he wore during the attack at the White House. He looks to be a young, white male, only a few years older than Catherine herself. His eyes look around in confusion. "What…what is happening?" His voice has an other-worldly echo. "Where am I? Why can't I move?"

"You're dead," Catherine replies.

The ghost of the terrorist appears to think for a moment. He
starts to recall the events at the White House and his sacrifice for
the Eye of Ruin. "I...remember now." His speech is seems labored.
"Why have you called me here?"

Communicating with the dead is more subtle than animating
a lifeless corpse. No one else in the room sees the spectral terrorist
or hears his voice, and when Catherine speaks to him, it is
unintelligible to them. Edward is starting to lose faith, as, from his
perspective, she has been casting her spell for too long with no
result. Unfortunately, he's not a man known for his patience.
"What's happening?" He lightly shakes Catherine's shoulder. "Is it
working?"

Andrea reaches across the body tray, and pushes Edward's
hand away from Catherine. "It's working," she says in defense of
the young Reaper. "I can sense the presence."

Catherine looks over at Edward. "What do you want me to
ask it...him...whatever?"

"Ask about his organization," Edward begins barking
demands. "I want names, places, targets. Get me as much
information as you can!"

Catherine, already flustered at the situation, becomes
overwhelmed at Edward's badgering. She grabs Edward's arm, and
as she does so, his eyes flash the same reddish hue of the spectral
terrorist. Edward recoils briefly from the shock of suddenly seeing
and hearing the ghost on the body tray. "Well...that's unexpected."
Edward says surprisingly calm.

"Sorry," Catherine responds sheepishly.

"It's okay," Edward says before looking down at the terrorist. "Can I talk to it?"

"It?" The ghost answers. "I'm right here, jackass."

"Really cute." Edward is stone-faced in his reply. "I want to know about your organization. Tell me about the Eye of Ruin."

"We bring destruction to the Cassus for the honor and glory of the Dragon King," the dead terrorist replies.

Cassus is a rarely used arcane term for people who cannot use magic. It's meant to be derogatory, but as very few people are familiar with the word, the effect is often lost. Edward actually knows the word, and takes no offense at it. He is more concerned with the second part of the statement. "What's the Dragon King?"

"He is the savior of magic," the specter answers with fervor. "The devourer of man; the one who will rain fire down on the unworthy and show the Cassus what true power is!"

While Andrea cannot see or hear the exchange that's going on, she can sense the magical energies given off by the summoned spirit. She takes the opportunity to see if she can glean anything from it. Most magical abilities require a verbal phrase or incantation to activate them. Some arcane talents also require somatic gestures or arm movements; however, there are a handful that can be used with far less effort. Transporters, for example, can teleport themselves great distances with just a thought. Prophets can usually glimpse through the eyes of another or even see into the future by merely focusing on an object or person. In this instance,

Andrea uses the potent magic radiating from the dead terrorist to channel her ability. She closes her eyes, taking a few deep breaths in and out before opening them again.

Andrea finds that she is no longer in the morgue at the DoS, but instead she's outside at the Lincoln Memorial in D.C.. Her visions can often feel like an intense dream or like they are actually happening. She feels the warmth of a sunny day, the Washington Monument looming over the reflecting pool in front of her. The entire area appears to be empty, and all is strangely quiet. Glancing down, she sees a stream of viscous crimson liquid flowing all the way to the base of the water below. She spins around in alarm to discover a grisly sight.

The white steps of this once sacred shrine now run red with the blood of countless bodies that have been eviscerated and strewn about. Every piece of nearly unrecognizable human flesh has been clawed, bitten, and mangled by some sizeable creature. Andrea's gaze follows the carnage up to the monument itself. The structure and its Greek inspired columns appear unscathed. The statue of Lincoln is hard to make out in the shadows of the inner chamber. In fact, it seems darker than usual except for the eyes of the sculpture that seem a little too life-like. Are they glowing? Andrea wonders if fear is getting the better of her. She is about to ignore it when suddenly the statue moves.

A colossal form snakes its way through the giant pillars with great celerity. What emerges is a reptilian beast covered in obsidian scales. It has a massive leathery wingspan that blocks out the sky overhead. Once in the open, the creature moves cautiously on all fours like a predator sizing up its prey; its razor-sharp claws eerily click on the cement with each step. Its head rests at the end of a long neck that serpentines back and forth in an almost hypnotic fashion. An elongated jaw is lined with rows of slick, black fangs. Two unnaturally green eyes lock on to Andrea. "A Prophet." the creature speaks in low, thunderous tone. "And a powerful one at that."

For a moment, Andrea is frozen in fear. She's never experienced a vision that could interact with her. She decides not to break the spell and push forward. After all, she thinks, it's just a vision; what danger could it pose? "What are you?" she asks.

"I'm the Dragon King," the creature answers.

Andrea senses other magic at play here. It feels as though an outside force has infiltrated the vision and reshaped it somehow. She knows magic is real, but as far as she's concerned, dragons are still creatures of lore. "No." She attempts to fight the illusion. "Something isn't right here."

The beast leaps forward. "You challenge the authority of a dragon?!"

The dragon breathes in deeply before aiming a jet of fire at Andrea. She doesn't attempt to avoid it, but rather makes a quick arcane motion with her hands. "You are not a dragon!" she shouts before uttering a quick spell. "Veritas visus!"

Just as the flames are about to envelope her, they vanish, along with the dragon itself. The scene of the massacre has also dissipated, leaving the monument unmolested. Andrea's heart is pounding in her chest, and she feels out of breath. She's not sure what she just encountered, but she knows what it wasn't. "You're no dragon," she repeats softly.

A man suddenly appears behind Andrea. He's a well-dressed, good-looking man with dark hair and eyes. He's so close to Andrea he is almost on top of her. She doesn't see him. He reveals a most wicked smile as he leans into her. "But I'm so much more," he whispers in her ear.

No sooner do the words escape his lips than a bolt of lightning surges through Andrea from behind, punching through her chest, arcing outward. This pain cannot be real, but she's never been in more excruciating agony. Her eyes shut tight, and she lets out a horrendous scream.

Andrea clutches her chest, still screaming. She opens her eyes to find herself back in the morgue. Her screams freak out the already nervous Catherine, who also starts screaming. Catherine releases Edward, breaking focus on her spell. This causes the spectral form of the dead terrorist to disappear, leaving only the charred remains behind.

Edward is in utter confusion. The morgue attendant jumps out of his chair, looking around in a panic. Once Andrea sees where she is, she stops screaming, and Catherine follows in kind. Edward sees Andrea's face is flush and covered in sweat. "What the hell was that Andrea?" He questions with little regard for her emotional state. "We were finally getting somewhere."

Andrea's still clutching her chest. She knows she wasn't actually murdered with a lightning bolt, but it felt like she was. Her chest burns, and she finds it difficult to catch her breath. "I…" she stammers. "I just saw…the…the Dragon King."

Edward waves to the morgue attendant and motions him over to Catherine. Catherine doesn't appear as bad off as Andrea, but she's rather flustered as well. "Can you take her upstairs?" Edwards helps the attendant guide Catherine towards the door. "And get her some water or something."

The attendant leaves the room with Catherine in tow. Edward is immediately back in Andrea's face. "What do you mean you saw the Dragon King?" He asks. "What did you see?"

"I saw…something," Andrea attempts to articulate through her shock. "Something terrible. We're dealing with magic I've never felt before. This guy, this Dragon King-"

"Wait, the Dragon King is a man?" Edward interrupts. "Did you see his face? Could you identify him?"

"No," She replies before attempting to correct herself. "I mean I didn't see him. I felt his…presence, but you don't understand-"

"Then do your job," He interrupts again. "Find him again, and let's end this."

Edward turns to make for the door; however he doesn't take one step before Andrea grabs him pulling him back. "You don't get it!" Andrea says frantically. "I think this guy can use more than one type of magic. That shouldn't be possible, yet he invaded my vision and used two powerful types of magic to push me out. This could be the most powerful sorcerer on the planet, and he seems to want all humans dead."

"Then I suppose it's good that I have a weapon of my own now," Edward boasts confidently.

"That girl is not a weapon!" Andrea replaces her fear with anger.

"If I wanted your opinion, I'd ask for it," Edward responds harshly.

"You're a real son of a bitch!" Andrea says as she forcefully pushes passed him and out the door.

Edward just shakes his head and laughs it off. Almost everyone that works for the Secretary has a strong distaste for his cold callousness, and he knows it. He likes it that way. He finds it easier to do his job when his subordinates are kept at arm's length. Even if someone got close, they would find he's pretty unfeeling. It's a trait that allows him to lie to Catherine so convincingly while keeping her detained without cause to continue utilizing her skills. He's also planning to serve up some false story to her parents so as to avoid any investigation into her disappearance. Most people would have reservations about doing such things; however, the only thing on Edward's mind at the moment is the taskforce he's been trying to get approved for the past three months.

When the Department of Sorcery was first created, it was meant to be more than just a monitoring center for people with magical powers. The Department was going to launch a nationwide police force with sorcerer officers called Guardians that would handle cases too dangerous for normal humans. Congress thought this gave sorcerers too much power and killed the bill immediately. Since that time, Edward has been carefully drafting a proposal for a small, elite taskforce of sorcerers that work exclusively for the DoS in a similar fashion to the Guardians, only with less legal oversight. The moment the first attack happened in Paris, he started putting pressure on the President for an Executive Order, but she resisted, knowing that such a decision would have major pushback. Edward is convinced that she'll have to agree now that there has been an attack on American soil.

## Chapter 5: Strange Company

Though the explosion only scarred the southern front of the White House, the President, Cabinet members, and all key personnel have been moved to an undisclosed location until a full investigation of the attack site has been completed. The facility is underground though you'd never know it from the inside. It's a labyrinth of halls, offices, and conference rooms that are extremely well lit. The walls almost seem to reflect the light, making it feel even brighter than it actually is. Most cubicles are sparsely decorated; each of them looking almost identical with basic office equipment.

The President wears a navy blue pantsuit and sits in a large rectangular room with a long glass wall along one side, allowing a complete view of the interior. Behind her, along one of the smaller walls, sits a large screen made up of six separate panels, each displaying a different muted news feed with the subtitles on. The President pours over a large open file folder. Wisps of hair have freed themselves from the bun she had styled in a hurry. Her exhaustion is apparent in both her sluggish movements and heavy eyes.

Eric is back on the President's guard detail, standing just outside the room; however, he's still shaken from the attack three days earlier. The fact that this is the first day he's been sober since the incident isn't helping his nerves either. He almost considered not coming in at all, perhaps never again. He doesn't feel fit to protect the President or anyone else for that matter. Had she not called personally to request his presence, he most certainly would've resigned.

Edward arrives at the underground facility with Celeste trailing behind him. She carries a stack of bulky binders topped with thick manila file folders, each filled with paperwork. The two of them are escorted through the countless hallways by a single Secret Service agent. Edward has a spring in his step and almost seems cheerful. Almost. He spoke with President Thompson this morning after having his taskforce pitch sent over to her. She didn't make him any promises, but she agreed to meet with him, and, most importantly to Edward, she sounded desperate for help.

Eric recognizes the Secretary as he approaches and opens the glass door leading in to where the President is. "The Secretary is here, Madam President," Eric says, pulling her attention away from her paperwork.

Eric steps in the room, holding the door open to allow Edward and his assistant to enter. The President stands up to acknowledge them. "Thank you for seeing me, Madam President," Edward says as he approaches the table end opposite Janet.

Eric steps outside and begins to close the door. "Agent Davis," the President says, halting Eric's exit. "I'd like you to sit in on this."

It seems such an odd request that Eric physically looks around to make sure she's talking to him. It becomes quickly apparent that she is, so he steps back in and closes the door. She waves everyone down to her end of the table. "Edward, I've been looking over the project information that you sent over," she says as she closes the file in front of her.

Eric makes his way to the President's end of the table, facing the glass wall so as to keep watch on the outer room. Edward and his aide sit opposite Eric, with Edward taking the seat closest to the President. Celeste breathes a sigh of relief when she finally sets down the heavy stack of binders and folders. "I'll get right down to it." Edward begins his sales pitch and picks up a binder to hand to the President. "In light of recent events, the United States needs this taskforce. We need a team that can go up against threats that use magic and if you'll just-"

"Who do you have in mind?" the President interrupts.

"I'm sorry?" Edward is completely caught off guard.

"I don't need to see anymore." The President declines the binder with a slight wave. "I am aware of what's at stake and what we're dealing with. I assume you already have a team picked out, and I'd like to know who they are."

"As you wish." Edward nods.

He slides the binder back over to Celeste and proceeds to take the stack of file folders, handing them to the President. She sets the files down in front of her and opens the top folder. It contains a photo and thorough dossier on Andrea, including her background, juvenile records, and medical history.

The file recounts how Andrea's parents abandoned her in Florida when she was no more than four years old and already showing signs of arcane affinity. It is presumed that her parents were not magic wielders and left her out of fear. She was in and out of foster care until her early teens when she landed in juvenile lock up for grand theft. There were no jails designed for sorcerers at the time, so she was frequently able to use her abilities to escape by seeing holes in the jail's security.

Andrea wasn't discovered by Edward until she was old enough to be tried as an adult and had found yet another new home in Carcer, the prison for sorcerers. Due to her troubled upbringing, she never received any sort of proper training in the use of magic until recently, and even then, no real education was given, as she's the first Prophet to work for the government. Despite this fact, she is quite natural at crafting new spells when the occasion calls for it.

"This one already works for us," Edward says as the President looks over the file. "She's on a work release program, using her divination magic for the DoS in exchange for a reduced sentence."

"Well, we're off to a great start," the President says sarcastically as she moves to the next folder.

This file includes a similar dossier, with the addition of a military history, for Anthony Taylor, a Lieutenant in the U.S. Navy. He's a young African-American with brash confidence in his eyes. "Lieutenant Taylor has been working for us for the past three months." Edward moves on quickly brushing aside the President's previous comment. "He's one of the finest Transporters the Navy has ever seen."

Edward isn't laying it on thick here. Military Transporters are crucial when it comes to getting supplies to the front lines quickly, and Anthony is one of the best. His apportation magic is strong enough that he's able to teleport large vehicles or shipping containers halfway around the world without the support of another sorcerer.

Anthony joined the Navy fresh out of high school because of his love for the movie *Top Gun*. He had dreams of being a naval aviator just like Maverick in the film. Unfortunately, Anthony discovered his magical talents at a young age and was honest about it when he signed up. He was sent for special training with a military sorcerer instructor who taught soldiers spells for flying and teleporting. For Anthony, it isn't a loss though. Sure, he's not piloting jets, but now he doesn't need the vehicle to take to the skies.

"He seems like a good candidate," the President says as she moves on to the next file.

This file is for a civilian; an Asian-American woman around the same age as Anthony. She is an Evo named Jasmine Yuen and, while she may not have military experience, she is rather deadly. Aside from being very good with fire-based attack magic, she also holds belts in kung fu, tae kwon do, akido, shotokan, and has advanced training in Brazilian ju-jitsu. The file also mentions that she is one of the top prize fighters for the Ultimate Magic Dueling Championship (known to most as the UMDC).

In the early 2000s the UMDC became a powerhouse in the world of entertainment by combining the thrill of magical exhibitions with the raw brutality of mixed martial arts. The concept sounds dangerous, but the UMDC has safety protocols in place for each bout. A Sentinel casts a barrier around the octagon to contain all attack magic while a Mender is on standby for any serious injuries fighters may suffer in the ring. Most fighters are Evos as their magic is "flashier" than other types, with the occasional Transporter thrown in to shake things up.

"Hmm, I recognize her," The President says upon seeing Jasmine's photo in her file. "A little high-profile for this kind of thing, don't you think?"

"Wait 'til you see the next one," Edward says under his breath.

"What was that?" the President questions.

"I said you should move on to the next one," Edward covers quickly.

The President looks suspiciously at Edward, but moves on to the next file. She immediately recognizes the man in the photo as Benjamin Baker, billionaire creator of U-Movie. Baker is a lanky Brit originally from London, but currently living lavishly in New York. While in England, he used his illusion magic to steal…a lot. He eventually got tired of the criminal lifestyle and decided to turn over a new leaf in America. After changing his name and starting a new life, he came up with the idea that would revolutionize the movie industry.

Where 3-D movies make the picture appear to come out from the screen slightly, U-Movie uses illusion magic and some state-of-the-art tech to allow the viewer to actually "live" the movie. Upon purchasing a ticket, viewers choose one of the film's main characters and then proceed to experience the movie's narrative as though they were a part of it. This innovation launched Benjamin into fame and wealth beyond his wildest dreams. "How do you expect one of the richest men in the world to agree to working for a secret government taskforce?" President Thompson asks incredulously.

"Howard Hughes worked with the CIA," Edward replies. "And besides, we have so much on his criminal exploits from England that if he doesn't play ball, we can easily have him deported and turned over to Scotland Yard or Interpol."

"Okay," Janet says as she closes the last folder. "Is that everyone?"

"I do have one or two more; however, I don't have files on them just yet," Edward answers.

"Well, who are they?" The President snaps back quickly.

Edward is visibly irritated by her pressing, but tries to conceal it. He shifts slightly in his seat before straightening up to answer. "One is a Mender named Emmanuel Henri." Edward rubs his hand where Emmanuel had cut him as he speaks. "And the other is…a Reaper."

"A Reaper?" Janet questions in disbelief. "You've actually found someone who uses death magic?"

"Yes, Madam President," Edward replies.

"There was no mention about death magic in the materials you sent over," she says in response.

"It's a rather new development," Edward says.

The President stands up rather abruptly, straightening out her jacket as she does. Eric and Edward immediately rise in response. Celeste looks around quizzically for a moment before standing as well. "I have two stipulations before I agree to anything." The President addresses Edward. "Number one: I want to meet this team."

"I can make that happen," Edward nods.

"Number two, and this is not negotiable," the President says while motioning to Eric. "I want Agent Davis to run the team should I find it acceptable and sign off."

Both Eric and Edward shoot the President a slight look of surprise. While Edward wants the President's support, he hates the idea of her having a spy in his ranks to report on every aspect of the taskforce.

Eric doesn't understand why he would be chosen for such an assignment after the White House attack, nor does he feel capable of handling the responsibilities in his current condition. He doesn't express himself verbally, but President Thompson can see the reservations in his eyes. She doesn't hang on this, however, turning her attention back to Edward. "Will that be a problem?" she questions.

"I can easily arrange a meet and greet with the team," Edward answers.

Celeste gives Edward a subtle, but incredulous glance. While the President doesn't appear to see it as her eyes are locked on Edward expectantly, Eric does. "And Agent Davis?" The President follows up.

Edward lets out a sigh as he answers. "If it will help get approval so we can begin to hunt these terrorists properly, so be it."

"Good." The President shakes Edward's hand. "Arrange the meeting and get back to me. Thank you for coming in."

"We'll get right on it," Edward says while giving Celeste a commanding look.

Celeste gathers up the binders and folders before following Edward out of the room. Eric follows Celeste and Edward to the door, closing it behind them. He turns back towards Janet. "Madam President, can I have a moment?"

"If it's in regards to the taskforce, then no," she replies curtly. "It's not a request, and it's not open for discussion. Whether you believe it or not, you are exactly the man to lead this team."

"But I've already failed at my job, and, as a result, a lot of people are dead."

It might be the lack of sleep or the pressure she's under from the terrorist attack, but Eric's self-doubt really gets under her skin. She moves towards him in an aggressive manner getting right in his face. "Knock it off! As callous as it sounds, your job was to protect me, and you did that. You're not the only one losing sleep at night because the events of that day play on a loop in your mind. The terrorists are responsible for those deaths. We both now have a chance to get justice, so I need you to stop feeling sorry for yourself."

While the President seems dismissive of Eric's emotional reaction to the deaths of many Americans, she feels the same pain rather deeply. She blames herself for the attack on the White House. She is supposed to be the leader of the most powerful country in the world, yet she feels rather powerless. She doesn't even really have much faith in Edward's taskforce, but she's willing to try anything if it can stop further attacks. She genuinely believes in Eric's abilities and thinks he can give the taskforce a better chance of success. It's too bad her faith isn't shared by Eric.

"Yes, Madam President," Eric says reluctantly.

Eric has been so lost in his own self-pity that he hadn't stopped to consider how anyone else might be feeling about the attack. While knowing the President's pain doesn't make him feel any better, it does at least make him willing to follow orders instead of quitting.

Meanwhile, Edward and Celeste make their way topside in an elevator. Celeste leans against the back wall to take some of the load off from mountain of binders and folders in her arms. Edward stands directly in front of the doors to the lift. He's looking down at the screen of his smartphone, positioned so that Celeste can't see it. An unknown number has texted a message that reads "Midnight."

Edward knows who sent the message, and, while it might seem cryptic, it's very clear to him. The text fills him with apprehension and anxiety though he doesn't show that on the surface. In fact, he doesn't react in any way. He doesn't even reply to the message; he simply stares at the screen until- "Why did you tell the President you could easily set up a meeting?" Celeste's voice snaps Edward back to reality. "You haven't even approached half these people."

Edward locks his phone and slides it into his inner jacket pocket. He looks back over his right shoulder to Celeste. "It won't be difficult," Edwards says with a smirk. "I'll have Lieutenant Taylor bring in Baker and Yuen, the FBI can collect the old man, and the girl is still in holding."

"But how do you know they'll agree to work for us?" Celeste questions.

"They don't have a choice."

## Chapter 6: Sneak Attacks

When Lieutenant Anthony Taylor woke up this morning, he didn't suspect he'd find himself in a literal hell before the day's end. It sounded like it would be a standard snatch and grab. He's done them before; in fact he's been specifically trained for it by the Navy. He also has extensive combat training so how did things go so completely wrong?

Anthony was assigned to apprehend and bring Jasmine Yuen and Benjamin Baker to a secret training facility for the Department of Sorcery. His first mistake was only skimming the dossier on Jasmine. While he has seen her fight on television, his arrogance caused him to miss a few crucial details about her full combat abilities.

Jasmine was taking a few moments to herself in the locker room before her UMDC prize fight in Dubai. The roar of the crowd watching the preliminary matches could be felt through the walls while she stood in front of a mirror in quiet reflection psyching herself up for the carnage that she knew would ensue. Her shoulder length black hair was tied back into a tight braid. The intensity of her brown eyes glared back at her, ready for anything. Unfortunately, that's when Anthony chose to teleport in and grab her.

The plan was to snatch her before her bout, making it appear as though she chickened out of the title fight. As Anthony found out, it wasn't a good plan. Before he could lay hands on her, he was greeted with an elbow to the throat, causing him to stumble back. For Jasmine, the fight was beginning early. She attacked ferociously, putting Anthony on the defensive. The blow to the esophagus really set the pace for the battle as Anthony was then unable to focus enough to teleport, instead relying strictly on hand-to-hand combat. The two were fairly evenly matched, exchanging blows and destroying the once pristine locker room.

The longer the fight went on, the more Anthony regretted his plan to apprehend this target. Jasmine is one of the UMDCs top female fighters, often challenging more than one opponent at a time. She loves the thrill she gets from each fight. To her, nothing is more exhilarating than when a battle provides her a significant challenge to overcome. Of course being one of the strongest females in the sport, she gets a lot of media attention. She puts on the act of the arrogant antagonist for the cameras when in reality, she is rather humble and respects most of the other fighters…unless they use cowardly tactics.

After a while of slugging it out, Jasmine got bored and decided to heat things up. "Ignis!" she said repeatedly, creating fire in her hands that she threw across the room.

This brings Anthony to his current predicament. Waves of heat emanate from the flames around the room, making him feel like he's suffocating. His only exit, short of scrapping the mission, is being blocked by a very aggressive Jasmine. Waiting to deliver the final blow, she stalks her prey. Each movement mirrors that of a serpent; the embroidered golden dragon coiling up from the left leg of her red fight shorts onto her top give her an even more reptilian appearance. The flames dance around her as though they obey her every command until the fire suppression system finally activates, showering the room in a fine mist. "Who sent you?" She finally addresses her attacker. "Qiang?"

"I don't know who that is," Anthony manages to choke out. "I work for the U.S. government."

Jasmine studies Anthony for a moment before taking a less hostile stance. "What do you want?"

Anthony notices Jasmine relax slightly and figures this is his only opportunity to grab her. He vanishes, instantly reappearing right behind her. She swings behind, but Anthony is ready for it this time, catching her arm. He quickly teleports them out before Jasmine can take another swing.

The spell instantly transports them to a brightly lit holding cell at a facility in Virginia. The room is empty with no windows or signs of any exits. The white padded walls have a grid pattern that travel to both the floor and ceiling. The lights in the upper four corners of the room change from hot white to a light blue almost immediately upon the room becoming occupied.

Jasmine breaks Anthony's hold on her and kicks him into a wall. He spins to face her before she can attack again. "Where are we?!" she shouts. "Take me back!"

"I can't," Anthony replies.

"We'll see about that," Jasmine says as she begins the somatic portion of a spell with her hands. "Inferni ignis!"

Jasmine's look of intensity turns to confusion as nothing happens after her recital of the incantation. It's a spell she has used many times, so she knows she performed it correctly. She tries again. Nothing still. Anthony stands down from his defensive position. "That won't work in here," he says.

Sorcerers are able to pull in arcane energy from the world around them and refocus it into the spells they cast. The government spent a lot of time and money into developing technology that is able to block to that ability. It only works on a small scale and, being experimental, isn't widely used. Carcer prison was the first facility to use the technology in cells and special anti-magic collars for transporting inmates.

"What the hell is going on?!"

Before Anthony can answer, a door-sized section of a nearby wall opens up. Two masked soldiers wearing heavy ballistic body armor enter through the doorway. Each one has an assortment of weapons including a combat knife, a holstered sidearm, two smoke grenades, and a taser. One guard holds a pump action shotgun loaded with bean bag rounds while the other wields a metal baton. "Against the wall!" One of the men shouts at Jasmine.

Jasmine backs up against the wall raising her hands in the air. "What do you want?" She pleads for an answer.

"That's not for us to explain," Anthony replies.

The two armed soldiers step between Anthony and Jasmine. Anthony backs towards the door. The soldiers follow after him, but keep their weapons trained on Jasmine. She sees where this is going and pushes off from the wall. "You are not leaving me in here!" she shouts as she lunges forward.

The guard with the shotgun fires at Jasmine, hitting her in the shoulder with a bean bag round and knocking her back into the wall. She collapses to the ground. The soldiers finish escorting Anthony out of the room, and the door closes behind them, engaging a mechanical lock.

"Was that necessary?" Anthony scolds the soldier with the shotgun.

"She attacked," the soldier says matter-of-factly. "I reacted appropriately."

"Right." Anthony lays the sarcasm down thick. "Can you at least get a medic to look her over? Make sure she's okay."

The soldier nods as Anthony straightens his form-fitting gray shirt before retrieving a thin metallic cell phone from his paramilitary pants. He makes his way down a narrow hallway leading to some elevators while calling Edward.

"Ah, Lieutenant Taylor, I've been expecting your call," Edward says from the other end of the line. "Do you have good news for me?

"Package one has been acquired, though she put up a serious fight," Anthony answers.

"A fight?" Edward sounds surprised. "Did you try asking her to come with you?"

"Um…" Anthony isn't even sure how to respond as the thought never even came to mind.

"I see," There's a slight sound of disappointment in Edward's voice. "What about package two?"

"I'll be collecting him shortly," Anthony replies.

"Good," Edward's tone changes to condescension. "Why not try a little tact this time?"

"Yes, sir," Anthony says before hanging up the phone.

Working for the Department of Sorcery the last three months has been pretty uneventful for Anthony. He's mostly been a desk jockey with the occasional need to actually transport something. Not quite what he expected when he made the jump from the Navy. During his time at the DoS, he's had very few interactions with Edward, and only started working directly under him in the past couple of days. The two of them do not get along very well. Edward hates jokes and pop culture references while Anthony hates humorless bureaucrats. It's a volatile relationship, but Anthony has the military discipline to play nice while Edward, for the most part, is just a jerk.

Anthony pushes the button to call the elevator. He needs to go give the file on Benjamin Baker one last look before he teleports to New York. He doesn't want a repeat of what just happened with Jasmine.

* * *

The Baker Building dominates the New York skyline. Aside from being one of the tallest structures in the city, it also magically projects clips from famous films on all four sides of the building twenty-four hours a day. It's a shining example of the success of Benjamin Baker's U-Movie empire. Every day starting at noon, Benjamin's favorite movie, *Clue*, streams on the building's southern wall, and it's currently about an hour into the film.

Benjamin's penthouse office takes up the top two floors of the building. Aside from the most lavish accommodations that money can buy, the vaulted ceilings provide ample room for a private theater for film screenings, a fully stocked bar, and a fountain in the center. There is also a desk, so Benjamin can justifiably call it an office. He had a holographic screen projector built into the top of it, for a three dimensional display of his computer screen. Benjamin sits in a large chair with his feet up on the desk. A designer blazer drapes on the back of the chair, and a keyboard sits in his lap as he types notes on it.

Anthony materializes near the fountain wearing the same tactical gear he wore in his encounter with Jasmine. Benjamin sees Anthony beyond his projection screen, but seems unalarmed. "Are you from catering?" Benjamin asks in his posh British accent.

"No, Mr. Baker," Anthony replies as he slowly makes his way towards Benjamin's desk. "I'm from the government. I need you to come with me right away. It's a matter of national security."

Benjamin takes his feet off the desk and stands up. He sets the keyboard on the desk before making his way towards Anthony, meeting him about half way. Benjamin extends his right hand in a gesture of peace. "Always happy to oblige," he says with a smile.

Anthony is relieved that this acquisition is going so well. He reaches out to shake Benjamin's hand only to grasp at nothing. This catches Anthony off-guard causing him to lose his balance and stumble forward into Benjamin. As he passes through it, the mirage of Benjamin dissipates into nothing, letting Anthony know he's been talking to an illusion.

"Damn Ghosts," Anthony says under his breath.

Benjamin learned to use his magical abilities at a very young age. His teacher introduced him to the arcane and a life of crime. Benjamin was a great student, learning over time how to cast a few minor illusions without having to speak the incantations. The moment he saw Anthony in his office, he turned himself invisible while simultaneously creating an illusory double in his place. The double can look and sound like the real thing, down to the horizontal crease on his black slacks from where the keyboard sat. It has no real presence, causing the illusion to end if it is physically interacted with. Stronger spells can make an illusion more interactive, but this magic was pretty basic.

Benjamin reappears near the fountain. He holds the real wireless keyboard in one hand while giving a sarcastic salute with the other. "Sorry ol' chap," Benjamin says. "But I already told Secretary Chamberlain where he can stick it."

Edward had approached Benjamin at a fundraiser a few weeks back regarding the taskforce. In typical Chamberlain fashion, he used no subtlety in his pitch, leading off with the fact he possesses information on Benjamin's criminal past. The conversation didn't go much further than that, as Benjamin doesn't appreciate being strong-armed into anything. After all, he left a life of being coerced by self-satisfying wankers a long time ago. Benjamin cut Edward off with a few choice expletives before walking away.

"You assume you have a choice," Anthony threatens.

"Multi duplis," Benjamin says while shaking his head in disappointment.

The room suddenly becomes very crowded as around forty other "Benjamins" appear throughout it. All of the images move and speak together, creating a rather eerie stereo effect. "Good luck finding the real me!"

Anthony lets out a defeatist sigh. "So much for tact," he mumbles to himself.

Anthony begins quickly teleporting around the room, grabbing at various Benjamins and causing them to disappear. As speedy as he is to shatter the illusions, more images of Benjamin continue to appear. Anthony blips throughout the vast penthouse for a few minutes, attempting to nab the real Benjamin before deciding his attempts are futile. He stops near the fountain at the center in the room. The thought occurs to him that Benjamin may not actually be any of the ones he can see. If Benjamin wants to play games, then Anthony has just the game for him.

"Omnia vectio!" Anthony speaks the words to a powerful incantation.

A low rumble spreads throughout the room. The intensity of the reverberation slowly increases, causing the exterior glass walls to waver. The entire floor begins to shake violently causing Benjamin to break his spell focus. One by one, his illusionary doppelgängers fade into nothingness, leaving the real him looking around in confusion. He assumes the tremor is a result of Anthony's arcane uttering since New York isn't known for having earthquakes; it has him concerned either way. He tries to make a break for the elevator, but is too late. Everything in the room seems to blink out of existence, leaving only the walls and anything bolted down.

The entire contents of Benjamin's office materialize inside a large training room. The fountain appears tilted, partially on top of a square sparring arena, spilling its contents all over the rubber mats that cover the concrete floor. Benjamin's desk sits among some rows of punching bags while the luxury seating from his personal theater has become fused with a wall. Moments after the chaos, the lighting in the room flashes red and is accompanied by an ear-piercing alarm. Benjamin is so horrified by what has become of his office that he doesn't seem to notice much else. "My office..." he mutters repeatedly.

A handful of armed soldiers, dressed in much the same fashion as the two men at Jasmine's holding cell, barge into the room responding to the alarm. Most of them are armed with automatic weapons. Anthony hustles over to the group with his hands in the air. "Everything's cool," he says trying to diffuse the situation. "Lieutenant Taylor bringing in a package for the Secretary. He wants him unharmed, but I'd get a collar on him before he snaps out of it."

One of the soldiers removes a metal collar from his belt, runs over to Benjamin, and clasps it around his neck. The collar is made with the same technology that is used in Carcer and the holding cells at this facility. The upside is portability, allowing prisoners to be transported without granting them access to use their magic. The downside is each unit is very expensive to make, and they tend to be buggy. Benjamin realizes what it is as soon as it's locked around his neck. He takes in the gravity of his current situation and handles it with the sophistication and class that he handles all his business with. "Please inform the Secretary that I accept his invitation," he says while straightening his white button down long-sleeve shirt.

## Chapter 7: The Gang's All Here

Even with a new job assignment and the President's pep talk, Eric continues to drink himself to sleep at night, trying to wash away his guilt. His hangover this morning isn't as bad as they have been, so maybe he's hitting the bottle a bit less. At least that's the thought running through his mind as he drives a government-issued black SUV to a DoS training facility located just outside of Langley, Virginia.

The compound has a concrete perimeter wall topped with barbed wire. This surrounds some barracks and a handful of other multi-story structures. Eric presents his identification to the two armed guards at the gate, gaining access to the facility. Upon driving inside, he notices the whole area is heavily patrolled by guards; many of them keep an anti-magic collar on their belts in addition to carrying assault weapons. This leads Eric to wonder if they are keeping people out or in.

Eric makes his way into a three-tiered parking structure before taking an elevator to a security checkpoint. He again presents his identification and is scanned for any weapons. Once through, he is led by an armed guard into a fairly unassuming one-story building with a beige exterior. It has very few windows; however, the automatic doors leading inside are glass. Upon seeing the thickness of the glass, Eric assumes it is at least bullet resistant.

Just inside is yet another security checkpoint with more heavily armed guards. It's at this point that Eric starts to get concerned about what the President has signed him up for. He's not even used to seeing this much security at the White House. His identification is checked yet again, and his fingerprints are scanned and run against the government database for verification. It's a tense few moments as the computer processes the information. The guards look ready to draw and shoot if there is even a slight software delay. Eric is finally cleared, given a badge, and granted access further inside the building. Even after gaining clearance though, he still has an armed escort following him to the elevators.

The elevator takes Eric underground to an expansive maze of hallways, each one similarly lined with doors to various rooms. He passes some living quarters, a mess hall, a medical clinic, an armory, and a handful of other rooms before arriving at a set of automated sliding metal doors. There is a guard on either side of the doorway. As the doors open, it becomes apparent why there is so much heightened security. President Thompson is standing inside the room next to Edward with two Secret Service agents nearby.

Eric enters what appears to be a circular "war room." A rectangular console rests at its center. The table-length top panel of the console is a digital display that can be angled towards a seating area arranged in an arc around half the room. The display is currently in a horizontal position and powered off so to function as a glass table-top. Edward stands directly in front of it, looking even more proud of himself than usual. His hands clasp the lapels of his gray suit jacket while he puffs his chest up as though he's challenging anyone in the room to test his authority.

The President wears a black pant suit and stands with her arms crossed. She has an expectant, slightly impatient look upon her face. Her demeanor eases a bit as Eric enters the room. Edward actually loses a bit of his steam upon seeing him, but attempts to hide this fact with bravado. "Ah, Agent Davis, you're just in time!"

"Mr. Secretary, Madam President," Eric says suddenly getting self-conscious about his wrinkled shirt.

Eric straightens his necktie in an effort to polish up his appearance. He shouldn't be surprised that the President is here since she's the one who wanted to meet this team, yet her presence has caught him completely off-guard. Now he's thinking that he's definitely still drinking too much. In an effort to avoid engaging the President directly, Eric wanders around the room. "This is quite the facility," he says looking over some of the computer workstations that sit opposite the viewing area.

"Yes," Edward says while keeping an eye on Eric. "This was initially set up as an arcane research facility."

"Well, they do say all the best research facilities are located underground," Eric replies with a dry sarcasm.

Nothing about what Eric has seen so far allows him to believe this compound was ever meant for only research. Even if the façade on the surface level was used for legitimate business, there's no way an underground research facility needs an armory stocked with tactical gear, body armor, and heavy weapons. There is always the possibility that the armory was added after the compound was repurposed, but the room didn't look makeshift.

The doors to the room slide open, allowing Andrea to enter from the hallway. She looks uneasy with the procession that follows her in. Catherine, Emmanuel, Jasmine, and Benjamin are escorted into the room; each wears handcuffs, an anti-magic collar, and a matching blue jumpsuit. Each prisoner's emotional state is vastly different from the next. Emmanuel is calm, knowing there's nothing he can do at the moment. Catherine is terrified and just wants to go home. Benjamin is irate and wishes to make a formal protest. Jasmine is calculating her odds for survival if she chokes out one of the soldiers with her handcuffs and makes a break for it. This sorcerer "chain gang" is led by two armed soldiers and followed up by Anthony.

"Is this your team, or is this place also doubling as a prison?" Eric quips at Edward.

President Thompson is appalled by what she is seeing; more so than that, she's angry that she allowed herself to be tricked by Edward's song and dance. Janet considers herself a tolerant, understanding person, but once you piss her off you'd better look out. "Edward, outside," She says in an imposing tone. "Now."

Without a word Edward sheepishly follows Janet and her two Secret Service agents into the hallway, the sliding doors closing ominously behind them. As soon as the door is sealed, Eric approaches Anthony, who he recognizes from his file. "Are the cuffs and collars really necessary?"

"Yes," Anthony replies while motioning to Jasmine. "Especially for that one."

Jasmine lurches forward, but is halted by the barrel of a rifle pointed at her head. Andrea steps in, pushing the soldier's gun barrel down towards the floor. "Knock it off," Andrea says aggressively. "These people have done nothing to deserve being held this way!"

"Is that true?" Eric presses Anthony.

"Technically, yes, they are being held against their will," Anthony answers. "But they are needed."

"Okay, get these things off them right now," Eric orders. "You can't expect people to work with you if you treat them like this."

"I would strongly recommend against that," Anthony warns.

"Noted. Now release them."

"I don't actually have that authority."

"Then who does?"

Almost on cue, the doors open, and Edward walks back into the room. His arrogant bravado has been replaced with sullen scowling. He is followed by the President and her Secret Service entourage. She looks very cross, eyeing Edward sharply as she walks. "Mr. Secretary, can we get these collars and cuffs removed?" Eric inquires.

"We'll get to that." Edward glances back at the President before addressing the group. "Ladies and gentlemen, please give me an opportunity to explain what is going on. I'm sure you have many questions-"

"I have a question," Catherine interjects. "Why should we believe anything out of your stupid, lying mouth?"

"Catherine, I apologize for not being honest before…and for not taking you home…and for detaining you in a holding facility, but you have to trust me here-"

"Trust you?!" Catherine interrupts again. "You've kidnapped us and now you want us to trust you?!"

"Listen." Edward tries to maintain what little composure he has left. "Some very nasty people are doing some very nasty things and are hurting a lot of people. I need your help to-"

"I can't continue to listen to this," the President steps forward. "Everyone, I apologize for the treatment you have received thus far. I wasn't aware anyone was being detained against their will."

Janet eyes the guards expectantly. "I want their restraints removed immediately."

The guards look to Edward then back to the President before carrying out her orders. "Madam President, if I may-" Edward protests.

"You shut up!" The President snaps at Edward before turning towards Catherine and softening up. "Catherine, is it? How old are you?"

"Fifteen," Catherine shyly answers.

Everyone in the room gives Edward a collective look of disgust. "Hallway," the President's imposing tone returns. "Now."

Edward's jaw tightens, and it's clear that he is cursing internally. But, he acquiesces, following her and the Secret Service back into the hallway. The doors seal pretty tightly, but muffled shouting can be heard from the other side. Eric tries to ease the tension as the group's handcuffs are removed. "My name's Eric Davis. I'm sorry about all of this. I'm sure the President will get everything sorted out and get you out of here."

"Was he referring to the terrorist attacks?" Benjamin asks as his cuffs are removed.

"Yes," Anthony answers before Eric is able.

"He never mentioned terrorists when he tried to sell me on this taskforce initially," Benjamin says while rubbing his wrists. "What exactly does he want us to do?"

"The taskforce's responsibility is to seek out and eradicate the terrorist threat."

"Whose idea was it to involve a 15 year old in such an undertaking?" Jasmine speaks up.

"I don't know," Anthony replies.

Everyone's handcuffs are removed and the guards start to remove their collars, starting with Catherine. "You don't really seem to know what's going on here," Benjamin directs his statement to Eric. "What do you have to do with all of this?"

"I was brought in by the President to train the team," Eric answers. "However, we were misled about your involvement. We were told everyone volunteered, and nobody mentioned a child."

"I'm not a child," Catherine says indignantly.

The guards finish removing everyone's collars. Emmanuel stretches before taking a seat. Andrea moves over to Catherine to see if she is okay. Jasmine begins sizing up the guards while also keeping an eye on Anthony. Benjamin continues asking questions as he approaches Eric. "So the plan was for the six of us to take on an entire terrorist network with your training? Are you a military man?"

"Former military," Eric answers. "Currently with the Secret Service."

"And what makes you qualified to train an anti-terrorist taskforce?"

Jasmine has been remaining silent and emotionless since being brought into the room. This is a con. She is filled with rage and has her sights set on Anthony. She's been waiting for the right moment to strike, and now she has it. In one deft move, she incapacitates a guard, and before the other one can react, she launches another attack. She delivers a snap kick to his knee, taking him to the ground, and follows it up with an elbow to the back of his head, rendering him unconscious. She wastes no time, conjuring an orb of fire that hovers just above the palm of her right hand. "Sphaera ignis!"

***

Outside in the corridor, Janet is giving Edward a dressing down of a lifetime. "You intentionally withheld this from me! You've been detaining this girl and went out of your way to keep that information a secret. You're done. You are done as Secretary of Sorcery. When I get done with you, you'll be lucky if you can work as a temp secretary!"

"She's the Reaper, Janet," Edward tries to defend his actions. "The girl is the Reaper."

"So you also withheld that the Reaper is a teenage girl…"

"Yes, and I should've come clean about that fact from the start, but I have the consent from her parents, and didn't think it would be such a big deal."

"Her parents gave permission for her to serve in a secret government program for sorcerers?"

"Yes."

"I want to meet these parents, and it better not be like today's meeting."

"I'll make the arrangements."

"Now I'm going to go back in there, and anyone who doesn't want to be involved will be released. You will do whatever it takes to make it right with them. After that, we'll see if I wish to proceed with this program and if you have a future."

"Yes, Madam President." It pains Edward to be so agreeable, but he can tell now is not the time to push any more buttons.

***

Anthony considers himself a quick individual with lightning reflexes and the ability to teleport from place to place in an instant, yet in this moment he feels frozen in place. He stands helpless as a swirling globe of fire propels towards his face. It all seems to be happening in slow-motion: every rotation of the sphere as it edges forward, every flicker of the dancing flame. The heat from the small fireball increases at an exponential rate. Just before it hits Anthony's face, the ball explodes against an invisible force. To his surprise, the magical flames have not affected him.

While relief and a bit of confusion wash over Anthony, on the other end of the room Jasmine is furious and begins summoning another flaming orb to hurl. "Sphaera ignis!"

"Praesidium!" Eric throws up another protective barrier, but this time encasing Jasmine rather than surrounding Anthony. "Stand down. I've placed a barrier around you, and if you throw that fire the only person you're going to hurt is yourself."

"Look, I'm sorry for what happened," Anthony pleads with Jasmine. "I was under orders!"

"You think I'm pissed about your little cheap shot in the locker room?" The floating fireball dissipates as she begins testing the boundaries of the invisible barrier around her. "That fight cost me…more than your life's worth!"

"Looks like we're about to have an interesting bout *here*," Benjamin jokes. "Anyone got any popcorn?"

"You can't keep this barrier up forever, and when it comes down," Jasmine points from Anthony to Eric as she speaks. "He dies and you walk away with a severe limp."

"Did you just make a *Weird Science* reference?" Benjamin asks with enamor.

"Shut up!" Jasmine shouts in response.

"Everyone needs to just take a breath and calm down." Eric tries to take control of the situation.

The doors to the room open again with Edward, the President and her two Secret Service agents entering once more. As soon as they see the scene within, the agents draw their pistols and move into a defensive position, shielding the President. Surprisingly, Edward jumps into the fray, trying to diffuse the hostility. "Everyone please give me a chance to explain." His words seem to fall on deaf ears. "I promise this can be a lucrative opportunity for many of you."

"Lucrative?" Benjamin is skeptical. "I'm wealthier than everyone in this room combined."

"You actually fall into the 'don't have a choice' category," Edward says with a shrug.

"Not helping," the President says.

As everyone around her grows increasingly hostile, Andrea's eyes turn completely milky white. As this happens, she suddenly gets a vision of an attack on the compound. Sometimes sorcerers will have passive abilities that don't require an incantation, often working on reflex. As a Prophet, Andrea will sometimes get minor visions of the future. She has no control over how far into the future she will see, or if she will have a vision at all. In her current vision, she sees many masked men, some Evos and others just heavily armed, appear out of nothing and kill everyone except for Catherine. The attack happens in this room, and everyone is dressed as they are now, leading Andrea to believe these events are impending. The vision takes only a moment and her eyes revert back to normal. "We need to get out of here now!" Andrea screams getting everyone's attention. "Something's coming!"

"Get the President out of here and send back up!" Eric instinctively barks orders to the Secret Service agents.

The air crackles, and a flood of outside air rushes into the room as a massive portal opens, swallowing up the console at its center. Before anyone can react, twelve masked men clad in black body armor rush into the room. The eight men in front lead the charge, firing M4A1 carbine rifles modified with close quarter battle receivers, making them ideal for fighting in confined spaces. The four men carrying up the rear are Evos who waste no time launching magical bolts of fire and arcane energy.

Eric creates a barrier in front of Edward and the President. He wasn't fast enough to save the life of his fellow Secret Service agents as the hail of bullet fire cut through them. The bullets are then halted as they impact the invisible barrier behind them. Everyone else dives for cover behind the metal chairs. The sound of gunfire summons the facility guards that were waiting outside the room. They grab the President and Edward, escorting them out into the corridor. One of them calls for backup into his radio as they move.

"Get the girl!" one of the masked Evos commands the others.

Two of the armed terrorists make their way towards where Catherine is hiding. Andrea intervenes, punching one of the soldiers in the face and delivering a kick to the other's gut, knocking him backward. A bolt of blue arcane energy zips across the room, striking Andrea center mass with enough force to throw her into a wall, knocking her lifelessly to the ground.

In combat, soldiers have very little time to think or plan. Most of what they are doing is reacting. Anyone who's been in combat enough learns to keep cool and think under the pressure. Anthony is dealing better than the civilians though he has no weapon and no plan. Eric remembers the files on everyone in the room and has at least an idea of their strengths and weaknesses. "Anthony, Benjamin, take the gunners from behind!" Eric takes command. "Jasmine, with me!"

Benjamin creates multiple images of himself, drawing fire from the terrorists. Jasmine runs to Eric, who throws up a smaller shield-like barrier in front of them so they can move with it. They begin skirting the armed terrorists, making their way toward the Evos. Eric deflects incoming bullets and spells while Jasmine pops out to throw fireballs at the enemy. With the terrorists completely distracted, Anthony grabs Benjamin and teleports behind the armed soldiers.

Catherine has been unable to move since the shooting started. Even with being able to speak to the dead, she has never felt more fear than she does right now. Gunshots and small explosions echo off every surface, louder than thunder. Tears stream down her face while she clings to the base of one of the chairs, hoping it will provide some semblance of comfort, but none seems to come.

Emmanuel slowly crawls over to Andrea. "Vitae animus," he whispers an incantation to determine her condition.

He can sense that she's alive, but she has a very serious concussion. He places his palms on her head and utters the words "Corpus integro."

Emmanuel's palms glow brightly for a moment as healing energies transfer into Andrea. He can sense the concussion damage fading, but something else is keeping her unconscious.

With surprise on their side, Benjamin and Anthony manage to disarm two of the soldiers and knock them out. Anthony uses the carbine to take down two more of the terrorists, but it draws the attention off the decoys and back to him and Benjamin. Anthony teleports them out of harm's way just as the soldiers open fire.

Four DoS guards enter the room from the hallway and open fire on the invading strike team. The two teams of highly trained soldiers exchange fire while attempting to avoid each other's bullets and the volley of evocation magic being thrown around the room.

Eric and Jasmine manage to close the distance between them and the terrorist Evos. Now that they are in melee, Eric drops his barrier and starts swinging haymakers. The Evos were not expecting someone to bring punches to a magic fight, and it takes them a moment to adjust. Two of them never get the chance as Jasmine drops one with a knee to the ribs and an elbow to the throat while Eric takes down the other with a haymaker. They may have very different fighting styles, but the two strangers work well together.

Anthony creates a flank with DoS guards, causing the remaining armed terrorists to be shot down in the crossfire. The two remaining Evos see that the battle is not going their way. They quickly look at each other before looking up. "Fluctus inpulsa!" the two Evo shout, creating a deafening shock wave that knocks the occupants of the room to the ground.

Everyone in the room is disoriented, but while on the floor, Eric sees that the room's ceiling is about to collapse from the sonic damage. "Omnia praesidium!" Eric yells, creating a shell-like barrier over part of the room.

An avalanche of steel and concrete fill the room. Eric's barrier takes the brunt of the impact damage, but it collapses after the main cave-in. Dust and debris create a visibly impenetrable cloud. The two Evos were outside of the area of destruction and move directly towards Catherine as though they can see through the gray. One of the Evos grabs a carbine off the ground, using the butt of the weapon to strike Catherine in the head. The other Evo picks up her unconscious body, and the two make a quick retreat back to their entry portal, which closes as soon as they are through.

When the dust starts to settle, coughing can be heard throughout the room. Eric manages to pick himself up. "Is everyone okay?" he asks while scanning the room.

"He's going to need a doctor," Benjamin says, revealing he's standing next to Anthony, who lies on the ground with a sizable gash carved into his upper left leg by a jagged piece of metal that is still protruding from the wound.

"They took the girl!" Jasmine says while quickly looking around in hopes that she is proven wrong.

"Let's get Anthony some help," Eric says while climbing over debris towards Anthony and Benjamin. "Maybe Andrea can track these bastards after."

"Dis one is not okay," Emmanuel says.

Everyone looks over to see Emmanuel carrying Andrea. Just like everyone else in the room they are covered in concrete dust. "Somet'ing is keeping 'er asleep," Emmanuel says while inching towards Jasmine who is making her way to him to help. "I may not be able to help 'er.

## Chapter 8: Befriending the Devil

A single cone of light breaks the darkness. It starts out as a pinhole high up and expands into a circle of light large enough to reveal an unconscious Catherine lying in the center of it. She slowly starts to come to, rubbing her head where she was struck with the rifle. Everything is a bit foggy. She has no clue where she is or how she got here. She's both weak and frightened, but manages to stand briefly until she notices the room swaying back & forth. She realizes it's not the room that's moving. She sinks back to the ground and tries to get her bearings. She can't seem to stop shaking, nor does she feel confident enough to venture into the darkness. Finally, she decides that, while unlikely to yield positive results, she should call out for help. "Hello?" Her voice is a trembling whisper. "Is anyone there? I just want to go home."

"There's no need to be frightened, child." A deep voice echoes throughout the darkness. "I'm not going to hurt you."

Two glowing green orbs with vertical black slits pierce the darkness behind Catherine as the head of the black dragon from Andrea's vision slithers into the light. It pauses just long enough to form a sort of twisted smile with its fanged maw before retreating into the black void surrounding the pillar of light. Catherine doesn't see the creature, but can feel the ominous presence of something watching her. She spins her head, looking over her shoulder, finding little relief that nothing is there. "Who-" Her words catch in her throat. "Who are you?"

"I have many names." The voice seems to come from everywhere. "Terrorist to my enemies. God to my followers. But Damian was the name given to me at birth. It's reserved only for my friends…and I'd like for us to be friends, Catherine."

Catherine continues looking around the dark, trying to pinpoint where the voice is coming from to no avail. After everything she has gone through, promises of friendship mean very little. "Then why are you hiding?"

"I hide for your benefit," Damian's monstrous voice still fills the darkness. "Most find my appearance…terrifying."

"Are you disfigured or something?" Catherine asks with a child's naivety.

Damian breaks into laughter, finding a great deal of humor in her question. "I suppose that depends on your outlook," he answers.

Catherine's fear has faded and is now replaced with curiosity. "Then let me see you," she boldly demands.

"As you wish," Damian says with a tone that implies she might regret her decision.

The darkness recedes, giving way to the long stone hall of a medieval castle. Light now pours in from outside through high embrasures carved into the stonework. Two massive wooden doors, barred with a thick oaken beam, sit at one end of the room. Opposite the doors is a throne made from solid gold that is well too big for a normal man. The room is otherwise barren, lacking even the basest of luxuries.

The lustrous throne casts a very large shadow behind it. There's something odd about the shape of the shadow, however. Catherine squints to try and make out what she's seeing, only to be startled when the shadow moves. The glowing green eyes of the dragon appear once again as the creature winds its way out of the shadow towards Catherine. To even her own surprise, she is not afraid, but rather awestruck by the sight of the scaled beast before her. She'd read about dragons in storybooks, yet even in a world filled with magic, they seemed fantastical. Could this be a real dragon? "Cool!" she says with wide eyes.

"That's the spirit," the dragon responds.

As the creature walks towards Catherine, parts of it begin to flake off and vanish like ash blown away in a breeze. What's left by the end of its journey is an attractive man in his mid-thirties. His hair is as black as the scales of the dragon he appeared as only moments ago. His dark green eyes no longer glow, but they are locked on Catherine, whose mouth now hangs open. He stops before her, extending a hand. "Hello Catherine." His voice has changed, now sounding like that of a Londoner. "Damian Westonbrooke at your service. Also known as…the Dragon King."

What Catherine didn't notice while ensnared by the presence of the "king" was that the room had also changed in appearance. She is no longer standing in a castle, but in a circular room with a stained glass dome ceiling. Long corridors branch off in all directions, revealing rows and rows of books. While the contents of the library are very old, it's obvious they are well cared for. The scent of ancient books washes over Catherine, and she finally realizes the change. She marvels for a moment before remembering that she's a prisoner. With a strange man before her, in place of a fictitious animal, her boldness retreats, leaving only fear.

"Why have you kidnapped me?" She tries to be brave in the face of her captor.

"Kidnapped?" Damian responds as though he's been wounded by her words. "I haven't kidnapped you. I have liberated you from those who sought to exploit your abilities for their own personal gains."

"Isn't that what you want too?" She isn't buying his benevolence.

"You're quite clever, Catherine," Damian says with slick confidence. "But no. Unlike the government, I'm going to give you a choice. A real choice."

"Then I choose to go home," she replies quickly.

"If that's your desire…" there is disappointment in his voice.

Damian waves his hands, and a framed wooden door appears in the center of the circular room. Catherine recognizes this door. It's the front door to her house. She rushes forward and grabs the handle. "But you should know," Damian's voice halts her from turning the handle. "I could teach you to control your abilities. Think of it. No more unwanted conversations with the dead. No more accidental undead servants. You could live a normal life…if you just let me help you."

She is torn by his words. On one hand, she was already taken in by Edward who lied about helping her, so why should she trust a man who sent armed men to kidnap her? On the other hand, she would give anything to be more normal. If nothing else this man demonstrates strong mastery over the arcane which is more than she could say for Edward. If Damian is true to his word, she'll make him prove it. She releases the door handle and faces her would-be mentor. "I'll stay, but I want to see my parents."

"I'll make the arrangements," Damian replies with a warm smile.

"And I want you to explain just how you are going to help me," Catherine says with determination.

"Follow me."

Catherine obeys, following Damian through a maze of book-filled hallways until they reach a small room with a square table at its center. The walls on all sides seem to go on forever as they reach all the way to the high ceiling. Each wall is adorned with shelves of books both new and old. A tall library ladder sits in front of one of the bookcases. Damian steps up onto the ladder as he speaks. "The problem with magic today is that most sorcerers innately figure out a few spells or magical abilities," Damian says while pouring over the collection on the shelves. "But they never advance beyond that. Why do you think that is?"

"They don't read enough?" Catherine replies with teenage sarcasm, causing Damian to chuckle.

"That's partly true," he says while pulling a few books off the shelves. "It's not that they aren't reading enough; it's that they aren't reading the right things. How much do you know about the book resurgence?"

"Not much. Someone discovered magic in books, and suddenly everyone was buying them again."

In 2008, an inexperienced sorcerer accidentally stumbled across a new magical incantation while reading an old copy of Rudyard Kipling's *The Jungle Book* in a New York coffee shop. The spell summoned a tiger right in the middle of the shop, creating quite the scene and making headlines all over the world. The idea that magic came from books got into everyone's heads, and they started tracking down all the hard copies they could. Up to that point, print was a dying art with most books transitioning to digital mediums. The book resurgence saw a big boom in publishing once more, though it was fairly short-lived as very few discovered any magic. Even other spellcasters weren't able to duplicate the results from reading *The Jungle Book.*

"Yes, but very few found what they were looking for," Damian continues as he steps down from the ladder. "Many assumed that a book must be magic if the content of the book was about magic. This led to the insane popularity of a particular boy wizard; however, there was no magic in those books I'm afraid."

"Then what makes a book magical?"

"Magic doesn't just appear in books." Damian sets the books he gathered from the shelf on the table. "It has to be scribed by a powerful sorcerer, and even then can only be seen by a sorcerer of the same type."

"But wouldn't people recognize a magic spell if they saw one?"

"No. The knowledge is worked into the text of the book. For example, J.R.R. Tolkien has a number of summoning spells scattered throughout *the Hobbit* and the *Lord of the Rings* books, but to the average reader, they are just great works of fiction. If a Shepherd were to read the text though, the spells would reveal themselves."

Shepherds wield summoning magic allowing them to call people and animals instantly to a location near them. The summoned are also typically under the influence of the caster, doing things for them they might not otherwise do. The strongest Shepherds have been known to call creatures not of this world to their aid. It's rumored that those summons have inspired some of the greatest monsters in books and movies.

"Tolkien was a Shepherd?" Catherine asks in dumbfounded wonder.

"A powerful one who legend claims could not only summon creatures from other realms of existence, but was also a friend to the denizens of those realms."

Catherine feels herself getting pulled in by the spectacle of it all. She has to remind herself to stay on the point. "What does any of this have to do with helping me learn control?" she asks.

"To learn control, one must have a better understanding of the thing they seek to master," Damian sternly answers. "What's in these books will give you that understanding."

"Fine," Catherine says with a touch of attitude. "Then what would I read for Reaper magic?"

"There aren't many known tombs containing your discipline," Damian picks up a book from the stack he set on the table. "But I'd start with this."

He hands Catherine the book, revealing that it is an original copy of the 1919 edition of *Tales of Mystery and Imagination* by Edgar Allen Poe. Even just holding the book, she can feel an energy of sorts tingling in her fingertips. She immediately pulls out one of the wooden chairs and plops down at the table, opening the book to its first page.

"I like your eagerness," Damian says. "I'll be back to check on you in a while, Catherine. I'm going to go see about getting your parents here."

Catherine looks up at Damian with a smile on her face. She can't help but feel trust for this man who seems so genuine in his actions. "Cat." She says to her new friend. "Call me Cat."

"Alright, Cat," Damian replies. "I'll be back soon."

Catherine immediately dives back into her book, anxiously looking for answers to her mysterious abilities. Damian makes his way back through the book maze to the central hub of his library. The door he created is still there, and with another wave of his hand, it changes from a wooden house door to a rusty metal door with a port window that one might find on a large boat or tanker. This is a teleportation gate created by one of Damian's subordinates and then made to look like a door with illusion magic. The portal opens with no effort on Damian's part, and he steps through.

The other side of the gate finds Damian on the bridge of a ship. Sunlight pours in through the windows, and the Manhattan skyline can be seen in the distance. The vessel appears as run down as the metal door implied it would be. It's a cargo boat, bigger than a yacht, but smaller than most ships of its type. It hasn't seen much care, though there are a few patches where the blue paint hasn't worn off or been rusted over.

Three men are on the bridge when Damian arrives, two of whom are in their twenties. One sits with a headset on at a communications station speaking to the harbor patrol. Another is at the helm with his eyes firmly fixed on the waters ahead. The third man is Jared Cross, a powerful Evo in his late-thirties. He sports a high and tight military haircut. Jared's face is fixed in a permanent scowl complimented by a nasty scar on his left cheek. He wears brown pants and a light blue collared shirt with the sleeves rolled up. He looks to be in charge of the other two.

As Damian steps onto the bridge all attention is turned to him. He gives the area a quick look over before approaching Jared. "Launch the next attack."

## Chapter 9: Calm Before The Storm

After the attack at the DoS facility, the President is being escorted, under protest, back to the secured underground site. She wanted to stick around to make sure everyone was okay and lead the charge on rescuing Catherine, but the Secret Service wasn't having it. She was rushed out of the facility and into a black armored limousine. She finally realized her security team was correct in their course of action. She couldn't tell how much she was actually shaken up by the experience. After all, this was her second near death experience in under a week. When adrenaline starts flowing, the fight or flight instinct kicks in, and in her case, it was fight. Now that the adrenaline has stopped pumping, her thoughts of heroism have faded with it.

While en route, the President receives a phone call from the Secretary of Defense. "Janet, I just heard what happened," Allen says. "And with these terrorists getting more aggressive, I really think we need to discuss this new initiative."

"I don't have time for this, Allen," she replies while rubbing her head in frustration.

"You need to make time, Janet." Allen's tone gets more irritable. "Do you really think the American people want to trust the nation's security to a ragtag group of warlocks?"

"Warlocks, really?" The President raises her voice. "How would you like to become the Secretary of Sanitation? Because you're working your way to it very quickly! I've come to expect more from you than hate-fueled slurs."

The term "warlock" dates back to a time when anyone wielding magic was thought to be in league with the Devil. It's never been a popular nickname in the eyes of magic-kind and while there are still some that believe magic is the Devil's work, the term is mostly used by non-sorcerers as an insult against sorcerers.

"Listen, I understand you're trying to do this 'right side of history thing,' but you need to understand that people with powers such as these cannot be trusted. We need to know who has magical aptitude, where they are at all times, and how their abilities can be used to benefit us with zero risk. Project Revelation provides this and more with-"

"Do you hear yourself?!" The President is in utter disgust. "Do you also wish we still had slaves, and that women weren't allowed in politics?"

"Of course not-"

"Now, you listen to me, and listen good. Sorcerers have existed long before you or I were born. They have endured nothing but fear, persecution, and prejudice because of men like you. You may be trapped in the '60s when they still didn't have rights, but during *my* presidency, *we* will work for peace and acceptance. Is that understood?"

There is a long silence from Allen's end of the line. "I said is that understood?" Janet repeats herself.

"Yes, Madam President," Allen finally answers in reluctant defeat.

"Good," the President promptly hangs up the phone.

\*\*\*

Since the attack on the facility, the injured have been moved to the small medical facility located just down the hall from the war room. The room isn't terribly big, as it was never intended to handle large-scale medical emergencies. Four exam tables line one wall with drab green curtains separating them. Opposite the exam tables are three metal cabinets with glass doors for easy viewing of the medical supplies within. There are also two chairs against the same wall, separating the cabinets from each other.

Anthony sits on one of the exam table while Benjamin stands near him. Anthony's left pant leg has been cut off, revealing his leg is no longer injured. There is some dried blood, but other than that, there isn't even a scar. The crimson-stained debris that had pierced his leg now rests on a small table tray nearby. Anthony used apportation to remove the object without causing additional tearing before Emmanuel mended the wound with his magic.

Having a wound mended can be a rather painful experience depending on the severity of the trauma. Magical healing causes the cells to regenerate at an accelerated rate. It isn't so bad having small cuts mended, but regrowing bone or reconnecting muscle tissue are often more painful than the initial injury itself. One of the major benefits of mending, aside from almost instant healing, is that since there is no scabbing, there is usually no scarring either. Anthony stares at his leg in amazement. "Have you ever been healed by a Mender before?" Benjamin asks.

"No way," Anthony replies. "The military can't typically afford them. It's weird. It kind of tingles."

Andrea lies unconscious on the next bed over. She's hooked up to a monitor, and a DoS nurse watches her vitals. Eric, Jasmine, and Emmanuel stand opposite the nurse, looking on with concern. "I healed de internal damage." Emmanuel addresses the nurse. "I do not know why she is still asleep."

"I'll arrange to have her transferred to another facility for an MRI," the nurse replies before leaving the room.

Emmanuel gives a quick look to Jasmine and Eric before looking back to Andrea. "I don't know what is holding 'er, but I feel magic here. I do not t'ink a hospital will help."

"I saw what hit her," Jasmine says. "But all I detected was some focused arcane energy. Nothing that would render some kind of magical coma."

"She was very brave comin' between those men an' dat young girl," Emmanuel says.

"I want to know why that girl was targeted in the first place." Eric says aloud, but seems lost in his own thoughts.

Almost on cue, Edward comes strolling into the room as though he hasn't a care in the world. "How is everyone?"

Eric steps out from behind the curtain of Andrea's exam table, glaring at Edward. "Can I talk to you outside?"

"Alright." Edward anticipates what's to come.

Edward motions for Eric to lead the way. He follows Eric into the hallway, the automatic doors closing behind them. Eric spins around quite aggressively. "What the hell was that back there?"

"A small security oversight," Edward says nonchalantly. "I'll try to get some additional anti-magic barriers set up in key rooms, so it shouldn't be a problem again."

"Goddammit!" Eric loses any cool he was trying to maintain. "We just got ambushed in your *secret base*! We have two dead Secret Service agents, one of your people is in a coma, a teenager has been kidnapped, and you have the nerve to call it an oversight?!"

"Who do you think you're talking to?" Edward gets right in Eric's face.

"I don't care what you're the secretary of." Eric doesn't back down. "If you don't start giving me some answers, real answers, I'm going to knock you on your ass!"

Edward realizes the man before him is someone he can't intimidate. Eric's eyes have the ferocity of a rabid animal. Believing that his threat is genuine, Edward decides to toss him a bone so he'll back off. "Fine." Edward takes a step back from Eric as he replies. "The girl is the key to all of this."

While still furious, Eric is now overcome with confusion which seems to ease his tense demeanor a bit. "What do you mean?" he questions.

"She's a Reaper." Edward answers.

And just like that, the rabid animal is back. Eric turns and puts his right fist into the corridor wall as hard as he can. His fist appears to stop an inch from the wall as a small invisible barrier of magical force encases his hand, protecting it from the impact. He pulls his hand back leaving a smooth bowl-shaped dent on the white surface.

Just like Andrea's random visions, Eric's own ward magic innately protects him sometimes. He discovered he was a sorcerer when he was ten years old. He and his younger brother, Alex, were playing on the sidewalk when his brother tripped and fell into the path of an oncoming car. Eric rushed over pushing his brother out of the way, getting hit by the car himself instead. To his surprise, the vehicle seemed to hit the air in front of him. The force of it still knocked him to ground, giving him some pretty severe road rash on one side, but the cushion that appeared between him and the car absorbed its kinetic energy, preventing what would've most likely been a lethal impact. Since that day, these barriers automatically manifest from time to time when he's in danger; however, they are never consistent enough for him to rely on their protection.

The commotion has caused everyone inside the medical room to begin eavesdropping near the closed door. A couple of DoS guards have also taken interest from down the hall. They move up with weapons drawn. Edward sees them over Eric's shoulder and gives them a signal to stand down. Eric has both fists balled up, but he keeps them at his side so as to not lash out again. "So we've just handed an already unstoppable force someone who has the ability to raise an army of the dead?!" Eric's volume is making it easy for the audience in the next room.

"It's never been confirmed that Reapers are *that* powerful." Edward attempts to sound confident. "Besides, that's why I put this team together. For just such a situation. They can get her back."

"Team?" Eric almost laughs. "There's no team here. None of the people in there want to be here! *I* don't want to be here!"

"Then get out," Edward retorts. "Run back and cry to the President. I don't need a man who let 174 people die on this team, anyway."

Edward knew it was a low-blow, but he needed to end this conversation as the alpha, and it worked. All of Eric's rage melts away, revealing the broken man beneath. The entire scene of the White House attack plays out again in his mind, leaving him speechless for a moment. He has no fight left for Edward, choosing instead to retreat. "Go fuck yourself," Eric says before pushing passed Edward in the direction of the elevator.

***

Andrea finds herself standing on Liberty Island, at the square base of the statue's pedestal, in the middle of the afternoon. She's staring up at the green, copper face of Lady Liberty, some 250 feet in the sky. Her wonderment is short-lived as the scene on the ground in front of her draws her gaze. Bodies lie everywhere. Tourists and Liberty Island guards decorate the ground in gruesome fashion. Many have been shot while others have been burned or electrocuted.

Just beyond the bodies, at the base wall of the massive monument, ten sorcerers in dark robes stand in a line; some have assault rifles slung on their backs. They all face the wall and appear to be in a deep meditation. Chanting can be heard emanating from the group, but Andrea can't make out what's being said. She can feel they are drawing in an immense amount of arcane energy. A dangerous amount. She needs to stop them, but she can't seem to move. The intensity of the power they are harnessing is reaching hazardous levels. Again Andrea tries to move, but she goes nowhere. She attempts to call out for the sorcerers to stop; however, no sound escapes her lips.

Suddenly, the incantation stops. The ground begins to shake as all the robed figures explode in a mountainous burst of blue light, obliterating the Statue of Liberty and engulfing Andrea along with it.

***

The occupants of the underground DoS facility's medical room just heard the heated exchange between Eric and Edward. The next few minutes have been spent in awkward silence. Everyone half expected Edward to gloat after his testosterone-fueled victory. Instead, they heard him head off down the hall opposite the direction they heard Eric go.

After a few more moments of silence, Emmanuel walks back over to Andrea's bedside to keep an eye on her vitals monitor. Jasmine and Benjamin sit in the chairs opposite the exam beds. Anthony is now walking around on his newly healed leg, and looks rather silly with one leg naked almost all the way to the groin. He keeps putting additional pressure on the mended leg as though he doesn't trust it to function properly.

Benjamin's boredom finally gets the better of him. He leans over to Jasmine. "So," he starts off. "UMDC fighter eh?"

"Probably not anymore." Jasmine directs her displeasure at Anthony.

Anthony stops messing around upon hearing her words. "I'm sorry about ruining your fight," he says earnestly. "I was under orders. I'm actually a big fan, and even though I regret the way it all went down, it was pretty sweet getting to throw down with Jasmine 'the Assassin' Yuen."

"You're lucky I didn't kill you," she replies.

"Oh I know."

"Yeah, don't apologize to Benjamin," Benjamin chimes in sarcastically. "He's rich. He can just buy another office."

"Don't be such a baby," Anthony responds with some sass. "I put the office back afterwards and left it just as I found it…mostly. I wouldn't have needed to transport it in the first place if you hadn't been trying to hide from me."

"I'll remember that the next time I'm being kidnapped," Benjamin says, crossing his arms.

"I'm sorry," Anthony says, though less genuinely than in his apology to Jasmine.

It looks as though Benjamin is about to say something snarky, but he's interrupted by Andrea suddenly sitting up in her bed. Jasmine and Benjamin jump to their feet, prompting Anthony to turn and see what's happening. Andrea is breathing heavily and appears covered in sweat. She's looking around, unsure of where she is. Emmanuel sees her confusion and attempts to offer some exposition. "You are okay," he states. "You were knocked unconscious and are now in da hospital…sort of."

Andrea quickly gets her bearings, as she is familiar with the facility. She has visited here many times to run training exercises. Anthony offers to help as she attempts to stand up. "We have to move," Andrea says as she gets to her feet. "I had a vision of the terrorists attacking the Statue of Liberty. I think it's happening today."

"We have to tell the Secretary," Anthony responds.

"Are we forgetting that they took the girl?" Jasmine says.

"Catherine?" Andrea's heart sinks.

"Yes," Anthony answers. "And nobody's forgetting that fact, but the Secretary must be alerted about this attack. He can mobilize a team to intervene."

"There's no time. I got the feeling this was happening very soon. Maybe now. *We* have to do something. Can you teleport us directly to Liberty Island?"

"I can, but what are you and I going to do?" Anthony says with apprehension. "I'm no strategist."

"What about that bloke that was supposed to train us?" Benjamin asks.

"He left. You heard him," Anthony says. "Wait. Are you planning to go with us?"

"Do you know how much U-Movie stock would skyrocket if the CEO helped save the Statue of Liberty? Count me in."

"Eric left?" Andrea inquires.

"Yeah, he and the stuffed shirt got into it pretty good, and he took off," Jasmine answers. "But he couldn't have gotten far."

"Videre vera," Andrea says while making an arcane gesture with her hands.

Andrea's eyes go completely white for a few moments. It's quite an unsettling thing to see up close for the first time. Benjamin didn't notice it when it happened in the war room, but now he has a front row seat, and he doesn't like it. "Is she looking into my soul?" he says while trying not to stare at her. "I feel like she's looking into my soul. Please make her stop."

"He's on the second floor of the parking structure," Andrea says as her eyes revert to their normal color. "Can you teleport us there?"

108

"I think you hit your head too hard," Anthony answers. "You are talking crazy."

"Come on, Maverick," Andrea replies. "It's time to buzz the tower."

Andrea and Anthony haven't worked together a lot, but enough for her to know his weakness. "Dammit Andrea," he says shaking his head. "You had me at 'Maverick.' Omnia vectio."

\*\*\*

Moments later, Eric approaches his vehicle inside the three-story parking structure. He reaches for the driver's door handle, but stops short. He's having a battle of conscience. He wants to dive head first into a bottle and drink Edward's words away, but he also doesn't trust the man to carry out a rescue operation for Catherine. He thinks he should, at the very least, follow up with the President and get her involved.

Before Eric can open his door, Andrea, Anthony, Emmanuel, Jasmine, and Benjamin materialize out of thin air a few parking spaces away. They see him at the car and rush over to him. He hears the hurried footsteps and spins around, ready to strike at a potential threat. "Agent Davis, hold up," Anthony says waving at Eric.

Seeing who it is, Eric lowers his guard while shaking his head over the fact that he almost took a swing at one of them. "What's going on?" he asks.

"The Eye's going to attack the Statue of Liberty," Andrea says, approaching him. "We're going to stop it, but we need your help."

Suddenly, all of Eric's self-doubt is replaced with determination. If there is even the slightest chance he can prevent more loss of life by this organization, he's going to try. "When's the attack?" he asks.

"I don't know exactly. My vision wasn't that clear, but we need to go now."

"I saw an armory on the way downstairs earlier," Eric directs his question to Anthony. "Can you take us there?"

"I'm so getting court-martialed for this," Anthony says with a sigh. "Omnia vectio."

In the blink of an eye, the entire group appears to vanish as they teleport back underground.

***

The entire group steps out of the ether and into a rectangular room containing a small arsenal. The metallic south wall of the room has a sliding door leading to a hallway. The wall opposite the door is lined with lockers, each containing a suit of ballistic body armor - good for stopping bullets, bad for stopping magic. The center of the room is filled up with steel weapon racks and lockers. A variety of assault rifles, small arms, and ammunition are secured on the racks. Additional armaments, including combat knives and explosives, are stowed in the lockers. Eric quickly glances around the room before turning his attention to Andrea. "Do you have any other details on the attack?" He inquires. "Did they have weapons and, if so, what kind?"

"Some of them had rifles," Andrea replies. "But I think they were all Evos."

"More magic and guns," Eric says with exasperation. "Great. Vests for everyone."

Eric and Anthony distribute lightweight Kevlar vests to everyone from the lockers. Eric's having second thoughts about bringing Emmanuel along as he helps him into a vest. "Are you sure about this?" Eric asks. "It's going to be dangerous."

Emmanuel knows that he is old and, as a result, constantly underestimated. It gets tiresome after a while. "I know dat." Emmanuel is slightly annoyed. "All da more reason for me to go. Someone has to tell da world how you died."

Eric lets out a small chuckle. "On second thought, having a Mender on hand will be useful," he says. "But you keep your head down."

Anthony is first to the weapons. He retrieves a carbine from the rack and holds it up for the others to see. "I know most of you are civilians," Anthony says, gathering everyone's attention. "But does anyone other than Eric have experience with the M4A1?"

Andrea takes the rifle from Anthony and snags an empty magazine cartridge from a locker. She demonstrates her proficiency with the weapon by quickly loading the mag and pointing out both the safety and rate of fire switches on the rifle. "A little," she says with a cocky smile.

"Fulgor." Lightning arcs between Jasmine's hands as she speaks the arcane word. "These are the only weapons I need."

Anthony hands one of the rifles to Eric before offering one to Benjamin. While Benjamin spent plenty of time around guns during his time in the London criminal underworld, he never used anything quite as high-tech as an M4A1. "Do you have a handgun?" Benjamin asks, pushing the rifle away. "I'm more useful with small arms."

Anthony keeps the assault rifle for himself. He pulls a Beretta M9 handgun from the rack and hands it to Benjamin. "That more your speed?" he asks.

Benjamin takes the gun. The weight and length of it is slightly more than he's used to, but it will do in a pinch. "Thanks," he responds.

Eric goes over the plan while Anthony loads magazines with ammunition and distributes them to the team. "Stopping the terrorists is priority, but there will still be civilians on the island, and we need to keep them safe. Our first objective should be to alert security on the island. Should things devolve into violence, it's better they know we're not with the terrorists. There will be a lot of ground to cover, so we'll split up into two-man teams. Benjamin, you're with Andrea. Jasmine's with Anthony, and Emmanuel, you're with me. Also, best not to announce our presence by appearing in the open. Benjamin, do you have something that can cloak our presence?"

"Oh, he's got something," Anthony says, thinking back to his office pursuit of the illusionist.

"Coetus occulti," Benjamin performs the somatic parts of the spell while speaking the words. "There ya go. You can't tell, but we're all invisible right now. I mean, not to us, but anyone who is not us can't see us. You're just gonna have to trust me on this."

"Okay." Eric looks around at everyone. "Last chance to stay here. I won't hold it against anyone since we don't know what we're walking into, but this is part of what I do, so I have to go."

After what seems like a very long silence, Jasmine finally speaks up. "Let's go kick some ass!"

## Chapter 10: Give Me Liberty

It's mid-afternoon on Liberty Island; the national monument is bustling with tourists who have journeyed far and wide to hear the story and take pictures of Lady Liberty. The population is a mix of both young and old with many families seeing the sights today. Scattered throughout the crowds, on all four sides of the statue's pedestal, are members of the Eye of Ruin doing their best to be inconspicuous. They slowly make their way towards the four support walls of the statue's base. They have gone unnoticed thus far.

Eric, Anthony, Andrea, Jasmine, Benjamin, and Emmanuel appear on the northwest side of the island, about fifty feet from the walls of the pedestal's foundation. While Benjamin and Andrea have to dance around a bit to avoid colliding with some tourists passing by, no one seems to notice the group's presence. This is probably best since they are outfitted with the weapons and armor from the DoS facility.

Each member of the group begins scanning their surroundings for anything suspicious. Andrea was hoping to have an edge in finding the suspected terrorists since she saw them in her premonition; however, no one is dressed in ominous cloaks.

As a member of the Secret Service, Eric has an eye for when someone doesn't belong. As casually as the terrorists are moving towards their target, he picks up on it. His eye was already drawn towards the walls, as they would be the most ideal place to strike if one's goal was to bring the statue down. "I see them." Eric points out the potential terrorists. "They'll be making their way towards the walls. Let's split up. Andrea and Benjamin take the northeast. Anthony and Jasmine take the southwest. I'll notify security. We only engage if necessary."

"Lame," Jasmine says shaking her head.

"Full disclosure-" Benjamin interjects. "Once I move away from the rest of you, the invisibility will wear off."

"Let's work fast then," Eric says. "Try to blend in."

"Right," Anthony says sarcastically, motioning with his assault rifle.

Anthony places a hand on Jasmine's shoulder, and they both vanish into a quick flash of light. Andrea and Benjamin expeditiously make their way towards the northeast side of the statue. Eric doesn't wait for his magical concealment to vanish before moving towards one of the island's security patrols. He is followed by Emmanuel who moves a much slower pace. Shortly before reaching the two-man security team, Eric surpasses the boundary of Benjamin's invisibility spell, causing the guards to draw their weapons on him. "Freeze!" one of the guards shouts at Eric.

Eric stops in his tracks and holds his gun up in the air in a non-threatening manner. "Listen," Eric starts out. "My name is Eric Davis. I'm a member of the Secret Service. We received word that there is an impending attack here. I've located the suspected terrorists and can point them out. I need you to notify all security personnel on the island."

Unfortunately, the guards are not buying Eric's story. To them, he looks like he could be the terrorist spinning a tale since they caught him. "Put the gun down!" The guard says. "I'm calling it in."

Before the guard can reach for his radio, rapid gunfire immediately followed by screams erupt from behind Eric and Emmanuel. They all look back to see three of the terrorists have moved next to the wall of the pedestal while four others have pulled out MAC-10 machine pistols and begun firing on the crowd. The terrorists are both men and women from various nationalities. Though they are dressed in nondescript clothing, they must have teleported onto the island in order to get their weapons through security.

People like to think they'll be brave in the face of danger, but in an actual life or death situation, one finds out who they truly are inside. Panic spreads quickly throughout the crowds of tourists. Self-preservation wins out as many people push others out of the way as they attempt to flee, even trampling some in the process.

The guards are military trained and manage to keep their cool a little better, though they weren't prepared for this. "Are they with you?!" one of them shouts at Eric.

"No!" he shouts back. "They are the ones I was telling you about! You need to alert every officer on the island now!"

Eric turns to make his way into the chaos. "Don't move!" Eric stops at the guard's words. "You're not going anywhere until we get this sorted!"

Eric looks back over his shoulder with a stone-cold glare. "I'm going," he says. "I'm gonna try to save as many lives as I can. You do what you need to do."

Eric takes off in a run towards a group of people who are under assault. Emmanuel gives the guards a shrug before following after Eric. The two guards look at each other then back to the scene of violence before them. "Fuck!" One of the guards says. "Call it in!"

The guard begins moving forward. "Where are you going?" the other guard questions.

"To help that guy!" he responds before running off.

***

The scene on the southwest side of the statue is worse than where the group first appeared. It looks as though a couple security patrols already attempted to intervene with the Eye of Ruin and were killed by fire; most likely from one of the Evos. Here, four Evos stand in a line, facing the base wall. They are chanting something inaudible while three others, also armed with machine pistols, fire on the fleeing crowds. It looks as though there may have been one or two more terrorists, but they were dispatched by the security team before they were killed. The area is mostly clear as many tourists have already escaped the area or were shot down.

Anthony and Jasmine appear far enough away from the terrorists to not immediately draw their attention. The carnage causes them both to pause for a moment. Jasmine was ready to fight some terrorists, but the reality of the situation didn't hit her until now. This isn't a bout in a ring somewhere. Actual lives are on the line, and it's causing her stomach to sink. She manages to push it down and replace the feeling with anger. Anthony has seen his share of violence, but he has never seen this much innocent death up close. As bleak as things look here, he knows it's going to get worse. "There's going to be more of them along the southeast wall," he says. "I can take them if you can handle this."

Jasmine's confident in her ability to kick ass in close quarters, but these men and women would mow her down before she could close the distance. She needs the element of surprise. "Yeah," she says looking skyward. "But I'll need a lift first."

Anthony looks up, unsure of what Jasmine has in mind. Time is short so he puts his arm around her waist pulling her in close. "Praevolo," he says.

With a burst of air beneath them, Anthony and Jasmine launch into the sky with blinding speed. He stops their ascension about 150 feet in the air. "Now what?" he asks.

"Position me over the ones with the guns," she replies.

Anthony quickly yet gracefully glides Jasmine to a position above the armed terrorists while maintaining their current height in air. "Alright," Jasmine says with a slight moment of hesitation. "Drop me."

"Are you crazy?!" Anthony questions.

"Don't be such a pussy!" Jasmine finds her confidence once more. "Drop me!"

Anthony's pretty sure this is a terrible idea, but he needs to get to the southeast side of the island, so he lets her go. He then wastes no time, teleporting away.

Jasmine finds herself rocketing towards the earth below. It's a much different experience than she expected. The movies make freefalls seem like they last forever, but this felt like the blink of an eye. She's almost on the terrorists when she enacts her plan. "Incaendo rivus!" she shouts with her palms open towards the ground.

Fire streams from her hands as though they were each a flamethrower, engulfing and incinerating the three armed terrorists below her. The force of the fire and the heat from the flames slow her fall, allowing her to touch down on the ground rather gently, like an angel descending from the heavens on fiery wings.

The screams of their compatriots cause the four Evos to stop casting their spell and turn their attention to Jasmine. She is now almost within hand-to-hand distance, but the Evos don't intend to let her get that close. The four sorcerers begin launching a barrage of elemental attacks in her direction. After years of fighting other magic-users in the ring-sized energy sphere for the UMDC, she finds it easy to avoid this uncoordinated arcane assault. She swiftly moves in on her opponents, discovering they are adept at wielding magic, but not at close-quarter combat.

This is where Jasmine thrives. Her favorite UMDC bouts are when she faces multiple opponents at the same time. The surge of adrenaline makes her feel hyper-aware. Suddenly, everything seems to be moving in slow-motion. Every move made by her opponents is telegraphed and easily avoidable. This fight is no different. She takes one of the Evos out of the fight right away, leaping in with a scissor kick that knocks him to ground. His head hits the concrete hard, rendering him unconscious. Jasmine kips back up to her feet while avoiding another ball of fire thrown at her. She grabs one of the terrorists who's attempting to cast a spell, spinning them in front of her to act as a shield. The grappled Evo is hit by an icy blast thrown by one of his allies, freezing him in place. Jasmine then jumps out from behind the frozen terrorist, landing a double kick to the heads of the two remaining Evos at the same time. This disorients both men, allowing Jasmine to easily knock them out.

***

Benjamin and Andrea arrive at the northeast wall, unnoticed by anyone, as they are still under the effect of Benjamin's invisibility spell. They find eight terrorists locked in a heated battle with Liberty Island security officers. Half of the terrorists are armed with MAC-10s while the other half is wielding magic. Andrea raises her carbine in preparation to fire at the unsuspecting terrorists. "Whoa!" Benjamin exclaims. "If you start shooting, you'll become visible, and, in case you haven't noticed, there ain't a lot of cover between us and them."

Benjamin no sooner finishes expressing his concerns when a thunderous crack echoes throughout the air as one of the Evos arcs a bolt of lightning through all of the security officers. The six guards convulse violently before dropping like smoldering ragdolls to the ground.

"We have to do something!" Andrea pleads. "I need a distraction!"

"I've got an idea," Benjamin says before uttering an incantation. "Grandis allucinatio."

The terrorist Evos are about to turn their attention to the base wall when the Liberty Island guards who were electrocuted appear to stand back up, readying their weapons to fire. For a moment, the terrorists look on with dumbfounded, horrorstruck faces. Before the guards can shoot, the terrorists open fire on them yet again. To the surprise of the armed men, their bullets seem to have no effect. "There's your distraction," Benjamin says.

Andrea unloads an entire clip of her carbine at the terrorists, dropping three of them. The remaining Eye of Ruin members spin around, trying to figure out what is happening. They lock eyes on Andrea as she reloads; however, before any of them can react, Benjamin lays down a covering fire with his Beretta, revealing himself to the terrorists in the process. While Benjamin does manage to take one down, three armed terrorists and one Evo remain, taking aim at him. "Oh bollocks," Benjamin says with a cringe.

In a panic, Andrea grabs Benjamin's arm, speaking words she's never spoken or heard before. "Falsum posterum!"

Benjamin feels a wave of fatigue wash over him as though arcane energy were being siphoned out of him. At the very same moment, the armed terrorists all look oddly at their weapons before ejecting their current clips. This behavior seems odd as the clips they remove still appear to have bullets in them. This also distracts the Evo long enough for Andrea to shoot her now reloaded weapon, eliminating the remaining terrorists.

Unsure of whether he is alive or dead, Benjamin slowly opens his eyes and checks himself for bullet holes. He lets out a sigh of relief when he discovers he's unharmed. "What the hell happened?" He looks to Andrea for answers.

Andrea isn't completely sure of what she did or how she did it. "I…I think I made them think their guns were empty." Her statement sounds almost like a question.

"I didn't know Prophets could plant a vision in someone's mind," Benjamin says.

"They can't," she responds as though she doesn't believe her own words. "Come on. Let's go check on the others."

***

The southeast side of base structure is the most populated area of the island, as it's the direction Lady Liberty faces, and on a normal day, makes a great photo spot. The current scene is far from picturesque. The area is still rather crowded with tourists who are cowering or injured. A handful of terrorists lie dead on the ground, having been shot by the island's security forces. The danger is no less imminent as four Evos have barricaded themselves near the base structure with a magical wall of fire protecting them from the security officers. The four Eye of Ruin fanatics are already well into their communal spell that will detonate with enough destructive force to take out this entire section of the island. Even if the other teams don't succeed, these four could still destabilize the Statue of Liberty enough to take it down.

Anthony teleports to the area, about 25 feet outside of the fire wall. He sees the Evos on the other side and can feel the amount of arcane energy being gathered by them. He knows he has to act fast if he's going to save all the people in the vicinity. He looks around, then up, and finally back towards the terrorists. "No way," he says with determination.

Anthony disappears in a flash of light, reappearing on the other side of the fiery blockade near the four sorcerers. They are too deep into their spell ritual to notice him. The arcane energy being pulled in by their incantation is reaching critical mass. He has to get them out of here now! "Omnia vectio." As Anthony speaks the words, he and the four sorcerers vanish.

Almost immediately, all five men reappear extremely high up in the Earth's atmosphere. The temperature is near freezing, and the air is very thin. The sudden sensation of falling causes all four

Evos to stop chanting and open their eyes. Were they not plummeting to their deaths, the view would be breathtaking, as they can see all of Manhattan, Ellis Island, Liberty Island, and everything else around them. The only solace they can take is the fact that it's too late to stop the spell they started. They will explode before they ever come close to hitting the ground. "Thanks for flying!" Anthony shouts with a smile before teleporting back down to the ground.

***

Back at the northwest side of the statue, Eric and two of the island security officers fight together against the terrorists. As with the other attack points, the Evos are being protected by the armed men and women who don't appear to have magical abilities. The four magic wielders focus on their nearly completed incantation. Emmanuel has been aiding the fight by healing injured tourists. He stays low and avoids being anywhere near the path of gunfire.

Five more island security officers come rushing to the gun battle. A hail of bullets is exchanged with casualties on both sides. Eventually, the superior numbers turn the tide of the standstill, and the armed terrorists are put down. The security staff cautiously assumes a tactical position around the Evos, getting ready to put them down. Eric senses the power built up in the Evos and fears what shooting them might do. "Stand down!" Eric halts the guards' gunfire. "I think shooting them will set off the explosion. Let me try something."

Eric takes a few steps towards the Evos while performing the hand motions needed to complete his spell. "Omnia praesidium!"

Eric encases the four Evos in a barrier much like the one he used on Jasmine back at the DoS compound. Emmanuel knows what Eric is attempting, but he fears the magic being summoned is stronger than his barrier. "Dat won't work!" Emmanuel calls to Eric. "De combined power of dere explosions will shatter your barrier like glass! Make individual ones!"

"If it's as strong as you say, I'm not sure I can sustain four barriers at once," Eric responds while focusing to keep his current spell in place.

Emmanuel may not be a Sentinel, but he's been using magic long enough that he has an innate sense of how all forms of magic work. The basic concepts of magic are fairly similar across all schools of the arcane and can be applied thusly. "Focus!" Emmanuel shouts. "You know de base spell. Picture in your head what ya need to do. You can craft a stronger spell even wit'out de words."

Eric can feel the volatile power inside his barrier reaching an apex. He takes a breath, visualizing his single barrier becoming four. As he concentrates, the normally invisible shell of his magical construct glisters with flecks of blue light. The shell walls between each Evo start to bow inward until they close off from each other and create individual barrier cells. The blue light fades, and the barriers are no longer visible to the naked eye.

The security officers relax their guard slightly, as they hope the danger has passed. The feeling is premature, as a surge of lightning passes through Eric from behind, striking all of the security officers. The energy of the bolt is dispersed enough to remove its lethality, but it does render everyone except Eric unconscious. The shock momentarily breaks Eric's concentration, and his barriers around the Evos fluctuate, but hold. Keeping the barriers up until the Evos detonate is crucial. Eric can't even look behind to see his attacker. Emmanuel, however, sees him clearly.

Jared Cross stands about twenty feet behind Eric. He's not dressed as subtly as the other Eye of Ruin followers on the island. He wears black paramilitary fatigues and a tactical vest outfitted with grenades. He has an automatic shotgun strapped to his back and casts his spells with while wearing armored gloves. Another bolt of lightning expels from the space between his palms, striking Eric once again. The pain brings him to his knees, but he keeps the barriers up. "You can't hold out forever," Jared taunts.

Emmanuel moves towards Jared, attempting to draw his attention away from Eric. It works, but only momentarily. Jared throws a bolt at Emmanuel, striking him in the side. Emmanuel stumbles to the ground. Jared prepares to hit Eric again with his arcane lightning when something catches his attention. Four large explosions light up the sky way above Liberty Island. This distraction gives Emmanuel a chance to cast a healing spell on himself. He stands back up in front of Jared again, his palms now glowing white. "You 'ave lost dis day," Emmanuel says. "Your friends 'ave fallen. Surrender before you get hurt."

Jared recognizes this old sorcerer as a Mender and finds it adorable that he thinks he can take on an Evo as powerful as himself. "What are you going to do old man?" Jared asks with a laugh. "Heal me to death?"

"Da t'ing about Menders is we can heal wounds, yes," Emmanuel says with cold calculation. "But we can also reopen old ones."

The light emanating from Emmanuel's palms turns from bright white to black. As it does, Jared's brash confidence crumbles. He drops to the ground, screaming. Every battle scar on his body, both internal and on the surface, torn open. Blood pours out of his face from the now open wound on his cheek. After a few moments, the pain is too much and his body goes into shock.

While this is happening, the four Evos in Eric's barriers explode. The sound is deafening, but the concussive force and destructive fireballs of each stay contained within. Eric releases his spell and collapses the rest of the way to the ground in pain and exhaustion. The light from Emmanuel's palms reverts back to its bright white and as it does, the gash on Jared's faces closes, though he remains unconscious. Emmanuel makes his way over to Eric to check on him. "Are you okay?" he asks.

"As long as we stopped them," Eric weakly replies.

"I t'ink we did," Emmanuel says with a hopeful tone.

\*\*\*

The sun sets behind Lady Liberty, creating an auburn skyline. The light on her back casts a dark shadow on her face and the southeast portion of the island below. The island buzzes with police, FBI, Homeland Security, and members of the press. Jared Cross and the few surviving Eye of Ruin members are taken into custody. The majority of injured civilians were ferried or teleported off the island to receive medical attention. Staff members from multiple forensic pathology centers have been brought into help with the dead. While the devastation could've been much worse, 31 people still lost their lives in the attack.

Eric, Emmanuel, Jasmine, Andrea, and Benjamin wait in a medical tent that was set up as a temporary facility while people were being taken off the island. It isn't much: just a few rows of cots, some of which are occupied by Liberty Island security officers. There are also two tables on either end stacked with first aid supplies. Eric sits on one of the cots, trying not to move. Emmanuel took care of his burns, but his muscles are still very tender. The others stand around him with somber faces. They did a lot of good today, but no one's in the mood to celebrate. Much like Eric with the White House attack, everyone feels like they could've done better. Like they could've saved more lives.

Anthony appears at the entrance of the tent and moves towards the group at a quick pace. He is wide-eyed and moves as though danger is right behind him. "Heads up," he whispers as he approaches.

"What were you thinking?!" Edward's voice booms from outside the tent.

Despite the pain this causes, Eric promptly stands up. Edward barrels into the tent like a bull charging a matador. He locks eyes with Eric before getting right in his face. "Running an unauthorized op, stealing military weapons and armor, and endangering civilians. I could have you locked up for the rest of your life!"

"We had intel that there was an imminent attack," Eric responds. "There wasn't time to track you down for authorization."

"You are not part of the team, Davis!" Edward shouts. "You don't get to make those decisions!"

"But we saved lives," Andrea comes to Eric's defense. "Doesn't that mean anything to you?!"

"Obviously, saving lives is a good thing," Edward takes his tone down a bit. "But this situation could easily be spun to show the DoS in a negative light."

"We wouldn't want that now, would we," Benjamin says sarcastically.

"If the Department of Sorcery comes under further scrutiny, this team won't exist," Edward snaps back.

"You mean this team that none of us asked to be on?" Jasmine interjects.

"You know what?" Edward explodes. "I'm done playing nice!"

"This was nice?" Benjamin jabs again.

"You may not want to be here, but you *will* work for me! I've got the goods on all of you, and if you don't play ball, two of you can spend the rest of your days in Carcer while another goes on the run from the Triad. Do I make myself clear?!"

"I think I've heard just about enough!" a familiar female voice booming with authority speaks from behind Edward.

His face goes white as a ghost. He quickly spins around to see President Thompson standing behind him with her Secret Service escort. If looks could kill, Edward would be dead where he stands. "Madam President," Edward almost stumbles over his words. "I…I had no idea you were coming here."

"That's because I don't answer to you," she replies coldly.

Edward realized how stupid his statement was as soon as it left his mouth. He was legitimately surprised that she was here so quickly, especially after the events that happened earlier today. "You're right, of course." He back-peddles. "My apologies."

"Save it," she responds by putting her finger in his face. "I've glimpsed behind the curtain one too many times today, and I don't like what I'm seeing. Who are you to treat these people this way?!"

Edward feels his treatment towards these sorcerers is justified. The Department of Sorcery already has a low public opinion and, despite the thwarted attack, he sees this as a public relations nightmare. He can hear reporters' questions in his head. *"Why would you only send a six-man team to stop a terrorist threat? If you had knowledge of the attack, why did you wait so long to act? Is combating magic with more magic really the answer?"*

He doesn't feel he is wrong in reacting the way he has, but he also knows that his opinion doesn't matter at the moment. Still, it's not in his nature to back down from a fight, and he's already bent to her will once today. "Do you know what they've done?!"

"Yes," the President responds with a cooler tone. "They've saved lives."

"With no regard for rules or protocol," Edward argues. "Their actions could've made things worse, and in some ways, they did! The press is going to have a field day with this."

"Well." President Thompson is exasperated. "It's nice to see you have such faith in the team you assembled. I'm done, Edward. I'm just done. This project is no longer under your control."

Her words stab at Edward like a knife to the gut and, in that moment, his thoughts turn very dark. He briefly wishes she'd been blown up at the White House, so he could run things his way. He quickly realizes how horrible those thoughts are and dismisses them as a result of his anger. He wants to shout and throw things, but he knows he'll only make things worse. Best to save face. Besides, he knows he has an ace in the hole if he can just exercise some patience. He decides to take the high ground…sort of. "You'll regret this decision," he says before pushing passed the Secret Service agents to exit the tent.

Janet looks over the entire team before landing her gaze on Eric. The tent is awkwardly quiet for what seems like forever. No one knows what to say to the President of the United States, especially after her exchange with the Secretary of Sorcery. Eric isn't sure if they'll be in trouble for their actions today, but he doesn't want anyone else to be taking the heat for it. "Madam President, I know we broke protocol, but when we found out, we had to act," Eric says stepping in front of the others as if to shield them from a verbal lashing.

"The Secretary is not wrong," the President responds. "This event will be a media storm; however, when I give my official press conference, I'm going to tell them the truth. That the six of you are heroes. Don't let anyone else tell you otherwise."

"Thank you," Eric says.

Janet smiles warmly at the group. "I have to go," She says. "I need to make a statement before the press speculate anymore about what happened. I want to see you all tomorrow the Department of Sorcery at 10am to debrief."

"Yes, Madam President," Eric answers while the others simply nod in agreement.

"Good," Janet replies before exiting the tent with her bodyguards.

## Chapter 11: Guardians

Emmanuel, Jasmine, and Benjamin are escorted through the halls of the Department of Sorcery. It has been less than 24 hours since they thwarted the attack on Liberty Island. They've all had a shower, a decent night's sleep, and a change of clothes. They are led through the bright hallways by a young male DoS staffer. As he walks, he keeps looking back at Jasmine with a sort of bashful admiration. She assumes he's just a UMDC fan and decides to ignore it unless he says something.

After a short while, they come to a wing of the building that looks to be unused. A closed set of glass sliding doors separate, the hallway from a large room filled with empty workstations. On the floor just beyond the glass door is the image of a medieval style shield with a sword passing behind it in a downward direction. "What is this place?" Benjamin asks.

The staffer pushes a button on the wall to open the sliding doors before turning to face Benjamin. "This was to be the command center for the Guardians," he answers.

"The Guardians?" Benjamin questions further.

"Yeah." The staffer prepares to disappoint Benjamin. "If you don't already know about them, I'm not allowed to discuss it. In any event, the President is waiting for you in the intel center near the back."

"Thanks," Jasmine replies.

She spoke to him, and now he can't help but say something. "You were amazing yesterday!" the staffer says to Jasmine with excitement.

"Huh?" Jasmine reacts in confusion.

"At the Statue of Liberty," he clarifies his previous statement.

That helps, but Jasmine is actually a bit more confused now. "Were you there?" she asks.

"Oh no." The staffer realizes she's unaware of what he's talking about. "The video on the news of you taking out the terrorists. It's on like every channel."

Jasmine isn't really sure how to respond to this news. "Um…thank you."

"Anyway, sorry, you shouldn't keep the President waiting," he says. "I'm just a really big fan."

Benjamin motions for Jasmine to go through the door first. She does and is followed by Benjamin and Emmanuel, leaving the staffer behind. They walk around the left side of the cubicles that make up the middle of the room. The perimeter of the work desks is made up of various other rooms, each with a glass door and inner wall providing complete transparency. Every door has a small placard on the glass wall next to it. Many of them are blank with only a few having the name of the room on them. Considering how much staff occupy the rest of the building, the emptiness is here is a bit eerie.

They round the back side of the workstations, finding more empty rooms. In the far corner is a room containing large screens on three of its inner walls. There is a massive horizontal touchscreen workstation in the center of the room that appears to affect what appears on the wall-mounted screens. The President stands at the station along with Eric, Anthony, and Andrea. Eric is wearing his Secret Service suit while Anthony is in his service uniform. Andrea is dressed much more casually than the other two, wearing jeans and a blue long-sleeve shirt. The President sees Jasmine, Benjamin, and Emmanuel outside, waving them in.

Upon entering the room, Benjamin immediately recognizes the tech being used at the workstation. The system is running satellite tracking and facial recognition using a picture of Catherine. It doesn't appear they've been able to find her yet though. The President rounds the table once everyone is in the room. "Thank you for coming," she says. "I know I told you all this was a debriefing, but that was a lie. After seeing what you all accomplished yesterday, I want to see how I can convince you to join the taskforce, even if just until we can find Catherine and bring her home. I'll not be threatening anyone. If you want to walk away, you are free to do so. Just know that should you stay, you will not have to work with the Secretary. I have taken over operational control of this program. You'll be answering directly to Eric, who will be answering to me. That's it. That's my pitch. If you stay, we start right now trying to track down the Eye of Ruin. If you decide to leave, I thank you again for what you did yesterday, and you know the way out."

For a moment everyone looks around the room waiting to see if anyone else leaves. No one does. "Good." Janet moves back around to the other side of the work table as she talks. "This wing will function as your base of operations. I'll have some staff brought in to assist with search operations."

"What are the Guardians?" Benjamin can't go on without knowing.

Janet finds the question surprising, but has no problem answering it. "When the Department of Sorcery was first opened, it was supposed to be more than it is today," she says. "The Guardians were going to be a nationwide sorcerer police force meant to deal with matters too dangerous for their human counterparts."

"What happened?" Jasmine asks.

"Congress," she answers.

"Catherine's face hasn't popped up anywhere," Eric tries to get back on topic. "Which means we're probably not going to have any luck with conventional technology. One of the terrorists has been identified as Jared Cross. He has a history of radical behavior and is on multiple watch lists. He also has a list of some nasty known associates we should look into."

"I'd like to question him," Andrea speaks up.

"I'll make a call and set it up," the President says before heading towards the door. "Eric, the team is yours."

Without waiting for a response, she leaves. There is a moment of hesitation from Eric when this happens. He still doesn't feel worthy of this job, but his desire to save Catherine outweighs his guilt. "Alright." He snaps to. "Anthony, you take Andrea to Carcer. The rest of us will rundown Cross's known associates."

"Yes sir," Anthony says.

"We flying or teleporting?" Andrea asks.

"I thought we'd drive," Anthony says with a smile. "It's not that far."

"You don't have to tell me," Andrea replies in a disheartened tone. "Let's go."

While Andrea and Anthony leave, the rest pull up the digital file for Jared Cross on the main screen. The photo of Jared looks to be a youthful military picture from a time before he had his facial scar. The file contains his date of birth, physical statistics, military training, his criminal offenses, and a list of his known associates. The first name to appear here: Damian Westonbrooke. Benjamin's eyes grow wide upon seeing this name. "Damian Westonbrooke?" Benjamin says louder than he would've liked.

"Do you know who that is?" Eric asks.

"I've never met him, but everyone in the London underground knows the name Damian Westonbrooke." Benjamin answers. "He's a master criminal and a Ghost."

Aside from downplaying his knowledge of Damian, he also lies about knowing him. It's not like they were friends or anything, just criminal co-workers. They pulled multiple jobs together before Benjamin turned over his new leaf. He doesn't think it's noteworthy to mention, so he tries to change the subject. "Who else do we have on this list?" he asks.

\*\*\*

A short time later, Anthony and Andrea arrive at Carcer Prison located in Arlington County, just a brief drive from the Department of Sorcery. The massive 30-story steel cylindrical tower dwarfs every other surrounding structure. The building has no windows, and the metal surface is almost as reflective as a mirror, making the building hard to distinguish from a distance. The reflective prison has a 12-foot high perimeter wall topped with cameras and guard towers.

Carcer was designed and built two years before the Department of Sorcery was opened. It didn't start out the technological marvel that it is today. Magical dampening technology wasn't developed until the facility had already been opened for a year. Originally, sorcerers held at the facility were placed into drug-induced comas to ensure they couldn't use magic. The technology to negate magical energy was commissioned by the government specifically for the prison. Once it was developed, the anti-magic fields were placed throughout the entire tower preventing any magic from being used inside the building. Outside, they use more traditional forms of security.

Anthony and Andrea are escorted to Warden Trace McRory's office. While the exterior of the prison is bright polished metal, the interior couldn't be more contrary. The walls are dull, the lighting is poor, and the curved hallways seem like an unending labyrinth within the circular structure. The Warden's office is fairly close to the entrance, but the building's layout would make it difficult to find one's way back without a guide.

The Warden's office is just as dismal as the rest of the interior only with slightly better lighting. The room is rather barren, containing a desk with a phone & computer monitor on top of it, two filing cabinets, and three metal chairs. One of the metal chairs is behind the desk with McRory sitting in it. The Warden is in his late thirties. He wears his age heavily on his face and his light-brown hair is starting to gray. Unlike most of the staff at the prison, he is a sorcerer, and it creates a lot of internal struggle for him. He understands that some people are a danger to others, but he doesn't much care for locking up his fellow magic-users.

He is just getting off the phone as Andrea and Anthony are sent inside the room. Trace chuckles upon seeing Andrea. "Oliveros," he says without standing up. "It doesn't surprise me that you're back here. What does surprise me is that it's not in a collar."

"Always a pleasure, McRory," Andrea replies.

"That's Warden McRory to you, criminal," he snaps back.

"Warden, we're here to speak to a prisoner," Anthony jumps in before things escalate.

"Yeah I know." Trace stands. "I received a rather unexpected call from the President a short while ago telling me to prepare prisoner Jared Cross for your arrival. He's being transferred to interrogation room three as we speak."

"Will he be collared?" Anthony asks.

"No need," Trace answers. "Magic doesn't work anywhere in this building. Trust me. I'm a Builder and I can't create a damn thing within these walls."

Builders use conjuration magic, allowing them to create inanimate objects out of nothing but arcane energy. The process can be physically exhausting on the caster if they create something particularly large or in abundance. Builders can make good money working in construction or for manufacturing companies when they're not being driven off by non-magic workers who think their jobs are being taken.

"He's not lying about that," Andrea adds.

"So what's your plan?" Trace asks as he moves around in front of his desk. "Gonna ask nicely? This guy hasn't spoken a word since he was brought in last night; what makes you think he'll talk to you?"

"Let us worry about that," Anthony answers.

"Hey, it's your time to waste." Trace motions to the door. "Come on. I'll show you the way."

Trace and one of the facility's guards lead the way through the maze of halls up one floor to the interrogation rooms. He types a code into a keypad that automatically opens a thick metal door revealing Jared Cross inside the room. He's seated behind a small table and handcuffed to a rod that runs along its surface. Aside from a few cameras in the upper corners and an empty chair across from Jared, the room is otherwise empty. "He's all yours," Trace says, motioning Anthony and Andrea into the room.

The heavy security door seals behind them once they enter. Jared doesn't appear worried by their presence. He wears a gray jumpsuit with an eight digit number printed over a barcode where you'd normally find a pocket. A smile creeps across his face as he looks up at his guests. "Well, well, well," he says. "The saviors of Liberty Island. To what do I owe the pleasure?"

Andrea flips the metal chair around and proceeds to sit on it backwards. Anthony stands next to her doing his best to look imposing. Andrea locks eyes with Jared and the two begin a lengthy stare down. It's Anthony who finally breaks the silence. "Tell us about your organization."

"I'm afraid you're going to find this conversation rather disappointing." Jared shifts his gaze from Andrea to Anthony.

"You're just making things harder on yourself," Anthony says while crossing his arms. "If you cooperate-"

"You'll cut me a deal?" Jared laughs. "I know where I am, flyboy. Carcer is the Guantanamo for people like us. I'm never seeing the sun again, so I have no incentive to talk."

Andrea's temper gets the better of her; she jumps up tossing the chair to the side. "Where's the girl?!" she roars.

"Oh, you needn't worry about that." Jared doesn't even flinch. "You're too late."

"Too late for what?" Anthony asks.

"Too late to stop your worst nightmares from coming true," Jared replies aggressively. "The Eye of Ruin will purge this world of those unworthy to serve the Dragon King. We'll use the power of death to raise an unstoppable army!"

Andrea slowly makes her way around behind Jared. "I suppose we should've expected a crazy answer," Anthony replies, shaking his head.

"We'll see who's crazy when the Dragon King is ruling your world as a god," Jared says with the utmost conviction.

"Still you, I'm guessing," Anthony says.

Andrea suddenly wraps her left arm around Jared's throat, grabbing him by the hair with her other hand. She jerks his head back before Anthony can intercede. "Tell me where Catherine was taken, or you won't live to see the reign of your god!"

"You think I fear you over him?"

Andrea slams Jared's face down on the cold steel of the table top. "How about now?" she asks.

The door to the interrogation room opens, and Trace comes rushing in, followed by a guard armed with a stun gun. "Hey, you can't assault the inmates!" Trace shouts. "Hands off!"

Anthony puts his hands in the air. "I was standing over here the whole time," he says.

Andrea releases Jared. The impact on the table lacerated the inside of his lip. Blood runs down his chin. He spits some blood out on the table before looking up at Andrea. "Oh, I'm going to remember this," he threatens.

"You two have to leave," Trace addresses Andrea and Anthony.

A second guard arrives at the interrogation room and escorts Andrea and Anthony out of the building. Anthony hasn't said anything, but he's clearly not happy with the way things went down. Unfortunately, Andrea isn't saying anything either. Anthony wants an explanation or an apology, but none are being offered. By the time they reach the car, he can't keep it in any more. "You want to tell me what the hell that was about in there?!" he asks, stopping Andrea short of her destination.

"He deserved it," she replies matter-of-factly.

"I'm not disputing that, but you got us thrown out of there before we got anything out of him."

"He wasn't going to tell us anything," Andrea says while reaching into her pocket. "And now we don't need him to."

After pulling her hand out of her pocket, she opens it to display a small tuft of short hair. "Is that his hair?" Anthony asks with a tone implying he might not want to know the answer.

"Yes," Andrea answers moving past him towards the passenger door of the black DoS sedan. "And now that my magic isn't being inhibited, we're going to get some answers."

Anthony's entire mood changes. He's not opposed to breaking the rules; he just wants to be a part of it. He moves in between Andrea and the car blocking her once again. "Just let me know the plan next time," Anthony says before opening the car door for her. "I could've helped. Maybe broken one of his pinkies or something."

\*\*\*

Meanwhile, across the Potomac River at the 1789 Restaurant in Washington D.C., a meeting is happening between the Secretary of Defense and the Secretary of Sorcery. A secluded establishment popular with politicians for its private dining rooms, it is the perfect place for a working lunch away from prying eyes. The restaurant is normally closed to the public at this hour; however, Allen has booked a room for lunch. He and Edward have the Garden Room all to themselves. The room's floral printed walls and lattice covered floor-to-ceiling windows make the whole meeting seem so much more innocent than it actually is. The room can hold around twenty people, making it feel very empty with only two men sharing the end of a large table.

Allen and Edward have known each other for many years, climbing the political ranks together. While they aren't exactly friends, their political positions have often aligned. They are also similar in temperament and their penchant for wearing designer suits. It wasn't until Edward took the position as Secretary of Sorcery that Allen distanced himself. These days, it's unusual to ever see them together.

Allen enjoys a medium-well rack of lamb with a glass of red wine. Edward has a succulent plate of duck in front of him, but has yet to touch it. He's not particularly hungry at the moment. "I warned you that taking that position would be nothing but headaches," Allen says before taking a drink of wine.

"*I* could've taken care of this Eye of Ruin situation," Edward grumbles. "But she's tied my hands and taken over my operation. That taskforce is mine."

"Here's the thing." Allen cuts into his lamb. "The President's naïve and optimistic. Unfortunately, that's not what runs a country. Men like us have a responsibility to make sure things that need to be done get done. Sure it makes things easier to have the President's blessing, but not having it never stops me, nor should it stop you. Project Revelation is almost ready."

"We've been over this before," Edward objects. "I'm the Secretary of Sorcery; I can't support a program that detains and experiments on sorcerers."

"I don't need public support," Allen replies. "I have backers. I have facilities. I have staff. The only thing I don't have is test subjects. All I need from you is a few names."

"I can't just give you names."

"I know you have watch lists for potentially dangerous warlocks," Allen says. "Just give me some names from that. I'll be doing you a favor by removing threats."

"I don't know." Edward rubs the back of his neck while shaking his head. "If anyone were to find out, the blowback would be-"

"Would you listen to yourself?!" Allen slams his knife and fork on the table. "These freaks are dangerous so long as we don't have the means to combat them! Project Revelation would remove the need for your taskforce and put the power in our hands. Think of it; an entire army of soldiers than can do what these warlocks do, but using tech instead of magic. We'll ensure our country's safety with the ability to exert our dominance over any other nation that opposes us."

Allen truly believes he has the country's interests at heart. He doesn't so much hate sorcerers as he is jealous of them. He's extremely envious of what sorcerers can do and believes their power would be better suited in his hands for America. This blind zealousness allows Allen to deliver an impassioned speech, but Edward isn't so easily swayed by mere words. Besides, patriotism is one thing, but he knows who Allen really looks out for. "And what happens to me once Revelation gets the DoS shut down?" Edward asks.

"When this is over, you can pick your position. We'll use the results from Revelation to track down and eliminate the terrorists. Once the world sees our results, you and I will be calling the shots around here. Not the President, not the Senate or Congress. Us."

As delusional as the idea sounds out loud, it makes a lot of sense in the minds of both men. Perhaps it's Edward's still fresh anger at the President, but a power grab could work if handled delicately. It will mean making nice with and cozying up to the President so he can stay in the loop on the taskforce's investigation. It seems a small irritation for the potential rewards. "I'll get you a list," Edwards says before cutting into his duck with a renewed appetite.

***

Back in the Guardian wing of the Department of Sorcery, Eric is still going through every part of the file on Jared Cross. Benjamin has gotten bored and is pestering Emmanuel. "All I'm saying is, according this file, this bloke's a real badass," Benjamin says. "And according to Eric, you took him down while he was stopping the bombs from going off. I just want to know how you did it."

"I didn't," Emmanuel responds. "He slipped an' fell."

"They found his blood all over the scene, but not a scratch on him!" Benjamin replies in disbelief. "If that isn't some weird Mender magic, then I don't know what is."

"He must've fallen down da stairs." Emmanuel sticks to his story.

"That doesn't make any sense!" Benjamin gives up. "Alright fine, don't tell me."

Benjamin storms out of the room to bother Jasmine, sulking the entire way. Eric looks away from the large wall monitor to Emmanuel. "He's not wrong," Eric says. "That really makes no sense. I'd come up with something different should we face an official inquiry."

"Eh," Emmanuel shrugs.

Eric pulls himself away from his work entirely. He looks Emmanuel over as he approaches him. He's normally very good at reading people, but this old man is a mystery. He obviously wants people to underestimate him. The question is, why? What is he hiding? "You are an odd one, Emmanuel," Eric says.

"Why do you say dat?" Emmanuel raises an eyebrow.

"I can't say exactly." Eric circles Emmanuel as he talks. "The file on you mentions no military or law enforcement background, yet you're cooler under pressure than some of the most seasoned soldiers I've known. You were able to teach me things about my magic I never knew were possible, but you're not Sentinel. And I heard what you said before Cross 'fell down the stairs.' Of which there weren't any nearby, I'd also like to point out. I don't know what any of this means other than to say you are an odd one, but I'm sure glad you're on our side."

"I am an old man, and I've seen many t'ings in my time, so very little surprises or frightens me. And I was guessing when I 'elped you at the Statue of Liberty. I didn't t'ink it would actually work."

Not exactly the response Eric was expecting. "You mean you didn't know making individual barriers would contain the explosions?" Eric asks with a sinking feeling in his stomach.

"No," Emmanuel says with an innocent smile.

"We could've died!"

"But we didn't," Emmanuel says, giving Eric a pat on the shoulder before walking away.

Benjamin finds Jasmine in one of the numerous cubicles out on the main floor of the Guardian wing. All of the tiny workstations are identical, each containing a computer screen and a phone on the desk top. As no one has ever used this section of the DoS, there is no personality or decor anywhere. It seems the wing was wired and functional as Jasmine has logged onto a computer. She watches a news clip on the internet. An attractive brunette news anchor sits on the right side of the screen with a cell phone shot video clip playing next to her as she reports. The footage is of Jasmine taking down three of the terrorist Evos using her martial arts skill. "While the White House has not released the identities of the anti-terrorist taskforce, this amateur footage has surfaced showing UMDC fighter Jasmine Yuen fighting the terrorists on Liberty Island. The UMDC reports that Yuen was scheduled for a title fight in Dubai earlier in the week, but vanished before the match started."

The anchor continues on in her report, but her voice is cut off by Benjamin. "Holy shit!" His exclamation startles Jasmine. "That was you?! You didn't even use magic! I'll tell you what. If you don't want to go back to the UMDC, I could make you a star."

"What?" Jasmine is actually unaware of who Benjamin is. "What are you talking about?"

"Do you know how much people would pay to do what you did in that video?" Benjamin's excitement is very transparent. "How'd you like to lead the next big U-Movie action blockbuster?"

"I don't appreciate your jokes." Jasmine shuts off the computer monitor. "I just lost a major purse for this hero crap, and I don't know where that leaves me with the UMDC."

"I'm not joking," Benjamin says. "And there is no way the UMDC drops you after coverage like that. You're a national hero whether you want to be or not. Hell, once all our names are released publicly, I expect U-Movie stock to be stronger than it already is."

Jasmine starts to realize that Benjamin may not be messing about. She stands up. "You work for U-Movie?"

"I created it, love," he says with smile. "And I could pay you ten times what a title fight would for just one movie. What do you say? Money. Fame. What more could you ask for?"

A flood of emotion washes over Jasmine. She's never thought about acting before, but the idea of it is exhilarating. She doesn't need the prestige; even in the UMDC, she fights for the thrill, not the fame. The money, on the other hand, is something that she could definitely use. Most of the money Jasmine's made from fighting has been gone to the Chinese Triad to pay for the lives of her mother and sister.

Jasmine was born in Shenzhen, in the Guangdong Province of China. Her family was poor, and her father died when she was very young. When she was a teenager, her mother became very ill, making things harder on her and her sister. She held many odd jobs in an attempt to put food on the table while her mother underwent treatment. It was at this time that she discovered she could make good money fighting in illegal tournaments. This is also when she discovered her evocation abilities.

After her mother recovered, she wanted something better for both her daughters and that thing was to move to America. Only, they had no money to do so. Jasmine had met many unsavory characters at underground fighting rings, including Triads and Snakeheads. Snakehead gangs specialize in smuggling people, often to wealthier countries. Jasmine took all her winnings and paid a Snakehead named Sung Qiang to bring her, her mother, and her sister to America. Unfortunately, once stateside, Qiang raised the price of their transportation, keeping her mother and sister until Jasmine could pay. And pay she has. But the Snakeheads continue to raise the price, threatening harm to her family should she not keep paying.

Jasmine hates Qiang, but everything she has is because of him. He arranged for her citizenship. He made the connections with the UMDC for her. Of course, everything he's done for her has only been to benefit himself. Once her family is safe, she vows to put an end to their operation so that no one else has to suffer in the same way her family has. "Okay," Jasmine says to Benjamin. "But I get to do all my own stunts."

Before Benjamin can answer, Andrea and Anthony enter expeditiously through the glass doors. Andrea rushes past Jasmine and Benjamin without so much as a glance. Anthony looks over at them without breaking stride. "We think we got something," he says, walking by.

Benjamin and Jasmine look at each other and then back at the ops room. Jasmine hops out of her chair, and they both run after Andrea and Anthony. Once in the back room, Andrea goes straight to the touchscreen workstation where Eric continues to pour over suspect files. She waves her hand which grasps Jared's hairs in it. "I need a world map," she says to Eric.

Without questioning why, Eric opens up a digital globe on the touchscreen which also appears on the wall screens. The others approach the table. "Allow me," Benjamin says as he touches the side of the touchscreen cabinet.

Benjamin's hand glows briefly, and as it fades, the flat image of the Earth suddenly materializes above the table as a three dimensional image. The hovering Earth is slightly transparent and slowly rotates. "Just think about the location you want, and it will highlight on the globe," Benjamin says to Andrea.

Andrea opens her hand containing Jared's hair, palm up. She holds her other hand a few inches above that, palm down. A couple minutes go by while she concentrates with her eyes closed. As she does this, the 3-D globe stops its rotation and begins moving erratically. The illusory image finally stops with Africa facing Andrea. She opens her eyes and points to a spot in the Egyptian desert. "This is the last place he was before attacking Liberty Island," she says.

Eric looks at Anthony. "Is that enough info for you to teleport us?" he asks.

"I can work with that," Anthony answers.

"Then let's suit up and take a little field trip."

## Chapter 12: False Flag

Catherine has lost track of time inside Damian's library. She would be happy in a normal library with such an expansive collections of books, but the addition of magical knowledge makes it even more enticing. She sits in the same place Damian left her and has been making her way slowly through the Edgar Allan Poe book given to her. She is pretty far into the book when glowing magical runes appear to her as she reads through its written text. Even though the arcane writing is foreign to her, she can somehow understand its meaning.

By using a portal, hidden by his own illusion magic, Damian appears in the library as though he has the abilities of a Transporter. His emergence out of thin air startles Catherine for a moment. He notices her fright and tries to appear less imposing by offering a smile. "How's it going?" he asks. "Are you hungry? Can I get you something?"

While Catherine appreciates the hospitality that has been offered to her, she's anxious and quite impatient, though she doesn't want to be rude. "No thank you," she says with a shrug. "Did you get a hold of my parents?"

"We're working on it," he replies, quickly changing the subject. "Have you learned anything?"

"I found something about detecting magical energies in *The Fall of the House of Usher*," she says, looking around while standing up, "which led me to wonder where we are exactly?"

"How do you mean?" Damian questions.

"Putting what I learned to use, I detected that everything around us is radiating magic," she says while motioning to the book. "And thanks to the helpful guide identifying magical auras, it seems that we're surrounded by illusion magic. I'm guessing that's to hide where we really are. So...where are we?"

"You catch on quick, Catherine," he says warmly. "I can see there's no point in hiding the truth from you."

With a snap of his fingers, the façade of a library vanishes, leaving a very large, brightly lit room. There is a metal table with six chairs where the wooden table once stood. A few bookshelves line the walls, but nowhere near the collection that was seen previously. A set of white double-doors are fixed along the southern wall with a single door on the adjacent east wall. "Did you learn anything else?" Damian asks.

"Just something about making the living appear as though they're dead," Catherine says with frustration. "But that still doesn't answer my question. Or help me learn how to control this. And when am I going to get to see my parents? You promised I could see them!"

"I'm working on that," Damian says calmly. "But we've hit a snag. It seems the government has picked them up and is holding them."

"What?!"

"Let me show you," Damian says, pointing towards the double-doors.

Catherine cautiously follows Damian out the doors through a series of windowless fluorescent hallways until they arrive at a room populated by a handful of the Dragon King's followers. Elena Volkov is a tall blonde with her hair tied into a bun. She looks all business, wearing gray slacks with a black button-down top. Standing next to her, and dressed quite a bit more casually, is Devon Black. Sporting jeans, a black t-shirt, and a blue hoodie, Devon is in his mid-twenties and appears to be about ten years younger than Elena. Calling these two "followers" is a disservice to their importance in the Eye of Ruin.

If Damian had a second-in-command, it would be Elena. She's a very skilled Prophet who formerly served in the Russian military. Devon is the Transporter who penetrated the White House's security for the attack on the President. While Elena is completely loyal to Damian and his cause, Devon tends to buck the system every chance he gets. If he wasn't so talented, Damian would've gotten rid him already. The three other men in the room appear to be the muscle; each wears black military-style fatigues and carries an automatic shotgun.

The room itself is for meetings. There is a round table with a top that looks to be carved from polished black stone. Around it sit a number of leather chairs, one noticeably larger and more comfortable than the others. The room is otherwise unfurnished. Upon Damian entering the room, the soldier types tense up as though they fear being accused of slacking off. Elena and Devon, who were having a private chat, stop what they're doing and focus on Damian's entrance, though they don't tense up like the guards. "Cat, these are two of my most devout comrades, Elena and Devon," Damian says pointing, out each one. "They have been the ones tracking down your parents."

"Thank you," Catherine says to them.

"Elena, I want you to show her what you showed me," Damian directs.

"Are you certain you wish to see?" Elena asks Catherine with a thick Russian accent. "It will not be easy to watch."

"Let me see them," Catherine says with a nod.

"Then have a seat." Elena motions to one of the chairs at the table.

Catherine takes a seat at the table while everyone else remains standing. Elena moves opposite Catherine at the table so they're facing each other. She places her palms onto the smooth black surface of the table and begins her incantation. While this is happening, Damian positions himself behind Catherine. "Oculus eminentia," Elena says, causing a disc of white light to appear roughly a foot above the table.

The colorless void is slowly replaced with an image of an interrogation room. The angle is similar to that of a security camera mounted in the corner of the room. An older man in a blue suit stands with his back to Catherine's vantage point. Beyond him, she sees her parents. They are an extremely generic middle-aged couple. Her father is an accountant, and her mother is an executive assistant, neither of which is prepared for the situation they find themselves in. The look of fear and confusion on their faces immediately affects Catherine, bringing tears to her eyes. The man in the suit circles around behind her parents revealing himself to be the Secretary of Sorcery, Edward Chamberlain. Though the image is silent, it is clear he is shouting at them. "What's he doing to them?!" Catherine angrily shouts.

"He's using them to get to you," Damian says.

"But why would he take them?" Catherine questions. "He knows I was taken by you."

"And he's hoping this will draw you out," Damian answers. "But he doesn't realize that we're going to go in and get them out just like we did you."

"But we can't keep losing people for these endeavors," Devon speaks up. "How many did we lose just trying to free her?"

"He makes a good point," Elena adds on.

Damian lets out a sigh of defeat. "You're both right, of course," Damian says earnestly. "But I made this girl a promise, and I don't intend to break that vow. Whatever we need to do to free her parents, we'll do it."

Suddenly, all of Catherine's apprehensions about Damian vanish. She doesn't really understand the gravity of her situation, and, while she definitely doesn't approve of the Eye of Ruin's past actions, the fact that they will risk their own lives for her parents means everything. "Is there some way I can help?" she asks.

"You needn't get involved," Damian says. "We'll figure something out."

"But they're my parents," Catherine protests. "I want to help."

"I'm afraid I'm not sure how you could," Damian says with concern. "You're untrained, and I'm not going to send you into the field like that. Magic is out of the question so there isn't-"

"I can use my magic if you'll just show me how to control it!"

Damian looks from Catherine to his two advisors for guidance. "I'm not in love with the idea, but having a couple of undead soldiers go in would be a zero risk operation," Devon says.

The scene in Elena's viewing portal continues forward. After Edward finishes yelling at Catherine's parents, who are both in tears at this point, a guard comes in to forcefully remove them from the room. Catherine can't look away. Even after her parents are pulled from the room, she stares at Edward, still standing in the interrogation room. She already hated Edward for essentially kidnapping and lying to her, but torturing her parents like this is too far. "I'll do it," she says with steely resolve.

"Are you sure?" Damian asks. "I can teach you the basics of arcane control, but I have no knowledge of necromancy. That part will be up to you."

"I'm ready."

***

A couple of hours after taking Catherine to begin her training, Damian returns to the meeting room. The guards have gone, but Elena and Devon sit at the round table, having been joined by one of Damian's favorite enforcers. Ava Thorne is a twenty-seven year old rarity. She is one of only a handful of women to serve in the Army Rangers. She's an imposing figure even when sitting at a table. Her frame is smaller than that of a body-builder, but her lean muscle is rock solid. She's slightly shorter than Elena and visibly looks to be the yin to her yang. While Elena has light blue eyes and long hair that she regularly keeps neatly tied back, Ava is a short-haired brunette with brown eyes.

Like most members in the Eye of Ruin, Ava is a sorcerer. She's a Builder. Most Builders use their abilities for construction; however, Ava applies conjuration magic to her field of expertise in a different way. On the battlefield, she combines conjuration with gunplay for deadly results, creating blockades that she can shoot through or around, while keeping herself safe. It's one of the things Damian finds most attractive about her. Most men find her aggressiveness emasculating, but Damian thinks a lover that can serve as a bodyguard just makes good business sense. Though the two share a bed on occasion, they never let on about their relationship. Damian is a strong enough Ghost that he feels he's able to prevent even a powerful Prophet like Elena from seeing his true emotions and intentions.

All three occupants are working on laptops. They look up as Damian enters the room. "Report," he states approaching the table.

"Elena was right," Devon starts off. "They took Jared to Carcer. While scouting, I saw the two DoS sorcerers she said would be there. I ported back and gave her my report."

"I believed their Prophet was trying to use Jared to track us," Elena says. "So I did what we discussed in that event. If they follow her vision, they'll walk right into a trap."

"Very good, but I don't want to take any chances," Damian responds. "Devon, you and Ava head to the site. I don't want anyone left alive. I don't care that they're sorcerers, they're no better than the Cassus they protect."

"On it," Devon says as he stands. "You ready?"

Ava nods and stands up closing her laptop in the process. She and Devon exit the room. Elena rubs her eyes with her right hand while closing her laptop with the other. She stands up and stretches before yawning. "How does the training go with the girl?" she asks.

"She doesn't realize how powerful she is," he answers. "But she's also a quick study. With just a little more time, she will be ready to serve her purpose."

"She could also be a dangerous enemy if not handled properly," Elena says.

"It won't get to that." Damian sits down at the table. "We have other matters to discuss. We're going to have another go at the White House, but I want some reinforcements first. We need to hit Carcer. Everyone in there must have a grudge against the government and should easily join our cause."

"That will be no trouble. The perimeter has guards, but they only use the anti-magic tech inside the structure."

"We may have to wait a bit to strike though. All government facilities are bound to be on high alert after Liberty Island. Everything is falling into place, and I don't want to jeopardize that."

"When do you want to go?"

"I'm not sure. Ideally, once the girl is ready, but I need to look into something first."

## Chapter 13: Chasing Ghosts

It's just after nine in the evening, local time, when Anthony's portal opens up on a sandy dune in the Egyptian desert. Clad in black fatigues and lightweight ballistic body armor, Eric is first through the shimmering gateway. He is armed with a carbine. Jasmine and Andrea follow him through, Benjamin and Emmanuel behind them. All four are wearing their own clothing; however, they too, wear the same body armor as Eric. Anthony is last through the portal with it closing behind him. Anthony is dressed identically to Eric, right down to the armaments. Much like when they journeyed to Liberty Island, Jasmine and Emmanuel opt not to carry a firearm.

Aside from a lone, single-story brick structure near their landing site, the desert is vast with no signs of civilization as far as the eye can see. For a moment, everyone's attention is drawn to the sky instead of the building. The intensity of the stars is so much more brilliant when there's no light pollution to wash it out. The chill in the night air brings everyone's attention back down to Earth. They quietly move towards the brick building which has one single door entrance on the face of it. As they get near, they can see that the door is made of metal, but has fatigued from years of being blasted by wind and sand. The bricks making up the walls look rather old and eroded as well. "Are you certain this is where he came from?" Benjamin asks skeptically.

"This is what I saw in the vision," Andrea replies.

"We've got to follow every lead," Eric says.

Over time, sorcerers learn to recognize the presence of nearby magic. It's not always distinct, nor can one always determine the type of magic in use. However, most sorcerers can usually recognize magic of their own school. Benjamin is getting a sense of very strong illusion magic radiating from the brick structure. Illusion magic can be trickier to detect as it is intended to obfuscate or deceive, but, in this instance, the arcane energy is so intense it creates a beacon for anyone who can sense its type. "Benjamin, can you make us invisible?" Eric asks.

"Umm…I could," Benjamin answers. "But I'm not sure how much it would help us. I'm picking up illusion magic so intense that whoever cast it would be able to detect my spell, just as I have theirs. We'd probably have more of a surprise going in without it."

"I am sensing a dozen or so heartbeats from inside," Emmanuel says.

"You can detect heartbeats?" Jasmine asks in surprise.

"Yes," Emmanuel answers. "It is very useful when one's job is to heal da sick an' dying."

"Okay everyone, be alert," Eric says. "Something doesn't feel right here."

Eric tests the metal door to find that it's unlocked. While the door opens easily, it makes a loud groan as it does. Eric stops and waits. He's expecting the sound to bring someone to investigate it, but no one comes. After a few minutes, Eric enters through the open doorway, followed by the others, with Anthony bringing up the rear.

Beyond the front entrance is a dark hallway made of the same aged brick as the exterior. The hall is wide enough to travel two by two; however, the group chooses to move single file. A flickering light can be seen at the end of the hallway, the glow of which provides just enough visibility to make out a handful of doorways on either side of the corridor. Eric moves up to the first door which he finds is closed. He is preparing to open it when Emmanuel stops him. "The heartbeats are coming from de room at de end of de hallway," he says in a whisper.

"Let's move," Eric whispers back to the group.

The entire group slowly makes their way down the hallway, stopping just outside the closed door at the end of it. Eric looks at the handle on the relic of a door. Everything about this whole scenario feels like a trap to him. He decides it's not worth risking the team's life. "I don't like it," he whispers back over his shoulder. "Let's head back outside and see if there's another way in."

Anthony turns to lead the way outside, but is now blocked by a metal door that wasn't there before. The others see this as well and begin looking around the hallway in confusion. To everyone's surprise, they are no longer in the hallway, but in a dark room. "You can't leave yet, the fun's just starting," a female voice says from the darkness.

Everyone looks towards the darkness. "Lux!" Jasmine shouts, creating a bright glowing orb of light in the center of the room, illuminating the entire area.

Ava stands with six Eye of Ruin sorcerers ready to attack. It's obvious they weren't expecting the light spell as some of them shield their eyes from its brightness. The room is otherwise empty, and now, being exposed, Ava immediately acts. "Voco moerus!" she exclaims while making arcane gestures with her hands.

As she finishes speaking, walls of stone rise up from the ground in front of her and the other Eye of Ruin members. Anthony and Eric open fire, but their shots strike the thick stone and have very little effect. The entire room erupts into chaos as magic and bullets fly back and forth. Eric shields his team with his defensive wards while Ava conjures more stone and steel protective blockades in front of her team. Jasmine exchanges bolts of fire and lightning with a handful of the enemy evocation sorcerers.

While the others are battling, Emmanuel stands back by the door with his eyes closed. He looks to be speaking some arcane words that require undivided focus. Just as he sensed the hearts beating in the structure when they first arrived, he does that now, but with more refinement. He's using each person's heartbeat to track them in the compound. Every heartbeat is in this room except for one. This last one is tricky to lock down as it seems to appear and disappear in different areas at an alarming pace. This leads Emmanuel to the conclusion that he's dealing with a Transporter. "There is a teleporter nearby!" Emmanuel shouts.

Now that he's aware and looking for it, Anthony can sense the dimensional rifts being created by the other Transporter teleporting around. As the sorcerer appears, Anthony is able to transport to him. It's Devon Black, who immediately takes a swing at Anthony upon seeing him. Watching two Transporters fight is very difficult to follow. Initially, the two men test each other, teleporting behind and throwing a punch they hope will land before the other detects it and teleports out of the way. This dance of blips goes on until they learn each other's rhythms, and then the fight changes completely. Instead of avoiding each other, they reach a point where they are countering each other's counters and actually making physical contact between teleports. The end result is a hyperactive boxing match that takes place all across the room. The two start off pretty evenly matched, but Anthony's combat training does come into play, giving him the edge. After a while, he finally seizes the advantage and is able to grapple Devon preventing him from teleporting away.

Jasmine and one of the enemy Evos happen to cast the same spell at the same time. Two bolts of lightning streak from opposite sides, clashing in the middle. The two bolts meet with such power that it creates an explosion of arcane energy and a deafening shockwave that knocks almost everyone in the room to the ground. Benjamin was standing near a side wall and was knocked into it; however, rather than impacting the wall, he passes through it as though it wasn't there, landing him in the sand of the desert outside. He looks around for a moment to get his bearings. After standing up, he examines the wall closer. It is solid to the touch, but there is something artificial about it. Benjamin realizes the magic he's been sensing is the building itself. The whole structure is an illusion.

Illusion magic affects the mind of a subject, causing them to see, hear, smell, taste, and touch things that aren't there. When interacting with a strong illusionary object in a normal way, the brain makes the body think it's touching what it sees, but if you don't see the illusion or you try to interact with it in a way that would defy physics, the effect fails. When Benjamin was thrown into the wall, there was nothing there to actually stop his forced momentum, so he passed through it. Now that he is aware of the spell, he can ignore the illusion entirely or attempt to undo the magic with a spell of his own.

Back inside the brick compound, everyone is slowly getting back to their feet to battle further. Ava's blockades were knocked down or destroyed by the explosion, and before she can cast new ones, the building surrounding everyone vanishes, revealing the starry Egyptian night sky. Ava, Devon, and the other Eye of Ruin sorcerers knew the building was an illusion and are only momentarily thrown off by its disappearance. Eric and the team, on the other hand, are a bit more shocked by the effect. Devon knows the battle could now easily turn to his enemy's favor and decides to retreat. Though he also knows coming back to the Dragon King with news of failure could mean death as well, so he has an idea that will kill two birds. He teleports directly in front of Eric with malicious intent. "Phasma percutio," Devon whispers the words before phasing his hand directly into Eric's chest.

Phasing is a form of apportation where the object or person is rapidly teleported in and out of the material plane of existence giving it a physical presence albeit one that can pass through solid objects. Devon's hand doesn't actually tear Eric's flesh but the phasing does interrupt his heart. Eric's eyes widen as he gasps for air. He feels as though a knife as been plunged into his heart, which has stopped beating. As Devon removes his hand, Eric drops lifelessly onto the sand. The other members of the team look on in horror.

Devon teleports back near the members of his side and opens a man-sized portal to the real Eye of Ruin headquarters. The sorcerers begin falling back into the gateway. Anthony sees this and leaps into the air, flying speedily towards Devon and Ava. Seeing him approach, Ava summons a dense pillar of sand from the ground that rises up directly under Anthony. The column strikes him in the face, and knocks him into the air. As he falls back to the ground, Ava and Devon pass into the portal that closes immediately after.

Emmanuel rushes over to Eric's body to examine it. Andrea and Benjamin make their way to Anthony to check on him. Jasmine slowly walks up behind Emmanuel, expecting the worst. "Is he okay?" she asks.

"His 'eart has stopped," Emmanuel looks back at Jasmine. "He is dead."

"Can't you do anything?"

"I cannot, but I believe you can."

"How can I help?" Jasmine kneels down by Eric's body.

"He 'as only been dead for moments," Emmanuel answers. "I believe you can shock his 'eart to get it working again."

"I've never done something that controlled," Jasmine says with doubt. "I just shoot lightning bolts at people."

"You can do it. Just do de spell as you know it, but picture de desired effect in your mind. Make sure to breathe. Focus as you cast, and you can modify de spell."

It sounds a lot to ask, but she's willing to try if it could save a life. Emmanuel rips Eric's shirt open, exposing his chest. Jasmine places her hands on Eric's chest with her palms touching his skin. She closes her eyes before taking in three deep breaths. She envisions the lightning barely sparking from her hands into Eric's body. She takes one more big breath, exhaling very slowly before opening her eyes and saying the word, "Fulgor."

A jolt of electricity surges from Jasmine's hands into Eric's chest, causing his body to lurch, though he remains lifeless. "Again," Emmanuel says.

Jasmine shocks the body again, causing it to jump once more, but with the same end result. Emmanuel urges her to keep trying, so she repeats the process three more times before Eric's eyes fly open, and he sits up with a gasp. He coughs and struggles to catch his breath for a few minutes.

In meantime, Andrea has checked Anthony for a pulse and finds that he's alive, but unconscious. He does have blood coming out of his nose and mouth, leading her to think the damage is worse than she initially thought. She looks over to see that Eric appears to be awake, so she calls for Emmanuel. "Anthony's alive, but he's not looking good! I need you over here, Emmanuel!"

Emmanuel quickly makes his way over to Anthony and examines him. "He 'as a pretty bad concussion," Emmanuel says.

He places a hand on Anthony's forehead and whispers a few arcane words. His hand glows brightly for a moment before the energy transfers from his palm to Anthony. The others look on as though his eyes will pop open while he spouts a quote from his favorite movie, but he remains still. "I 'ave healed the damage, but he will be unconscious for a while," Emmanuel explains, addressing their concerns.

Jasmine helps Eric to his feet. Even though his chest and lungs are on fire, he feels pretty good for having been clinically dead a minute ago. He scans the surrounding desert, wondering where the Eye of Ruin went. "What happened?" he asks.

"They 'ported out right after you went down," Jasmine answers.

Eric is furious with himself. How could he lead the team right into a trap? He shouldn't have rushed the operation. He believes his over-eagerness to bring Catherine home has left them stranded in the middle of the Egyptian desert. And to make matters worse, the realization that the building is gone has just now fully hit him. "The compound was an illusion?" he asks, thinking out loud.

"Yeah," Benjamin answers.

Something about all of this isn't adding up for Eric. "But why would your vision of the past have an illusion in it?" Eric directs his query to Andrea. "Why would the terrorists be launching their attack on Liberty Island from an imaginary compound in Egypt?"

Now that the question has been asked, everyone wonders what's going on. Benjamin came from a world of liars and thieves, so he is the first to be suspicious. He starts moving aggressively towards Andrea. "Did you lead us into this trap?!" he asks angrily.

"What are you talking about?" Andrea is completely taken aback.

"You had the 'vision' that brought us here," Benjamin accuses. "Are you working with the Eye?"

"Fuck you," Andrea responds. "I saw the structure in the vision; I don't know why it would be fake!"

"Perhaps de vision was false," Emmanuel interjects.

Everyone stops and looks at Emmanuel. "Like an illusion inside a vision?" Benjamin asks incredulously.

Even in a world where magic use is fairly common, the idea of illusion magic being used on divination magic seems ridiculous. "How would that be possible?" Eric asks.

"It is rare, but powerful sorcerers are able to combine magic," Emmanuel says. "Like mixing illusion wit' divination to create a false vision in someone's mind."

Andrea thinks back to what she did to the terrorists back on Liberty Island. "That's what *we* did!" she exclaims while motioning to Benjamin.

"What now?" Benjamin asks in confusion.

"I don't know how, but we implanted a false vision of the guards' guns being empty," she clarifies.

"Interesting," Benjamin says.

"Yeah, but the skill needed here…" Jasmine trails off unable to fathom the power required.

"Two masters," Emmanuel says in response. "But de Ghost would have to be de stronger of the de two for all of dis."

"How do we find sorcerers that powerful?" Jasmine asks.

"I know one," Benjamin says with a sigh.

"I want a full report on that, but we need to focus on getting out of here first," Eric says. "Since we don't know how long Anthony's going to be out, we need to figure out another way to get Stateside."

"Does anyone have cell service?" Benjamin jokingly asks.

## Chapter 14: Snake in the Grass

To say Damian is disappointed would be an understatement. He sent two of his best, along with a team of Evos, to handle something that he considers a minor problem. Hearing that they failed to completely eliminate the nuisance is not the news he was expecting. He stands silently in his office with Devon and Ava before him. He's been quiet long enough for Devon to fear the worst.

Damian's office is simple, yet sleek. The walls and furnishings are all black with little to no décor. There is a dark wooden desk and bookshelves filled with books new and old. There are window frames on two of the walls, but there are no windows. Damian uses these to project illusions of any scenic view he desires. The fact that they are currently blank is yet another bad sign for Devon and Ava.

The door to the hallway opens, and Elena walks into the room, stopping half way between everyone. She stands by the desk, facing Devon and Ava with the same judgmental look on her face that Damian is currently wearing. Devon can't take the suspense any longer. "This was not our fault." He breaks the silence. "Why wouldn't you send a Sentinel with us? This team is better than you let on, and they were gaining the upper hand."

"You know very well why," Damian says with a calm intensity. "If you can't avoid some magic spells thrown your way, then maybe I don't need you."

"Look, I killed their leader," Devon tries to defend his actions. "And Ava might've taken one of 'em out as we left. That should count for something."

Damian doesn't respond, instead looking to Elena for confirmation on Devon's claims. "They both live," she says in her deep Russian accent.

"That's impossible!" Devon raises his voice. "I stopped his heart. I watched him die!"

"Then someone brought him back," Elena says matter-of-factly. "I see him in future events."

Devon throws his arms in the air in dramatic fashion. "Oh, well if she sees it then it must be true," he says sarcastically.

Having a powerful Transporter has been a tremendous help in setting up the Eye of Ruin's strikes, and, while Devon hasn't been part of the organization as long as the others, he's made an impact with what he can do. Unfortunately, he has a problem with authority even when that authority is anti-authority. He constantly clashes with Damian. He isn't as enamored by "the Dragon King" as Damian's other followers, often thinking he knows better. He's cocky, and his faith in his own abilities makes him feel untouchable.

"Devon, you're not helping the situation," Ava says, putting a hand on his shoulder.

Devon pushes her hand away. "Whatever," he says with an attitude. "You'll be fine. You're his favorite."

He turns to leave the room. "If you walk out that door, you won't like the consequences," Damian threatens.

Devon spins around to face Damian. "Fine," he says before teleporting out of the room.

Damian looks at Ava, then glances at Elena. He needs to address this dissidence, but right now, he doesn't have the time. "Ava, you're dismissed," he says waving her off.

Ava leaves without a word of protest. Elena gives Damian a long discerning look. She already knows his intentions for Devon, and she does not approve. "Is that really necessary?" she asks.

Damian can sense her magic, and even though he has no way to protect himself from her powers once she's already inside, he turns his back on her in defiance. "Stop gleaning my future," he says. "I'll talk to him before I do anything drastic, but I have a meeting to get to. I need you to work with her while I'm gone. She's getting stronger, but she's not yet where we need her."

"I'll do what I can," she answers.

***

It's late afternoon back in Virginia at the offices of the Pentagon. Allen Barber sits in his massive office, reviewing some files. The dark mahogany furnishings of his office make it look more like a gentleman's smoking den than the workspace of a public servant. A crystal brandy decanter set rests atop a small table near the desk. The stuffed heads of two antlered animals are mounted to plaques on either side of the door leading out of the room.

Allen sits at his desk with his suit jacket resting on the back of his chair. His tie is uncharacteristically loosened, and his sleeves are rolled up. He's in the middle of reading some personnel files he shouldn't have. Not the files Edward sent over, but ones he pulled some strings to acquire. He's interrupted by a phone call from his secretary, telling him that Texas senator Patrick Cobb is here to see him. It's an unscheduled visit, but he doesn't think much about it since he and the senator have mutual political interests. Allen slides the files into his top desk drawer and tells his secretary to send him in.

Allen's secretary, an attractive brunette young enough to be his daughter, opens the door from the outside, allowing Senator Cobb to enter. He's an older man with rather unkempt graying hair and a beard to match. He wears a brown suit and, almost as if directly from the stereotype handbook, a bolo tie with a silver cow skull clasp. The secretary closes the door after he passes the threshold, leaving the two men in privacy. Allen stands and comes around to greet his guest. "Patrick, you s.o.b.," Allen says extending a hand. "It's been a while. Have a seat."

They shake hands before Patrick sits in one of the two chairs in front of the large desk. "What brings you by?" Allen asks as he makes his way back to his chair.

"I thought we'd talk about Revelation," Patrick replies.

The statement halts Allen in his tracks. Officially, the only person to be told about Revelation was the President. Even when he was shopping the idea around for backers, he kept the details vague and never mentioned it by name. How could this senator know about it? The answer to his question is soon revealed as the older man sitting before him slowly morphs into the much younger Damian Westonbrooke. While Allen is shocked to see him in his office, the man now in front of him is no stranger. "What the hell are you doing here?" Allen asks with hushed irritation.

"You don't return my calls, so I thought we should have a little face-to-face," Damian replies sardonically.

"You shouldn't be here," Allen says making his way to his office door to lock it.

Damian stands. "I wouldn't have to be here if you kept me updated," he shoots back. "What's the status of Revelation? Where are my Sentinels? Why do you have animal heads on your wall?"

"Very cute," Allen replies sarcastically. "Revelation is moving along fine. We've been able to extract the magic from your volunteers; however, there were some drastic side-effects."

"Such as?"

"They died."

"All of them?" Damian asks with surprising indifference.

"Yes, all of them."

"Does the tech work?"

"It does."

"Then I guess the sacrifice was worth it."

As civil as these two are acting right now they actually hate each other. How is it then that Project Revelation has them working together? The answer is simple: they're using each other for separate end results. When things come to a head, there will be blood; it's just a matter of who decides to strike first.

The Eye of Ruin is actually a machination of Allen's. When the Department of Sorcery was created and governmental steps were taken to make sorcerers a more accepted part of society, he knew he needed to do something. What better way to push his own agenda than to create a terrorist threat that he alone has the solution to stop? Damian popped up on his radar a year before he took the position of Secretary of Defense, when he was in charge of Homeland Security. Damian was a mercenary on Interpol's watch list. Not much was known about him, but his reputation for using his magic nefariously if the price was right kept him on Allen's mind. Once the technology was ready, and he had the financial backing, he made his approach. He offered Damian a lot of money to work the nations of the world into a frenzy, posing as a radical anti-humanist sorcerer. What makes the plan so perfect is that Allen has no intention of paying Damian, but rather destroying him and the Eye as the endgame to cover his bases.

On the other side of the story, Damian was an arcane hired-gun working primarily out of London.  He worked mainly with other sorcerer criminals until their organization was raided by Scotland Yard.  At the time, there was no way to hinder a sorcerer's abilities, so the orders were "shoot to kill."  Very few magic-users survived the bloodbath, and it forever changed Damian.  He was already a brutal son-of-a-bitch in the criminal world, but this lit a fire in him to see his kind as the master race.

When Damian came to the United States for work, he was approached by Allen.  He agreed to the proposition with the stipulation that any technology created by Revelation be shared with him.  Outfitting himself with hardware that would allow him to use other types of magic would make him a god in the eyes of his fellow sorcerers.  Damian was already the man Allen wanted him to become and just didn't realize it.  He intends to use Project Revelation to outfit the Eye of Ruin with additional magic weaponry in order to destroy the government and ensure that magickind rule over humankind.

"Yes, I suppose it was worth it," Allen says in a still irritated tone. "Now will you leave?"

"Not so fast," Damian holds up his hand as if to halt him. "I want a tour of the research facility."

"That's out of the question," Allen replies.

"I want to make sure I'm not just sending sorcerers to their deaths for no reason before we proceed any further," Damian rebuts. "If you don't like it, then I suppose the media will want to hear all about your true nature."

"You can't threaten me," Allen attempts to appear imposing. "Who would believe you over me?"

No sooner does he pose the question than the entire room bursts into flames. Allen finds himself alone in a vortex of fire. He can feel the flames pulling the oxygen out of the air. He feels as though he's about to pass out when a loud crash comes from above as the roof is ripped off his office. A gigantic reptilian creature blocks the light of the sun trying to enter from outside. The head of the beast slinks forward, causing Allen to stumble backward to the ground. Its fang-filled jaw is larger than Allen's whole body, and he can feel its hot, rancid breath on his face. The monster opens its mouth, prompting Allen to believe he's to be its next meal. He shuts his eyes tightly, expecting the worst. "I will make them believe," a booming, guttural variation of Damian's voice shakes the room.

Allen opens one eye to peek at the impending doom to discover his office looks normal. There's no trace of the towering creature nor any signs of fiery destruction. Allen is cowering on the floor, but it's Damian standing over him, not a dragon. Damian extends a hand to help Allen up. "Your point is taken," Allen says begrudgingly as he stands.

"Good," Damian says contently. "Let's go."

"Right now?!"

"Yes. If we go from here, you know I'm not armed, I know you're not armed, and you don't have time to set up anything interesting for me."

Allen hates this idea, but he doesn't see having much of a choice. This is one of the exact reason he hates magic-users, but he knows if he plays along just a bit longer he can put this warlock in the ground where he belongs. "Fine," Allen says in a gruff tone. "Let me get my jacket."

***

It's well into the night before Damian makes it back to the Eye of Ruin compound. His trip to Allen's Revelation laboratory was a very successful endeavor. He garnered a basic understanding of the magic extraction & redistribution process, was able to covertly leave with one of the Allen's devices, and most importantly, he now knew where the lab was located. Once Catherine has learned to make the dead walk at her command, they will be making an unscheduled visit back to the facility.

Damian knows that his move today was an aggressive one, and, while his goal now seems within reach, this is the time to be most cautious. Allen will not forget this and will most likely take measures to ensure it can't happen again. Then there's also the DoS taskforce to worry about. These sorcerers are posing a bigger threat than he anticipated. Perhaps he's going about this the wrong way. Maybe aggression is the answer in this case. These sorcerers might see his point of view and join his cause if he handles them correctly. He decides it's worth looking into, but right now he has some internal problems to deal with.

Damian finds Devon getting out aggression in the weight room. This large room is outfitted with a row of punching bags, a small boxing ring, three treadmills, and a full set of free weights. Devon unleashes a barrage of blows against one of the punching bags. It looks as though he's been here a while, having worked up enough of a sweat to soak through his workout shirt. Damian walks into the room, standing between Devon and the exit. "I was wondering when you'd show up," Devon says, a bit out of breath.

"I warned you there would be consequences for your defiance," Damian says.

"Consequences," Devon laughs sarcastically. "Everyone knows that's code for death."

"Often, yes," Damian says with a nod. "But we need a Transporter, and I told Elena I'd talk with you before I reacted irrationally."

"So what, you're going to apologize and make nice with me?"

Now Damian starts laughing. "No, I'm still going to kill you," he stops laughing.

Devon doesn't actually fear Damian the way the others do. Sure he doesn't know him as well, but all he's seen him do is make illusions. Illusions can't hold up to what he can do. "I'd like to see you try," he says, moving a bit closer to Damian. "I'll bet you're not even here. I'm guessing I'm talking to a projection right now."

"I'd only send a projection if I were afraid of being hurt."

"Your mistake," Devon says before teleporting away.

He reappears behind Damian, delivering an elbow to the back of his head. To Devon's surprise, he strikes an invisible force field a few inches away from his target. Pain shoots throughout his arm as hitting the barrier feels like elbowing a steel wall. Devon winces and quickly teleports back to his starting position about ten feet away. "You've never had the faith in the Eye that the others have," Damian says raising his right arm to reveal a metallic bracer on his wrist.

The technology of Revelation is advanced, but also limited. Magic is too complicated for science to recreate an entire magical style with all its various abilities. Revelation allows them to infuse one spell into a device that can replicate the spell repeatedly, but with a slight recharge time. In this case, the bracer took on a personal barrier spell. The mechanical cuff has a small green light on it to indicate it's operational. As the shield is invisible, there is no other way to know it is working. "And it's that doubt that will be your undoing," Damian threatens.

"So I can't hurt you, so what," Devon remains confident. "You'll never be able to touch me."

"Nor do I intend to," Damian says with a shrug.

Devon finds himself lifted into the air as a sharp pain stabs into his back. He looks down to see the coned tip of a concrete spike protruding from his chest. Devon's agony is only rivaled by his confusion. How could Damian have the ability to do this?

He feels himself being lowered back down to the ground. He's extremely weak and near death, but he's being propped up by the massive spike run through his back. He coughs up blood while struggling to breathe. Just before he loses consciousness, Ava leans forward from behind him. "You were right," She whispers in his ear. "I am his favorite."

With that, Devon dies. Ava dismisses the spike she conjured, causing it to reform into the ground from where it came. This causes Devon's body to collapse into a bloody pile on the floor. Damian stares at the corpse for a long moment, almost as though he were regretful, until he completely assuages that notion. "We're going to need another Transporter," he says. "It looks like Carcer's going to fall sooner than expected."

## Chapter 15: Bruised But Not Broken

Two days have passed since Eric and the team were ambushed in Egypt. The journey back to the United States was quite a fiasco. The Department of Sorcery has no power to operate outside of the country, so when Eric was able to call in, Edward had to reach out to the Central Intelligence Agency for support. Well, in actuality, he didn't have to, as the DoS almost always has access to a Transporter that could've easily brought them home, but he wanted to stick it to Eric and blame it on bureaucracy.

The CIA is constantly running covert flights in and out of other countries. In previous years that meant hitching a ride on a cargo plane to get to the States, but the introduction of magic to the world changed the face of air travel. Unfortunately, the CIA didn't have a Transporter available on such short notice. Even though they can travel anywhere in the world instantaneously, Transporters are very sought after and typically stay extremely busy. The CIA had to direct the team to an airport.

Airports the world over still function much the same as they always have with the exception that they now have a terminal for

*Instaports*, a very expensive teleportation service that transports you from one airport to another in the blink of an eye. The CIA was able to provide passports and cover stories for the team while Benjamin covered the cost of Instaporting the whole group back to Dulles International Airport.

Anthony remained comatose until they were back on home soil. He awoke about 24 hours after they returned, finding out then the severity of the hit he took. On the surface he seems fine, having all his motor skills intact. The trouble starts when he tries using magic. He can't seem to find the command words he's looking for, and, when he does, nothing seems to happen. It's as if his brain has lost his knowledge of the arcane. Even innate abilities he could once do without reciting an incantation are now gone. The doctors believe this could be just a temporary thing, but then again, they don't have an understanding of what gives somebody the ability to use magic, so their hopefulness is just that.

After hours and hours of debriefing back at the DoS, Benjamin, Jasmine, and Andrea were released, each with their own government escort. Andrea went back to the hospital to check on Anthony. Benjamin paid for him and his DoS babysitter to Instaport back to New York so he could get some work done. Jasmine was in an unusual position as all her personal effects were left in Dubai when she was taken. She's managed to use a phone at the DoS to call her promoter, Lou Sykes.

Lou is a short, stocky former boxer who represents a handful of big name fighters in the Ultimate Magic Dueling

Championship. Lou saw Jasmine fight when the Triad first paid to get her on a fight card. He saw in her a strength that reminded him of when he was a young fighter and signed her immediately. He coined her nickname and pushed for her to get the big fights. He molded her fight persona and refined her fighting style by getting her the best trainers. He's a guy that genuinely cares about his fighters, having once been in their place. More than that, he knows of her situation with the Triad and helps when he can. "Where are you?" Lou sounds excited. "Are you okay? Do you need anything?"

"Lou, I'm okay," Jasmine replies in a tone that sounds opposite her statement. "But I'm concerned about my family. Missing that fight put me in a bind, and I don't have the money to pay Qiang."

"I know," he says. "I took care of it."

Ever since becoming her promoter, Lou has acted as a sort of surrogate father to Jasmine, but she'd never ask for him to help with this kind of thing. "You shouldn't have done that," Jasmine protests. "I don't want Qiang to have an excuse to come after you."

"I wasn't going to stand by and let your mom and sis get hurt," Lou says. "But you can't keep letting him stretch this out. We should get this authorities involved. Maybe some of your new government friends."

"You know I can't do that," she says, wishing it were an option. "Qiang would kill them at the first sign of any cops, and, even if they lived, they would be deported. I'm not even here legally, and Qiang would definitely take me down with him. I just have to keep paying until I can figure something out. Fortunately, I may not have to worry about the money for long."

"You're damn right about that," Lou emphatically agrees. "The UMDC has been calling non-stop to set up another fight! After your superhero antics at the Statue of Liberty, you're a hot commodity right now."

"I've got something better than that," she says with a bit of glee.

"Really? Do tell."

"The head of U-Movie has offered me a contract to make some action flicks."

"Oh, shit!" Lou hostilely exclaims.

"What's wrong?" Jasmine asks, unsure if it was her news that upset him.

"Um…some English guy called here a bit ago, claiming to be the boss at U-Movie," Lou regretfully answers. "But I thought he was yanking my chain, so I hung up on him. I'm so sorry! I can call him back though. I've got the number on my phone. In fact I'll call him as soon as we hang up!"

Jasmine laughs at situation. Partly out of joy that Benjamin wasn't blowing smoke up her ass about the movie deal, and partly due to Lou's flustered apology. "It's okay, Lou," she says. "Thank you for everything."

While there is some solace in knowing she will have plenty of money to pay the Triad for her mother and sister, there is also that nagging feeling that once they find out the situation, Qiang will demand more and continue this torturous process. Lou isn't wrong. Her new acquaintances from the DoS would be perfect to help if she felt she could trust them with her secret. Even if she got over her fear of deportation, now is not the time for such requests. Things in Egypt didn't turn out well, and who knows if that will mean Edward regains control of the team.

***

The events of the past few days have been strongly encouraging Eric to hit the bottle once again, but he's been fighting the urge. He has a meeting with President Thompson and Vice-President Murray in just a few minutes to go over the unsanctioned trip to Egypt. The President's tone was not a pleasant one when she called. Eric thinks he may be setting a record for gaining and losing a command position.

While the southern face of the Presidential Residence is still under construction after the attack, the Oval Office was left entirely intact. Most of the blast force was pushed outward over the lawn leaving the southern portions of the East and West Wings unscathed. The President has insisted on working back at the White House rather than the secured underground site. She will in no way give more power to the Eye of Ruin by living in fear.

Being very familiar with the layout of the White House, Eric knows he's being taken to the Oval Office Study, the working office of the President which adjoins to the more ceremonial Oval Office. While the Oval Office is constantly photographed, and therefore elegantly decorated, the study is a more conventional workspace. It's a small suite that can hold maybe four people comfortably, accessed by a corridor outside the Oval Office.

Upon arriving at the study, Eric finds the President seated in a cushioned leather chair behind a small wooden desk. She wears one of her usual pant suits with the blazer hung on a coat rack in the corner of the room. Standing to her left, and hovering over her shoulder, is Henry Murray, the Vice-President. He's a portly gentleman with a slight receding gray hairline. He's almost always seen wearing a blue or gray three-piece suit with the vest being stretched to its limits.

The study isn't typically used for meetings and isn't designed for it. The desk is flush with the wall right next to the entrance door. There are two other chairs in the room across from the desk on either side of a small end table decorated with a lamp and a phone. The President looks up from the desk when she sees Eric standing at the door. "Agent Davis," she starts off. "Please come in."

Eric steps into the office, and the President motions for him to sit in one of the chairs. He does so, and Henry sits in the chair next to him. The President sits back in her chair and spins it around to face the two men. She looks directly at Eric, and there is a long awkward silence before she asks her question. "What happened?"

Eric fidgets in his chair before answering. "With all due respect, Madam President," he says. "It's all in the report."

She reaches back, grabbing a bound stack of papers off the desk. "This, yes," she says while waving the document. "This is the official report. I want to hear from you. I want to know why you thought it was a good idea to zip off to Africa on an unsanctioned op without consulting me."

The line of crap that most people would try to sell in his position is that he was looking out for her by giving her plausible deniability, but Eric is not most people. "I was caught up in the prospect of catching the Eye at their home base and rescuing Miss Moore," he says earnestly. "We had actionable intel, and I moved on it without giving it a second thought."

"Actionable intel?" Henry speaks up. "The report said you saw a vision of the enemy compound?"

Henry is a former Indiana Governor who has very little knowledge about what sorcerers do. He knows of magic, and sees it in use every day, but he's never gone out of his way to learn anything about it. That being said, he believes, just as the President does, that having these abilities doesn't make someone less human, and, just like the rest of humanity, some people are good while some are bad. Janet likes him as her VP because he's very analytical and impartial when he provides her with council. If he's asking questions, it's to legitimately understand a situation better. "Yes," Eric answers Henry's question. "Andrea used her magic to see an image of the enemy HQ and tracked it to Egypt. We later discovered the image was a false vision implanted by someone else."

"With an illusion spell?" the President asks.

"No, illusions do affect the mind, but this was more invasive," Eric tries to explain. "It was magic within magic if that makes any sense. We think that two sorcerers, probably a Ghost and a Prophet, combined magic to create the false vision specifically for Andrea to see."

"I don't like what I'm hearing here." The President's tone becomes desperate. "Magical bombs, kidnappings, and now this? I'm not sure we're equipped to deal with this. Eric, I didn't bring you here today for disciplinary action. While I am disappointed in how you handled the situation, the CIA's involvement kept it quiet, so we're okay there. But this report has me very worried."

"It should," Eric replies. "These people are very organized, and I guarantee they're not done. I can tell you this though: that was a hit squad that was intended to take us out, and they failed. We've gotten their attention which means we pose a threat to their endgame. I also believe we have a lead on one of them."

"Another vision?" Henry asks with touch of skepticism.

"No, one of the team used to work with a Ghost that he thinks is capable of the illusion used on Andrea," Eric answers. "He's reaching out to former contacts to try and track him down. If you keep us on this, I promise we won't make any moves without your approval first."

This is just what the President needed to hear to reassure her of her decision to put Eric in charge. "You have twenty-four hours to turn up this lead." The President stands as she speaks. "And I want you sharing information with the FBI, CIA, Interpol, Homeland Security, even State and local PD if it'll make the difference."

Eric and Henry stand. "Yes Ma'am," Eric says.

Janet dismisses Eric, closing the door behind him after he leaves. She looks to Henry. "What do you think?" she asks.

"24 hours is generous." Henry sits back down. "Congress is going to pass that law; of that I have no doubt. The majority was already leaning that way, but the recent attacks have swung the vote, even with your team's intervention on Liberty Island."

The bill Henry is referring to would require any person with arcane ability to register with a national agency that would keep tabs on their activity. It would also provide funding to law enforcement agencies across the country for special divisions run by non-magic officers to police the sorcerer community. This force would have authority to detain and interrogate anyone even suspected of having arcane abilities. Congress has always wanted a police force specifically for the magic community, but they rejected the Guardian program since it would be run by and use sorcerers as the officers.

Janet has been against this bill, as she knows the kind of message it sends. To her, it hearkens back to the times of McCarthyism and the House Un-American Activities Committee when the government could make accusations of subversion and treason without evidence. "You know I'm going to veto it," she replies.

"And that's your prerogative, but I think that will only buy you a bit of time before they push it through without your blessing." Henry states the reality of the situation.

"Do you think taking down the Eye of Ruin will change anything in the eyes of Congress?"

"I doubt it," he answers.

The President lets out a long sigh. She knew the answer before she asked the question. She doesn't want her administration to go down in history as starting the biggest witch hunt since the Salem Witch Trials. That was a time before the existence of magic was widely known, but a series of prosecutions were held accusing people in colonial Massachusetts of practicing witchcraft. The hearings, based on rumors, religious overzealousness, and false accusations led to the execution of twenty innocent people. "What about public opinion?" she asks. "Surely quelling the threat by using sorcerers should buy a bit of goodwill. I mean, people already use items and technology infused with magic in their everyday lives; I just don't see how there can be so much hostility towards all magic-users from one small radical cell."

"Well, sure magic is accessible," Henry replies. "But typically to those with money. Aside from those fancy movies, and even those are a bit on the spendy side, magical services are reserved for the wealthy. The majority of people may see the benefits of magic, but it doesn't really affect them in a positive way."

"But terrorism affects everyone..." Janet finishes Henry's thought for him while falling back into her chair.

"Exactly," Henry affirms with a nod.

\*\*\*

At Benjamin's office in New York, he's been on the phone trying to reach some of his former criminal associates in London. It's the first time he's been back to his office since it was teleported away. As Anthony stated, he did bring it back, but nothing looks right. Everything is slightly askew, and the once beautiful fountain is bone dry with the flooring near it ruined by water damage.

Benjamin's not having a lot of luck reaching anyone helpful. The five hour time difference has not helped his cause, not to mention he burned a lot of bridges when he went straight. He finally manages to reach a fence named Nigel Richardson who used to sell stolen merchandise that Benjamin would acquire, though this was back then Benjamin went by a different name. Nigel was a weasel who always low-balled the thieves he worked with so he could keep a higher cut of the profits, but he and Benjamin parted on amicable terms. "Well, well, Benny Baker, now is it?" Nigel says in a thick Londoner accent. "Been a long time you ol' sod. Let me guess, you got somefin' you need moved on the black market. What's your pleasure?"

"I actually don't do that no more," Benjamin replies, slipping into the speech pattern from his criminal days. "I'm trying to track down an old mate."

"I see." the disappointment in Nigel's voice is heavy.

"But I can pay for the information," Benjamin adds.

"Now you're talkin'." Nigel's tone improves greatly. "Shall we talk terms?"

"What's it going to cost me?"

"Depends on who you're askin' about," Nigel answers.

"I'm looking for Damian Westonbrooke."

There is silence accompanied by just a bit of static. The pause is long enough that Benjamin thinks he was hung up on. "Hello?" he asks.

"Ten thousand pounds," Nigel finally answers.

"Done. Where do I send it?"

Nigel wasn't expecting Benjamin to agree to the amount so easily. While U-Movie is international, the name Benjamin Baker at its head is not. Nigel wasn't aware of Benjamin's wealth, but he must be doing well to part with so much so easily. Greed was always one of the reasons Nigel didn't keep many clients for repeat business, and it was about to show itself again. "Did I say ten?" Nigel back-pedals. "I meant twenty thousand."

"Seven thousand," Benjamin counters.

"But you just agreed to ten!" Nigel says in a huff.

"That was before you raised the price." Benjamin knows he's in complete control of the conversation now. "If you'd like to keep haggling, my offer will drop to five."

"Seven's good," Nigel quickly says to lock in the current price. "I'll text you the account number."

While they remain on the phone, Nigel sends his account information to Benjamin, who in turn sends an electronic payment in the amount of seven thousand pounds. "And sent," Benjamin says to affirm the payment is on the way. "Now what can you tell me about the current whereabouts of Damian?"

"Not much I'm afraid," Nigel responds. "He was buildin' a right proper criminal kingdom until Scotland Yard burned it to da ground. Word is he packed up and went across the pond to start fresh. Don't know if he too's livin' under a fancy new name like you, but I doubt it. He was always too proud to use an alias."

"Anything else?" Benjamin asks already knowing the answer.

"I may 'ave more, but we're going to need to negotiate a new price," Nigel responds, thinking he now has control of the conversation.

His comment is met with utter silence. "Hello?" he asks.

There is no answer, as Benjamin has hung up on him. It's not much to go on, but knowing that Damian is in the United States means he is mostly likely the Ghost working with the Eye of Ruin. Even when they were young, upstart criminal wannabes, Damian was always more skilled at using illusion magic. His temperament also leads Benjamin to believe he would be the perfect recruit for an anti-human terrorist organization. With his new information, Benjamin grabs his DoS escort and heads back to Virginia.

*\*\**

Bright and early the next morning, the whole team is assembled in the situation room of the Guardian wing at the Department of Sorcery. Anthony has joined them. He was released from the hospital last night, and, even though he still can't access his arcane powers, he brings his military experience to the table.

Eric and Benjamin stand at the head of the touchscreen table which displays a mugshot of Damian, along with his Interpol file. Andrea, Emmanuel, and Jasmine are huddled at the foot of the table with their attention fixed on the other two. Anthony leans against a wall, looking on with his arms crossed. "This is Damian Westonbrooke," Eric states. "He's currently our only potential lead. He's a Ghost with a lengthy criminal record."

"He and I used to be acquainted," Benjamin adds. "And I have reason to believe he's here in the country. He has the skill needed to pull off the kind of illusion we saw in Egypt."

"Question," Andrea interjects. "How do we find a criminal who can make himself look like anyone?"

It's a valid question. A Ghost that doesn't want to be found won't be. A Prophet might be able to track one down if they had something tangible to work with, but even knowing where to find one is a long way off from catching one. They're on a time crunch, but Eric doesn't have the first idea what to do. "I'm open to any ideas," he says.

Emmanuel has been using magic for longer than he can remember. He's had many powerful mentors who have exposed him to many different types of magic. This allows him to think about the arcane in a way that most do not. "I might be able to help wit' dat," he speaks up.

No one really knows when or where magic began, nor do they know how or why it exists. Science hasn't been able to explain it or fully replicate it, and even the most dedicated researchers of ancient magic have yet to scratch the surface. The one thing that everyone believes is that arcane energy exists throughout the universe. It is this energy that a sorcerer is able to draw in and create the effect of a spell. What very few realize is that there is a different kind of arcane energy within every sorcerer. When this energy is tapped, it increases the effect of the spell tenfold. Emmanuel just happens to be one of the few sorcerers in the world who knows this. "I can help you focus your power." He addresses Benjamin before looking to everyone else. "Dis technique can help you all if you are willin' to learn."

"It's not gonna hurt is it?" Benjamin asks.

"If you think it's going to help us track down this lead, we'll try it," Eric says while glaring at Benjamin.

"I need everyone to close their eyes," Emmanuel instructs.

"I am not holding anyone's hand," Andrea protests before doing as asked.

"Now t'ink about when you are casting a spell, but do not focus on de spell itself. Reach out wit' your mind and feel de magic energy all around you. It exists everywhere and in everyt'ing. Dat is what creates all magic. We are merely instruments to channel it."

Everyone else in the room has had little to no formal training with an arcane mentor. Those that have, received a crash course from a sorcerer who themselves was lacking any knowledge outside of the few spells they could cast. The idea that magical energy is used to cast spells is nothing new, but the idea of that energy being the same before it is harnessed by a sorcerer is quite a revelation to this group. "Do you feel it?" Emmanuel asks the group.

With the exception of Anthony, everyone says yes in one form or another. He's in a rather low place at the moment. He feels as though he no longer belongs on the team without his ability to apportate. It would be easy to pass blame for his current condition, but the only person he's angry with is himself. If he hadn't blindly flown at that sorcerer in Egypt, he wouldn't have been blindsided by her spell. Everyone is telling him his military experience makes him invaluable, but he thinks they're just too polite to tell him they don't need him anymore.

Believing everyone is focused properly, Emmanuel continues. "Now switch dat focus from outside to wit'in, but keep your mind open to da magical energies. Each sorcerer has their own unique energy inside, but dey do not use it. Dis will feel different dan what you felt before. If you can draw from both sources of power when you cast, you will see a vast difference in the produced spell. Shields will be stronger. Fires will burn hotter. Visions will be more precise."

"Is there any kind of drawback to doing that?" Benjamin interrupts. "Otherwise, why wouldn't you cast like that all the time?"

"Dere is," Emmanuel replies. "Using da power too much will age your body much faster dan normal. Look at me. I am only twenty-six years old."

Everyone's eyes fly open, and their mouths hang open in shock. "Are you having a laugh?" Benjamin is clearly taken aback. "Why would anyone use magic that would make them look like you? I mean, I don't mean you; I mean old, like you."

Emmanuel bursts into laughter. "You should see da look on your faces right now!" Emmanuel continues to chuckle. "I was joking."

The mood in the room lightens, and everyone enjoys a brief laugh. Benjamin lets out a sigh of relief. "You got me good, old man," he says. "So, is there no drawback then?"

"Using one's own energy does tire da body," Emmanuel answers. "You will need rest after casting a spell in dis way; however, if you use too much internal energy all at once, it can kill you."

Benjamin starts laughing at what he assumes is another ribbing by Emmanuel. No one else appears to join in the fun. "Why are you laughin'?" Emmanuel chides. "I am bein' serious. You could die."

"Oh…" Benjamin stops laughing.

"Ready?" Emmanuel asks, once again in a jovial tone.

"You want me to try it right now" Benjamin asks in disbelief.

"No," Emmanuel says. "I meant to practice. You would die for sure otherwise. Is dere a place we can all go?"

"There's a spell testing room downstairs," Andrea answers. "It's meant for what you are proposing."

***

The team has relocated to a testing facility built in one of the sublevels of the Department of Sorcery. The room is circular in design and reinforced with the strongest materials available to help contain any magic used within. The dome-shaped ceiling is high enough that the sources of light cannot be seen, only the illumination they provide. There is an observation room along a small section of wall, separated by thick blast resistant security glass, though there are currently no spectators within.

For the past few hours, everyone has been aggressively training, though not all are using Emmanuel's technique. Anthony and Jasmine spar with each other using various unarmed combat styles. Eric, Andrea, and Benjamin take turns attempting to draw from their own energy when casting, giving each other an opportunity to recover after. Emmanuel monitors and talks them through each attempt to ensure no one goes too big too soon. He knows it's risky teaching them this kind of power, but it's clear to him that the sorcerer constructing entire illusory buildings must be privy to the same knowledge.

Over time, a sorcerer can build up endurance for siphoning one's own vitality when crafting a spell. The normal practice of such magic leaves a sorcerer temporarily enfeebled, often short of breath and unable to stand afterwards. Emmanuel has conditioned himself to do it with very little exhaustion after, though, at his age, he still doesn't prefer to exert himself like that often.

Eric has just finished an attempt at strengthening a personal barrier. He sits against the wall a short distance from Emmanuel. His breathing is labored, and it looks as though he couldn't stand up even if he tried. Benjamin stands up, looking a bit worse for wear, but managing. Emmanuel approaches him before he can begin another attempt. "Dat is enough practice," he says motioning for Andrea to stand. "Now we will do da real t'ing."

Anthony and Jasmine stop sparring and suddenly take interest in what the others are doing. Andrea stands up with a bit of confusion on her face. She steps forward before Emmanuel guides her next to Benjamin. Her expression turns from confusion to concern. "Don't worry," Emmanuel assures her. "No hand holding, I promise. You are going to attempt to combine your magic again, but dis time to track down Damian."

"Then what was all this 'focus on your inner energy' nonsense?" Benjamin asks.

"It was not nonsense," Emmanuel says with an uncharacteristically stern tone. "Now shut your eyes."

Benjamin shrugs and closes his eyes. "Andrea, try to cast da spell you used before to track da terrorist," Emmanuel instructs.

"But dis time, you need to split your focus between da incantation and Benjamin's arcane power. Try to draw on it. Benjamin, while she does dat, you must picture Damian in your mind while channeling your energy to Andrea."

Both sorcerers go through the motions, but after a few minutes of trying they still feel no connection. Benjamin finally gives up and opens his eyes. "It's not working," he says with a shrug.

"You give up too easily," Emmanuel responds.

Andrea grabs Benjamin by the shoulders and pulls him to face her. "We've done this before," she says. "We can do it again."

"Alright, let's try," Benjamin says in response.

The two attempt to perform the combined spell once again, and, just as before, it seems as though it's not going to work. It's at this point that Andrea's mind wanders from casting the spell to thoughts of what might happen to Catherine if they fail. She remembers the constant fear she felt being passed around the legal system as child with no one to care about her or where she'd end up next. She can't even begin to imagine what Catherine must be feeling as a captive, but Andrea refuses to let her feel as abandoned as she once did.

Benjamin feels the arcane essence pervading within him suddenly sucked out nearly causing him to collapse. At that same instant, Andrea feels a sensation similar to a jolt of electricity pass through her, and she gets a picture in her mind. It's a vision of a place she's very familiar with: Carcer Prison. She also gets a clear image of Damian standing out front with a group of his followers. The vision fades, and she feels as drained as Benjamin.

Anthony and Jasmine rush over to make sure Benjamin and Andrea are okay. "Did it work?" Jasmine asks.

"Carcer," Andrea says weakly. "He's going to Carcer."

## Chapter 16: The Fall Of Carcer

Normally, Damian would be more calculated when staging an attack on a Federal facility, but he's been feeling particular emboldened as of late, even with the Eye's diminished numbers. In his mind, Carcer Prison is the biggest symbol of hate against the magic community, with the Department of Sorcery running a close second. He wanted the Eye's first attack to be on Carcer, but Allen demanded they start out of the country. Now, Damian feels the balance of power has shifted, and he will decide where his people strike. What better way to recruit new sorcerers to your cause than by liberating a bunch being held by the government?

While the interior of Carcer is designed to hinder magical energy, the exterior of the prison is built with a more practical application: defense. It may not look it, but the building and surrounding perimeter wall has some of the most state-of-the-art security measures on the market. The wall itself is built from the same materials as the exterior to the prison, but without the reflective effect. This material is a magical metal created by Builders that science has been unable to replicate. While it's not immune to the effects of evocation magic, it is resistant to them. It would take a very powerful sorcerer, using some strong spells, to penetrate it.

The wall is patrolled by armed guards, each equipped with an assault rifle and an anti-magic collar for apprehending any potential escapees. The guards are backed up by hidden gatling-style sentry guns that rise up from the top of the wall. The rotating barrels of these large caliber weapons can fire up to 6,000 rounds a minute and are computer controlled by an operator inside the prison. If all of this isn't enough, Carcer also staffs a handful of sorcerers as guards to use magic against magic if it comes to it.

It's late afternoon, and one of the guards is battling the glare of the sun as he patrols the western wall of the compound. While squinting against the bright rays, he sees a black spot on the horizon. He blinks hard before shielding his eyes with his hands as he looks again. The spot appears to be getting bigger. He quickly retrieves a pair of binoculars and looks once again. What he sees through the magnifying lenses causes a chill to run down his spine.

A massive scaly black beast, with an impressive wingspan, flies briskly towards the prison. The guard almost drops the binoculars as he does a double take. He grabs his radio. "Incoming!" he shouts in a fluster.

The guard starts pointing out the incoming flying beast as guards on other walls take notice. The prison's exterior cameras also angle towards the commotion while the sentry guns ascend from their nests. A blaring siren echoes throughout the perimeter as the entire prison goes into lockdown and the main entrance gate seals shut. Additional armed guards emerge from within the main prison tower, making their way up to the ramparts where their fellow forces are braced behind the parapets, awaiting the impending attack.

The titan of a black dragon barrels toward the prison with increasing speed. The sentry guns are the first to open fire once the creature is within their optimal range. The explosion of gunfire drowns out all other sound in the area including the alarms. Shortly after the opening volley, the guards also train on the dragon and open fire. Countless rounds appear to strike the beast having no effect, though the guards continue to try.

While everyone's attention is focused on the sky, they don't see the real threat approaching on the ground below. Just outside the wall, under the cover of an invisibility spell, Damian, Ava, and nearly thirty Eye of Ruin followers wait to launch their attack. The Carcer security continues to dump ammunition into the illusionary beast with no results. A wave of panic starts to take hold of them, but they stand their ground.

Damian gives Ava the signal to begin the assault. She approaches the wall, touching it with her hands. Builders can analyze the material makeup of an object by touch and recreate it with their magic. Powerful Builders can also remove materials by magically dissolving them. After a moment of studying the unearthly material in the wall, Ava begins her incantation, "Figura materia."

A small vertical seam appears on the wall between Ava's hands. It begins to stretch, reaching almost to the top and bottom of the wall, followed by the sound of cracking and metallic crunching. A tremor resonates throughout the defensive barricade as it begins to disintegrate along the seam. The narrow crack opens up to a massive void, providing enough of an opening for Damian's forces to rush into the exterior of the compound.

A handful of prison guards realize something is amiss and turn their attention away from the flying beast. They look down from the wall to see the unnatural opening below. At first they see only the tear, but it isn't long before Damian's forces launch their attack, removing their shroud of invisibility. While Carcer's security is trained to deal with sorcerers, they were not prepared for a surprise attack of this scale. A group of guards are taken out immediately in a combination of evocation magic and gunfire.

The sentries and wall guards shift focus from the black dragon to the prison yard. War has broken out between the Eye of Ruin and the security forces on the ground with a very clear winner. A few Builders create barriers to soak up bullets while the Evos counter with elemental magic. Bursts of fire, shards of ice, and arcs of lightning lash out from behind concrete barricades, killing guards by the score.

During the chaos, Damian and Ava, who are still invisible, have made their way to the reflective wall of the prison structure. Ava looks to Damian. "Bring it down," he says to her. "I'll cover you."

Ava presses her hands against the warm reflective metal, once again speaking her incantation. As before, a small fissure appears in the wall structure and starts to elongate. The crack spreads to about eight feet in length before suddenly coming to a stop. Ava feels resistance as though her magic is being battled, and she sees her work begin to undo itself. For a moment she's confused. She wonders if the building's security could be doing this somehow. Is there some sort of new technology that can actually reverse the effects of magic? She shakes off her self-doubt and refocuses her efforts on opening the wall.

What Ava cannot see is that on the other side of the wall, Warden McRory stands using a counter-spell to keep the wall closed. It's a dangerous gamble on his part, as he had to disable the anti-magic barriers on the ground floor of the facility so he could wield his magic against her, but he saw no choice after seeing what she did to the outer wall on the security feed. Trace is a powerful sorcerer in his own right, but he doesn't get to practice his craft nearly as much as he'd like. He struggles when Ava starts to push back from the outside.

The battle in the yard intensifies, and things are looking grim for the prison forces until four black SUVs race up to the front gate of the prison and additional sirens heard approaching in the distance. As they slide to a stop, Eric, Jasmine, Anthony, Andrea, Benjamin, Emmanuel, and two teams of DoS soldiers pour out of the armored vehicles. Everyone's wearing some form of ballistic armor, with the team in vests and the soldiers in full body armor.

As per usual, Jasmine and Emmanuel carry no weapons; however, everyone else is outfitted for a full-scale assault. Even Benjamin has opted to carry an assault rifle instead of a pistol.

Eric orders everyone to move on the opening in the perimeter wall. The group advances, though they cannot help but take notice of the gargantuan obsidian creature in the sky. "Do we need to worry about that thing?" Eric asks Benjamin as they run.

"No, it's only an illusion!" Benjamin replies.

As if on cue, the dragon rears back and releases a stream of scorching fire from its maw, engulfing three guards atop the wall. Their screams are heard for only a moment before the smoke clears revealing their grizzly fate. Benjamin did not think it was possible for an illusion to kill someone in that way, and it shows in his stunned expression. "I thought you said it wasn't real!" Eric shouts.

"I don't know what just happened!" Benjamin says. "There's definitely illusion magic coming off that thing!"

"Shit!" Eric says as he prepares to create a large barrier. "Avoid the dragon! I'll try to shield us!"

The reinforcements continue towards the wall opening while Eric creates a large umbrella-shaped barrier above them. Their appearance reinvigorates the prison's waning security team, who now fight harder than ever. While the fray is still in the favor of Damian's forces, the guards have managed to subdue a couple of his sorcerers.

Damian grows impatient with how long it's taking Ava to break through the wall. "Hurry up!" he growls.

Ava has managed to open a crack in the prison wall wide enough to see the man inside causing her so much trouble. "It seems someone's trying to stop me!" she angrily replies.

Ava uses the same attack on Trace that she did on Devon, but he senses it and manages to avoid a killing blow. Her spike pierces his leg which breaks his concentration allowing Ava to open the wall further. While this is happening, Damian commands the dragon to unleash few more fiery volleys on the wall, leaving most of its defenses destroyed or in ashes.

Ava gets the prison structure open enough to send someone inside. "It's open!" she calls to Damian.

"The time has come my children!" A guttural voice booms from the dragon's mouth. "Your sacrifice will liberate our oppressed brothers and sisters! Show them the power of dragon fire!"

At this command, three of the Evos break from the rest, running for the opening in the prison wall. Eric and Anthony see them and move to intercept while the rest join the battle. One of the Evos notices the oncoming opposition and preemptively shoots out a ball of explosive flame. Eric takes the brunt of the blast which throws him back hard into a concrete blockade. His personal barrier activated, preventing what would've otherwise been a lethal attack, but the force of it renders him temporarily incapacitated. Anthony fires back in response with his carbine, killing the sorcerer who launched the spell. The other two terrorists make it inside the prison.

Ava continues to remove more of the prison's base wall, but, in doing so, she has to solely focus on that. Damian has become distracted by the sense of a familiar arcane presence; he's removed his invisibility while surveying his surroundings. This gives Anthony enough time to follow the suicide sorcerers into the prison.

Just inside the opening, he finds the Warden, who has managed to get himself upright. He's created a temporary cast around his wound and conjured up a wooden cane that can double as a weapon. "McRory, are you okay?" Anthony asks.

"I'll be fine," he says through a wince. "We need to get after those assholes! Follow me!"

"Maybe I should take point," Anthony replies, displaying his firearm.

"Good call." Trace motions for Anthony to go first.

Back outside, Emmanuel makes his way around, healing injured guards while Jasmine and Andrea help level the playing field against the Eye of Ruin. Eric makes his way to his feet again and rejoins the fight, shielding the DoS soldiers and prison guards from projectiles.

Amidst the carnage, two individuals seemed fixed in a strange trance, slowly looking around the chaos until they lock eyes. Benjamin and Damian haven't seen each other since they worked together in London, and even then, they didn't pay each other much mind. But meeting again after all this time, on opposite sides of a battlefield, makes things interesting. "Kaelan Burrows," Damian says in acknowledgement.

"I don't go by that name no more," Benjamin replies, slipping back into his old idiolect. "You still go by Damian?"

The two men circle each other as they speak. "To some," Damian says with a wicked grin. "But you can call me the Dragon King."

"That's what I always liked about you, Damian," Benjamin says with a hint of sarcasm. "Your humbleness. Nice touch with the dragon by the way. You've gotten better since our last job."

"You have no idea what I've become," Damian replies.

"Why don't you enlighten me?" Benjamin challenges.

Damian lets out a laugh. "If you want enlightenment, just open your eyes! You're fighting for a system that oppresses our kind. They paint me as a terrorist, but they are the ones who persecute and incarcerate without cause! I am a liberator. We've worked together before, Kaelan; stand with me now and help free our brothers and sisters."

"It's Benjamin…and I don't stand with murderers that kill innocent people to push their own agendas."

"Pity," Damian says before making an arcane gesture. "Fulgor!"

Lightning arcs from Damian's hands striking where Benjamin stands. Much like the guards' bullets against the dragon, it appears to have no effect. The bolt passes through him which surprises Damian. Benjamin smiles as his image fades away, revealing he was just an illusion. "Seems I'm not the only one who has gotten better," Damian says while trying to sense where Benjamin might actually be. "I couldn't even sense the illusion. It's a nice party trick, but let me give you a taste of true power. Deus fulgor!"

The battle briefly pauses as everyone outside gets that eerie feeling that danger is looming: their skin tingling or the hair raising on the back of their necks. The air all around becomes charged with static, and small surges of electricity can be seen jumping off of metallic surfaces. A dark cloud forms directly over the prison tower and with it, the rumbling of thunder. The gray mantle crackles with electricity, foreshadowing what's to come.

Eric looks over to see the source of this ominous presence to find Damian floating about six feet off the ground. His hands are held towards the sky, and his eyes are as white as the lightning he's calling. Eric knows he can't let this spell be finished. He takes aim with his rifle, ensuring it will be a headshot, and squeezes the trigger. To his surprise, the bullet reflects off an invisible barrier surrounding Damian. Eric doesn't understand what's happening. He can't detect any Sentinel magic in the area other than his own. He unloads his entire clip at Damian, just to be sure, but the bullets are once again repelled. Since that plan has failed, Eric quickly decides it's time to protect who he can against what's about to happen. He tries to apply Emmanuel's lessons as he creates a barrier large enough to cover all his allies.

\*\*\*

Anthony and Trace have caught up to the two Evos inside the prison, but with one of them injured and the other without magic, they are at quite a disadvantage. Sensing that they are being followed, the two Evos create a wall of flames between them and their pursuers. The impediment only lasts a few minutes as the prison's fire sprinkler system activates, extinguishing the flames, but it gave the Evos the time they needed to escape. Fortunately, Trace knows his facility and where someone is most likely to strike at. "I think they're going for the backup generators," he says to Anthony. "If they're trying to free prisoners, they'll need to disable those and cut the main power."

"What happens when all the power goes out?" Anthony inquires as they move.

"A bunch of pissed off sorcerers will be able to use magic again," Trace answers.

"Aren't there other systems in place to avoid that?" Anthony asks.

"As soon as I saw that beast on the monitors, I sent guards to each cell to outfit the prisoners with the collars, but it will take time to get them all."

Trace leads the way towards the elevators that lead to the basement level of the prison. Before the doors can open, a voice comes in over the Warden's radio. "Sir, we're getting reports of weird electrical activity all throughout the building!" The voice is accompanied by a lot of static.

Trace grabs his radio, shouting into it. "Get those prisoners collared now!" He pulls the radio away from his face before looking back to Anthony. "We may want to take the stairs."

\*\*\*

The roar of thunder echoes from the gray mass swirling above the prison tower as electricity builds up within it. No one is really sure what's going to happen. This kind of phenomenon has never been seen in the natural world, and, despite his years, not even Emmanuel has seen an evocation spell this powerful before.

Eric calls for everyone to gather close to him in an effort to shield them from what's to come. He's not even being specific at this point; he doesn't want to see anyone struck by this thing. Everyone stops fighting momentarily in an effort to find sanctuary under Eric's umbrella-shaped barrier. Unfortunately, the cloud explodes before everyone can make it to shelter, releasing a cyclone of lightning that engulfs the entire prison spire and sends out a shockwave that can be felt miles away. Damian and Ava appear unaffected by the electricity, but anyone else not inside the prison or under Eric's barrier is immediately flash-fried before being obliterated by the concussive force.

As planned, all the power at the prison goes out, leaving it extremely vulnerable to magic until the emergency generators kick on. Almost as if on cue, a section of the prison's mirror-like wall, fifty feet up, starts to glow red as though it's being super-heated. Within moments, the glowing metal melts away, revealing Jared

Cross in his gray prison jumpsuit behind it. He leaps from the structure, slowing his dissent in a similar fashion to Jasmine back on Liberty Island.

Upon seeing where Jared was held in the prison, Ava turns her attention from the base walls to the area where his cell was. She's working at a much faster pace now, exposing multiple cells in a matter of moments. The prisoners within the cells peek outside, unsure of what's happening, but they quickly realize it's a prison break and begin looking for a way down. One of the prisoners is a Builder, magically creating metal stairs to the ground. Another prisoner is a Transporter who teleports herself and a few other prisoners out of the cylindrical tower.

Gia's a short-haired bank robber in her mid-twenties who's been locked in Carcer since it opened. She would love to see it burned to the ground and goes directly to the man she believes is in charge. "What's the plan here?" she boldly asks Damian.

"Bring it down," Damian answers before shifting his focus back to Eric and his team, who are back on the offensive.

***

Flames dance throughout the basement of the prison as the Evos attempt to keep Trace and Anthony at bay, so they can complete their task. Trace has created some walls to hold back the flames while he and Anthony plan their attack. They know the electricity's out already since the fire is the only source of light in the basement currently. For some reason, the backup generators have not automatically turned on as they are set to do when there is a loss of power. Trace tries to keep calm, but he's panicking at the thought of the prisoners figuring this out. "We need to get those generators on right now!" he says to Anthony.

"If we don't stop those Evos, that will be the least of our problems," Anthony replies. "I've seen guys like these before. They're going to blow themselves up, taking us, and possibly this building, down with them! Where are those reinforcements you called?"

"Probably stuck dealing with the prisoners now," Trace answers. "I think this is up to us."

"If you can keep us shielded, I'll take them out," Anthony checks his weapon as he speaks.

Trace nods before manipulating the fortifications he's created. The material of both the walls becomes malleable where they connect with the ground, sliding along the surface with ease. As Trace moves forward, the walls keep pace about a foot ahead providing portable cover.

They enter the generator room to find yet another obstacle between them and the two Evos. A solid sheet of ice, at least a few feet thick, blocks their way forward. Anthony gives a sigh of frustration at the sight of it. The Evos thought they were being clever, but failed to realize that ice is a solid that's easy for a Builder to exploit. Trace holds his hands in front of the ice before making a motion as though he were opening a curtain. "Emoveo forma." Upon uttering the incantation, the ice parts in the middle, creating a doorway.

The opening reveals both Evos deep in an incantation. Anthony recognizes this as the same thing the sorcerers were doing at the Statue of Liberty. Knowing they must be close to drawing in the energy required for detonation, he rushes into the room, shooting one of the sorcerers. While the shot hits its mark, killing the sorcerer, it also releases some of the energy that was already harnessed, knocking Anthony back into what's left of the ice wall. He drops his rifle from the force of the blow. While he scrambles to retrieve it, the other Evo realizes the situation is dire and decides to blow his top early. "Obcisor displodo!"

The Evo's skin glows like the sun, causing darkness to retreat from the room entirely. The spell creates a transmutation in the Evo's cells, changing them into a highly volatile state and creating a living bomb. Once this single use spell has been started, there is no turning back. Trace reacts by quickly duplicating the material of the prison's metallic exterior wall and thrusting it at the Evo, crushing him between it and the wall of the underground structure. This doesn't prevent the explosion, but it dampens it enough that it doesn't destroy the room or bring down the building on their heads. The shockwave of the muffled detonation still rocks the foundation, creating a momentary earthquake for anyone inside or nearby the prison.

Trace flicks on a flashlight from his belt as he finds himself now back in darkness. He helps Anthony to his feet after he dove behind the ice to avoid the Evo's explosion. The two men look at each other as if to say "I won't say we peed ourselves if you won't," before turning some power on. The generators hum with life which causes the overhead fluorescent lights that aren't broken to flicker on. Both men take a moment to gather themselves before they make for the elevator.

\*\*\*

The sirens heard earlier finally deliver on their implied promise with the arrival of the police at the outer wall of the prison. Six squad cars and a SWAT van unload their armed officers who storm the yard of the prison. Inside the perimeter, a group of escaped prisoners have joined Damian's forces in taking on Eric's team and what remains of the DoS soldiers. The police are taken aback as more magic is being thrown around the yard than they had ever expected to see in one lifetime. Fortunately for them, the dragon no longer hovers in the skies, having vanished when Damian needed the energy for the lightning storm.

Even though the sentry guns have been destroyed or disabled, a few of them sputter and whir in place as they attempt to operate, signifying the power is back up. Damian knows things will only get worse from here. He grabs the Transporter that was freed. "Can you get us out of here?" he asks.

"Where?" she replies.

"Anywhere, but here," he states.

Gia nods before creating a large portal behind them. The scene on the other side of the gateway is a seaside dock somewhere. It's nighttime, and not a soul can be seen anywhere in view.

Damian approves of the location. "Get to the portal!" He shouts over the combat. "Or get left behind!"

The Eye of Ruin sorcerers, along with the escaped inmates, flee towards the picturesque rift. Jasmine is quick to take down anyone turning their back on her to run. Ava creates concrete barricades to hinder Eric's team and the police while they escape. Most of the fleeing sorcerers make through the portal with only a few getting shot down by law enforcement.

Damian is the last one through the rift. He backs in, waving at Eric while flashing his signature grin. The gate closes before an enraged Eric can get to it. He lets out a furious roar and kicks at the ground to vent. He looks back to see devastation that was wrought by the attack. While the prison still stands, it's riddled with massive holes and is undoubtedly no longer structurally sound.

Anthony and Trace make it back to the surface about the time that the military and additional Department of Sorcery reinforcements arrive. All of the remaining Carcer prisoners are rounded up and outfitted with collars, if they weren't already wearing them. They are escorted off-site to a temporary holding facility located at the Department of Sorcery.

It's hard for Eric to see this as anything short of another failure. Even preventing most of the prisoners from escaping, the loss of life and the fact that Damian's people got away again makes it feel like they're fighting a losing battle. This is a rare moment for Eric, though. Instead of wallowing in self-doubt, he focuses on how much worse the situation would've been had they not intervened at all. He's angry, yes, but he's turning that anger into resolve. They're going to catch this maniac and stop him from hurting anyone else.

## Chapter 17: Double the Fun

The day after the prison break, there is a maelstrom of press, supporters, and protesters outside the Department of Sorcery hoping to catch members of the President's taskforce on their way in. The press conference the night before praised the DoS's proactive efforts to track down the Eye of Ruin which led them to interrupt another of the terrorists' plans. The White House Press Secretary also noted that the same team involved in thwarting the Liberty Island attack was utilized here. This news inspired sympathizers and infuriated detractors, leading to the mob scene today.

The team was smuggled into the building via an underground tunnel along with Warden McRory, who's in a wheelchair after his leg injury. Magical healing is much faster than traditional medicine, but that isn't without downtime. Newly mended flesh, no matter how quickly it's achieved, needs to relearn how to function properly. Trace feels fine and wants to be on his feet; after all, his injury was only slightly worse that Anthony's leg wound from the attack on the training facility, but he's under doctor's orders to remain in the chair for at least the next 24 hours.

Eric, Emmanuel, Anthony, Jasmine, Benjamin, Andrea, and Trace convene in the main work room of the Guardian wing. They're discussing possible means of recapturing the escaped convicts, Trace leading the conversation. Andrea and Eric are a bit tuned out. Andrea's biased against Carcer to begin, and she's also not a big fan of its warden. He wasn't cruel or malicious, but in her mind he's guilty by association of what the prison stands for.

Eric hasn't heard much of the conversation because he's too concentrated on yesterday's attack. How was Damian able to deflect his bullets with barrier magic? He wasn't able to sense any other Sentinels at the prison. He also can't get past the fact that if Damian is an illusionist, how was he throwing around evocation magic? "Even though we have trackers implanted in each convict, we're having a bitch of a time pinpointing them," Trace reports. "We believe the Transporter is continuously teleporting them to throw off the tracking satellites. Inmates aren't aware of these trackers, so I'm not sure how they would know to avoid detection."

"Maybe they're just paranoid, so they keep moving," Anthony offers up.

"Or maybe someone saw something they shouldn't," Andrea says.

"That's unlikely," Trace replies. "Prisoners are put under before the procedure and the implant is injected subcutaneously, leaving no mark or scar. I'll bet you didn't know you have one."

"What?!" Andrea jumps up in outrage.

"With your record, did you really think the DoS would let you out without a way to monitor you?" Trace doesn't mean to be a jerk, but it comes across that way.

Andrea's incensed to the point of lunging at Trace, but Jasmine holds her back. "He's not worth it." She attempts to calm Andrea down.

"Who else knows about the trackers?" Benjamin asks. "Is it possible that Damian could have someone on the inside?"

"I mean, I guess it's possible, but where would you start looking?" Trace asks.

"How was Damian able to call the lightning?" Eric interjects with his own thoughts.

The entire room pauses in confusion, looking to Eric for some elaboration. He stands and begins pacing briefly before looking directly at Benjamin. "You said he's a Ghost, but we know the lightning wasn't an illusion," Eric says trying to work out the mystery as he talks. "It looked as though the evocation was coming from him. How is that possible?"

It's not a thought anyone had really given until now…well, one person had, but he also knew the answer the moment he was near Damian. "He can use bot' illusion an' evocation," Emmanuel finally answers.

First, he brings the knowledge to enhance magic using unheard of techniques, and now he speaks of one person being able to use two kinds of magic; the group is really starting to wonder about the life Emmanuel has lived to this point. "That's impossible." Benjamin says what everyone else is thinking.

"But you 'ave seen it," Emmanuel says, motioning away as if Carcer were right outside the window. "Evocation an' illusion are firmly under his control."

"He never used any evocation back when I knew him," Benjamin continues to argue his point.

"Bot' magical types do not always manifest at de same time," Emmanuel explains. "De *magister dualis* are very rare an' should not be underestimated."

Magister dualis, much like most arcane incantations, is Latin. It means dual master, and it's a term known to very few. There have always been legends circling the arcane world about spellcasters who can use more than one kind magic; however, nobody in the modern world can say they've ever seen them. The prospect makes Damian even more dangerous if it's true.

"Someday, I want to know how you know so much about these things," Jasmine says.

"A teacher of mine encountered one long before my time," Emmanuel says, trying to brush it off as though it's nothing. "I've just 'eard stories. Dat's all."

"What about his ability to deflect bullets with no effort?" Eric questions. "There wasn't any protection magic in that yard, so how did he manage that?"

"There was something odd about that," Andrea says. "I could sense magic, but it was very faint."

"I don't know what dat was, but I don't t'ink it was magic." Emmanuel rubs the back of his neck as he ponders what it might actually be.

"I need to report this to the President," Eric says. "Warden McRory, can you keep working on tracking the escapees? Andrea, see if you can use your abilities to help."

"What about the rest of us?" Jasmine asks.

Eric looks back before walking out the door. "Rest up because things are going to get far worse before they get better."

***

Over the past couple days, Catherine has done nothing but pour over every book in Damian's personal collection, searching for necromancy spells. When she hasn't been doing that, she's been practicing the spells she does know and getting guidance from Elena. The task of going through Damian's books has been a daunting one. Since there are no other Reapers, there is no one to tell her where to look. Damian's recommendation was entirely based on a rumor he once heard that Edgar Allan Poe was a Reaper. While it turned out to be true in that instance, she hasn't had a lot of luck since.

Catherine finally tracks down the spell she is looking for in a copy of *Dracula* by Bram Stoker. Upon finding the incantation, she laughs out of frustration because she intentionally avoided the book, thinking it would be too on the nose. Of course, having the spell and using it are two different things. The idea of animating a dead body and working it like some kind of morbid marionette gives her the creeps. If it weren't for the thought of helping her parents, she would've given up already.

Damian showed up at the compound yesterday with a bunch of faces Catherine hadn't seen before. She wasn't made aware of the attack on Carcer prison, and, in her naivety, she was easily convinced they were just new followers of the Eye. Damian and Elena are the only two people Catherine really trusts in this bizarre world she's been forced into, so when they're not around, she keeps to herself.

Today, she's gone looking for Damian to report her findings, but finds Elena in his office instead. As Catherine enters the room, Elena covers up some blueprints she was working on. "Hello, Catherine. What can I help you with?" she asks.

"I um...I think I found the thing that will help get my parents out," Catherine says shyly. "Is Damian around?"

"He is away taking care of some important business, but he will be back in a while," Elena smiles warmly as she stands up from Damian's desk. "Did you want to show me what you found?"

Catherine gets a little squeamish. "I'm not really sure how." She fidgets with her hands as she speaks. "I would need a...a dead body...and I...I don't know where to find one...and I really don't want to go looking for one."

Elena comes around to the front of the desk where Catherine stands. She softly laughs at Catherine's awkwardness and places a hand on her shoulder. "It is okay." She begins walking with Catherine out of Damian's office. "It is natural to fear what you can do, but you must try if you are to learn. I will be with you the entire time."

Elena's words make Catherine feel a bit more at ease while they walk to a large cold storage locker near the kitchen. This particular unit is not used to store food, but rather corpses of the Eye's fallen brethren. What Catherine doesn't realize is that this room was stocked with bodies specifically for her to test on. This walk in refrigerator has a rack on either side, each with four shelves and on each shelf lies a body. Elena points to one of them at random. "Will this work?" she asks.

"I guess," Catherine answers with a shrug.

Elena gives a tug on the side of the tray, and it slides out about two feet, displaying the entire body. Elena steps further into the room, allowing Catherine to approach the body. "Go ahead," she says. "I'm right here."

Catherine takes a moment, looking down at the body. She doesn't recognize the man, but he's clothed in the dark military fatigues she's seen some of the guards wear. Charred partial corpses notwithstanding, this is the first dead body she's been close to, and it's surprisingly pinker than she thought it would be. She was hoping that the proximity would help her get past her fear of this thing opening its eyes, but now that she's looking down at the lifeless husk, she really doesn't want it to come to life. This isn't the same as just bringing some frogs back life for a few minutes; this is animating and controlling a human being. What if she can't control it? Will it attack her? She looks over at Elena, who gives her a nod of encouragement. Taking a deep breath, Catherine holds her hands over the body and speaks the incantation she learned. "Falsum vitae."

A bright green aura surrounds the body for a moment before fading away. Beyond that, nothing else happens, leading Catherine to think she messed up somehow. She's getting ready to try again when her fear becomes reality. Both eyes shoot open, giving Catherine such a shock that she lets out a shriek and jumps towards Elena for protection. It doesn't take a divination spell to see this young girl's fear, and, while Elena doesn't possess any maternal instincts she's that aware of, she immediately steps between Catherine and the body to shield her.

Realizing that she may have overreacted, Catherine peeks around Elena to see what the animated corpse is doing. To her surprise, it lays still, staring blankly upward with its milky eyes. "It looks like you were successful," Elena says proudly.

"Yeah, but now what?" Catherine questions.

"Make it do something," Elena replies.

"How?"

"Think of what you want it to do," Elena instructs.

Catherine pictures the body sitting up in her mind, and without delay, it does just that. She remains standing behind Elena throughout the entire process, as she's still freaked out by everything she's doing. She makes the body stand up and walk out of the refrigeration unit. She then goes through a number of movements including having the animated corpse walk the hallways and manipulate objects like door handles.

Elena can clearly see Catherine's ill at ease. Unfortunately, her years in the Russian military have made her hard and lacking empathy to things such as fear. She knows Catherine would be much further along if it weren't for this weakness. She also knows that being forceful with Catherine wouldn't help matters, so she tries a different approach. To help make Catherine more comfortable, Elena has her make the corpse do some silly things like stand on one foot and pose like a glamorous model. This works, and for a bit, Catherine forgets about the gravity of her power, letting the magic flow more easily through her.

***

Allen Barber makes his way back to his office after a morning of meetings at the Pentagon. With the attack on Carcer, there's a push for the military to get more involved in Department of Sorcery matters. Even though Allen didn't approve the strike on the prison, it seems to have worked in his favor. Having a few more sorcerers on the run to take out later, along with Damian, isn't so bad if it gets him what he wants. This move by the Eye of Ruin does mean Allen needs to step up his surveillance on Damian so he's not blind-sided again.

Allen's just settling down at his desk when he receives a phone call. He recognizes the voice on the other end as one of the security officers at the Revelation facility. "Mr. Secretary?" the officer asks.

"Yes, what's going on?" Allen replies.

"Well…" The guard pauses as though he's not sure if he should speak. "You uh, said to call if you ever made an unscheduled visit to the facility."

"Yes."

"You um…you showed up about an hour ago," The officer says with the slightest quiver of fear in his voice. "I would've called sooner, but I wasn't told until just now."

"Thanks for your call," Allen says coldly before hanging up the phone.

After showing Damian the Revelation facility, he took precautions just in case, and it seems it was a wise decision. It suddenly occurs to Allen that Damian could've worn his face other places, like the Pentagon. Allen begins sweeping his office for anything out of the ordinary. He expects to find a hidden listening device or camera, but everything looks just as he left it. The last place he looks is in his desk drawers. He's about to close the top drawer when he notices the slightest little oddity. Inside the drawer are the files on the DoS's taskforce. Allen's very particular about his files and paperwork. He knows that he left these ones stacked in alphabetical order, but now Anthony's file, which was on the bottom, is on top. In Allen's mind, that means Damian went through these files.

The good news is these aren't the files Edward provided him; he keeps those securely off-site. Damian won't be getting access to a list of sorcerers with criminal backgrounds any time soon. And he's not too worried about having the personnel files on the taskforce discovered, as he's the Secretary of Defense and could easily explain it. No, what has Allen concerned is why Damian would go through the files secretly. If he wanted information on the team, Allen would've provided it, so he speculates that Damian's not adhering to their deal. What does Damian need with the DoS saps? Is he trying to turn them? Allen decides to take action at the very thought of it. They can't be used against him if they're dead. Besides, Revelation could really use some more test subjects.

## Chapter 18: Something Wicked This Way Comes

Eric drops by his apartment on the way back from his meeting with the President in order to get a change of clothes before he rejoins the team at the Department of Sorcery. His debriefing went smoother than he anticipated. The President praised the team interceding at Carcer and offered an additional 48 hours to track the Eye via the escaped prisoners.

Eric lives in an upscale one-bedroom located in the Downtown D.C. area. His living room and kitchen are separated by a bar-style counter with two tall chairs in front of it. A laptop is set up on the countertop as though it's used as a desk. The front room has the basest of furnishings. There is a couch, coffee table, and a small entertainment center with a tv on top of it. A short hallway extends off the living room, leading to a bathroom on the left and the bedroom on the right.

It's early evening when Eric makes it home. He changes out of his suit into jeans and a red button down shirt. Before heading out, Eric calls the DoS to check in with the team and see if they want him to pick up some food on his way. He gets a hold of

Benjamin who informs he is the only one around. Anthony went to pick up Andrea, who was still off with Trace, while Jasmine and Emmanuel went back to the hotel to freshen up. Since there are no requests, Eric decides he'll pick up a couple of pizzas, and people can eat it if they want. He lets Benjamin know he'll be back soon and hangs up.

***

For the better part of the afternoon, Andrea has been stuck working with Trace at a Carcer tracking facility located a couple blocks away from the prison itself. The inside of the building's non-descript exterior is a network of powerful computers linked to satellites that monitor the tracking signals embedded into the inmates. Normally this tracking center is manned by a staff of two, but in light of the current situation, it's all hands on deck. The entire room is filled with technicians, analysts, and a mathematician who's been brought in to look for patterns in the jump locations. No one has had any luck locking down a position. Even when a signal pops up long enough to dispatch local authorities, it's gone before they get there.

Andrea has been given some items that belonged to the escaped inmates in an attempt to predict where they're going. Her magic has allowed her to see the escapees' destinations a few times before they arrived, but not with enough foresight to enable a capture. Law enforcement has yet to arrive while anyone was still around.

A short while ago, Anthony called to tell Trace he was coming to pick up Andrea so they could get back to investigating their way since the tracking appeared to be a dead end. Finally having a moment, he pulls Andrea aside into a break room to let her know. "Lt. Taylor's on his way here to pick you up," he says with the deflated sound of defeat. "Seems we're not making enough progress this way."

"Thank God," Andrea replies with relief.

"What do you have against me?" Trace asks, a bit irritated.

"Are you serious?" Andrea's in disbelief.

"If it's about earlier, I was just stating facts." Trace defends his words. "It wasn't personal."

"Don't you get it?" Andrea gets in Trace's face. "You work for a government that is trying to segregate and oppress our kind!"

"So do you."

"No, no, no. I don't have a choice. I'm here so I stay out of Carcer."

Trace has never thought of Carcer as a way to oppress sorcerers. He believes in the justice system, and if someone commits a crime, they should serve their time. Carcer simply had the means to prevent criminal sorcerers from escaping. "So you're saying you're innocent and should never have been there?" he asks.

"Not innocent, but I don't deserve Carcer," Andrea replies.

"But when you were held at normal jails, you used magic to escape, so why is it wrong for the government to develop and implement technology that prevents magic-users from using their powers in jail? By your logic, murderers that can use magic should be held in cells they can easily escape. We've never treated prisoners poorly, and I'm not going to apologize for working somewhere that keeps people safe from the dangerous members of 'our kind.' Have a good evening, convict."

Trace promptly turns and exits the room, leaving Andrea in stunned silence. She hates being called "convict," and it cuts deep when she hears it. What's more troubling is that his words made a lot of sense. She's always been so blinded by her hatred of being a prisoner there that she never even considered the necessity of Carcer. It ultimately doesn't change her view on the prison, but maybe she won't direct so much animosity towards those who work there.

Anthony arrives to collect Andrea within the next ten minutes. He checks in with Trace before they leave. There are still no tracking updates, but Trace lets him know he'll call if anything changes. It's also very clear that there's more of a divide between Trace and Andrea than he last saw, only this time Andrea looks more guilty than angry. She says nothing as they leave.

The two sit in silence as Anthony drives the government SUV through surprisingly empty streets back to the Department of Sorcery. Andrea sits in the front passenger seat, staring out the window. Anthony wants to know what happened, but he's afraid to push, so he instead tries to get her talking without asking anything. "Don't worry," he says. "We'll find them."

Andrea looks over at Anthony, but before she can respond, it feels as though a bomb goes off outside her door. Glass shatters, the metal of the door buckles, concaving as the entire vehicle is knocked across the intersection it was passing through. Andrea manages to see a large armored truck outside her window. The truck must've run the light and hit them. Just before she blacks out, she sees what looks like armed soldiers exit the vehicle, advancing on the SUV.

Andrea jerks in her seat, realizing the entire car accident was a vision and hasn't actually happened yet. She recognizes they're almost to the intersection where they get hit. "Stop the car!" she shouts, grabbing Anthony by the arm.

Anthony slams on the brake pedal, causing the SUV to skid to a stop just short of the intersection. He frantically looks all around, but sees nothing. There are no other cars on the road and they have the right-of-way, so he's baffled. "What the hell was that about?!" his voice almost cracks as he asks.

"Someone's coming," she answers still looking ahead at the intersection.

Anthony follows Andrea's gaze, trying to see what she's looking for. As he does, a large, gray armored truck with blacked out windows skids into the intersection. The truck power-slides into a ninety degree turn towards them. It pulls up directly in front of the SUV to block its path. Four soldiers file out of the rear compartment of the truck, advancing in military fashion. They are all wearing full tactical gear with helmets and armored face masks.

The two lead soldiers are armed with automatic shotguns, firing into the engine block of the SUV so they can't flee.

Inside the vehicle, Anthony grabs the 9mm sidearm stored in a hidden compartment for emergencies. He also tosses his cell phone to Andrea before forcing the passenger seatback down and ushering her into the back seat. "Get down!" he orders.

Andrea rolls into the back, staying low. She redials the first number in the phone. Anthony opens the driver's door to fire at their attackers. Strangely, they are not shooting back. Instead, the two soldiers in the rear move up, taking point with body-sized ballistic shields protecting them.

Andrea hears someone pick up on the other end of the phone, but, before she can say anything, a pair of headlights appears from behind the SUV, moving at a rapid pace. The lights are from another armored vehicle that slam into the SUV's rear bumper. The impact throws Andrea into the rear window, causing her to drop the phone to the floor.

The force of the crash also pushes the DoS vehicle forward which knocks Anthony to the ground. As soon as he is down, the armored soldiers move in to subdue him. He puts up a struggle, but four to one goes in the soldiers' favor. They cuff him, collar him, and sedate him just to be safe.

The world is spinning when Andrea opens her eyes. She hears footsteps outside the car, but she's too disoriented to know what's happening. Her head is throbbing. She touches her head where she hit the window glass. It's wet. She pulls her hand away to see it is now covered in blood. The back door to the SUV opens, and the last thing Andrea hears before losing consciousness is: "Get her collared and then make sure she's okay. We need them alive."

\*\*\*

Under normal circumstances, a government paid lodging would be something inexpensive and nearby, but the President made arrangements for the DoS to put up the non-local members of the team at the Ritz-Carlton, Pentagon City. It's easily the nicest hotel Jasmine or Emmanuel has ever stayed in. Their rooms each have a king bed, a large wall-mounted flatscreen tv, a bathroom with Italian marble décor, and all the amenities one could want.

The two checked in to their separate rooms a couple hours prior to get showered and change clothes. Neither one was really prepared with any kind of overnight bag, so they acquired some DoS uniforms to change into until they can get some new clothing. Emmanuel waits until the last possible minute to change into it, as he's been enjoying the plush complimentary bathrobe that came with the room.

Benjamin, Jasmine, and Emmanuel all have adjoining suites with a scenic view of Arlington. Benjamin stated he probably wouldn't use the room, but it was provided to him regardless. Jasmine and Emmanuel meet in the hallway at 7pm, as per their agreement, to head back to the Department of Sorcery. The make their way to the elevators and in turn down to the lobby.

The entrance hall of the hotel is rather quiet. There are customers about, but not with the hustle and bustle of a busy hotel.

Jasmine and Emmanuel start making their way from the elevators towards the glass double-door entrance. As they walk, something catches Jasmine's eye. It was only a glimpse, and just for a split-second, but she thought she saw a snake tattoo on the desk clerk's neck. Aside from the fact that it's a different clerk from when they arrived, this one is also an Asian male. She might just be paranoid from all the recent things they've been handling, but what she thinks she saw happens to be the brand of the snakeheads that have her mother and sister. "We may have a situation," Jasmine whispers to Emmanuel as they keep walking.

"What is wrong?" Emmanuel whispers back.

"Just go out front and get the car," she answers. "I got this."

Jasmine breaks off from Emmanuel, making her way to the front desk. Emmanuel continues to the main entrance, but stops before going outside to look back at Jasmine. She stands before the Chinese desk clerk, who slowly looks up from his computer screen. Just before he greets her with a smile, there is the faintest of moments where his true visage is visible. This is not a hotel clerk before her. He's got a hard set to his jaw and a hint of malice in his eyes. This is a killer. "How can I help you, Miss?" he says with a heavy accent.

Jasmine isn't buying into the ruse. She knows what she saw, and she'd recognize Qiang's calling card anywhere. She doesn't even waste time with words. She grabs the clerk by the collar and pulls him over the counter. Her own body weight and momentum allow her to throw the clerk into the center of the lobby floor. As soon as she does this, the handful of guests and other staff that were mulling about immediately stand, revealing that no one in the lobby is who they appeared to be. The clerk kips up off the ground with expert agility. "You shouldn't have done that," he says, removing his staff jacket.

What has become of the hotel's actual staff or customers is a mystery, but everyone here currently is a Triad snakehead. There are eight in total, including the fake desk clerk. They begin to surround Jasmine, but these men aren't sorcerers and know that she could easily take them all out which is why they have insurance. The thug who was masquerading as the clerk appears to be in charge of the others. "Qiang would like to see you," he says. "You've been avoiding him since you skipped your last fight. He is most disappointed and may have to take it out on your mother and sister."

"I made arrangements to pay him," Jasmine says with attitude.

"And it was received, but you must be taught that breaking the rules has consequences," he replies.

"Okay," she says regretfully. "I'll go."

Emmanuel isn't entirely sure what's happening, but he's heard enough to know that Jasmine shouldn't be leaving with these men. He rushes forward from the front door, pushing past a couple of the gangsters who pay the old man no mind. "What are you doin'?" Emmanuel asks with a raised voice. "You cannot let dem take you."

"I don't have a choice," Jasmine replies. "If I don't go, they'll kill my family."

"You do 'ave a choice," Emmanuel argues. "But lettin' thugs push you around is not one of dem. We can get your family back."

The lead snakehead gets bored and wants blood. He brandishes a small knife and lunges at Emmanuel. Jasmine pushes Emmanuel out of the way and disarms the thug using a knife hand block. She's about to counter with an elbow when he wags a finger at her, reminding her of what's at stake. Jasmine lowers her arms, allowing him to hit her with a haymaker. She goes down and appears unconscious.

Emmanuel ducks down to check on Jasmine. "Mind your own business, old man," the snakehead taunts, "before you get hurt."

Emmanuel has never been a fan of people who push others around for their own benefit, but using someone's family as leverage is inexcusable. This also isn't his first run in with members of the Chinese mafia, so there's already bad blood. Emmanuel stands. "She may 'ave reason to not fight you, but I do not."

Emmanuel steps into a fighting stance which causes all of the thugs to burst out laughing. "You are funny." The snakehead continues to laugh. "What can one old man do against us?"

"You are right," Emmanuel answers. "Renovo!"

Signs of Emmanuel's advanced age begin to vanish as his hair color turns from gray to dark brown. His thin frame becomes covered with dense muscle, and his once mildly sagging skin grows taut over it. The old man before them has transformed into a much younger one, in peak physical condition. No one has time to marvel at what just happened because Emmanuel immediately strikes the lead snakehead in the throat before delivering a spinning back kick into his torso. The attack launches the gangster back into his own people.

It rarely comes up nowadays as Emmanuel prefers not to fight, but he is a master of six different martial styles including Haitian machete fencing, Brazilian capoeira, and Chinese kung fu. Having sized up his opponents, he intends to use capoeira and change it up when necessary. He goes into the esquiva lateral, defensively weaving side to side very rhythmically, waiting patiently for his eager challengers to move in.

The lead snakehead gets back to his feet. He's enraged that he was just made to look a fool in front of his subordinates. "Kill this warlock prick!" he shouts, pushing his men forward.

Seven of the thugs rush in with the lead one holding back. Emmanuel twirls into the air, performing a butterfly kick, both his feet leaving the ground and hitting three of the incoming goons in one sweeping motion. He comes out of the leaping kick into a roll before going back on the defensive. The rest of the thugs attack, but with movements like a wild tornado, Emmanuel systematically takes them apart.

The spell Emmanuel cast not only restored his youth, but also put his body in the best state that it can be, making him stronger and faster than even the most seasoned athlete. This is part of his success against the snakeheads. Even being as skilled as Emmanuel is at martial arts, he would be hard-pressed to take out seven trained killers without that extra magical boost.

After making short work of the cohorts, Emmanuel turns his attention to their leader. "Your turn for a lesson," Emmanuel says.

This criminal enforcer was already looking crazed, but Emmanuel's words trigger some deep rage. He charges, tackling Emmanuel to the ground. The two men grapple with each other trying to get the upper hand. Emmanuel's not very good with wrestling or grappling and knows this so he mostly uses his energy trying to get away from his opponent.

The two men finally separate and get back on their feet. Within a moment, they are back at each other striking, blocking, and counter-striking aggressively. This Triad thug is putting up a much better fight than his lackeys, but he's also attacking in anger, getting more enraged the longer they fight. Emmanuel exploits this by switching styles suddenly and landing an axe kick to his enemy's shin which shatters the bone. The thug lets out a scream as he drops to the ground.

Emmanuel kneels down next to the Triad gangster. This man, who was an alpha tough guy only moments ago, now nurses his broken leg on the verge of tears. His leg is in very bad shape. Nothing has punched through the skin, but it is bent in a way most unnatural for a human limb. Emmanuel points to the wound. "Dat looks painful," he says, trying to hide a smile. "But I am goin' to show you mercy."

Emmanuel holds his palm just over the leg, whispering an incantation. His hand takes on a bright white aura for a moment, and the Triad bites down to avoid screaming again as his tibia reforms underneath the skin and muscle of his leg. After repairing the damage that he's done, Emmanuel stands. "Should I let you go, what will you tell your masters?" Emmanuel asks.

"I will tell them to kill you all, starting with her mother and sister," the gangster says, defiantly.

"Dat is what I t'ought," Emmanuel says, shaking his head with disappointment.

While Emmanuel hates everything that Triads represent, he also doesn't generally act on impulse. He's not a vengeful man, but a calculated one. He knows that these men fear their bosses more than any pain he can dole out. He also knows that if they are allowed to leave, Jasmine's family will be executed immediately, and a death warrant will go out for her. Emmanuel kicks down on the gangster's leg, breaking it once again. He's not vengeful, but he can be wrathful.

The thug's agony is ended rather quickly as Emmanuel strikes him in the chest. It isn't a normal punch though. His fist takes on an onyx-like aura, swirling between dark and light. It looks to draw something out of the snakehead before ending his life. Killing these men won't necessarily stop the execution of

Jasmine's family, but it will buy them a bit of time while the Triads try to figure out what happened to them. Emmanuel makes his way around the room, dispatching the rest of the gangsters in a similar fashion before Jasmine wakes.

There is a moment of sheer panic when Jasmine's eyes open. She tries to ignore the drumming in her head while she tries to work out where she is. Before long, she realizes she's still in the lobby of the Ritz. The panic returns when she sees all of the thugs on the ground. Emmanuel stands over them; however, the magic has worn off, returning him to his elderly state. Jasmine's not sure what has happened here, but she finds it difficult to believe an old man could take out eight Triad enforcers. That's the least of her problems right now. However these men were put down, it has put her family in jeopardy. She quickly gets to her feet. "What happened?!" she frantically asks.

"I could not let dem take you," Emmanuel answers.

"That was not your call to make!" Jasmine shouts. "They're going to kill my mother and sister now!"

"No, we will save dem," Emmanuel tries to calm Jasmine down. "I 'ave a way to track dem. We just need to get Andrea."

"How can you track them?" Jasmine questions, still flustered.

"I absorbed a bit of each one's life essence," Emmanuel says. "Andrea can use 'er magic to see where dey 'ave been. Den we go an' get your family back."

The idea of finally getting her family free from the clutches of Qiang and his snakeheads is very relieving. Seeing these goons dead also brings her a bit of satisfaction, but until her family is actually rescued, she cannot relax. "Then let's go!" Jasmine exclaims.

"You call Eric," Emmanuel says while looking around the lobby. "I will look to see if anyone was hurt when dese men showed up 'ere."

Emmanuel finds a couple staff members and some guests tied up in a supply room behind the front desk. No one has any serious injuries. While he assists in getting the hostages untied, Jasmine grabs the desk phone and calls Eric. "Eric, is Andrea back?" She asks as soon as she hears the phone answered. "I need to talk to her."

"She and Anthony never made it back to the DoS," Eric answers. "We found the SUV, and it looks like they were attacked en route. We're not sure where they are, but we're gonna find them. Are you and Emmanuel still at the hotel? I'll come get you."

## Chapter 19: Revelation

Anthony's eyes slowly open, revealing the world around him to be a bright blur. He can feel that he's in motion, and as his eyes begin to adjust, he can make out what appears to be overhead florescent lamps rushing by like lane indicators on a freeway. He has no idea where he is or how he got here. The last thing he remembers is getting attacked in the SUV. Anthony's concern immediately switches from his surroundings to the whereabouts of Andrea. Upon attempting to look around, the first thing he notices is that he's wearing a thick metal collar which he assumes is an anti-magic unit. He tries to sit up and discovers that he also can't move his arms or legs.

Everything comes fully into focus giving Anthony a better idea of his surroundings. He finds himself strapped down to a gurney being wheeled down a long hallway. He's being escorted by two men in military fatigues and a dark-skinned man in a white lab coat who notices him looking around. "It seems our patient is awake," he says with a smile. "I'd save that energy if I were you."

"Where am I?" Anthony asks while still trying to free himself.

"Seeing as you don't need to know that, I won't be telling you," the man continues in his jovial tone.

That's not going to stop Anthony from probing. He's trained to try and get any information he can. Anything might be relevant. "Will you at least tell me who you are or why I'm here?"

"Well we are going to be spending some quality time together, so why not," he answers. "I'm Doctor Randall, and you're here so we can extract some of that beautiful magic of yours."

Elijah Randall is not a medical doctor, but a biologist and engineer who has studied magic extensively. Though not the inventor of anti-magic technology, he has managed to reverse-engineer it to develop the machine that extracts spells from sorcerers and infuses them into gear. Elijah's morally ambiguous when it comes to the methods of magical research. He didn't originally set out to hurt people, but science sometimes requires the breaking of a few eggs, and he's found he enjoys being the one to do it.

"Where's the girl?" Anthony presses further.

"Don't worry, she's up after you," Elijah says with delight. "But your military file says you're a teleporter which gives you priority."

Elijah's answer does provide Anthony with some insight. Whoever's behind this is well-funded and has access to sealed military files. Unfortunately, that doesn't narrow it down as much as he would like. It also tells him that they don't know about his injury. He'll go along with this for now since he's pretty sure he doesn't currently have any magic for them to take. "Lucky me," Anthony replies sarcastically.

Anthony is wheeled into a room straight out of a horror film. The stench of scorched flesh is almost palpable throughout. In the center is a metal chair with neck, arm, and leg restraints attached to it. The chair itself has small bits of something blackened on it in various places. Around the chair is a square cage with cylinders atop it on every corner. Each cylinder is capped with a metallic ring giving them a similar shape to that of a Tesla coil.

Outside of the cage are large, almost archaic-looking, machines that could be straight out of Victor Frankenstein's laboratory. Inside one of the machines sits an empty glass chamber. A series of heavy cables connect the machine cabinets to a computer workstation about six feet away. Whatever the purpose of this device, it's apparent that it generates a lot of electricity.

Anthony decides he doesn't want to find out how magic is extracted by this thing. He waits for the guards to undo his restraints and stand him up. He doesn't struggle, but goes along willingly, so the guards are less alert. Elijah steps over to the computers while one of the guards proceeds to open the cage around the chair. With only one person holding him, Anthony makes his move. He rears back, throwing the guard off-balance before delivering an elbow to his gut. The other guard reaches for his stun-stick, a baton with a taser at the end, but Anthony lands a kick to his chest first, knocking him into the metal cage wall. Anthony then makes a break for the door. He doesn't get very far, however, as a jolt shoots down his spine from the collar, rendering him disabled.

The guards collect and strap Anthony into the extraction chair. They make sure the restraints are extra tight as payback. Once locked in, his collar is removed. Elijah walks over to the front of the cage, peering in at Anthony. "I'll bet you weren't expecting that," he says with glee. "I modified the anti-magic collars with extra security. I've never actually seen it used before though, so thank you."

"I aim to please," Anthony grunts, trying to hide how much pain he's in.

"So glad to hear that," Elijah says, moving back to his computer console. "It should make this whole process much easier."

\*\*\*

The command room at the Department of Sorcery is almost as busy as it was the day of the White House attack. All staffers on hand are scouring security feeds, reviewing the accident report, and corresponding with local law enforcement in an effort to locate Anthony and Andrea. While the team that took them cleaned up the scene, leaving no shell casings, they did have to leave the government SUV, and there was no covering up what they did to its engine block. Unfortunately, there isn't much else to go on at this time.

After picking up Jasmine and Emmanuel from the Ritz-Carlton, Eric takes them back to the DoS to meet with Benjamin and to join the search for their missing teammates. Celeste greets them as they enter the command room, giving a rundown of the progress so far. She's not dressed in her usual professional manner. She was at home, winding down from the day when she got a call and came straight in. "Have they checked traffic cams and nearby security footage?" Eric questions.

"They've searched for it, but no footage exists," she replies.

"As in there were no cameras in the area?" Eric asks quizzically.

"As in someone wiped the footage," Celeste answers.

"Who the hell would be able to do that?" Jasmine asks with a raised voice.

Jasmine is on the verge of having a full on meltdown. Despite Emmanuel's assurances that her family will be fine, the disappearance of Andrea has her freaking out inside. She explained to Eric that she and Emmanuel were attacked by thugs, but she left out the part about the Triads and her family being held captive. She feels the less people that know about that the better. It's not that she doesn't trust Eric or Benjamin; she's just trying to keep them out of it to protect them.

Celeste doesn't know who wiped the footage, as anyone in a high enough position could have the data erased. Even a talented and motivated computer programmer could've done it. Either way, it's troubling. "I don't know," she says.

"Have you checked with Warden McRory to see if he has anything?" Eric asks.

"I spoke to him personally," Celeste replies. "He didn't know anything, but he is on his way over."

Everyone's attention is pulled towards the room's entrance as the automatic doors open to reveal the Secretary of Sorcery. Edward dons one of his usual suits; however, he's missing his tie at the moment. He, too, was called at home, though he was working in his study at the time. As he steps into the room, he locks eyes with Eric. The tension between them has not subsided, but now is not the time for further drama. Edward looks past him at his staff. "Where are our people?" he asks.

Eric can't think of what Edward would have to gain by kidnapping members of a team he created, but something has been bugging him since he picked up Jasmine from the hotel. He got a look at the bodies of the dead assailants, taking note of their matching dragon tattoos. This got Eric thinking of when Edward threatened someone with the Triad. He noticed there was no mention of a Triad affiliation in Jasmine's file, and he can't imagine Emmanuel having one, but someone must. Based on how she's been acting, Eric's money is on Jasmine. Did Edward deliver on his threat because he lost control of the team? The timing on this attack seems very suspicious. Edward may have nothing to do with it, but Eric's still going to ask.

Edward's in the middle of getting briefed by his staff when Eric approaches. He put a hand on Edward's arm and leans in closely. "I need to speak to you privately," Eric whispers.

"I do love our private chats," Edward says with a sarcastic sigh. "Conference room?"

Eric nods, and the two men adjourn to the back where the conference room is. While the glass wall may keep the sound in, there's no visible privacy to speak of and the entire command room is waiting for a show. Eric and Edward stare each other down for what seems like an eternity. "Something on your mind?" Edward finally speaks up.

"Did you have a hand in this?" Eric asks.

Edward is genuinely baffled by the question. "What?" he asks with wide eyes.

"Jasmine and Emmanuel get attacked by what I'll wager are members of the Triad on the same night Anthony and Andrea get attacked," Eric spells it out for him. "Then all footage that might help find the culprits gets wiped out. Not many people have the power to do that or the knowledge of Jasmine's past to hire the Chinese mafia."

The news of Triad thugs being involved is unsettling to Edward. He actually has a pretty good idea who might have the knowledge and the means to do what Eric's accusing him of, but implicating Allen would spell his own doom, so he reveals nothing. "I don't know what you're talking about Agent, and I don't appreciate the implication," Edward says.

"You've hated me since the beginning, and I'm sure that was only compounded when the President handed your taskforce over to me," Eric says moving towards Edward. "My question is, are you the kind of man who would act on that hate?"

"Davis, we're on the same team." Edward holds both hands up to halt Eric. "You're right. I don't like you, but as long as you do your job and stop these terrorists, you've got nothing to worry about from me. Now can we get back to searching?"

Edward doesn't wait for a response, abruptly turning and walking out of the room. As he does, all eyes that were fixed on the conference room quickly look in random directions. Edward's met by Celeste, who begins filling him in once again on the search status thus far. Benjamin approaches Eric as he exits the conference room. "What was that all about?" he asks.

"I'll tell you later," Eric replies.

Everyone in the room gets back to searching. Once Edward is fully up to speed, he steps into a quiet corner of the room to make a phone call from his cell phone. It's a short call. So short that it's hard to know if he's talking to a person or leaving a message. "We have to talk," is all he says before hanging up.

After about twenty minutes, Trace McRory shows up at the command room. He has a look of urgency on his face as he scans the room for a face he recognizes. He makes his way hastily to Eric upon seeing him. "Eric," he says catching his attention. "I think I know where they are."

Eric looks around to see if anyone else is in earshot. Everyone is so involved in their work that they don't appear to have heard what Trace said. Eric grabs him, ushering him back towards the main door. "Not here," he whispers.

Eric and Trace slip into the hallway. Eric checks the hall for cameras while Trace looks around in confusion. "What's going on?" Trace asks.

"Internal problems," Eric replies in a tone just above a whisper. "I think someone here may have a hand in our recent bad luck, and I don't know who to trust."

"Well, I might be able to cheer you up," Trace replies. "Remember I mentioned that Andrea's outfitted with a prisoner tracker?"

Trace pulls a small handheld device out of his pocket and presents it to Eric who takes possession of the device. "Signal's still pinging?" Eric asks.

"It cut off while I was on the way here, but we have the last known location," Trace says. "What do you want to do? If someone here was in on the kidnapping, they'd probably know about the tracking implant. She might not even be where the tracker last pinged."

"We still need to check it out," Eric says. "I'll get my team, but let's keep this quiet for now."

"I'm coming too."

***

Andrea finds herself in one of her least favorite places: a cell. The square room is well lit and contains only a mattress and a toilet. There are no windows, and the only door is electronically sealed with no inside handle. Andrea is not restrained in any way, but she is outfitted with an anti-magic collar. She's also had her belt, shoelaces, and anything metallic removed.

Andrea doesn't know where she is, having woken up inside the cell already, but she has no intention of staying here. With the exception of Carcer, she's never been in a prison she couldn't escape. Her biggest obstacle currently is the collar. She is familiar enough with the device that if she had something to pick it, she could remove it. She realizes that when they searched her, they overlooked her underwire bra which contains a thin strip of rigid metal. "Amateurs," she says while removing her bra.

Andrea rips the metal strip out of the bra and proceeds to remove the collar. It takes her multiple attempts, as she can't actually see the locking mechanism, and she even shocks herself once before getting it. With the collar removed, she can once again access her divination magic. She touches the door and speaks an incantation, allowing her to see through the eyes of the guard who last touched it. This was how she escaped prison previously. She was able to avoid the guards by not only seeing where they were but also where they would be.

Andrea launches her plan by pounding on the door repeatedly and screaming, as though she were being stabbed to death. Through her magic, she sees the guard outside the door look over and shout, "Shut up in there!"

Andrea continues screaming and pounding until the guard is so incensed he opens the door. In his rage, he misses the fact that her collar is off as he moves to strike with his stun-stick. Andrea can see his intent before he acts, allowing her to easily avoid the attack. She turns the tables by electrocuting the guard with his own weapon. While he can't move, she chokes him to unconsciousness. She takes the guard's weapon, his keycard, and his boot laces before locking his body in the cell.

The halls of the Revelation facility are like a maze. The white walls have no distinguishing characteristics from one walkway to the next. Andrea got some sense of the proper path to the exit while she was in the guard's head, but not much else. She's not sure if Anthony is in one of these rooms or not, but she wouldn't be able to look herself in the mirror again if she didn't check. She decides the best course of action would be to make her way to the exit and work her way back.

Shortly into Andrea's search, the sound of screaming starts echoing through the halls. Her heart sinks because she knows those screams are coming from Anthony. She breaks into a sprint, trying to track the noise to its source. Unfortunately, the guard she locked in her cell is not the only one patrolling the facility grounds. She turns a corner, nearly colliding with two guards who immediately give chase.

\*\*\*

Meanwhile, in a room not far away, Anthony feels as though he's being ripped apart from the inside out. Elijah has been demanding that he cast a teleportation spell, but rather than admit he can't, he instead refuses. This would draw the ire of most men, but Elijah isn't like most others. When his requests get declined, a warped joy spreads across his face, almost causing Anthony to second-guess his defiance. Not that he could recant now; even if he were to tell the truth, he knows this maniac wouldn't believe him.

Each time Anthony refuses to cast a spell, Elijah flips a switch on the console he stands behind, causing the coils atop the cage to throw lightning into the cell below. There's something almost arcane about this electricity in that it creates ten times the pain of getting electrocuted while only doing a tenth of the damage to flesh and organs. Most subjects relent after one shock, but being unable to do that, Anthony has suffered through three so far.

The actual magic extraction of the archaically designed machine has nothing to do with the cage or the coils. The chair itself acts as a sort for grounding device for sorcerers, siphoning off arcane energies before they can coalesce into the desired spell. The magic is then redirected into a containment canister located outside the cage. Another machine takes the captured energy and infuses it into a channeling tool that holds it in a loop, allowing the spell effect to be used over and over.

Allen Barber told Damian that extracting the arcane energy results in the death of the sorcerer. This fact is entirely false, a point which Damian discovered when he returned to Revelation masquerading as Allen. While it's true that Damian's volunteers didn't survive the process, it had nothing to do with the extraction. Allen ordered their deaths after the procedure was complete, a directive that Dr. Randall was eager to carry out, although he made the deaths as slow and painful as possible.

"You're more resilient than most," Elijah says with a crazed smile. "And while I enjoy that, I can't imagine you could be. Why not cast a little spell and end your suffering?"

There isn't any point on Anthony's body that isn't in searing pain. He feels like a slab of meat being slow-cooked in a barbeque smoker, only the vapors rising off him don't have a delightful hickory aroma. If there is one thought keeping him going at this point, it's that he doesn't want Andrea to suffer through this. He thinks if he can just hold out long enough, maybe a miracle will happen. Eric and the others must be searching for them by now. "I'm having…a great time," Anthony manages to say. "Why don't you come have a go?"

"Intriguing offer," Elijah replies, flipping the switch once more. "But I'm fine over here."

***

Andrea's pursuers have increased from two to four, though she has managed to keep hidden from them. She knows it's only a matter of time before someone sounds an alarm, if they haven't already. While staying ahead of the guards, Andrea's also made her way towards the sound of the screaming she keeps hearing.

Andrea reaches the room that seems to be the source of the noise. She touches the door and speaks her incantation. Just like at her cell, she sees through the eyes of one of the guards in the room. Anthony sits before her, strapped to a chair in a cage. He's being electrocuted. Andrea ends her spell, looking back the way she came. The guards chasing her will be rounding the corner any moment. She doesn't have a lot of time for planning, so she improvises, pounding on the door before her. She then quickly darts down the hall and around another corner.

Four guards with stun-sticks at the ready come running from around the corner down the hallway. Just before they reach the door, it opens, and one of the two guards from within the arcane extraction room steps out with a puzzled look on his face. "What's going on?" he calls to the other guards.

"We think we've got a test subject on the loose," one of the guards reports.

The guard at the door looks back into the room. Elijah has just finished shocking Anthony for a fifth time. Anthony hangs limp in the chair, only being held up by his restraints. He's conscious, but barely. Elijah looks over at the guard to find out what's ruining his fun. "Someone's out of their cell," the guard says.

"Both of you get after them!" Elijah barks. "We can't have any of these freaks wandering the halls!"

The two guards in the room with Elijah rush out to join the other four in their search. Andrea uses the opportunity to circle around, making her way back to the extraction room. She remembers seeing where Elijah was positioned, and she hopes he's still in the same place. Bursting into the room, Andrea hurls her stun-stick like a spear. It misses her intended target, but comes close enough that Elijah drops to the ground as a reflex to avoid being struck. This gives Andrea the time she needs to clear the distance from the door to the computer console. She leaps over the four foot workstation, kicking Elijah in the head as he stands back up. He goes down hard, but not before pushing a small button on the underside of the desktop.

Anthony suddenly feels his restraints being released one at a time. He manages to lift his head just enough to see Andrea's face. For a moment, he thinks she's an illusion until she starts helping him up. He's so weak he's not really much help in trying to stand. Andrea's struggling to hold him as Anthony has both height and weight on her. She can see he's got nothing in the tank, but if they're to make it out, she needs him to try. "Talk to me, Goose," she says.

Anthony's never been on this side of a rescue mission, but he's been in Andrea's place before, and he appreciates what she's trying to do. He gives her every ounce of strength he can muster in order to right himself. "I'm Maverick," he says weakly. "You're Goose."

"Then let's get out of here, Mav," she replies.

Andrea and Anthony slowly make their way towards the exit. They don't encounter any guards, and it looks like they're going to make it out until they round the final corner. Standing between them and the steel double-door exit are four heavily armed soldiers. Each soldier wears ballistic body armor and has a strange metallic device with a slight glow on their utility belts. The two soldiers in the front point automatic shotguns at Andrea and Anthony. The other two soldiers back them up with 9mm pistols. Andrea and Anthony give each other defeated glances. "You've got this, right?" Anthony attempts to joke.

"Yeah, I'm all over it," Andrea jokes back.

"Down on your knees!" one of the soldiers shouts.

The doors behind the guards suddenly burst inwards from the force of a fireball. While this draws the soldiers' attention, the flames do not seem to affect them in any way. Eric, Benjamin, Trace, Jasmine, and Emmanuel step out from the smoke. The soldiers open fire on them, but their bullets are absorbed into a barrier created by Eric. Trace and Benjamin return fire, only to discover their own bullets have a similar effect on the security team.

Eric is once again baffled by the presence of protective barriers without the presence of the magic. Anthony on the other hand now knows exactly what's going on. "They're outfitted with tech that can mimic barrier magic!" he shouts to warn everyone.

"Let's see if they can block this," Trace says stepping to the front of the group. "Inaedifico!"

The walls on either side of the soldiers come alive, stretching around and ensnaring them like an octopus's tentacles.

As the wall material snakes around the soldiers, it melds together, cutting them off from the hallway, but leaving just a narrow passage for Andrea and Anthony to pass through.

More guards come around the corner from the direction Andrea and Anthony are fleeing. "Move!" Eric shouts.

Anthony starts limping forward with the assistance of Andrea. The guards take aim with pistols and proceed to fire. "Maceria!" Trace says, creating a thick stone wall between the guards and his allies.

Hearing the impact of the bullets into the stone behind them, Anthony and Andrea pick up the pace as much as possible. They squeeze through the narrow opening between the new cylindrical walls in the hallway. Gunfire erupts from behind those walls as the soldiers attempt to shoot their way out. A round grazes Andrea's right arm before Eric has a chance to cast a barrier behind them. Benjamin and Jasmine move up to help them both to the door, allowing the whole group to exit as a team.

Anthony and Andrea discover the prison-like facility is actually a warehouse on a secured lot amongst other inconspicuous buildings. Dark asphalt stretches out to the surrounding perimeter fence, and a handful of unconscious guards are scattered across the top of it. Powerful flood lights along the tops of the buildings, and on posts near the fence, keep the darkness of night at bay. The team cautiously moves towards the gate where their SUV is parked on the other side.

Out of the corner of his eye, Eric catches a quick glint in the darkness. Silently stopping the others with a hand motion, he stares more intently into the shadows of the buildings ahead. There's a sort of ripple in darkness as something moves. The movement is low to the ground and calculated. Eric realizes it's a trick meant to draw their attention. He glances back at the opposite buildings to see a nightmarish creature stealthily approaching.

It's hard to see the beast's body as its massive mouth covers everything else when looked at directly on. The maw of this thing is almost a perfect circle, large enough to easily swallow a grown man whole. The entire mouth is lined with row upon row of jagged teeth that surround a long barbed tongue protruding from the throat at the center of everything. It's not immediately apparent how the thing sees with its mouth wide open until Eric notices two eyes just above the gullet. "Behind!" Eric shouts.

The others turn to see the beast. Those at the rear have a slightly different angle on it and can see the body behind the mouth. The creature has a body similar to that of a maneless lion with the exception being its three tails, all of which seem to be prehensile. "What the fuck is that?!" Benjamin shouts in response.

"I don't know," Eric replies. "Just shoot it!"

Eric, Benjamin, and Trace open fire on the beast, but discover how quick it is. In the blink of an eye, the creature repositions so that all the projectiles are directed at its mouth. The circular rows of teeth begin to rotate rapidly, like the blades in a blender. The bullets get pulled into this vortex of teeth and seem to have no effect on the creature. "That's not good," Trace states the obvious.

Jasmine conjures a ball of flame, hurling it at the beast. The fire also gets pulled into the tornado of teeth dissipating on impact. "So…" Benjamin seems almost speechless. "They eat bullets and fire? Do you wanna try lightning?"

The creature that was stalking in the shadows steps into the light, revealing that it's a second of these missile eating beasts. Eric motions everyone back and they quickly comply. The beasts now stand between them and their escape. "Suggestions?" Eric asks.

"Dere is a Shepherd around," Emmanuel states while looking around for said individual. "Dey are responsible for dese t'ings."

"Great," Benjamin says in exasperation. "Now we're dealing with real magical monsters. Eric, how do I get out of this team? It's bad for my life expectancy."

The creatures start to advance. The team decides to retreat back into the building, but they are cut off by more security approaching opposite the beasts. Eric throws up barriers to halt enemy gunfire while Jasmine and Trace attempt to slow the creatures with various evocation and conjuration spells. Nothing seems to work as the missile eaters absorb or easily overcome the spells thrown at them. It looks as though the entire team will be killed or captured.

Anthony has reached his breaking point. Between losing his magic, the failure of stopping the Eye, and being slow roasted like a movie theater hotdog, he can't take anymore. He has to do something! His rage makes him run so hot it feels like his blood is actually boiling. He starts to feel pain within, just like when he was strapped to the extraction chair. He lets out a shrieking cry of agony as an explosion of electrical energy shoots out of him, encircling the entire team before collapsing back in on Anthony, creating a nova-like flash. When the light fades, the entire team, including Anthony, is gone.

## Chapter 20: Reunion

Allen is beginning to find Edward's need for constant meetings a bother. The two of them shouldn't be speaking now that the political climate surrounding arcane matters is a powder keg waiting to explode. In fact, if Edward didn't know so much about Revelation, he would've ignored his request this time around. He's certainly not buying lunch.

It's around two in the morning when both Secretaries meet at a downtown D.C. parking structure. Edward gets into the back of a black limousine to find Allen seated facing him with an expression of boredom on his face. Once inside, the vehicle begins moving, though the tinted glass partition is up, so the driver isn't seen. "What's so important that we just had to meet?" Allen asks, maintaining his look of disinterest.

"Did you have members of my taskforce attacked tonight?" Edward asks while fighting the urge to grab Allen forcefully by the collar.

The question definitely has Allen's attention. Should he say *no* and risk looking like the liar he is? Should he say *yes* and explain why he thinks the team is traitorous? If he does that, he'd have to explain why, and he's definitely not going to tell Edward about his involvement with the Eye of Ruin. He decides to probe further to find out what Edward knows. "Why would I have your team attacked?" he asks.

"I don't have that answer, Allen." Edward leans forward as he replies. "But you certainly have the means and motivation."

"I had nothing to do with it, Edward." Allen lies very convincingly. "Why are you so concerned about it anyway?"

"It's my team!" Edward shouts.

"Was," Allen replies. "Was your team. Now they belong to the President and her boy toy, Eric Davis. Besides, I read their files. Sounds like whoever orchestrated this did you a favor."

"Did me a favor?!" Edward is livid. "They're people, goddammit! Sure they're assholes, but that's no excuse for having them kidnapped or executed! And how the hell did you access their files? I didn't give you those."

"That's adorable," Allen chuckles. "If I want access to sealed files, I get them. I wasn't about to let the Department of Sorcery put together a pseudo-military taskforce without knowing who would be on it."

Edward's starting to feel that he may have backed the wrong horse. Allen's always been ruthless in politics, but Edward never realized just what a sociopath he really is until now. While Edward wants to further his own political career and agenda, the thought of good people being killed as a result of it makes him ill. "I can't do this anymore," he says. "I want my files back and that list."

"No," Allen replies coolly. "I'll be hanging on to those. If you want out, you're out, but consider those insurance should your new moral compass guide you somewhere that would negatively impact me."

As much as he'd like to fight on this point, Edward knows his hands are tied. If he tries to bring down Allen, his own career will go up in flames. He ponders how he managed to get himself in this position, and more importantly, how he can get out of it. This isn't the time or place to push how far Allen will go for his own ambitions. "You have nothing to fear from me," Edward tries to assure Allen. "Just know the door swings both ways. You try to take me down, and I'll bring you with me. Take me back to my car."

Allen pushes a button on a small panel next to his seat. The car slowly comes to a stop. Edward looks out the windows, trying to figure out if they're already back in the parking structure. To his surprise they're just parked on a D.C. street somewhere. The driver opens Edward's door from outside. "You can find your own way back," Allen says motioning for Edward to leave.

Edward lets out a frustrated laugh before getting out of the car. Allen's phone rings as the driver closes the rear door. It's the Revelation facility calling. Allen answers the phone, "What's going on?"

"Sir, there's been an incident," the voice on the phone reports.

"I'll be right there."

Edwards receives a call on his cell phone from Celeste as he watches Allen's limo speed away. "Has there been any progress?" he asks after answering the phone.

"Sir, you should get back to the DoS right away," she says on the end.

"Can you send a car?" Edward asks. "I got flat tire. I'll text you the address."

***

Catherine has been waiting at the Eye of Ruin compound with great anticipation for the past few hours. Damian promised Catherine he would rescue her parents if she would provide him some undead troops. She did just that, animating eight dead sorcerers and commanding them to obey Damian's orders. He then departed to storm the DoS with his new soldiers, liberating Catherine's parents. Catherine insisted on going with them, but Damian was firm on her staying behind to remain safe. She eventually conceded so the operation could get started.

It's been hours since they left, and Catherine can't sit still any longer, fervently pacing back and forth in the library. Something must've gone wrong, she thinks. It shouldn't have taken this long. Maybe she messed up the spell and the soldiers went lifeless in the middle of the operation. Has she doomed both her parents and Damian?

Elena happens by the open doorway to the library on her way to Damian's office when she notices Catherine's frantic treading. Over her time here, Catherine has spent the most time with Elena who has overseen her training. This has resulted in a kinship between the two. It's not a feeling Elena's comfortable with, as she typically avoids emotional attachments, but it's crept up on her regardless. She also knows that Catherine can be a powerful ally, and a point will come in the near future where this girl will have to choose where her loyalty lies. Being kind to her could make the difference between her being a friend or a foe.

"You will wear through the floor like that," Elena says as she enters the room.

"I can't help it," Catherine says without breaking stride. "I'm worried."

Elena approaches, forcefully stopping Catherine in her tracks. She sits her down at the reading table. "There is nothing to worry about," Elena says with a hand on Catherine's shoulder. "I have seen their success in a vision."

"Are your visions always accurate?" Catherine asks, showing a bit of relief.

"Most of the time," Elena says honestly.

Perhaps honesty wasn't the right choice for the situation as Catherine's face washes over with anxiety once more. "So there *is* a chance I messed something up?" Catherine questions with dread.

"Why do you not believe in yourself?" Elena asks.

"I don't know," Catherine shrugs. "I'm new to all of this. I was raised thinking that sorcerers were bad, so when I discovered that I was one, I was ashamed. I kept it to myself and tried to ignore what I was. It wasn't until coming here that learned it's okay."

Upon saying this, Catherine realizes that while she has fear of her parents not returning, she also has fear about how they'll react if they do. Will they be happy to see her? Will they be accept her and be proud of her, or will they condemn her for being magic-kind? These thoughts spiral into her fears and create quite the emotional storm within, causing her eyes to tear up. Elena can see the conflict, but has no idea what will calm her. "The world is a harsh place, child," she says. "And it does not get better when you grow up. You must learn to trust in yourself, regardless of what others say or do because inevitably, people will let you down. You have power like no other. We have both seen this, so no more doubts. No more tears."

Elena's words are not the comfort that Catherine was looking for, but somehow it helps. It occurs to her that when she arrived, she was a victim and now she's not. She has knowledge about who she is in the world of magic and fellow sorcerers that she can trust. Catherine decides then and there to no longer live in fear. If her parents can't come to terms with who she is now, then they can be without a daughter. "Thank you, Elena," Catherine says while abruptly standing up.

To Elena's surprise, Catherine wraps her arms around her in a heartfelt hug. She's really not used to this, but Elena gives in to the moment and hugs her back. As much as Elena has given Catherine the tools to survive, she in turn has received something from this young girl as well.

When Elena joined the Eye of Ruin, she was in a dark place. She had only known the life of a soldier until she was cast out for being a sorcerer. Russia has taken a much more radical anti-magic stance than the rest of the world. Elena was a trained killer with no country to fight for. She came to America in hopes there would be change, and, while its military embraces magic, there was still so much bigotry everywhere else she began to resent humans, cursing them as the Cassus. Damian sold her on a better future with magic-kind in the seat of power.

Since becoming Damian's right-hand, their campaign of fear and terror has been non-stop. Elena doesn't question or regret their actions, but she does acknowledge all the violence has made her even more emotionless than when she started. She's an unfeeling cog in the Eye of Ruin war machine and it wasn't until seeing Catherine's vulnerability that she discovered her own.

Elena convinces Catherine to return to her quarters to try to get some rest until Damian returns to the compound. Her room is very plain, much like military barracks. There is a twin bed, locker, dresser, and a desk with a wooden chair. At the back of the room is a small bathroom that adjoins with the quarters next door.

Catherine tosses and turns in her bed, but can't seem to fall asleep. She's restless from a mix of anxiety and excitement. The compound is particularly quiet right now which makes the noise Catherine suddenly hears from the bathroom even more unsettling. It sounds like some very wheezy, labored breathing. She's never heard the sound before, nor is she aware of anyone having asthma. Nevertheless, she gets up and goes to the door. "Are you okay in there?" she asks, after knocking on the bathroom door.

There's no answer. She knocks again. "Hello?" she asks hoping for a response.

Again, there is no answer, and the breathing has also stopped. It sounded serious, so she decides to open the door in case someone has passed out. The room is dark as she enters it. She flips on the light to find the bathroom is empty. She knocks on the door to the adjoining room. "Is anyone in there?" she asks.

She gets no response and assumes that someone must be messing with her until the sound of wheezing starts coming from back in her own room. Catherine spins around quickly, rushing into the room in hopes of catching the culprit. The room is empty, and now she starts getting a bit weirded out. A cold chill shoots down her spine. "Liar," a raspy voice whispers in her ear.

Catherine turns to see who's talking, but again finds nothing. She lets out a slight yelp when a knock at her door gives her a scare. The door opens, revealing Damian on the other side. He enters the room with a look of concern on his face. "Is everything okay?" he asks while looking around.

"I'm fine," she answers, unsure of what just happened. "I just…had a bad dream."

"Well, I may have something to cheer you up," Damian says while extending a hand for Catherine to take hold of.

Catherine was so disturbed by what just happened that it only now hits her that Damian is standing in her room which must mean that he got her parents. She doesn't take Damian's hand, but rather darts past him into the hallway. To her disappointment, the hall is empty. "They're not here," she says sullenly.

"No, they're not," Damian replies while walking into the hall himself. "But they are in the conference room."

The walk to the conference room feels like it takes an eternity for Catherine. All the emotions that have been battling within her the past few hours are at their strongest now. She stops short of the double-doors to the room, taking a couple of deep breaths to calm down. Damian puts a hand on her shoulder. "It's going to be okay," he says.

Catherine finally pushes the meeting room doors open. Sitting at the round table, in orange prison jumpsuits, are her parents. They look as though they've had a rough time, as they're unkempt and borderline malnourished. As they turn towards the sound of the door opening, all the tension on their faces melts away at seeing Catherine. They both spring up and run over to embrace their daughter. Tears stream down her mother's face, and her father isn't far off. This is exactly how Catherine hoped their reunion would be, but it's not what she expected. She's so overwhelmed with joy that she can't help but cry as well.

Gia is also in the room, sitting on the opposite end of the polished-stone table. She stands up when Damian enters the room. She's no longer wearing her Carcer prison suit, having acquired some of her own clothes. She wears ripped up, stone-washed jeans and a purple shirt with word "RAMONES" over a picture of the band on the front. She walks over to Damian, and they share some hushed words before she leaves the room.

Damian grabs both door handles and prepares to close up the room with him outside of it. "I'm going to leave you three for now," he says. "Let me know if you need anything."

"Thank you," Catherine replies.

Damian closes the doors, leaving Catherine alone with her parents. He escorts Gia back to his office, where they find Elena waiting for them. Damian moves past his desk to his chair. Gia and Elena sit opposite him. "It was a very successful test." Damian is elated. "She's ready."

"We may have a problem with the facility," Elena replies.

"What are you talking about?" Damian questions.

"While you were gone, I had a vision of the government's team discovering it," She answers.

"Is this a future event, or has it already happened?"

"Already happened."

"Alright," Damian says in contemplation. "Looks like we're going to need to do this extraction right away."

"We need to talk about that," Elena says in a serious tone.

Damian gets the feeling he's not going to like this "talk." He looks to Gia. "Can you start prepping the troops to mobilize?" His question is more of an order. "We may be heading out shortly."

"Fine," Gia says before teleporting out of the room.

Damian stands and walks around to the front of his desk before leaning back on it. "What's the problem?" he asks.

"The girl would make a strong ally," Elena says. "Would it not be better to have access to all her power rather than extracting a bit of it?"

"Where is this coming from?" Damian questions, suspiciously.

"Nowhere," Elena stands up defensively. "I just see a lot of potential in her."

"She may have potential, but making her a member of the team was never part of the plan," Damian says while easing Elena back into her chair.

Elena pushes Damian off to remain standing. She steps away from him, stopping at the door with her back to him. "That is hypocrisy," Elena says scornfully. "You claim to be making a better world for sorcerers, but does that not include her?"

"She can live in it," Damian replies, hoping to quell Elena's fury. "But I won't jeopardize her safety in creating it."

It would be a very noble sentiment if he actually meant it. Sometimes Damian forgets that he and Elena have spent so much time together she can see his true intentions no matter how convincing the lie. "You don't fear for her safety," Elena faces Damian. "You just fear *her*."

Elena's not wrong. Reapers are the strongest type of sorcerer, and even with his ability to wield both illusion and evocation, Catherine could most likely take him down. It's this fear that prevents him from embracing Elena's pitch. The only way he trusts her power is if it's in his own hands. "What would you have me do?" Damian raises his hands in frustration. "All it would take is one teenage mood swing for her to disrupt our plans."

"Taking her in would prevent her from turning on us," Elena pleads. "She has very little connection with her parents. The only reason she wants to see them so badly is because she is scared. If you change course, *we* could form that unbreakable bond with her."

"What's done is done," Damian replies with a shrug. "I can't take that back now. We proceed as planned."

Elena doesn't question Damian's actions very often, but she feels that it's becoming a more frequent event. She wants to believe he's acting for the good of their mission, but recent visions of Damian sacrificing the lives of their Sentinels to Revelation and murdering Devon for disobedience are making her question his "noble intentions." Elena also knows there is no changing his mind once it's made up, so she yields for the time being. She still believes what they're doing to Catherine is a mistake, but the Eye is Damian's organization, so it's his mistake to make. "As you wish," she says.

\*\*\*

Back in the work room, Catherine sits with her parents, sharing stories of their recent experiences in what feels like a dream scenario. They've never been so caring or complimentary to her before. She believes it's just the joy of freedom being projected onto her. They didn't even bat an eye when she told them of her magical abilities. It seems peculiar considering the negative stance on magic-users they've held her entire life. Perhaps they finally see the benefits since it was magic that rescued them.

"Sweetie, the man who rescued us mentioned you don't really want these gifts you have," her mother says.

"They are pretty creepy," Catherine replies. "And they are the reason we're all in this situation to begin with."

"Cat, this past week has been a nightmare, but it's brought us all closer together," her father says. "I know we've been against magic, but in light of all that's happened, if you want to keep these abilities, you have our blessing."

This is just how she wanted them to react, but something about what he said confuses her. "What do you mean keep these abilities?" she asks.

"Hon, she doesn't know," her mother says.

"Sorry," her father apologizes before elaborating. "While we were being interrogated, we heard talk about a government project that can remove magic from someone permanently. We mentioned it to the man who rescued us, and he says he thinks he knows where the facility is. He thought you might want to go through the procedure once we were back."

"But you don't have to if you don't want to," her mother adds on.

"Whatever you choose, you have our support," her father hugs her.

Catherine wishes someone would pinch her, so she could know if she were awake or not. Could she really be free of these necrotic powers and finally live a normal life? All her desire to be independent fades away, leaving behind the little girl who just wants her mommy and daddy. "I…I don't want them," she says fighting back tears again.

## Chapter 21: Hunting We Will Go

Anthony finds himself in another hospital bed. This time, at the Department of Sorcery in one of their first aid stations. When his body released the burst of electricity back at the Revelation compound, it teleported the entire team back to the DoS, but left him unconscious. He has since woken up, but has been assigned bed rest, as his muscles are very weak from all the electric agitation.

After looking Anthony over, Emmanuel attempts to make sense of what happened outside the Revelation facility. Eric waits with him, looking on in hopes of good news. "I 'ave cast a spell dat will speed up 'is recovery time," Emmanuel says.

"That's good," Eric replies. "Does he have his magic back?"

"I do not t'ink so," Emmanuel answers. "His ability to draw in outside arcane energy 'as been cut off which is why he cannot cast. Somehow de torture stored up de electrical energy inside 'im allowing one spell to be used in an emergency when 'is emotions ran high."

"So...he's not better..." Eric laments.

"No," Emmanuel affirms. "I am afraid not."

Emmanuel and Eric leave the DoS to meet everyone back at Eric's apartment. He sent everyone over with a key before he and Emmanuel checked on Anthony. Until they figure out who they can trust, Eric doesn't want to discuss anything at the Department of Sorcery.

Upon arriving, Eric can see that morale is low and everyone is physically worn out. Andrea's gunshot wound was healed earlier by Emmanuel, but she keeps rubbing her arm where she was struck. Jasmine sits on the couch looking fidgety, as though she has somewhere to be. Benjamin's at the counter, slowly picking toppings off of the cold pizza that Eric had picked up earlier. Trace shouts at someone on the other end of his cell phone. He hangs up and throws the phone shortly after Eric and Emmanuel arrive. "Easy, those things aren't cheap," Eric says.

"We finally got a location lock on those trackers," Trace responds in a foul tone. "Only when the Marshals got there, they discovered they'd been following the trackers themselves. They'd been dug out and attached to a drone that seemingly was going through portals that had been left open for brief periods. Looks like whoever was running it just stopped. I guess they thought we'd chased our tails long enough. The worst part is this definitely means there's a mole. Either in the Marshals service, the prison staff, or at the DoS."

"At least that narrows it down," Benjamin says sarcastically.

Jasmine is too overwrought to be focused on the information being presented. She steps up to Eric hastily. "I need to attend to a personal matter," she says forcefully.

"We're in the middle of a serious situation right now," Eric replies. "What sort of personal matter?"

"It's personal," Jasmine answers with a tightened jaw.

"You're going to have to do better than that," Eric crosses his arms.

"I can't talk about it."

"Then you can't go."

"You want to try and stop me?"

The entire mood of the room becomes very tense. Jasmine looks ready to throw blows and Eric looks ready to defend himself. No one is seated any longer in case they need to jump in and separate them. Emmanuel pushes between Jasmine and Eric with surprising strength for his stature. "Enough of dis!" he exclaims. "Jasmine, tell 'im, or I will."

It takes a few moments for Jasmine to actually stand down, but when she does she reluctantly relays the story of her family and the snakeheads to everyone in the room. She has a hard time trusting, but it does feel good to get it off her chest. The people in this room have been some of the most trustworthy she's met. If there is a chance of getting her family back, maybe it lies with them.

"When I fought de t'ugs, I absorbed a bit of their life essence," Emmanuel says. "Enough dat Andrea could use it to track dere previous whereabouts."

"Shit." Eric lets out a deep breath. "Okay, I need to report this facility we found to the President right away. Benjamin, can you work with Warden McRory? See if you can figure out another way to track the escaped convicts. Jasmine, you, Andrea, and Emmanuel have four hours to see what you find out about these snakeheads. If you find them, have the DoS provide you with a Transporter, but I don't want you going after them without me. Call me as soon as you have something and we'll go together. Are we clear?"

Everyone agrees before dispersing on their tasks. Eric leaves to head over to the White House to meet the President. His information could be given over the phone, but just like at the DoS, someone might be listening that shouldn't be. A face to face is the only thing he'll trust.

Trace and Benjamin remain at Eric's apartment brainstorming ways of tracking the convicts or the Eye of Ruin. Benjamin shares everything he can remember about Damian from the days they ran together in London.

Jasmine, Andrea, and Emmanuel head back over to the Department of Sorcery. They head to the arcane training room so as not to be disturbed. At this hour, no one will be using it. When they arrive, Emmanuel explains to Andrea what they need to do. "You will cast your spell normal," he instructs. "But you will draw de energy from me similar to de way I taught you do draw it from Benjamin when you combined magic."

"Okay," Andrea answers with uncertainty.

Accomplishing a combined spell seemed like a miracle the first time, and she's not sure she can do it again. Knowing now the difference between her own arcane essence and that of the world does give her a confidence that didn't exist previously, and when she starts focusing on these energies, she surprisingly detects Emmanuel's almost immediately. It's impossible to ignore the bright arcane aura emanating from within him. Andrea draws from it as she was taught, providing her visions from the eyes of the snakehead thugs. She catches brief glimpses of the events at the hotel before time starts moving backwards. The gangsters pass through a shimmering gateway into what appears to be a gambling den.

A thick cloud of smoke fills the poorly lit room, making it difficult to see at first. When the view finally clears it becomes obvious they are in a mahjong parlor. A few dozen Chinese men, both young and old, are scattered about at various wooden tables, smoking heavily. They gamble while playing the tile-based game of calculation and chance. The raucousness of these inebriated gamblers allows the gangsters to pass through with little notice.

The thugs pass through a set of double-swinging doors leading into a busy commercial kitchen. A handful of cooks prepare a number of fish-based traditional Chinese entrees. This room may be even dingier than the gambling den. The once white walls have a brownish tone and are blackened near the inferno-like stove on top on which sits two massive woks. Cooking grease is everywhere, making the floor slick and the entire building a fire hazard. The thugs move swiftly through the kitchen, passing another set of double-doors leading to the front portion of a restaurant.

This room doesn't have the same seediness as the kitchen or back room, but is rather well decorated in red and jade green with gold trim molding. Decorative lanterns hang from the ceiling, providing soft light on the round tables below. Intricately carved Chinese dragons hang from the walls around the room as though they are keeping watch on the dining room. The restaurant is open and quite busy, with the exception of one table that is sectioned off by a room divider with plum blossoms painted on it.

Still moving in reverse, the gangsters make their way out of the restaurant, but as they do, the lead thug looks back at the secluded table and catches the eye of one man in particular. This dark-haired Asian looks younger than he actually is, even through his scowl. He wears all black, with a button down shirt that is showing more chest than it should, though it almost looks like he's wearing another shirt under it as tattoos cover his skin up to his neck. The man nods to the thugs and points to the kitchen. The thugs then pass through the front door of the restaurant to the sidewalk outside.

The men are in front of the Forbidden Palace restaurant in what appears to be Chinatown somewhere. Andrea notes the address before continuing to scan through images from the point of view of the thugs until it becomes clear that they are in Los Angeles, California. She never sees anyone who might be Jasmine's mother or sister, but she figures the restaurant might be a good place to start.

Andrea ends the spell and relays what she saw to Jasmine and Emmanuel. Jasmine is familiar with the restaurant, having met Qiang and the snakeheads there once or twice to make payments. She is fired up on hearing this news and shuffles the other two off to find a DoS Transporter to take them to California. This is completely against what Eric said to do, and, while Andrea sees herself as a rebel, it doesn't feel right. "Shouldn't we call Eric?" she asks as they hurriedly make their way to operations.

"There's no time!" Jasmine says, dismissing Andrea's inquiry.

Andrea's not the only one having reservations about Jasmine's impulsive behavior. Her emotions and fear are superseding her judgment which means all bets are off when she is face to face with her family's captors once more. Emmanuel guesses, in her current state of mind, Jasmine will act in one of two ways. She'll either crack from fear, catering to their demands, perpetuating the problem indefinitely, or she'll lash out from frustration, creating an enemy of the entire Triad organization.

Arriving at operations, the three find the graveyard shift working. All is quiet, and only a few technicians with low clearance sit at computers crunching data. Fortunately for Jasmine, the DoS does keep a Transporter on site 24 hours a day for emergencies. It's sort of an on-call position where they just hang out in a break room until their services are needed. One of the technicians directs the trio where they can find the teleporter.

Jasmine wastes no time, running down a couple hallways towards the break room with Andrea and Emmanuel in tow. The room they find the Transporter in is built for overnight stays. It has two cots up against a back wall in front of which sits a small couch facing a tv. There is also a small round table next to a kitchenette in the corner that includes full-size refrigerator. The man they're looking for sits on the couch, watching a cooking show on cable. He's dressed in blue slacks and a white long sleeve shirt that has a light blue grid pattern on it. His full head of dark hair and the van dyke beard on his face is well groomed. There is a security badge clipped to his shirt pocket with his picture on it. The name on the badge reads Rion Parsons. He jumps up in a huff when Jasmine barrels into the room. "Are you the Transporter?" Jasmine asks rather rudely.

Rion's not sure who this person is, but she's intense, and he doesn't want to piss anyone off. "Yes," he answers. "What's going on?"

"We need an immediate transport to California," Jasmine replies while handing him a small slip of paper. "Here's the address."

"Just one way?" he asks, looking over the address.

"No, we'll need an exit as well," Jasmine replies.

"Okay," Rion says while getting out his cell phone to plug the address into a search engine.

Transporters, especially more inexperienced ones, need a visual indicator as well as an address in order to successfully teleport to a location. While Rion looks for an image of the restaurant as a reference point, Emmanuel pulls Jasmine aside. "We need to talk about dis," he says.

"Look, I know Eric said to wait for him, but I can't," Jasmine replies curtly. "You're not going to get in trouble for this because I'm going alone."

"Dat is what I t'ought you would say," Emmanuel says with a sigh.

Before she can turn back to tell Rion to hurry up, Jasmine finds herself in a choke hold and a rather good one at that. She's very skilled at hand fighting, knowing a dozen different ways to break a hold, but she can't even find wiggle room in this one. Emmanuel has positioned himself in such a way that even if she were to go limp, forcing him to hold dead weight, he could easily lower himself while maintaining his lock. The last thought through Jasmine's mind before she blacks out is "who is this guy?"

Andrea and Rion look on in stunned horror as Emmanuel lowers Jasmine onto the couch. He sees their faces and attempts to diffuse the situation. "She will be fine," he says. "She's just takin' a short nap."

"What the hell did you do that for?" Andrea asks.

"She was not t'inkin' clearly," Emmanuel answers. "I will go in 'er place."

"She's going to murder you when she wakes up," Andrea says earnestly.

"Dat may be true," Emmanuel says. "But it would seem our team motto is dat it is easier to ask forgiveness dan permission."

"Would someone like to tell me what the fuck is going on?!" Rion asks in a panic.

"I am commandeering da mission," Emmanuel replies. "Same location."

"Okay," Rion says with the pitch of his voice indicating otherwise.

"Give me ten minutes," Emmanuel says.

Rion has never been less sure of anything his entire young life, but he saw how this old man put the beat down on the "imposing chick," so he goes with it. He opens a shimmering portal with a street view of the Forbidden Palace restaurant on the other side. It's late there, and there is little to no street traffic. "You sure this is where you want to go?" Rion asks. "They look closed."

"Dey are open for da business I am seeing dem for," Emmanuel answers.

"Okay." Rion finds himself repeating the word, but still not really feeling it. "I'll open it again in ten minutes, but I'm not going through after you."

Emmanuel takes a look back at Andrea who looks very worried and not just for him, but for Jasmine's family. "Don't worry, I 'ave dealt wit' dese types before," Emmanuel says with a smile before walking through the portal.

***

The President is none too thrilled to be woken up at 3am, but Eric made the matter sound like it was a life or death situation. She throws a robe on over her modest blue pajamas and makes her way to the Roosevelt Room. Located near the Oval Office, this meeting room holds a large conference table and is furnished with reproductions of classic English Baroque styling. The walls are an off-white with white trim adorned with various paintings and plaques. One end of the room is rounded off with a fireplace and doors on either side. The President is informed that Eric is already waiting for her inside as she approaches.

She finds Eric pacing furiously in long strides as he waits for her to arrive. She motions for the Secret Service to wait outside the room before closing the door. "If you wear a hole in the carpet, it's coming out of our pay." She attempts to lighten the mood. "Now what is so important that I'm losing out on the little sleep I already get?"

Eric collects himself while the President sits down at the long table. Light pours onto the wooden surface from a false skylight above. She motions for Eric to join her. He sits and proceeds to bring her up to speed about the attack on the team, the removal of the tracking chips from the Carcer escapees, and the secret facility kidnapping and extracting magic from sorcerers.

The President gets a sick feeling in the pit of her stomach knowing now that there might be a traitor in her midst. The sensation is only made worse by the fact that she thinks she knows who it is. Allen Barber. Though the proposal for Revelation seemed speculative and didn't go over the science behind its pitch, the story of this facility sounds exactly like what Allen had dreamt up. She always knew of his animosity towards magic-kind, but she never thought he would go rogue and do something like this. "I need to contact the FBI and have Allen Barber brought in right away," she says as she stands.

"As in Secretary of Defense Allen Barber?" Eric asks.

"Yes," she answers. "I think he's behind this, but I want to be sure. You're going to take me to see this facility first hand."

The President motions for Eric to lead the way. He slowly stands looking almost like he shouldn't say what he's about to. "Um…Madam President," He says hesitantly. "Do you maybe want to get dressed first?"

In her shock and subsequent haste to act, she forgot that she is still in her pajamas. She takes a second to look down before looking back at Eric and nodding. "You coordinate with security in case he's spotted here," she replies. "I'll go find something more suitable for venturing outside."

\*\*\*

It's about midnight in Los Angeles when Emmanuel steps onto the sidewalk outside the Forbidden Palace. The entire block is done up with Chinese architecture meant to resemble the ancient world of the motherland. The design is a bit of a hodgepodge, mixing ceramic roof designs of the Tang dynasty with the pillars and columns of the Han dynasty, though the average American tourist would never know the difference. It looks to be straight from an old kung fu movie, and that's what generates business.

The sign on the glass door of the restaurant reads "closed," but Emmanuel can see light coming from within. He takes a chance and, to his surprise, finds it unlocked, though he doesn't make it more than a few feet inside before he is accosted by men with guns. It's clear they were expecting someone else, as they relax a bit upon seeing an old man. Emmanuel keeps his hands in the air just to be safe as they escort him to the corner table sectioned off by the decorative partition.

The man from Andrea's vision sits at the table in the same black outfit that would've been from earlier this evening. He sits alone at the table with a ledger and multiple stacks of cash. He counts a stack before making a note in the ledger. Four Chinese men guard the table at a distance, each one armed with either a machine pistol or an easily accessible blade. One of the escorts says something in Mandarin to the man at the table. He looks up at Emmanuel dismissively. "This is the second old man she's sent to fix her problems," the man says, also speaking in Chinese.

"No one sent me," Emmanuel replies in perfect Mandarin.

Every Triad in the room has a raised brow, and the curiosity is enough for the man at the table to stand up to take a closer look at his unexpected guest. "What do you want?" he asks, continuing the conversation in Chinese.

"Qiang, I presume," Emmanuel says.

Now he knows this old man is here for Jasmine as very few outsiders are privy to that name. "If you knew the danger of speaking that name without invitation you would run away, old man," Qiang says as a threat.

"Your name means nothing to me," Emmanuel replies. "But what does the name Haidi Guaiwu mean to you?"

One of the reasons Emmanuel is so adamant about helping Jasmine with the Triads is that the hotel incident was not the first time he'd encountered them. The details of Emmanuel's life would read like the script for an action-adventure movie. When he was a much younger man, he visited China, spending many years there. One of his sorcerer mentors was also a famous martial arts instructor and trained Emmanuel in both until the Triads attempted to shut the school down so they could buy the property for cheap.

Back then, Emmanuel was much more impulsive, acting on emotion rather than intellect. When the school was attacked and his master murdered, Emmanuel led a handful of his fellow students on a warpath against the local Triads. Emmanuel let the streets run red with Triad blood, giving him the nickname "Monster of Haiti." It took him hearing this name to realize what he had become. He left China and made a vow to live a life of peace. It's a vow that was only recently broken. Even though Emmanuel fled the country, the tale of the crazed Haitian not only remained, but spread like wildfire. It became a cautionary story that Triads told their initiates, and while it has waned in recent years, many of the high ranking gangsters still know it.

The only Triad in the room whose eyes acknowledge the name Emmanuel asks about is Qiang. He feels a bit of fear, but also doesn't want to believe that story is real. "It is a myth," Qiang responds.

"It is no myth," Emmanuel continues in Qiang's native language. "And if you do as I say, you will not have to find out the hard way."

Qiang motions for his men to stand down for the moment. "What do you want?" he asks hostilely.

"I want Jasmine's mother and sister brought to me unharmed, right now," Emmanuel says without backing down.

"I knew it!" Qiang shouts. "I knew that bitch sent you!"

"She didn't send me." Emmanuel stops Qiang's tirade. "If it were up to her, she would've come back with your thugs and would continue paying while you string her along. You and I both know that it will never stop so long as you have the power, so I am taking that from you. I killed the men you sent. If you harm her family, or if I ever hear you bother her again, I will kill all of you and burn down everything you care about. Do I make myself clear?"

Qiang is so enraged he can't even speak. If the stories of this Haitian are true, he can't risk pissing him off. He decides to cut his losses. He's already made a small fortune off of Jasmine's payments anyway. He nods to Emmanuel that he agrees. "Then bring them to me," Emmanuel demands.

Qiang begrudgingly orders two of his men to go fetch Jasmine's mother and sister. The guards disappear into the kitchen for a few minutes before returning with a two Chinese women, one slightly younger than Emmanuel, and the other around the same age as Jasmine. Both women are ragged and skittish. They don't know what's going; they live everyday in fear, so the idea of being released isn't on their minds at all. The guard pushes them towards Emmanuel who gently holds his hands out in a non-aggressive way. "It will be okay," he says in Chinese. "I will take you to Jasmine. You will be safe."

Tears immediately form in the eyes of both women. Could they really be leaving this hell they've known for so long? Emmanuel starts to guide them towards the front door, being sure to stay in between the women and the snakeheads. Just as they get to the door Qiang shouts from the corner, "Enjoy your victory today because this isn't over, Haidi Guaiwu!"

***

Back at Eric's apartment, Trace and Benjamin have been brainstorming ideas on how to recapture the Carcer escapees. It hasn't been a very productive meeting of the minds. Trace is a tad paranoid since finding out the prisoners removed their trackers. Every government agency that Benjamin suggests might be able to help, Trace immediately shoots down. The NSA is running some of the most advanced facial recognition software available, but Trace refuses to reach out because he thinks there are spies everywhere. Benjamin finally reaches a point of exhaustion. "Aren't you taking this a bit seriously?" Benjamin asks. "I mean, come on, you're the warden; it's not your job to personally track down these prisoners anyway."

Trace plops down on Eric's couch. "I know that, but these assholes came into my house and took my prisoners," he replies. "I feel obligated to do everything I can to get them back."

Benjamin makes his way over to the kitchen and begins rifling through Eric's fridge, which is almost as bare as his apartment. He finds some deli meat and cheese for making sandwiches, a leftover takeout container, an expired carton of milk, and three bottles of beer. Benjamin grabs one of the beers. "Appalling, simply appalling," he whispers to himself as he closes the door.

Benjamin heads around the counter back towards the living room. He tosses the beer to Trace who catches it. "It's not as if you designed the place." Benjamin attempts to make Trace feel better. "You just manage it. If a part of the system fails, it's not your fault…oh wait, no yeah that's your whole job isn't it? To make sure it doesn't fail."

"You can stop trying to cheer me up," Trace says before opening the beer and taking a big swig. "Besides, the system didn't fail. There's a mole I'm telling you."

"Isn't it possible they just divined the location of the trackers on the prisoners?" Benjamin asks as he sits down next to Trace. "The Eye has a very powerful Prophet working for them. They managed to give Andrea a false vision and anyone that strong could easily…"

"Did you intentionally trail off just then?" Trace asks.

"What?" Benjamin stands, as though he's just had an epiphany. "No, but I just got an idea.  What if we tricked them?"

"How do you mean?" Trace is not following.

"Andrea and I do what their Prophet and Damian did to her," Benjamin explains. "We give a false vision about the DoS finding some evidence at one of their jump sites that would compromise their actual location.  If it works, they might dispatch a team to the location to clean said evidence before it's discovered. Then we have a team waiting to apprehend on site."

"That might be just crazy enough to work," Trace says with renewed resolve. "Let's meet the others at the DoS."

"What about the 'spies'?" Benjamin asks sarcastically.

"Look if you're wrong, and this plan doesn't work, I'll be right back to 'they have eyes and ears everywhere'," Trace answers.

"Fair enough."

\*\*\*

Jasmine begins to regain consciousness, and the first thoughts through her head before she opens her eyes are that she's going to murder an old man.  She doesn't know what he was thinking, nor does she care right now.  Her eyes pop open as she springs up, ready to pounce, but her fury is cut down immediately. Her heart races, and she feels weak due to the sight before her. She is still in the break room at the Department of Sorcery, and while she expects to see Emmanuel there, she finds she's alone in the room with her mother and sister. Jasmine has no time to say anything before they both rush forward and hug her.

Jasmine's mother and sister wept quite a lot during their captivity. They were tormented and forced to endure foul living conditions while being in a constant state of starvation or dehydration. These are not those tears, but rather tears of joy at being reunited with Jasmine. Words are not even spoken at first. The three women just hold on to each other as though this all may be a dream that could end if they let go.

Jasmine's mother and sister relay the story of how Emmanuel rescued them and what Qiang said as they left. Jasmine sets off to find Emmanuel and Andrea, but she refuses to let her family out of her sight for fear they will vanish like the illusions she believes they might be. They make their way up to the Guardian wing to find Emmanuel and Andrea giving Rion a tour. His mouth is agape, and there is clear jealousy in his eyes. "So you guys get this whole area and I get a break room?" he asks in feigned outrage.

"We don't live here," Andrea replies. "It's just for operations."

"Still, how do I get this gig?" Rion asks. "I'm so bored where I am. Today is the first time I've actually gotten to transport someone...or anything since I took the job."

"We don't make those decisions, but we can put in a good word for you with our boss," Andrea replies with a bit of uncertainty in her voice.

"Oh my god!" Rion's ecstatic. "That would be awesome! Whatever you want teleported, I'll teleport it! I don't care, I just don't want to be stuck watching soaps in a tiny windowless room for ten hours a day."

Emmanuel notices Jasmine and her family at the entrance to the wing. "Unfortunately, right now you do need to go back to dat room," Emmanuel says while motioning in the direction of Jasmine.

Rion turns to see what's being pointed out. Upon laying eyes on Jasmine, he understands why he must leave. Things were pretty intense earlier, and he isn't a part of this. "Right," he says with a nod. "I'll follow up later."

Rion sheepishly walks out, passing Jasmine and her family as they move inward. Andrea has to stop herself from laughing when she sees Rion high-fiving himself with elation on his way out. Emmanuel moves up to meet Jasmine half way. "I am sorry for earlier," he says, expecting some form of retaliation.

Jasmine's no longer angry with him, just perplexed. "Why did you do it?" she asks. "They're not your family, and I could've handled it."

"Yes, you would've 'andled it and put a price on your and dere 'eads for de rest of your lives," Emmanuel answers. "I 'ave been where you were, and I wanted to spare you da feelin' that comes after you kill for revenge."

"Thank you."

## Chapter 22: The Best Laid Plans

Allen has been scrambling since he heard about the breakout at the Revelation facility. He's not sure who'll be coming, but he's certain someone will be. Fortunately, he has a handful of empty buildings registered to dummy corporations he can relocate his pet project to. Time is of the essence, so even though he doesn't like getting his hands dirty, he's on site to make sure no stone is left unturned. His normally pressed designer suit is wrinkled and marred by grease from moving equipment. Sweat beads heavily on his brow while his breathing is extremely labored. Though exhausted, he finds the act of putting in some hard work very patriotic.

A fleet of white windowless vans have just been loaded in the yard outside the warehouse. They are being watched over by a bunch of Secret Service knockoffs in black suits and sunglasses. Allen ventures back into the building one more time to make sure everything is accounted for before heading to the new site.

Allen finds Elijah in the extraction room. The last of the machines has been boarded up in a wooden crate and is being wheeled out by two of the sunglasses crew. "That looks to be everything, Doctor," Allen says. "Let's get out of here and let the cleaners do their work. I've left a surprise for anyone who may come after."

"Indeed," Elijah responds.

Allen and Elijah escort the extraction crate to one of the vans. The sky overhead is suddenly shrouded in a blanket of dark clouds. A heavy rain begins to pour down, causing many of the guards to remove their sunglasses. Within minutes, everyone outside is drenched. As soon as the extractor is loaded, Elijah hops in the van with it. Allen orders everyone into their respective vans, with orders to follow his limo. He then climbs into the back of said limo and leads the caravan out of the gated lot.

The new location is a good forty-five minutes away, but no one seems to be onto the original facility yet, so things are looking up. This close call has made Allen realize he needs sever ties to the Eye of Ruin and burn it to the ground. He can always find other "volunteers" for Revelation, but Damian and anything that could connect the Eye to Allen must be turned to ash.

About thirty minutes into the trip, Allen gets an alert on his cell phone. He reaches into his jacket pocket for the phone only to realize that it's not wet nor is it damp. In fact, it's not even cold. Allen pats himself down to discover that no part of him has any indication at all that he was in the rain just a half hour ago. His hair is completely dry and still gelled as it was when he left his home earlier in the evening. The reality of the situation slowly sets in, and Allen orders his driver to stop the car.

The eight white vans have also pulled over to the side of the unpopulated road. Allen emerges from his car looking up at the night sky. It's a very clear night, no clouds anywhere on the horizon. The bad feeling Allen had in the limo is growing. He runs to the van that contains the extraction machine, yanking open the back doors to find it empty. There's no crate, and there's no Elijah. Allen's not sure when, but, at some point, Damian must've been there and put up a very elaborate illusion. The extraction machine and the doctor to run it are still back at the warehouse.

As he runs up the line of vans, Allen shouts obscenities and orders for the guards to follow him. He hops into the limo and the driver makes a quick u-turn, heading back the way they came with the vans following suit.

Inside the limo, Allen tries frantically to call Elijah to warn him, but he's getting no answer. He's in such a fluster that he overlooks the missed call from his office. Allen's too worried about Damian's intentions to care about a voicemail. If Damian did something malicious, Elijah is most likely already dead. Allen plans to slap a collar on this illusionist and then gouge out his eyes with his own two hands.

*** 

Approximately thirty minutes earlier at the Revelation facility, Elijah sits in the extraction chamber waiting for crew members to come help him take the machine apart. He's surprised when Allen shows up instead. Elijah was previously warned that a Ghost might show up appearing as Allen, so the two arranged a key phrase and response. If "Allen" speaks the wrong response, Elijah will know he's dealing with a doppelgänger. "Secretary Barber, what an unexpected pleasure." Elijah grasps a pistol hidden under his workstation as he prepares to say the key phrase. "I recalibrated the machine sixteen degrees as you requested."

Elijah waits nervously for Allen's reply. He doesn't want to shoot someone. Sure, he has no problem torturing them; in fact, he sort gets off on it, but killing directly sounds so unscientific. Allen looks over at the extraction chair before turning back towards Elijah. "I thought we agreed on twelve," he answers.

Elijah breathes a sigh of relief when he hears the correct response. Unfortunately, he and Allen don't really understand how illusion magic works. Damian's magic affects the mind, often using its own thoughts and memories against itself. In this situation, Elijah's own thoughts fed him the proper phrase response through the illusion. "So we did." Elijah releases his grip on the pistol. "Are we moving this thing or what?"

"Yes, but some of the help is having a problem with one of the other devices," Allen says. "I need you to go set them straight. I'll wait here and get this thing loaded when they arrive with the crate."

"Never a dull moment," Elijah says before rushing out of the room.

While this scene was playing out for Elijah, a separate one was being projected in the same room, but for Catherine. Damian was able to smuggle Catherine, Elena, and Gia into the facility unnoticed due to a third, more potent, illusion that was affecting the entire facility. This is the one that convinced Allen he had the extractor. It's taking every ounce of focus for Damian to maintain three illusions of this scale, but once Allen and the caravan depart, he can drop one and focus more on Catherine.

Upon entering the extraction chamber, Catherine doesn't see the cold torture cell with a monstrous machine at its heart, but instead a brightly lit room with a chair similar to something one might see at a dentist's office. Gia waits outside while Damian and Elena walk Catherine into the room. "This is it," Damian says spinning around with his arms out like the showman he is. "This is where the magic happens."

Catherine approaches the chair. She looks at it for a moment. It doesn't look scary, but the concept of having magic removed sounds painful. "Will it hurt?" she asks.

"You may be tired after," Damian says warmly. "But I can promise you there will be no pain."

"And we will be here the whole time," Elena adds.

Catherine climbs into the chair while Damian steps behind the shiny computer console. "All you need to do is attempt to cast the most powerful spell you know," he explains. "This will allow the machine to lock onto the arcane source of your magic and remove it. Are you ready?"

If this machine works, she could be free of her grim abilities forever, so if she's having second thoughts, now's the time to act on them. Catherine takes a minute to reflect on everything that's happened to her recently. When she met Damian, she was afraid of these abilities, but after being taught how to use and control them, the fear has been replaced with confidence. In fact, only a few short hours ago, she was resolved to embrace being a sorcerer, but after being reunited with her parents, she longs to be normal again. She's twisted up inside. On one hand, she could be a regular teenager with parents who love her. On the other hand, she could use her magic for good. She almost laughs at the thought. What good can come from death magic? No, she thinks, she'll be better off without these gifts. "I'm ready," she says with certainty.

"Alright, begin casting the spell," Damian says.

Even without a corpse to focus on, Catherine starts the incantation while drawing in arcane energy. Damian, having familiarized himself with the process after watching Elijah on previous visits, starts the extraction process. Catherine feels the magic being drawn out from within her. It leaves her feeling the exhaustion of just having run an aggressive mile in gym class. "All done," Damian says.

"That was quick," Catherine barely utters while struggling to keep her head up.

Elena gets a vision of Allen pulling back into the warehouse lot with his fleet of vans and guards. He looks extremely hostile, and his guards are locked and loaded as they file out of their vehicles. Elena makes her way over to Damian. "Your friend is on his way back," she whispers.

"Have Gia take you and Catherine back," Damian responds in kind. "I'll finish up here."

Elena helps Catherine out of the chair. She is barely able to stand on her own and relies heavily on Elena to walk out of the room. Once they are gone, Damian drops the façade, revealing the sinister room beneath it once again. He pulls out a bracer similar to the one he's already wearing which contains the barrier spell inside it. He places the metallic cuff in the machine containing the glass cylinder that now has a gaseous darkness within it. The bracer fits directly under the cylinder that holds the spell essence.

Damian heads back to the console to complete the infusion process. He activates the sequence and a blinding beam strikes the cuff from the cylinder. The metal of the bracer glows as though it's being heated in a forge. After a few minutes, the cylinder is empty and beam ceases. A cooling liquid sprays onto the heated metal, creating a steam cloud that engulfs the entire machine. Damian waits patiently for the dense mist to disperse before collecting the object of his every desire.

The bracer is still warm to the touch, but Damian can't wait for it to cool completely. He puts it on and can immediately feel the strength of the magic within. Now that he has what he wants, Allen's usefulness has run its course, and Damian can think of no better way to give his new toy a test run than on some hired goons.

Just as in Elena's vision, Allen's limo and his army of vans roll back into the lot. Allen's angry, but he's not stupid. He falls back behind his legion of armed bodyguards while they advance on the main doors to the facility. Damian appears on top of the building to taunt his would-be attackers. "Allen, you brought friends!" he calls down.

The guards immediately open fire on Damian, unleashing a hail of bullets that hit nothing. The image of Damian vanishes, leaving the guards scanning the area for the real target. "They just never learn," Damian's voice comes from all around. "Catena fulgur!"

A bolt of lightning arcs from behind Allen, hitting the center most guard, before chaining to every other. The surge of the electricity causes each man to spasm, firing their guns uncontrollably in all directions. Some of them are killed by the friendly fire while the rest die from the electricity. Allen looks on in horror at the line of smoldering corpses as Damian appears behind him. "Look at the bright side," Damian says with a smile. "At least you don't have to pay them."

"You son of a bitch!" Allen shouts as he faces his tormentor.

"Come come, we both knew this day was inevitable," Damian says. "You're just upset that I have the upper hand."

"Go ahead and kill me," Allen says defiantly. "You'll just reinforce my entire stance on your kind."

"I don't care about public opinion, Mr. Secretary," Damian says menacingly. "I'm a terrorist, remember?"

"Then get it over with!"

"Oh I'm not going to kill you, Allen," Damian says as he raises his left arm with the new bracer on it. "They are."

Allen looks over his shoulder to see what Damian's pointing at. All of his guards are back on their feet, but something is not right about them. The way they're standing, staring blankly ahead as though they have no cognitive function. They seem catatonic until they all take a step forward in unison. It's quickly followed by another step and another until Allen realizes they are closing on him. With undead soldiers on one side and a psycho with magical powers on the other, Allen knows his time is up.

***

A short time later, the local police and FBI are swarming the scene. Red and blue flashing lights dance on the sides of the tall warehouses, illuminating the night sky. Dozens of uniformed officers have the perimeter taped off while two teams of FBI agents, clad in bulletproof vests and blue jackets with their moniker on the back, sweep the inside of the facility. A medical examiner's team investigates the horrific scene in front of the row of white vans.

Bodies are strewn about in a semi-circle surrounding the mauled remains of what appears to be Allen Barber. No one at the ME's office has ever seen anything quite like this, and they've seen just about every cause of death imaginable. They're equating it to a really nasty bear attack…only far more vicious. They've erected partitions to keep any press that may arrive from filming the grisly scene.

Eric and the President arrive ten minutes after the site has been secured on the outside. The President's security detail fans out so the President can move about freely with Eric at her side. She emerges from her armored limo in a tan pantsuit. She has no makeup on, and her hair has been hastily tied back. She is preceded by Eric, and they are both greeted by Special Agent Dana Richards, the lead on the scene. Just like her fellow agents, this forty year old, dark haired senior agent sports ballistic body armor under a blue jacket. "Madam President, we've secured the site." Dana walks and talks, escorting the President towards the warehouse entrance. "We've got quite the mess here, but the good news is we have a witness and a suspect in custody. The Secretary's driver claims to have seen everything. We have someone taking his statement as we speak. We also found an Elijah Randall wandering the halls. He seemed really disoriented and confused when we found him."

"And the Secretary?" Eric inquires.

"It's uh…not a pretty sight I'm afraid," Dana cringes at the thought of what she saw.

"How?" the President asks.

"We can't say for sure," Dana answers. "The ME's office is still going over the scene."

This isn't the news the President was hoping for. Sure she and Allen never saw eye to eye, and the realization of his depravity was bone-chilling, but she'd never wish harm upon him. It takes her a moment to fully process the news. "Um…anything else to report?" she asks.

"Each of these vans is loaded with heavy equipment," Dana reports. "We've got the lab boys on the way in to tag everything. We also found cameras posted around the area. I've got a team inside going room to room looking for the security feed."

"I'd like to see inside myself," the President says.

"With all due respect, Madam President," Dana replies. "I'd prefer if you waited until my team is done sweeping the entire facility."

Screams erupt from inside the warehouse, followed by the rapid sound of gunfire. More gunfire and screaming quickly follow. The Secret Service agents leap into action, surrounding the President and moving her back towards her car. The patrolmen and FBI in the area draw their side arms, aiming at the doors to the warehouse. The shooting and screaming from inside stop abruptly with a long moment of silent tension following. The doors finally fly open as an FBI agent comes barreling out of the building, pursued by the two nightmare creatures Eric had encountered here earlier.

One of the creature's tongues skewers the fleeing agent, pulling him into its enormous razor-toothed maw. There's a violent spray of blood, and the agent is no more. The rest of the law enforcement in the area open fire on the beasts, but again they seem to absorb the bullets in their mouths. People begin to panic, breaking formation to run. Their prey are scattered, and so the beasts prepare to strike. One of the lion-like animals lunges forward, only to smack into an invisible wall. The agent whose life was just saved by Eric's barrier collapses in a faint.

The other missile eater tries to jump in another direction only to be stopped in mid-air as well. Just like with the terrorists at Liberty Island, Eric has constructed a barrier designed to keep the creatures in. After a couple attempts to break out, the beasts become incensed. One of them presses its open mouth against the barrier and its teeth begin rotating like when it's devouring. Eric can feel the teeth acting like a drill against his magic shield. It won't take long for them to punch through. "Get back!" Eric yells to everyone in the area.

The police and FBI usher the medical examiners back to a safe distance without actually knowing what that might be in this situation. Eric has to think quickly, as he knows these things will kill everything if they get out. He decides to attempt Emmanuel's lesson by drawing from his own power. As he reaches for this internal energy, his thoughts are on both containing and destroying these things. His focus is shattered as the beast breaks through the barrier. It acts quickly, shooting its tongue forward at Eric, striking him in the leg. The pain is excruciating, causing him to drop the barrier altogether.

Eric feels the flesh in his leg tear as the beast begins to reel him in with its barbed snare. It's seeming like his flesh will give before he gets pulled in, so the second beast shoots its tongue at Eric, landing a better hit in his upper left shoulder. Now the creatures work in tandem, pulling him into their mouths. He knows when they finish with him everyone else is next, and he can't let that happen. He tries one last time to create a barrier from his own power. Maybe it was the adrenaline or the fear of failing to save more lives, but he feels the arcane force project from within him and surround the creatures again. The force of the wall closing up severs both creatures' tongues, sending them into a frenzy within the invisible sphere.

Contain and destroy. The words repeat in Eric's head until the barrier begins to shrink. It's a minor amount at first, but the beasts notice. It stops them for a moment as they begin to cautiously look around. It shrinks further, causing the missile eaters to freak out once more; this time, their range of movement has decreased significantly. The barrier continues to decrease in diameter until it suddenly implodes, crushing everything inside it into nothingness.

Eric can tell he's losing blood fast, but he takes a quick look around to see that everyone else appears unharmed. He can see the President shouting orders in the distance, and members of the medical examiner's team are running his way before he blacks out.

## Chapter 23: Life After Death

Damian returns to the Eye of Ruin's headquarters with a very
pleased smile across his face; Allen is out of his way permanently,
and he has Catherine's power while still retaining her trust. He'd
like to see Eric and his band of sorcerers try to stop him now.
They'll be crushed under his might only to rise as slaves in his
army. The thought of it makes him want to launch an attack right
now, but he has his sights set on the White House once again, and
impulsiveness will not win the day.

      The question now is what to do with Catherine now that he
has what he wants. Elena's point about her being a strong ally is
valid, but were she to turn, she would be a handful. It would be so
much easier to kill her than allocating time and energy to keep her
loyalty, especially since that commodity seems hard to come by
these days. Damian never thought Elena would question his
decisions, and yet, she has over this child. He has a suspicion that
if he were to kill the girl, he would have to kill Elena too.

      Damian decides it's too big a decision to make right now.
He'll wait until after he takes the White House to see what's in his

best interest. After all, once he has the country, finding a new Prophet should be no problem.

***

Catherine is back in her room at the Eye of Ruin's compound. Her parents have been moved into the adjoining room until they are all permitted to go back home. The mattress on Catherine's twin bed is uncomfortably firm, but she's resting easier on it tonight. Knowing that she'll soon be living a normal life back home has her drifting off until an unsettling whisper forces her eyes open. "Liar," it says.

Catherine recognizes it as the same voice she heard earlier before Damian arrived back with her parents. What creep is in her room again? She springs out of the bed, flipping on the lights to find no one yet again. Upon checking, she finds that the bathroom is also empty. Someone has to be doing this, she thinks to herself. This is a place filled with magic-users so the idea isn't farfetched. She decides to look into the hallway in hopes of finding this prankster, but before she reaches the door, she hears the sickly breathing that preceded the initial disturbance.

Once again, she spins in place, looking all around. The room is empty. "Who's there?" she finally asks.

"Liar!" the disembodied voice angrily repeats.

"I'm not a liar!" Catherine says back with some attitude.

"Liar," the voice continues. "Damian is a liar."

What is this voice she's hearing? What is it talking about? What has Damian lied about? "Who are you?" Catherine asks. "Show yourself."

"I am nobody," the voice responds, with an air of melancholy. "Because I'm dead."

Catherine doesn't know who's pulling this stunt, but she doesn't find it funny at all. "You...you can't be dead." She almost stumbles over the words. "I can't talk to the dead anymore. I can't."

"But I am dead," the voice says. "Murdered."

"Prove it!" Catherine demands. "Show yourself!"

"That's not up to me..."

Catherine knows she's going to regret it, but she was told her abilities were gone, so she has to try. She closes her eyes, thinking about the voice, visualizing it in her head. She sees a young man. He seems familiar. She sees short dark hair, a black shirt, and blue jeans. Catherine opens her eyes to find a ghastly sight before her. Devon stands in front of her with a large cavity torn into his chest. His entire mid-section is a bloody mess with broken ribs and entrails hanging out. His body is spectral with a green hue, though he stands and moves as though he were a physical form. It could be a really good illusion, but Catherine can sense this is a real ghost. "Devon?" she asks.

"The one and only," he says in a gurgling wheeze.

"Why are you here?"

"I don't know," Devon responds. "You drew me here. I died, then there was nothing, and now I'm here."

"I couldn't have brought you here," Catherine argues with the spirit. "Damian removed my magic abilities."

The most disturbingly disgusting noise resonates from within Devon's ghost as he attempts to laugh. "You don't really believe that, do you?" he asks. "Damian's had eyes on your abilities since our girl at the DoS tipped him off to your existence. You talking to me is proof that you still have your magic. He lied to you. It's what he does."

Catherine doesn't want to believe this about the man who went out of his way to rescue her parents. "No, you're wrong," she replies while shaking her head.

"Your loyalty is adorable," Devon replies. "Do you know what my loyalty got me? A spike through the back from our fearless leader's girlfriend because I questioned his plan. He's a monster, and you shouldn't trust him. I'll bet it was his idea for you to have your magic removed."

"It was my parents idea," Catherine rebuts. "After Damian freed them and brought them here."

"Look, if you believe in him, that's on you," Devon says. "But knowing that he's an illusionist, I'd take a closer look at those parents of yours."

The apparition of Devon starts to fade away. "Wait!" Catherine shouts. "Where are you going?"

"I already told you, kid, I don't know," Devon answers. "I'm not running this show."

The specter vanishes completely, leaving Catherine alone in her room, standing in stunned silence. She doesn't know what do with the information that's been presented. She decides to peek into the adjoining room via the bathroom. As she cracks the door, light bleeds into the room revealing her parents each sleeping on a different bed. They seem so peaceful that she decides not to wake them.

Suddenly Catherine is overcome by drowsiness. The adrenaline that spiked when she was startled is wearing off. She realizes that she hasn't slept in quite a while, and she's still not fully recovered from the magic removal process. She decides to get some sleep and talk with Damian and Elena about what she saw in the morning.

*** 

Elena is asleep in her own room when she has a strange dream. She sees Gia and the rest of the Carcer inmates that they liberated inside of a rundown studio apartment. The walls are covered with a floral wallpaper that is weathered and peeling in places. A drab brown couch sits atop a lime-green shag carpet. The escapees are passing through a doorway-sized portal in the middle of the room. The Eye of Ruin compound is on the other side of the gateway. Someone touches something they shouldn't before going through the gate. The portal closes after the last person passes through it.

Light coming in through a window shade turns to darkness before becoming light once more. This process repeats as if to signify the passage of a few days. Time seems to slow again when Eric and Andrea appear in the room. Andrea looks to be using her magic while feeling around the room. She stops when she finds the spot on the wall that was touched by one of the escaped prisoners. "I can track them wherever they go now," she says.

With that, the dream ends, and Elena wakes up knowing full well that it was a vision. She flips on the lights and immediately starts getting dressed. Her room is almost identical to Catherine's. Damian offered her a luxurious suite, but she refused it. She lives the same Spartan lifestyle as she did when she was in the military.

Elena finds Damian in his office seated at his desk. He's in the middle of planning his assault on the White House when she interrupts. "The government team may have a way to find us," she says as she enters.

"How?" Damian quickly stands.

"They'll use their Prophet to track the inmates back to us," Elena answers.

"We'll just misdirect them like we did before," Damian says like it's no big deal.

"Not this time," Elena answers. "She will trace us from something one our guest's touched at one of the decoy jump sites. Since we do not know when that will be, we cannot implant an illusion appropriately."

In an uncharacteristic fit of rage, Damian throws everything atop his desk to the ground. Considering how things have been going lately between the two, Elena covertly retrieves a small knife from her sleeve, keeping it hidden against her forearm should she need to defend herself. Damian rubs his palms over his face in frustration. "Things were going so well," he says. "Here's what we do. Have Gia figure out which jump site you saw. Send her and the rest of those morons to clean up their mess. Should they encounter our government friends, have them eradicate the problem directly."

"Da," Elena answers affirmatively in her native Russian.

"And just in case that doesn't go to plan, I'm taking a small team and proceeding with the revolution tomorrow when traffic around the White House will be at its peak," Damian says as he begins to gather up the desk items he knocked on the ground.

"Where will I be?" Elena asks.

"Right here," Damian answers. "I need you on comms working your magic to see any potential threats that may arise. Nothing will stop me this time."

"Don't you mean nothing will stop us?"

He doesn't. "I do."

***

Eric wakes up in a hospital bed to find Anthony sitting in a chair next to him. The room is small and brightly lit. There is an observation window to the hallway that is covered by a curtain, and the exit door is closed. Eric's injuries have been healed, by

Emmanuel no doubt, yet he's still in a hospital gown and hooked up to a heart monitor. Anthony is looking much better than the last time Eric saw him. He's back in his green flight suit and stands upon seeing Eric's eyes open. "Good to see you're awake, sir," Anthony says.

Eric slowly sits up looking around the room. "Likewise," he replies.

Considering his condition when he lost consciousness, Eric feels rather lucky to be alive right now, though his thoughts quickly turn from his own well-being to that of everyone else that was outside the Revelation facility. "Is the President okay?" he asks.

"The President is fine," Anthony answers. "The FBI lost a half-dozen agents to whatever those creatures were, but you managed to kill both of them."

"Did they find the sorcerer who summoned them?"

"No, no one else was on site. From the look of things, they were gone before you all showed up."

Eric stands, almost immediately regretting the decision when his feet touch the cold linoleum floor of the hospital room. "How are you doing?" Eric asks as he looks around for socks or slippers.

"Fine, considering, though I still can't seem to use magic," Anthony replies.

"Where's everyone else?"

"Benjamin, Trace, and Andrea had a plan to locate the escaped prisoners, so I told them to run with it," Anthony says.

"Jasmine went with them as back up. Emmanuel's in the waiting room, asleep."

It suddenly occurs to Eric that he never heard from Jasmine regarding her family. "Two things," Eric says. "One, I need to get out of this hospital dress and two, do you know anything about Jasmine's mother and sister?"

"Clothes we can get you, but I don't know anything about Jasmine's mother or sister."

Eric is given some hospital scrubs to be discharged in. His clothes were torn and soaked with blood, so they were disposed of by the hospital for sanitation reasons. Once released, Anthony drives Eric and Emmanuel back to Eric's apartment so he can get a change of clothes.

Along the way, Emmanuel fills Eric in on what happened with Jasmine's family. Eric's upset that they acted without calling him, but considering all the chaos of recent circumstances, he's just glad that her mother and sister are safe. Emmanuel leaves out the same details he left out when telling the story to Jasmine about his past with the Triads. Of course, the lack of detail as to how Emmanuel negotiated her family's release from the gangsters only makes Eric more curious about Emmanuel's past.

Eric tries to put in a call to the President, only to reach her secretary. It seems there has been a media firestorm ever since they got hold of the news about the Secretary of Defense being murdered by a sorcerer. In order to counter the effects that such news might have on an already volatile situation, the White House also released the information of Allen's deranged pet project.

The President wasn't convinced that was the smart play, but her options were limited, and her advisors were insistent it would help. As soon as the news broke about the Secretary, there were already reports coming in about violence against known magic-users in retaliation. Just as Allen predicted, he's being labeled as a martyr. Unfortunately, releasing the information about Revelation only made things worse. Trust in the government to protect the rights of magic-kind is all but gone, resulting in protests outside the White House and Congress.

Security has been ramped up at the White House while the President and Vice-President meet with other cabinet members to try and get a handle on a situation that is quickly spinning out of control.

\*\*\*

Meanwhile, at a flat in England, Benjamin, Trace, Jasmine, and Andrea lie in wait with members of the British Army and Scotland Yard. The apartment Benjamin and Andrea used in the false vision is located in Lancashire, England and one of the real jump points that Gia had used. The entire town is quite rundown with little police presence normally, making it an ideal spot for quick stops between crimes or escapes, as the case may be.

Since the Eye of Ruin gained international notoriety with their first attacks being in Russia, Paris, and Nigeria, the British government was more than willing to lend some of their own military and law enforcement if it could lead to making some arrests. In fact, the Queen lent some of her own personal magically-inclined staff members to bring the American team over and locate the flat.

Andrea waits outside the small one-story building with members of the police and military. It's afternoon here, but you'd never know it as clouds blot out the sun entirely. The exterior of this flat is as abysmal as the interior. Brown walls with white window and door fixtures look as though they haven't seen any care in decades. Old, discarded junk clutters up the patchy lawn. Even the concrete of the sidewalk is cracked and missing chunks here and there.

Inside the single room structure, Benjamin, Trace, Jasmine, and three British sorcerers wait to spring their trap. Benjamin has made them all invisible, and each person is armed with an anti-magic collar. The objective is to collar Gia if they come through so they can't get away. It's a great plan, except they don't know if their false vision actually worked. The only way to find out was to come here and wait, and, while they could've picked a jump point closer to D.C., this seemed less suspicious. Benjamin also pushed for England so he could feel the cold, muggy climate of home on his face for a bit.

They aren't waiting long before the air in the room begins to crackle with arcane energy. Seven figures materialize in the room. While not all of them, they are the escaped Carcer prisoners led by Gia. She seems especially agitated as though she was just chewed out and sent here under duress. "I don't know what one of you touched that can be tracked," Gia barks at the others. "But I want this placed torched. We're not taking any chances. Burn it all."

Trace has heard enough; without waiting or signaling anyone else, he reaches out and clamps his collar around Gia's neck, exposing him to the room. She obviously knows something's wrong, but she can't see Trace as he's behind her. One of the other escapees recognizes Trace from Carcer right away. "It's a trap!" he shouts.

Before anyone can react to his words, a few more collars get attached to the escaped criminals. Those that are still able to use magic do so to defend themselves. One of the former inmates is a mountain of a man with ward magic at his disposal. He was one of the few prisoners to get collared before the power was shut down during the prison break, so he didn't partake in the fighting as he couldn't use his magic. Once freed, he was fine working with his fellow criminals since it was beneficial, but that time has passed, and he knows there's no honor among thieves. He casts a barrier shockwave which creates a strong invisible wall and propels it out away from the caster at a rapid pace. This knocks everyone in the room, other than himself, backward into a wall. It's a force intense enough to blow out the windows and doors of the flat.

To everyone outside, it feels like a bomb just went off. They take cover while trying to get a report from inside. A few moments after the explosion, the large escapee comes running out the door. He's encased himself with a barrier spell allowing him to deflect bullets and plow through soldiers with ease. He gets half way down the street before one of the British sorcerers manages to make it outside the building to assist. He's the Queen's personal Transporter, Maxwell Davies, a short, pale individual with brown hair and a rather generic face. You'd not consider him ugly or attractive, just plain. What he lacks in presence, he more than makes up for in magical ability. He casts a portal around the fleeing giant and puts it in a loop, so no matter where he runs, he winds up back in the same spot. "Don't worry about him," Maxwell says to the soldiers. "He'll tire himself out."

Back inside the flat, Benjamin, Jasmine, Trace, and the two others have subdued the rest of the criminals. Gia may be collared, but she still puts up a fight: kicking, flailing, and biting until Jasmine just knocks her out entirely. All of the convicts are escorted outside, where they are given shackles in addition to their magical restraints. As predicted, eventually the large escapee loses steam and stops running in place, at which point, he is also apprehended.

Andrea examines each criminal, magically scanning them to get a vision of where they came from. Fortunately, the Eye was not as careful this time around, sending Gia and her crew directly from the main headquarters which Andrea determines is just thirty minutes northwest of D.C. in Bethesda, Maryland.

Andrea's just about to report the good news when she finds herself standing on the sidewalk just north of the White House along Pennsylvania Avenue. She's facing Lafayette Square, but recognizes where she is, having been through the area many times. Some kind of terrible disaster has happened to a large group of people in the street. Countless bodies are scattered across Pennsylvania Avenue while those who are still alive flee in terror.

A thunderous roar fills the air. It's a sound Andrea has become familiar with, so she's not surprised when she looks skyward to see the same dragon from Carcer and her previous vision. In reality, the dragon may be an illusion, but in a vision it could be a metaphor or a symbol that she must interpret. The creature unleashes a massive stream of fire on the White House, turning it to ash in an instant.

While Andrea's focused on the dragon, she feels a hand on her shoulder. She turns to discover a walking corpse grabbing her. It's a woman, but she must be dead; her head has been split wide open from an impact. Blood coats her entire face and pours down her clothing. The soft brain tissue below the skull has also be mangled, some of which hangs out of the opening. She otherwise still looks like herself except that she now also has no pupils.

As if this sight wasn't disturbing enough, Andrea looks past this undead woman to see that every other body has also risen. They stand in formation before slowing walking towards her. It's at this point that Andrea snaps back to reality. She's standing outside the flat in England, surrounded by soldiers who have the convicts secured in front of her.

Andrea quickly finds Benjamin. "We have to get out of here now!" she says with intensity.

"Why, what did you see?" Benjamin asks.

"I'll explain when we get back, but we have to go now!" she responds.

Benjamin can see her distress and hastily makes his way over to the soldiers in charge. He explains they have an emergency, and the military agrees to hold the inmates for the time being. Maxwell, who brought the team over from the States, opens a portal back to the Department of Sorcery. "Pleasure working with you, lads and ladies," Maxwell says as the team passes beyond the threshold.

The four step out into one of the official transport zones within the Department of Sorcery. While there's no way yet to prevent transport into a building, aside from the expensive and power sucking technology used at Carcer or having a Sentinel constantly placing wards all over, facilities instead can monitor for the energy and spatial fluctuations that occur from the use of teleportation or a gateway. Official transports are done in designated areas with specific coordinates so not to raise alarms. Unsanctioned gates, such as the one opened by Rion the night before, or by Anthony any of the times he's teleported the entire team in or out, raises an alarm that gets investigated and must be explained. Since this operation was official, it went through the proper channels, making building security very happy.

Andrea, Trace, Jasmine, and Benjamin meet Eric, Emmanuel, and Anthony in the Guardian wing. Eric is out of his hospital scrubs and back into his usual Secret Service uniform, minus the jacket. Benjamin gives a brief report on what happened in England before Andrea interrupts. "We're going to have to debrief later," she says frantically. "We've got an emergency. I know where the Eye of Ruin's hideout is, but while I was gleaning, I got a vision of Damian attacking the White House again. I saw his dragon illusion and fire and…"

"And what?" Eric pushes.

"And what could only be explained as zombies," she answers.

"Zombies?" Benjamin inquires. "As in-"

"Catherine must be helping them," Eric concludes.

"Maybe, but visions aren't always one hundred percent," Andrea says. "Sometimes they need to be interpreted."

"Do you have any idea when this attack will happen?" Anthony asks.

"No, but if it's anything like the last one, it'll happen soon," she answers.

"We need to contact the White House, and we're going to need Edward's cooperation on this," Eric says. "Mount up everyone. We're going to go take these bastards down before they have a chance to strike."

## Chapter 24: Castle Siege

Catherine wakes feeling refreshed and resolved to find out what the hell is going on around here. She avoids looking in on her parents as she doesn't want to be influenced by them before she has more information. As she marches down to Damian's office, she notices there are far fewer people walking the halls of the compound today. Another oddity is that the door to Damian's office is closed which is almost never the case. She knocks at the door, but receives no answer.

Deciding that the conference room is the next likely place to find him, she heads that way. Once again, he's not where she expected, but Catherine does find the next best thing: Elena. As she approaches Elena, it dawns on her that the room is different. The back wall of the room is about five feet further back and adorned with monitors. There is a large computer workstation under the monitors where Elena sits with her back to the door. The screens display various camera feeds from around the White House and surrounding streets. This area of the room must've been previously concealed by an illusion, but for what purpose?

Catherine quietly wanders further into the room with her gaze fixated on the computer screens. The angles don't appear to be news cameras nor are there any reporters or sound of any kind. They could be security or traffic cameras, but Catherine's not sure. "You are not very good at sneaking," Elena says without turning around.

Catherine realizes she's walked almost all the way to Elena without saying a word. "Sorry, I wasn't trying to be sneaky," Catherine says defensively. "I was just wondering what you're looking at."

"Do you not know the White House?" Elena asks.

"Of course I know the White House," Catherine replies. "I'm just wondering why you're watching it."

"I am following orders." Elena is intentionally being cagey.

"Do you know where Damian is?" Catherine sounds annoyed.

Elena spins around in her chair. She wants to get a visual read on Catherine after hearing her tone. Catherine's arms are crossed, and her face is as serious as a teen trying to look tough can be. "He is out," Elena gives the attitude right back. "I can let you know when he is back."

"This can't wait." Catherine's stubbornness will not be outdone.

Elena is not actually cross right now, but she is trying to avoid talking to Catherine. She really does need to focus on detecting any danger that might interrupt Damian's strike; however, deep down, she's afraid of why Catherine is in such a state of urgency. While Damian has placed an illusion on Catherine to help mask her magic, there is always a possibility that she figures out nothing was actually taken from her. If she finds that was a lie, it will make her question what else may be false which is why Elena didn't like this plan from the start. "What is the problem?" Elena asks.

"I don't think my magic was removed."

A string of obscenities in Elena's native tongue run through her head. "What makes you say that?" she asks remaining calm on the exterior.

"What happened to Devon?" Catherine changes up her questioning in hopes of getting a reaction.

This conversation is really not going in a good direction for Elena. While Damian didn't tell her what he did to Devon, she saw his intent before he acted on it. What's not clear is why Catherine would be asking about him. She only met him for the briefest of moments, and he's been dead for a while now, so this must have to do with her magic. "He betrayed the Eye and is no longer with us," Elena uncomfortably answers. "Why do you ask about him?"

"Because I spoke with him last night," Catherine answers. "He had some things to say, including the fact that he was murdered by Damian."

"It was not murder." Elena finds herself defending Damian's actions. "He broke the rules and faced the consequences."

"He was killed for breaking the rules?!" Catherine is appalled by what she just heard.

"The Eye has one purpose, and Damian will not let anyone stand in the way of it."

With the truth about the murder in the open, it sets in that what she saw last night must be real. "If he's dead, and I spoke to him, that means Damian never removed my magic!" Catherine is furious.

"Of course he took it." Elena bends the truth. "Why would he lie about that?"

Catherine may be young, but she's not stupid. Something's wrong here in a big way. "If he really did take it, then I guess a little test won't hurt," Catherine says before abruptly turning and running out of the room.

Elena knows where Catherine's going and chases after to stop her. She arrives at the cold storage to find the door is already open and Catherine inside standing over one of the dead sorcerer bodies. "Catherine, you do not want to do that!" Elena pleads.

At this point, Catherine is on the verge of tears; the only thing holding them back is the perfect cocktail of anger and betrayal brewing inside her. "Why not?!" she shouts. "What are you afraid of?!"

"I just do not want you to be hurt," Elena answers.

Catherine doesn't understand what Elena means with her response and proceeds to cast. There is a moment after she speaks the words that nothing happens and she thinks she may have overreacted, but that feeling quickly retreats when the corpse sits up on its shelf. It was a lie, and Elena was in on it. All at once, Catherine finds herself back in school with a class full of students laughing at her. She's so heated that she can't see or think straight; her hands are trembling as she balls up her fists. Her rage is then played out through the animated corpse. It stands and lunges at Elena, reaching for her throat. Elena's military training kicks in, and she fights the zombie off. The undead sorcerer continues to thrash at Elena getting stronger with each hit. It's not physically getting stronger, but the dead feel no pain so it can hit with all its might without fear of injury.

At some point, Elena gives up, allowing the undead puppet to grab her. She feels partly responsible for leading Catherine down this path. Maybe she deserves to die in this fashion. The zombie's grip on her throat tightens while Catherine looks on in combination of anger and fear. Elena looks over at this young girl she has wronged and, just before the strangulation cuts off her airflow entirely, says, "I'm sorry..."

Catherine has a moment of clarity when Elena starts to lose consciousness. She's not a killer. She's not part of the Eye of Ruin. She just wants to go home. She dismisses the spell, causing the zombie to fall lifelessly to the ground. Elena collapses as well, gasping for oxygen. Catherine rushes past her out of the room heading towards the sleeping quarters. She just wants to get her parents and get out of here.

Catherine runs into her parents' room to find them waiting for her. Seeing that she's upset, they wrap her in a warm hug between the two of them. It's like they knew exactly what would help make her feel better. "What's wrong, sweetie?" her mother asks.

"I just want to go home," Catherine says, still fighting back tears. "Can we just go home?"

"Of course, honey," her mother responds.

"Are we allowed to?" her father asks.

"I don't care if we are or not, I just want to go." Catherine is practically pulling them out the door.

"That's all I needed hear," her father asserts himself. "I don't care whose butt I have to kick, nobody lies to my daughter and gets away with it!"

And just like that, Catherine is struck by a world-shattering revelation. These aren't her parents. The comfort she felt mere moments ago melts away, leaving only despair. She begins thinking back to the moment they arrived here at the compound. Every interaction she's had with them, they've been everything she wanted them to be. Every emotion she's felt, they reacted to in just the right way, as though they were in her head and now it makes sense because they actually were. This is all an illusion.

What Catherine doesn't understand is how she couldn't sense the illusion magic like when she first did in the phantom library. With the blinders off, she really starts looking at everything around her. There is illusion magic coming off of everything; the floor, the walls, the ceilings, the furnishings, and yes, her parents. Damian was no fool. The moment he knew she could detect his magic, he overloaded her senses with illusion so that when he created the image of her parents, she wouldn't even notice.

Catherine can no longer fight it, and the tears pour from her eyes. Edward lied, Damian lied, Elena lied. They've all tried exploiting her because of her magic. She's never felt so broken and alone. Who knows where her parents actually are, or where she is for that matter. To add insult to injury, the illusory parents continue attempting to comfort her. "There's no need to cry," the illusory father says. "We're right here."

"You're not real," Catherine says slumping to the ground.

"Of course we're real," he says in response.

"YOU'RE NOT REAL!!!" Catherine screams at the top of her lungs.

The illusions only relent for a moment before starting up again. "We're as real as you need us to be," they say in unison.

Catherine closes her eyes, not wanting to see these false symbols of hope any longer. "I don't need you," she whispers to herself. "I don't need you."

The voices of her parents suddenly cease. Catherine slowly opens her eyes to find she's alone. The illusions are gone. All of the illusions are gone. Somehow she's broken Damian's enchantment and can now see the compound for what it really is. While the room is still as bare as it was before there are many slight differences. The walls are not painted, but plain concrete. The twin beds are just cots made from metal and military green canvas.

Catherine has never felt more hopeless. Now that she knows the truth, Damian will most likely have her killed, and honestly, she doesn't even care. She curls up completely on the floor while continuing to cry…waiting for this hell to end.

***

Elena finally recovers from the oxygen deprivation, wanting nothing more than to follow Catherine to make sure she's okay, but her duty to Damian trumps that choice. While she was near blackout, two visions appeared in her head. The first was of Damian being greeted at the White House by US military forces. They appear as though they've been expecting him.

The second vision was of Eric and his team attacking the Eye of Ruin compound. Both visions feel urgent, prompting Elena to sprint back to the conference room computer station. She grabs the headset, radioing Damian. "What's going on, Elena?" Damian asks over the radio.

"The White House knows you are coming," she replies. "I do not know how, but they do."

"I'll be more careful on my approach, but this changes nothing," Damian coolly replies. "Just more logs for the fire."

"We have also been discovered here," she delivers the other bad news.

"How?"

"I assume they captured Gia."

"Have Jared prepare the troops and wipe them out. There's no room for prisoners in my new world."

Elena makes her way to down to another section of the facility located underground. The entrance to the sub-level was hidden by Damian's illusion magic in case the main building was ever raided. It's here that the majority of this cell of the Eye's sorcerer-soldiers lives and trains. The sub-level is as large as the top level and is split into three sections. The smallest room is the kitchen and dining hall which is adjacent to the main living area. That large room is connected to the entrance and contains rows of beds with foot lockers at the end. There is a small sectioned off area for bathing and toilet facilities. The far end of the sub-level is the training area which is set up similarly to the one at the Department of Sorcery.

Each area is populated by a variety of sorcerer and non-sorcerer soldiers. They are young and angry at the world, fed promises of a better tomorrow where they'll have the power. Everyone is dressed in pseudo-military garb of a black or green color. While the majority of their forces don't wield magic, the ones that do are rather skilled with it. Amongst the magic-users are one Mender, three Builders, and six Evos. The rest of the Eye's sorcerers, including Ava, left early in the morning to accompany Damian to the White House.

Elena finds Jared on the practice range. He's getting out some pent up hostility on automated targets that lower down from the ceiling, moving around erratically until they are destroyed or switched off. Jared's lashing out with everything in his evocation repertoire: fire, ice, lightning, wind, and various other arcane energies. Elena calls to him from outside the training room. "Cross!" she shouts. "I need everyone topside! We are about to have company!"

Jared wipes the sweat from his brow as he walks towards her. This is the best news he's heard since being freed from Carcer. He's been wanting revenge, and, even if these aren't the same people that put him there, he's going to get it. "Oh we'll give 'em a proper greeting," he says with a menacing tone.

Back upstairs in a staging area that doubles as a supply depot, a large portal opens. The shimmering light from the magical doorway reveals a vast amount of crates filled with food stuffs and containers full of other survival necessities. Eric is the first person through the gateway, but he is quickly followed by Anthony and Jasmine. They each wear body armor and carry the standard issue carbine rifle. After a quick scan of the empty room, Anthony gives the all-clear signal to everyone else waiting on the other side of the portal. Benjamin, Andrea, Trace, Emmanuel, and a dozen DoS soldiers enter the room. Rion is the last one through the portal before he closes it. He looks around very nervously.

Rion joined the Department of Sorcery straight out of college and has no military training or combat experience. The job pays decently enough, and he thought it would provide him the opportunity for some fun travel. While this definitely isn't what he had in mind, it's more exciting than any other transport he's ever done. Anthony can see how jumpy Rion is, so, while everyone else advances towards the two exits out of the room, he approaches the young Transporter. "You okay?" he asks.

"Yeah, I just don't want to get killed, ya know," Rion answers.

"Don't worry." Anthony attempts to calm Rion's nerves. "You wait here. If anyone other than one of use comes through either of those doors, you teleport out of here."

"What about everyone else?"

"If they get to you, there probably aren't any of us left to worry about," Anthony answers.

"You got a weird way of cheering people up," Rion says with an eye roll.

"Everything's going to be fine," Anthony says with a pat on the shoulder. "Now, I gotta get on the highway to the danger zone."

"Is that a reference to something?" Rion quizzically asks. "It feels like a reference to something."

"That hurts, man," Anthony says before rushing off to join the others.

The exit doors go into two separate hallways that eventually meet up again further into the facility. Eric, Andrea, Benjamin, and Emmanuel head through the east door with six DoS soldiers while Anthony, Trace, and Jasmine lead the other six through the west door. They barely make into either hallway before all hell breaks loose.

Jared, along with about half of the Eye's sorcerers and soldiers, opens fire down the eastern hall. Eric blocks the initial volleys of magic and bullets with his barriers while his forces return fire and find rooms to duck into that are out of the line of fire. Jared catches sight of Emmanuel and Andrea, both of whom he'd personally like to kill. He sends a large fireball their way which is blocked by Eric's barrier, but the explosion knocks down the surrounding walls, opening the entire area up more.

***

The fighting in the eastern hall can be heard in the western corridor, and the explosion shakes the entire building; however, before Anthony's team can turn back to go assist the others, they are set upon by Elena's half of the extremists. Trace creates a wall between them and their attackers before removing the side walls of the hall to give his team places to go. Before he can join them, he feels a magical pull on the center wall he created. There's a Builder on the other side trying to remove the obstacle. Just like with Ava at the prison, he battles for control.

Elena's magic allows her to see the intention of her enemies to move around the sides and flank. She directs her Evos to create fire walls to obscure visibility while she has the non-sorcerers shoot through the fire on her command.

Upon seeing the walls of fire ahead, Anthony gets a bad feeling in his gut and orders everyone to fall back. Jasmine has an idea using a tactic from one of her UMDC matches. She positions herself behind Trace before creating a cyclone around herself. The force of the winds is violently making it difficult for Trace to keep his focus. The air almost pushes him into his own wall, but Jasmine breaks the cyclone, causing an explosion of wind that travels down both side channels towards the fire walls. The wind isn't strong enough to put the flames out, but it does blow them back, surprising the gunmen on the other side. The flames even lick the Builder, causing him to change tactics. He stops trying to lower the wall in front of him and instead erects two new walls along the sides blocking the fire.

Trace feels the resistance gone and uses the opportunity to move his defensive wall forward. He creates openings in the wall that allow Anthony and a few of the DoS soldiers to shoot through it as it slides forward. The enemy Builder isn't quick enough to create his own wall and is put down by gunfire. The victory is short-lived, however, as Trace feels the movement of his wall slow to a crawl before it freezes in place. The openings in the wall become iced over, obscuring any visibility they had.

***

The sounds of conflict have made their way to Catherine's room. She's still on the ground, feeling hopeless, when the rumble from the explosion causes her to sit up and look around. It was too short to be an earthquake. She then notices the distant sound of gunfire. Something big is happening, and this could be her chance to escape. That strong sorcerer who's in control of her powers finds her way back to surface, giving Catherine a plan.

After making her way back to the cold storage unit, Catherine finds the door has been left open. Elena left in such a hurry that she didn't bother to close it. The corpse that Catherine previously animated is still in a heap on the floor. The racks hold five other bodies, making a total of six. If Catherine's magic can't be removed, then she's going to use it to her advantage. She slides the racks out, providing room for the bodies when she takes control of them. A few arcane words and the six corpses begin to move; they first sit up before rising to their feet.

Catherine's squad of undead soldiers is not grotesque in appearance. They are all very pale with a bluish hue, but they've been otherwise preserved. They are dressed in the same black military-style clothing the rest of the Eye's forces wear. Each corpse has its own injuries from how they died, but nothing too abhorrent. They're mostly gunshot wounds to limbs and torsos. They file out into the hallway, followed by their puppet master, and form a wall of undead in front of her.

\*\*\*

Eric and his team had to launch this assault with very limited time and resources. The Department of Sorcery lent every guard they had working at the time which wasn't very many. Edward put out a call to local Bethesda law enforcement, the FBI, and Homeland Security, but it takes time for those reinforcements to travel out. Eric's team was hoping to catch Damian before he headed to the White House which meant they couldn't wait, so they made the jump with the hope that back up would arrive sooner than later.

Since Damian has yet to make an appearance, Eric believes they arrived too late.

Things in the eastern hallway are not going well for Eric and his team. Most of the DoS soldiers have been killed by Jared, who is on a warpath trying to reach Andrea and Emmanuel. Eric's barriers had been taking a hail of gunfire before getting shattered by the strength of the evocation spells thrown at them, and while Benjamin has been using illusions to hide the team, the sheer amount of destruction being sent their way means that even being unseen isn't satisfactory protection.

Eric knows if they keep at this rate, they won't survive until help arrives. "Benjamin!" he shouts back. "Focus on them, not us!"

Benjamin stops trying to obscure the team and casts a distraction instead. Illusory members of his team suddenly appear behind Jared's men with enough pomp and circumstance to draw the ire of the enemy. A handful of non-sorcerer terrorists get picked off, by Benjamin's real allies, when the turn to shoot the illusions. Jared orders a retreat into one of the nearby rooms to get out of their presumed flank. Eric and his team move up in hopes of boxing them in.

***

The fight in the western hall has gotten up close and personal. Guns have run dry, being exchanged for melee weapons and unarmed combat. The corridor and adjacent rooms are now one and the same as both Trace and the enemy Builder modify walls to suit their needs. Every surface is riddled with bullet holes as well as scorch marks and frost damage.  In the chaos, it's almost impossible to tell friend from foe at first glance.

Jasmine takes on two of Elena's Evos and one of the Builders.  Conjuration magic isn't permitted in the UMDC, so she doesn't have any experience battling against it.  It's proving a challenge.  She understands the mixing of martial arts with evocation, and she recognizes when other Evos are casting certain types of spells, but the Builder keeps creating constructs around her to both block and distract, giving the other Evos an edge in the fight.

Trace created a stone construct with a humanoid form, using it to charge the enemy line when they still had ammunition.  This gave the other enemy Builder the same idea and now the two of them engage in a surrogate battle via their magic golems.  With each punch or kick, stone breaks off of the moving statues, spraying nearby combatants with debris.

While the DoS soldiers engage the non-magical terrorists, Anthony is caught between Elena and the other Evo.  Elena is already a handful being military trained, but she's also able to anticipate almost every attack allowing her to easily avoid them.  The addition of the Evo just makes the fight that much more deadly; however, even in the face of possible death, Anthony can't help but sing the words to "Danger Zone" by Kenny Loggins after getting it stuck in his head from his quip a bit ago.

It becomes quickly apparent to Anthony that Elena's ability to avoid his strikes is more than just skill.  He's decides that she's the Prophet for the Eye of Ruin. She's using her ability to see what he's going to do next, so he knows he needs to surprise her somehow. He turns his attention away from Elena and towards the Evo. He positions himself between them before taunting the Evo. "You're the worst sorcerer I've ever seen," he says. "You couldn't hit me if you tried!"

The Evo takes the bait, charging up a fire blast to throw at him. At the last possible moment, Anthony drops flat, feeling the jet of fire pass over him, even scorching a few of his hairs. Elena was so focused on Anthony's future actions that she forgot to pay attention to her surroundings. She sees the fire too late to avoid it entirely. The blast hits her in the side knocking her backward into a wall. The Evo is in such shock about what just happened that Anthony has a chance to get in close, striking him in the throat and crushing his windpipe. Without the ability to cast, Anthony makes short work of the defenseless sorcerer.

\*\*\*

Emmanuel and the enemy Mender are both doing their part to keep their allies up and healthy, but the Eye of Ruin started with a numbers advantage, and it has yet to shift out of their favor. Having figured out the additional troops were illusions, Jared has rallied his team, and they have pushed Eric's back into the hallway. An Evo has sealed the exit behind them with an ice wall, and the only thing keeping Jared's forces at bay is Eric's barrier spell. When it goes, they will be completely exposed.

Catherine and her six undead bodyguards round the corner at the end of the hall, behind Jared's team. Jared notices the approaching zombies, but dismisses them as another illusion. He commands his team to continue their assault, as he feels the barrier is about to give way.

It's not clear from Catherine's vantage point what exactly is happening ahead. She sees one group of people attacking another group, but she can't make out who's on the other side. At this point, she doesn't even care; she just wants out, and she knows they'll try to stop her. While remaining back at a safe distance, Catherine directs her puppets forward to knock out anyone in her way.

The undead sorcerers shamble forward with surprising celerity, setting upon Jared's soldiers. Because the dead don't have the same physical limitations as the living, they can push themselves harder, faster, and without fear of exhaustion. While they're not killing anyone, they still pick Jared's soldiers apart with ease, leveling the playing field.

Andrea sees Catherine in the distance. At last they have finally found her, but she is definitely not the fifteen year-old she remembers. Andrea's about to report what she sees to Eric when her second-sight flips on and she gets another horrific vision of Damian destroying the White House. This prediction of the future comes with a much bigger sense of dread than the previous one. "Eric!" she shouts. "Someone needs to get to the White House right now!"

Eric quickly assesses the situation. He has a guess where the undead soldiers came from, and if they're attacking the Eye of Ruin, then Catherine hasn't sided with them as he previously suspected. With the zombie intervention, the only real threat left is Jared and a few sorcerers which Eric has faith his team can handle. "I'll go on ahead and coordinate with the military," Eric says. "Finish securing the compound and get Catherine to safety. Join me when you're done!"

Andrea and Benjamin nod in agreement before turning their attention back down the hallway. In order to get through the wall that's been constructed behind them, Eric decides to get experimental. He projects a small, but focused barrier around himself before charging the wall. The energy from the shield, coupled with the force of Eric's charge, starts to break apart the ice. It's takes a few more attempts, but he punches through it. He then makes his way back to Rion who teleports him to the White House.

Suddenly, Jared finds himself on the losing side of this fight, but he's out for blood. He sends his remaining Evos at the undead while he charges towards Emmanuel. He surrounds himself in an energy vortex that allows him to break through what remains of Eric's barrier. The swirling blue energy surrounding Jared knocks the last of the DoS soldiers out of his way as he rushes Emmanuel.

Emmanuel doesn't have time to get out of the way, so he braces for the impact. "Sicut densa metallum," he speaks a defensive incantation.

Emmanuel's bones and muscles temporarily take on the density of steel. As Jared connects with Emmanuel, he redirects the energy from his spell towards his target, blasting him through the wall beyond. To anyone watching, it looks like Emmanuel was vaporized by the attack. A smile crosses Jared's face, but he's not done yet. He starts preparing a spell to launch at Andrea while he turns to face her. To his surprise, she's looking his direction with a 9mm pistol trained on him. The intent in her eyes wipes the smile from Jared's face as she pulls the trigger. Not wanting to risk missing, Andrea unloads the entire clip at him.

Jared feels a few bullets impact his vest, pushing him backwards a bit. He thinks he's otherwise cheated death until a chill starts to take hold of him, followed by a stinging in his neck. He touches his neck, pulling his hand back to see it stained crimson. One of Andrea's bullets nicked his carotid artery, and he's quickly bleeding to death. He tries to super-heat the wound with a fire spell to cauterize it, but he's so weak the spell fails. He collapses to the ground, closing his eyes for the last time.

***

The battle on Anthony's side of the compound is nearing a close. Elena's non-sorcerer comrades have all fallen, with only one Evo and both Builders remaining of her sorcerers. Jasmine has managed to defeat one of the Evos on her, but the Builder continues to give her issues. Anthony has jumped into the fight alongside her, making it a more even duel.

Trace and the other Builder have left a wake of destruction in the path of their sparring constructs. The stone surrogates have smashed through multiple walls including an exterior wall allowing sunlight to pour in.

While Elena was taken out of the fight for a few moments, she received a vision of the FBI and local police arriving at the facility. As she comes back around, she can tell the Eye of Ruin has lost here. It's time to let Damian know this place is burned and make a speedy exit. While the battle continues, Elena sneaks back down the hall heading towards the conference room.

The Builder hassling Jasmine conjures up a concrete box, encasing both her and Anthony inside it. With their problems out of the way, the Builder and the Evo head off to give the other Builder a three on one advantage over Trace.

Inside the concrete prison, there is complete darkness until Anthony clicks on a shoulder mounted flashlight. There isn't much room to maneuver, but that doesn't stop Jasmine from trying. She furiously punches at the hard, rough surface until her knuckles bleed. She doesn't do well in enclosed spaces. To her, it feels like the walls are closing in, squeezing the oxygen out of the area. Anthony can see that she's becoming unhinged. "Whoa, whoa, whoa, take a breath," he says.

"I can't, there's no air!" she says in a fluster. "We gotta get out of here!"

Anthony's seen this kind of behavior before in combat situations. It's when that fear you weren't expecting hits you like a freight train; it's hard to stop and even harder to come back from. She's hyperventilating and will go into a full panic attack if he doesn't do something. "Jasmine, listen to me," he says taking hold of her. "Listen to my voice. You have the power to get us out of here, but you need to calm down. Remember Emmanuel's lesson on arcane energy. Find that source inside and use it to heighten one of your spells. Something that can get through these walls. I'll be right here the whole time."

Anthony's words catch her just in time to prevent her from fully shutting down. She runs through her combat spells to figure out what she could use that wouldn't kill the two of them in the process. She has one spell that adds a bit of arcane energy to her fists when fighting to provide a little extra kick. It's not enough to help punch through stone, but if she could enhance it, then maybe. She closes her eyes and tries to picture any place other than where she is. Once her breathing has regulated enough, she thinks back on Emmanuel's lesson. It takes a few moments, but she finally senses that inner energy he was talking about. She casts the spell, causing a bright red aura to surround her hands. She balls up her fists and begins punching at the walls once more. This time, within a few hits, the concrete starts to buckle, creating an opening on one side. After the energy dissipates, Jasmine can feel the fatigue mentioned by Emmanuel, but her adrenaline keeps her going so she and Anthony can quickly exit the box.

The two Builders and Evo are feeling confident about their advantage over Trace until the air outside the compound fills with oncoming sirens. All three of these sorcerers are familiar with the heralding that precedes law enforcement and they can tell by this blare that they won't be able to escape the numbers that are coming. As Jasmine and Anthony make their way over, the three sorcerers put their hands up while getting down on their knees to signal they surrender. It seems not everyone is willing to die for the Dragon King.

***

Catherine's zombies have incapacitated what was left of the Eye of Ruin sorcerers, and they stand fast as she decides if Andrea and Benjamin are friend or foe. She remembers they weren't exactly fans of Edward, but here they are, so they must be working with him. She's not going back. She's just about to give the order to knock them out as well when she hears running down the hall behind her. She glances back to see Elena sprinting out from the western hall where the two become one. She's headed in the direction of the conference room. All thoughts of Andrea, Benjamin, and even her undead puppets are immediately gone. Catherine's only concern is making sure Elena doesn't get away. She takes off after her at full speed with Andrea calling after her, "Catherine wait!"

Andrea and Benjamin get ready to give chase when they hear debris shuffling around by the wall where Emmanuel was blasted. The hole in the wall is still clouded by dust from the destruction. A cough is heard within the cloud before Emmanuel stumbles out from the visual obfuscation. The clothing where he was struck, center mass, by the energy beam has been burned off. His skin is also scorched and still smoking, but even while he slowly walks forward, his skin cells appear to be repairing themselves at a rapid pace. "Emmanuel, thank god, I thought you were dead!" Andrea exclaims with relief.

"Almost," he answers with another cough.

"We found Catherine," Benjamin interjects. "Will you be okay here by yourself?"

"Go," Emmanuel answers. "I will be fine."

Elena makes it back to the formerly hidden computer station and attempts to radio Damian. She gets no response, but before she can make a second attempt, she hears footsteps running up the hall towards her location. She stands, pulling a Makarov Russian service pistol from her belt. She makes sure to keep her distance from the door and waits to greet her mystery guest.

Catherine makes her entrance, but comes screeching to a halt when she sees a gun pulled on her. There is a moment of hesitation, but Elena lowers the gun when she notices the fear in Catherine's eyes. The two women stare at each other for a good long while. No words are spoken, but their expressions speak volumes. The pain of betrayal wells up in Catherine's eyes once again while Elena can't even make eye contact because of the shame she feels for her part in that betrayal. "Why?" Catherine finally breaks the silence. "Why go through all of this? Pretending to be my friend only to lie about removing my powers? What's the purpose?"

"Damian did take your magic, but not in the way he presented," Elena answers.

Catherine's emotional pain is all at once replaced with curiosity and confusion. "What do you mean?" Catherine asks while drying her eyes.

"There is a technology that can capture magic spells and allow them to be reused by someone other than the sorcerer who cast them," Elena says. "We trained you so Damian could take your ability to raise and control the dead. Even now, he is using it to wipe out the government."

Catherine feels like one of the girls at school who would fall for the bad boy knowing his reputation, but expecting she'll be the one he doesn't hurt. She knew up front Damian was a terrorist, but he convinced her that he was just misunderstood. He is a monster and a far worse one than Edward. She has to do something to stop him. She wouldn't be able to live with herself if Damian commits mass genocide using magic he stole from her. "Where is this happening?" she asks.

"First the White House, then everywhere else," Elena answers. "He is not wrong you know. We will always be feared and persecuted by those who cannot use magic. He is bringing about change."

"Change can't happen by becoming what you hate, so he sure as shit isn't right," Catherine says boldly. "And I'm going to stop him."

Almost as if on a reflex, Elena raises her gun at Catherine again. She's knotted up inside, not knowing what the right thing to do here is. She believes in what the Eye is trying to do and should shoot this girl where she stands to prevent her from stopping it, but on the other hand, Damian's been incredibly self-serving lately, proving the Eye's purpose may be a lie. "Are you going shoot me?" Catherine looks up at Elena like a wounded animal.

Elena's hand starts to quiver as the emotions she's ignored most of her life flood her heart and mind. "I could never shoot you," Elena says as she removes the clip from the gun tossing both in opposite directions.

Benjamin and Andrea rush into the room with weapons drawn. They both instinctively get between Elena and Catherine with guns trained on the former. "Get your hands behind your head!" Benjamin shouts.

"Catherine, are you okay?" Andrea asks, looking back at her.

"I'm okay, but we need to get to the White House right now," Catherine answers.

"What about her?" Benjamin asks.

Catherine recognizes the look of defeat on Elena's face that she herself wore just a short time ago. "She'll come along quietly."

## Chapter 25: Slaying A Dragon

Damian couldn't have asked for a better day to conquer the White House. Pennsylvania Avenue is packed with people there for an anti-magic protest. Vehicular traffic north of Lafayette Square is bumper to bumper. Even foot traffic in the seven acre public park is rather robust for it being mid-morning. The sun is out, but there is still a November chill in the air ensuring everyone is bundled up in coats and hats.

The north lawn of the White House is a symbol to every American, representing the greatness of their country. The famous face of the government has pristine columns and rows of windows resting under the nation's flag flying above the roof, the Washington Monument seen behind it in the distance. A beautiful in ground fountain is surrounded by a ring of bright red tulips and grape hyacinth on the well-kept lawn that stretches out to Pennsylvania Avenue. Clusters of trees to the east and west of the fountain have lost a few of their autumn leaves on the grass below, creating a rather beautiful scene. Damian can't wait to destroy the scene and rip this symbol open to reveal America for the monster he sees it as underneath.

He has positioned himself in the center of Lafayette Square, standing atop the rectangular stone base next to the statue of President Andrew Jackson on horseback. Four cannons circle the base on the grass as though defending the statue from danger. Outside of that is a low wrought iron fence to keep tourists off the grass. Passersby see only the statue, as Damian has made himself invisible while scouting possible dangers.

Ava and twelve Eye of Ruin sorcerers have accompanied Damian on what they are considering a suicide mission. They are his most devout and powerful followers, made up mostly of Evos. They have already been strategically positioned along H Street, north of the square, and on Pennsylvania Avenue near the protesters, south of the square. They await Damian's signal to unleash the full destructive power capable by the Eye of Ruin.

Sirens are heard in the distance as a fleet of red and blue flashing lights approach the protesting masses on Pennsylvania Avenue. Behind the impressive number of police vehicles is a convoy of military transports painted in the traditional green, black, and brown camouflage. Damian could not be more gleeful at the sight of the incoming police and National Guard. Had he known alerting the White House would've brought in this many donations to his army, he would've called the threat in himself.

The National Guard soldiers form a line on the sidewalk between Pennsylvania Avenue and the White House. Police officers in full riot gear, including body armor, helmets with visors, shields and batons, file out of their vehicles and form ranks to suppress the protest. Of course, the protesters have no idea about the real reason behind the police presence, so they push back. It doesn't escalate to violence, but it could get there very easily. All it would take is one little misunderstanding, and Damian has just the thing. "Ava, wall off the protesters and police," Damian speaks into his covert communication device. "All others prepare to attack on my mark."

Ava is also positioned in the park, but closer to the south side of it. She makes the somatic gestures for the spell as subtle as possible while whispering the incantation. "Moenia terrae."

The ground underneath the police and protesters begins to rumble until the earth punches through the asphalt, reaching towards the skies on all four sides of the terrified assembly. The hard rock stops growing about twelve feet up, leaving no means of escape for anyone inside. The National Guard is on high-alert now, scanning the area for the culprit, though for many their view is obscured by the large box in front of them now.

While no one can see inside the walls, screaming and the sounds of a riot breaking out can be heard from the outside. Damian thinks the fire has been well stoked, so the time has come to watch it burn. "Now," he commands his troops.

As Damian's massive illusionary dragon appears in the sky above the square, a series of large-scale magical attacks erupt, starting at H Street and working their way towards the White

House. A chain of fireballs explode along the multiple lanes of backed up vehicles in front of Lafayette Square, sending glass and metal shrapnel into the flesh of any nearby pedestrians. Most of the vehicle occupants are killed instantly, but the cries of those who aren't and are trapped within burning wreckage can be heard over the roar of the flames. As people flee the area or move in to help survivors, the four Evos positioned on H Street begin picking them off with a mix of arcane bolts and various elemental based spells.

At the same time Damian, a Builder, and two more Evos raze the public park. Statues are demolished, trees and lawns are burned, and anyone unlucky enough to be caught in the middle is violently put down. While there was a decent amount of foot traffic through the park, it isn't as densely populated as the other areas, so destroying it is more for the spectacle.

Ava and the remaining Evos move south of the square to continue the assault on Pennsylvania Avenue. Ava creates cover for herself and the Evos while they arc lightning down on the masses within the walled off area. As the Eye of Ruin murders dozens by the score, the National Guard soldiers are split on countering the attacks. Half of the soldiers are so intimidated by the black scaled beast of the skies that they don't notice much else. The other half sees the real threat and fire on sorcerers with M16 rifles.

Damian feels he has enough corpses to get the ball rolling. He activates the bracer with Catherine's magic stored inside. Slowly, as if straight out of a horror movie, the dead begin to rise.

Bodies begin to crawl from the steel wreckage on H Street. Some are mangled from physical trauma while others look more alive, having died from internal injuries. The most unsettling of the walking corpses are the ones that were burned alive. Charred flesh, exposed bone, some still ablaze and leaking fluids as they shamble south towards Lafayette Square to join the dead coming to life there.

As he directs the death magic towards Pennsylvania Avenue, Damian tells Ava to lower the walls she created around the protesters and police. The stone partitions recede back into the ground, revealing the horde within. Not everyone from this group had died, though the few that survived are now frozen in fear. These undead look the least monstrous since they were either beaten to death or electrocuted, but even then, a congregation of lifeless husks with solid milky eyes and nefarious intentions would frighten even the most hardened individual.

Within minutes, all of Damian's undead forces have amassed in front of the National Guard soldiers who, now being faced with a more disturbing threat, have lost interest in the dragon altogether. With hundreds of zombies at his command and many more soon to follow, Damian's victory is at hand. He gives the order to advance, propelling the grotesque mob forward. They are quickly stopped by something, though, before reaching the soldiers.

From one angle, the sight is almost comical as though countless undead mimes are attempting to "walk against the wind." However, the viewpoint of the soldiers is far more graphic. The zombies are pressed up against an invisible barrier, and, since they don't feel anything, they continue trying to carry out their orders. As a result, the pressure on those at the front is squeezing them like a tube of toothpaste, with the more delicate corpses almost exploding in a spray of blood and entrails on the barrier.

Damian halts his army to investigate the problem. He joins Ava on the northern sidewalk of Pennsylvania Avenue, and she raises the ground beneath them, creating a ten foot tall pedestal with a better view of the situation. Damian's happy thoughts of victory are replaced with sheer rage as he sees Eric stand on the White House lawn with other Sentinels and troops from inside.

Eric arrived inside the White House as the dead were being raised. By that point, the Secret Service had already moved the President, Vice-President and other executive staff to the secured bunker underneath. Having a rough idea of what was to come based on Andrea's vision, Eric filled in the security staff. All available sorcerers and soldiers not staying with the President joined up with Eric to try and stop the siege before it starts.

The thing about barrier spells is that they can only take so much concentrated damage before they collapse. And while they can be recast, after a while, the local energy from which the sorcerers draw for the spell would become depleted. The same goes for the battle magic being used to attack the barrier. In this situation, each side has something to supplement their magic use.

Damian's zombie army spreads out along the invisible shield that spans the entire north lawn of the White House, proceeding to thrash at it. All of Damian's Evos move up in a support capacity, bombarding the magic shell with everything they have.

On the other side, the military fires into the legion of undead in hopes of whittling them down. Unfortunately, unlike the zombies they've seen in the movies and on television, these don't drop when shot in the head. It's the magic that gives life to these unholy creatures, not a desire for brains and flesh. They will fight until there is nothing left of them to do so.

In all the chaos, a bullet does manage to slip past the wall of corpses, striking Damian's other Builder in the head. He thought he was safe near the back and has quite the look of surprise on his face as he dies.

Most of the men and women on the White House lawn feel fear and revulsion at the sight before them; however, there is one that feels only sorrow and regret. To Eric, these aren't monsters, just more people he failed to save. While Damian may be masked from sight, the fact that his dragon hovers in the air breathing fake fire on the world below lets Eric know he's present. Without a Transporter, Damian will not be able to make a quick getaway should he need to, and Eric wants to make sure he doesn't escape this time. He's going to make sure this psycho is locked in the most secured cell Carcer has to offer.

Unfortunately, the standoff is not going in the favor of the White House. Aside from the amount of kinetic and energy damage being slammed into the barrier wall, Ava keeps conjuring up stone doorways, effectively cutting small holes in the shield. The Sentinels are quick to seal them, but not before handfuls of the undead push through. This draws the focus of some of the soldiers who attempt to kill those that are already dead. Any soldiers killed in their seemingly futile efforts immediately rise again as one of the enemy.

After a solid ten minutes of bombardment on it and harassment behind it, the barrier buckles, giving the zombies free rein of the White House lawn. The Secret Service and National Guard begin to panic, breaking formation to either flee or fend for themselves in better tactical positions. Rather than pool their efforts to create another large barrier, the Sentinels start shielding themselves or small groups of soldiers near them.

To buy some time, Eric creates a flat wall-like barrier as tall and wide as can; however, rather than casting it on a vertical plain, he makes it on the horizontal. It starts off in the air about eight feet off the ground before he forcefully lowers it on the incoming undead mob. This flattens a good section of them, creating the horrendous sound of bones breaking, followed by a robustly juicy squish.

An enraged Damian reveals himself, still high on his stone pedestal, glaring down at Eric from afar. "Tear him apart!" Damian commands his undead directly towards Eric.

As the swarm of death closes in, Eric takes solace in knowing that while they are after him, they're not harming anyone else. He creates another barrier around himself and commands anyone else still alive to fall back to the steps of the White House. The throng of zombies washing over Eric's barrier is so densely packed, it blacks out the sunlight inside. The interior of the shell is deafening as the undead relentlessly smash and claw at it with their bloodied limbs. Eric can feel the barrier start to fail when all of the sudden the clamoring goes completely silent. He's not sure if he's still alive as everything is still in complete darkness. Light slowly starts to pierce the darkness within the barrier as the zombies disengage before becoming very still.

Damian's eyes grow wide with surprise. He checks the bracer to see if it's broken. The light on it indicates that the magic is still functional, confusing, him further. "KILL HIM!!!" he shouts in frustration.

Had Damian taken a bit more time with Doctor Randall to fully understand the technology he stole, he would know that while the devices can replicate a spell, the original caster of said spell will always supersede the knock-off when it comes to the casting of that spell. In fact, Damian doesn't realize what has happened until he sees Catherine standing on the steps of the White House looking directly at him as if to say, "Your move, bitch."

"I knew I should've killed you when I had the chance!" Damian calls down to her.

"You can try now," Catherine taunts. "But it looks like your army is now my army."

"And once I've choked the life out you with my bare hands, they'll be mine once more," Damian says before jumping off the stone platform.

He creates a strong wind underneath him to slow his descent to the ground. Ava and the rest of his sorcerers converge on his location in preparation to advance.

Catherine is joined on the white steps of the Presidential building by Jasmine, Benjamin, Emmanuel, Trace, Andrea, and Anthony. Eric also makes his way to the bottom of the steps, giving everyone a nod of acknowledgment and relief. Catherine seems distracted as everyone else is preparing themselves for what's to come. "Are you okay?" Jasmine asks.

"Yeah, but if I don't keep concentrating on this, he'll regain control," Catherine answers.

"We need to destroy that bracer he's wearing," Anthony says.

"Don't forget he's wearing the one with the barrier as well," Benjamin adds. "We have to get through that first."

"It should function like the spell," Eric says. "If we throw enough damage his way, it'll break and need to be recast. Not sure how the tech works, but we could be looking at a very narrow window between shields."

"So, are we gunning for Damian then?" Trace asks.

"He'll be concealing his true location," Benjamin says.

"And you can conceal ours," Eric says. "The difference is we have a Prophet. She might be able to pinpoint the real Damian."

"I'll try," Andrea says.

"Anthony, Jasmine, you keep the others busy." Eric lays out the battle plan. "Benjamin and Emmanuel, keep Catherine safe while Andrea tries to find Damian. Trace and I will try to draw him out if he's hiding."

The entire team is physically worn out, but they are drawing a line in the sand, and the determination in their eyes signals to the Eye of Ruin that they're ready for the real fight to begin.

Damian's Evos strike first with a volley of arcane energy bolts which are negated by a quick shield wall Eric creates in their path. Anthony and Jasmine return fire, he with his carbine and she with her favorite fire spells, as they make their way down the stairs to take position on the left flank.

Benjamin makes himself, Emmanuel and Catherine invisible while also creating mirages of the three of them that appear to run down the right flank. As predicted, some of the Evos begin attacking the illusions. While they are hidden from sight, Emmanuel and Benjamin slowly walk Catherine back closer to the doors of the White House in case someone gets clever and attacks the last place they were seen.

In turn, Damian also makes himself invisible and summons his dragon into the fight. At this point, everyone on the battlefield knows it is an illusion, but it's no less dangerous seeing as Damian can somehow cast his evocation spells from it.

Eric and Trace move directly forward while trying to madden their adversary into making a mistake. Eric is taking point on the antagonizing while Trace is more or less watching for any signs of the Eye's leader. "Is this all you've got Damian?!" Eric calls out. "You're nothing without your stolen magic. Just a common thug with a God complex trying to rule through fear!"

Andrea attempts to find Damian through his illusions, which is even more complicated than it sounds. Since his magic removes him as a focus point, she is instead glimpsing into the near future of every other person in the area, hoping that he will be revealed in one of those visions. It's not always exact, and the future is always changing, so her search may yield no results, but she tries anyway. As she casts the spell on Trace, she gets a violent vision of him impaled on a stone spike. Looking around, Andrea can see Ava casting a spell near the fountain in the center of the lawn. Without thinking, Andrea runs forward, dive-tackling Trace to the ground just as the earth erupts where he was standing, projecting a jagged piece of stone skyward.

Trace looks around in bewilderment to realize what Andrea just did for him. While she has proven to him already that she's not an average convict, he never thought she would risk her life to save his. Andrea quickly stands and helps Trace to his feet as well. There's no time to truly express his gratitude right now so he goes with a simple, "Thanks."

The few remaining soldiers and agents that Eric ordered to retreat back to the White House stand in the open double-doors to the structure. They may find magic quite intimidating, but their job is to protect, and they refuse to sit idly by while Eric's team gets overrun. They can see Anthony and Jasmine are currently pinned down by the eight Evos, so they break from their position to lend support. Using M16s and 9mm pistols, they fire on the Evos who were so concentrated on Anthony and Jasmine that they didn't even see it coming. Two Evos go down while the others falls back to redirect their attacks.

With room to breathe, Anthony and Jasmine give a nod of appreciation to their guardian angels before advancing on the enemy. Ava intervenes on behalf of the Evos, creating a wall to cutoff Anthony and Jasmine's support. The find themselves under fire once more and now there is nowhere to hide. Jasmine creates a wall of ice to absorb some of the blasts being directed at them, but it won't hold for long.

Anthony wishes he had his magic back, if even for a moment, to get them behind the enemy. He starts thinking about when they were at the Revelation facility and he gets an idea. "I need you to shock me," he says.

"What?!" Jasmine reacts to the bizarre request.

"I need you to hit me with a strong jolt of electricity while I try to teleport us behind them," he clarifies.

"Won't that kill you?"

"It could, but if we stay here, we're dead anyway!"

Jasmine agrees to attempt it. She puts her hands on his arms, trying to avoid direct contact over his heart. They both speak their incantations at the same time. The electricity coursing through his body is agonizing, but it's also very short-lived as the energy redirects into his spell, transporting him and Jasmine safely behind the attacking Evos. They are not immediately noticed, and, while the strain of the spell leaves Anthony incapacitated, Jasmine moves in, attacking the unsuspecting enemy.

Back over by the fountain, Trace has constructed a stone canopy to provide cover for him and Andrea against the constant streams of fire coming from the dragon. A good stretch of the once pristine green lawn is now a maze of large flame trails. Eric is out in that maze with a barrier protecting himself as he continues to taunt Damian, though so far he has yet to take the bait.

Andrea finally gets a vision of something she believes will force Damian into the open; however, Eric is too far away with the thunderous roar of all the fires for her to let him know. "We have to take down his Builder," Andrea says turning to Trace.

Trace sees Ava making her way towards Jasmine and the Evos. "I'm on it!" he shouts as he runs out after her.

Benjamin and Emmanuel also see everything that is happening. They would like to help, but they understand that if anything happens to Catherine, all hell will break loose. "Emmanuel, if I keep you invisible, can you go have a check on Anthony?" Benjamin asks.

"Yes," Emmanuel answers, already in motion towards the scene.

Jasmine has systematically picked apart the remaining Evos. The entire grouping was stunned by an electric bolt before they even knew she was there. From that point, she moved in close, and

it was pretty much over. She's about to turn back to check on
Anthony when a spike emerges from the ground, narrowly avoiding
her chest. The razor sharp rock stabs into Jasmine's shoulder; in
fact, the only reason she isn't dead is because she was in mid-spin.

A second spike rapidly sprouts from the earth in front of
her, but stops short of hitting her by less than an inch. Jasmine
stumbles back away from the crooked stalagmite while applying
pressure to her bleeding shoulder wound.

Ava feels that same resistance she did back at the prison.
She turns to find the source and finish him, but Trace is already on
her, tackling her to the ground. Both are trained in hand-to-hand
combat, but any technique they may have goes out the window as
their melee turns into an all-out brawl. Haymakers, elbows, knees,
biting, clawing; nothing is off limits.

Damian's attention is pulled away from Eric as he notices
the fight between Ava and Trace. It looks as though Trace is
starting to win. Damian redirects the dragon to go lend Ava
support. It hovers, waiting for the right moment to strike. That
moment appears when Ava manages to flip Trace off of her and roll
out of the way. "Ignis inferni!" Damian speaks the incantation,
prompting the dragon to breathe fire down on Trace.

A harrowing scream is heard within the flames, making
Damian realize something's wrong. The wailing is coming from a
woman. He immediately dismisses the fire and the dragon. At the
same time, Benjamin drops his illusion, revealing that it was

actually Trace who flipped Ava and rolled out of the way, leaving her to burn in Damian's fire spell.

Damian may feel little regard for most others, but he actually had some feelings for Ava, having shared a bed with her. Knowing that he just killed her because he fell for an effect from his own school of magic makes him blind with rage. Andrea's vision showed Damian dropping his invisibility out of anger, but it didn't show where his location was. He appears right in front of the fountain, erratically launching fireballs at the face of the White House. One of the blasts hits right next to Benjamin and Catherine, knocking them both to the ground.

Damian feels the resistance fade, and he has control over the undead once more. He directs them to attack any living thing that isn't him. The zombies begin moving in all directions, to kill as they have been directed. They have no regard for the trails of fire, walking right through them, some catching fire themselves.

Eric knows that if they don't drop his shield right now, they will not have another chance. He looks around the lawn for his team. Jasmine and Anthony are back on their feet, having been healed by Emmanuel. Trace is also upright, trying to wall off the walking corpses. Andrea is already shooting at Damian with an M16 dropped by one of the dead soldiers. Benjamin and Catherine are still down, but Eric can't wait for them. "Focus on Damian!" he calls out.

Damian feels his barrier wearing thin very quickly as he becomes the target of gunfire from Eric, Andrea, and Anthony.

Jasmine centers a beam of fire on the shield while Trace conjures shards of earth to stab at it. The shield breaks so fast Damian has no time to get a spell off. He moves his undead troops in front of him to absorb the onslaught.

Jasmine runs forward, using one of the zombies as a spring board to leap up in the air. While she's there, she calls down a lightning bolt in the center of the undead. It strikes true, hitting Damian and destroying both bracers. With no one to control them, and no magic animating them, the undead become the dead once more.

All of Damian's plans have been dashed by these lesser sorcerers. If he can't win, he'll make sure that everyone else also loses. The self-destruction spell used by the Eye's suicide bombers was taught to them by Damian himself. With his arcane source of power, Damian's bomb will be able to level the White House and part of D.C., but he'll need time to charge it up. "Fluctus tonitrui," Damian says, sending out a radial shockwave that knocks everyone to the ground, leaving them disoriented.

Damian then begins drawing in the energy for his final spell. What makes Damian's magic stronger than other sorcerers is that he draws power from someplace unknown to the sorcerers of Earth. In fact, it's unknown even to him. He discovered it after he gained the ability to cast evocation magic. He never questioned where it came from. He just loved the rush it gave him from using it. In his mind, he must be the closest thing this world has to a god.

Having experienced the effects of flash bang grenades in military training, Eric and Anthony are the first ones back to their feet. Eric recognizes what's happening. "Get everyone back!" he shouts to Anthony.

Similarly to when Damian called down the lightning storm at Carcer, he ascends into the sky as he gathers power. Eric's protector instincts kick in, allowing him to jump and grab hold of Damian. He pulls from his internal energy to create a barrier around both of them which pulls Eric into the sky with his target. By being at the center of the shield, he can maintain its integrity easier, and he's hoping to contain Damian's explosion with it.

Anthony helps everyone get to their feet. "Get inside the White House!" he directs the others.

"We have to help Eric!" Andrea argues.

Anthony looks up at the two men in the sky. He, too, recognizes the spell and the sacrifice Eric is making. "We can't..."

While the team reluctantly retreat, to safety, Eric and Damian continue rising into the air. Their animal instincts tell them to mangle each other with a show of brute strength, but they are so focused on maintaining their spells that they can only glare at each other and exchange words. Damian does take comfort in knowing once his energy peaks, the explosion will rip through Eric's barrier like tissue paper. "You've stopped nothing," Damian laughs. "This city will burn, and, even once I'm gone, another will take up my mantle until sorcerers rule this world like the gods we are!"

"We are not gods!" Eric counters. "It's assholes like you that make others fear us. You think you're building a better world? You're just making the one we live in worse for everyone besides yourselves!"

"Is that supposed to appeal to my humanity? I lost that when my magic evolved into what it is now. You're just jealous because I'm better than you. Your magic will never be as strong as mine, and I'll prove that shortly. Even if you'd killed me when I started the spell, it would've taken down half the White House, so you can imagine the devastation at full strength. I guess you're just not good at protecting people, Agent Davis."

Eric knows the truth of Damian's words. His barrier will not hold. He thinks through every spell and trick he knows trying to find a solution to lessen the destruction. He suddenly remembers what he did at the Revelation facility to the two razor-mouthed monsters. He caused his barrier to implode. He doesn't know if the creatures were killed or sent somewhere through magical means, but he knows they weren't around to hurt anyone anymore. Maybe he can do that here. He'll use every ounce of his own inner energy if he has to.

Back down on the ground, the team has made it safely into the White House, but no one wants to remain there. Even Catherine wants to get back outside and help. "He wants us to stay safe inside," Anthony says.

"We can't let him die!" Andrea shouts.

"If you let me out there, maybe we can get Eric out, and I can construct something to contain the blast," Trace pleads.

That plan actually sounds feasible, so after a moment of thinking on it, Anthony agrees. They all rush back to the entrance of the building. Looking up, they don't even see the two men any more. The arcane power Damian has built up radiates so brightly it makes Eric's barrier visible, creating a small second sun in the sky.

"I don't think anything is containing that," Benjamin says, fearfully.

There's a bright flash, and, for a moment, the large glowing orb in the sky expands. Everyone dives for cover, only to witness the shield collapse in on itself, leaving the sky empty. Eric's gone, but so is Damian, leaving the world a bit safer for the time being.

There is a long period where no words are spoken. Everyone just stares at the sky where the glowing orb was only moments ago. When the reality of the situation sets in, there is a communal break down amongst everyone. Eric saved them. He saved all of them, but at the cost of his own life. Did they deserve such a sacrifice? A few of them don't think so, but they're happy to be alive. Even as they celebrate life, the sight of death is all around them, sending a clear reminder that this can never happen again. Stopping Damian may feel like the end, but until all cells within the Eye of Ruin are stopped there's still much work to be done.

# Epilogue

In the weeks following the death of Damian Westonbrooke and the arrests of the known remaining Eye of Ruin members, Congress passed their law requiring all citizens with magical abilities to register with the Department of Sorcery. The President vetoed the initial bill, citing how her team was able to take down the Eye of Ruin when traditional law enforcement could not, as proof that sorcerers should be policing sorcerers. The bill was amended to reinstate the arcane police force known as the Guardians.

The media has been all over the events in D.C., spewing propaganda on all sides of any arguments to be had. Public opinion on sorcerers is still split since the raid at the Project Revelation facility. The death of Allen Barber has made him a martyr in the eyes of the anti-magic populace, with various media sources painting him as a true patriot just looking out for his fellow Americans. This has caused a small public outcry for Revelation-style research to be backed by the government.

On the opposite side of that coin, many now see sorcerers in a more positive light since Eric's death. His being a sorcerer and sacrificing himself to stop a monster of a man has him looking like a saint in the public eye. As with Allen, he has his detractors in the press, but the positive influence far outweighs the negative.

The President has been in non-stop meetings to prevent similar future incidents and giving press conferences in an effort to keep people calm. Aside from all of her political responsibilities, she personally reunites Catherine with her real parents. It turns out Edward had local authorities tell them that she ran away. While the reunion isn't the one she imagined in her mind, Catherine's parents are overjoyed that she's okay. When they first hear the news of her magical abilities, they grow a bit distant, but when they hear the story of everything she's been through, they soften and act like parents should for their child.

The President offers Catherine a job at the Department of Sorcery if she wants it, but Catherine opts to go back to Oregon with her parents. The President allows this with no fuss, but knowing the extent of what Catherine's magic can do, she can't just let them go. Catherine will be under covert surveillance for the rest of her life, to ensure nothing like what happened at the White House is ever repeated.

The President also makes arrangements for Eric's funeral at Arlington National Cemetery. At first, there was a rumor that Eric might still be alive somewhere, but during the cleanup efforts at the White House, a body was found that's believed to be his. Though it was burned beyond recognition, the dental records were a match. The funeral is a televised event with all senior White House staff in attendance as well as the entire team. Even Catherine attends it before heading back out west.

***

Back in Oregon, Catherine is adjusting to life as a celebrity at school. Her face is nationally known as "the girl who helped take down the Dragon King" and she kind of hates it. Sure she never enjoyed being an outcast, but now everyone wants to be her "friend" just in hopes to share in her spotlight. The one thing she does appreciate is the support she's getting at home. Her parents have been nothing but encouraging about her abilities, and they've never been closer as a family.

The President was able to keep Catherine's abilities out of the press, so that hopefully once the media coverage dies down, she can lead a somewhat normal life. The events of the last month have taught Catherine to embrace the arcane instead of fear it. She has no intention of raising zombies or carrying on conversations with dead people, but now the idea of those things doesn't keep her awake at night.

***

Aside from the Guardian police force, the President also keeps the taskforce running to keep looking for Eye of Ruin cells and other potential threats. With Eric now gone, Anthony reluctantly takes lead of the team. Andrea's sentence is pardoned by the President, ending her work release program with Carcer, but she opts to stay on the taskforce anyway, now as a paid employee. Jasmine and Emmanuel also decide to stay on, but Benjamin claims to be too busy running his business empire and only offers his services as a consultant.

Trace resigns as Warden of Carcer to join the DoS full-time. His official title: Secretary of Sorcery. It seems Edward's lie about Catherine's parents was the last straw for the President. He was promptly fired and lucky she didn't file any charges against him. Trace seemed like the perfect replacement, having the administrative experience from overseeing the prison.

\*\*\*

It's just after midnight at Arlington National Cemetery in Virginia. This hallowed 624 acres is the final resting place for veterans who died during one of the nation's conflicts, dating all the way back to the Civil War. The cemetery is run by the Department of the Army, a component of the Department of Defense and doesn't allow visitors after 4pm. Not that you would want to come here after dark. Most of it is not lit, and, on a night like this, where the moon keeps ducking behind the clouds, visibility is minimal. Though even in the dark, the countless rows of uniform marble headstones can be seen like rows of white dominoes waiting to be knocked over in spectacular fashion.

A slender figure approaches one of the headstones. The gender of this person cannot be determined, as they are cloaked in shadow. A bony hand, so thin it would look like a skeleton if not for the taut skin covering it, extends from the sleeve of a long dark coat, waving just over the marble marker. The nails on this hand are long and sharp, but otherwise undecorated.

As the hand passes over the gravestone, the ground begins to rumble. It feels like a minor earthquake along this row of the cemetery. The tremor grows in strength as the ground in front of every stone starts growing into a coffin shaped mound. When the earth finally ruptures skyward, grass and dirt rain down, creating a dense cloud wall along the entire row. The sounds of creaking wood can be heard within the earth. Low groans and gurgling add to the noise.

It takes a few minutes for the debris to settle enough to reveal the devastation. All of the gravesites have been torn open. Many of the stones have been overturned or have fallen into the hole before it. The darkness within the earth emanates with activity as the shrouded figure takes a step back while raising their hands up as though they are about to conduct a choir of the macabre.

Suddenly, a hand reaches out of one of the holes grasping tightly at the grass. The skin on this hand is a greenish-blue and is cracked in places. The fingernails peel off the tops of the fingers from the force of gripping the ground. What emerges from the grave is a man in a black suit. The face of this man is in a similar state to the hand. Dark fluids have oozed out of his eyes, ears, nose and mouth, drying in place. His short dark hair has fallen out in patches. Hard to say if this person was attractive in life or not, as their face is completely unrecognizable from what it once was.

The walking corpse pulls itself completely out of the ground and stands looking blankly forward. More of the dead climb from their row of graves, each in varying states of decomposition, with the worst being only skeletons.  Once the entire row has risen, the necromantic master of ceremonies continues walking forward to the next row of graves.  As this grim figure moves, the undead form ranks and follow it, revealing the mass of empty graves behind them.  An army of formerly dead soldiers march in unison under the command of their new general.

The mysterious Reaper stops once again waving their hand over another gravestone.  In the briefest of moments, the moon breaks free of its cloudy prison, providing just enough light to see the name inscribed on this marble marker: Eric Davis.